The Taste of Good Fruit

A NOVEL

by

MaRita Teague

West Bloomfield, Michigan

Unless otherwise indicated, all Scripture quotations are taken from the *King James Version* of the Bible.

Scripture quotations marked NIV are taken from the *Holy Bible, New International Version*®. NIV®. Copyright © 1973, 1978, 1984 by International Bible Society. Used by permission of Zondervan Publishing House. All rights reserved.

12 11 10 09 08 10 9 8 7 6 5 4 3 2 1

Cover design by Tracy McCutchion

The Taste of Good Fruit
ISBN 13: 978-1-57794-858-2
ISBN 10: 1-57794-858-0
Copyright © 2008 by MaRita Teague
www.MaRitaTeague.com

Published by Walk Worthy Press
P.O. Box 250034
West Bloomfield, Michigan 48325
www.walkworthypress.net

Printed in the United States of America. All rights reserved under International Copyright Law. Contents and/or cover may not be reproduced in whole or in part in any form without the express written consent of the Publisher.

Every branch that beareth fruit, he purgeth it,
that it may bring forth more fruit.

John 15:2

To Zedric, the love of my life;
&
To Kenneth and Rita Hinton, my wonderful parents;

For encouraging me through the purging
and helping me to bring forth fruit.

Acknowledgments

The old hymn says, "Without Him, I could do nothing; without Him, I would fail." Without the Lord, I couldn't have written the story and it certainly wouldn't have been published. I'm forever grateful for this tremendous blessing and give all glory to Him.

Zedric, my dear husband, you are the iron that helps sharpen me. My relationship with you has proven to me what wonderful blessings God can give us when we seek Him with our whole heart. Your unconditional love and support has made the difference. Noah, Joshua, and little one—you are my heart and I love you.

My parents, Rita and Kenneth Hinton, I love and admire you. You've had some challenges this year, but you made it through! God is good—42 years of marriage! Thanks for the reading, Mom. Thank yous to my other beautiful family members who have helped: Aleta, Landrian, Elicia, MiKelle, Kandace, Charles, and my totally terrific nieces and nephews.

Denise Stinson, my publisher. How can I tell you what it felt like when I received that first call from you saying Walk Worthy Press wanted to publish my book? I am so grateful. Thank you for your ministry and for believing in my story to see it through to publication. It's definitely not about being first but enduring to the end!

Thank you to the publishers at Harrison House and to Monica Harris, my editor.

Adrian Davis, thank you so much for reading the script and for your feedback, as well as your friendship. Love you and Kennedy.

My pastor, Superintendent Tony Campbell, the First lady, Missionary Joyce Campbell, and the entire Yeshua Church of God in Christ family. Thank you for your prayers and support. Also, thank you to Bishop Ted Thomas, Sr. and the entire First Jurisdiction of Virginia.

Anthony Watson for the website design; Brian and Denise Cannon for the pictures; Charlotte Teague, my sister-in-law, from Purseonality Boutique for the exceptional; and Dr. David Neff from the University of Alabama in Hunstville for guiding and inspiring me to improve my writing "bird by bird." An advance thank you to Audrey and Diane Hinton, Perry Hinton, as well as Denise and Willis Turner.

I also want to thank my mother-in-law, Evangelist Evelyn Penn, and father-in-law, Leon Teague, for blessing me with a jewel.

My dear friends who have prayed me through: Deacon Jeff and Sis. GloriaMcLeod and family; Elder Craig and Missionary Fannie Tillman and my precious godsons, Dillon, Jacob and Logan; Beverly Armour-Thomas; Missionary Jane Cornick; James and Izola Tillman; Derrick and Kim Jones; Lisa and Terry Downing; Lorrie and Edwin Smith; and Michelle and Gerald Hicks. A special thank you to those who helped me in Huntsville: Missionary Ann Downing; Lee and Dana Harris; Missionary Chantaye Knotts; Steve and Missionary Rochelle Hendricks.

Dr. Elton and Edna Amos and Old Landmark COGIC; Dr. Terrell and Pearl Harris and the True Light COGIC; Dr. Mattie Thomas of Alabama A&M University; Pastor Wilson and Bethel AME Church; Dr. Jean Goodine of Northern Virginia Community College; and Dr. Joyce Pettus—all of whom have helped me along the way.

Mata Elliott, Leslie J. Sherrod, and Yolonda Tonette Sanders, my fellow writers and lifetime friends. Thank you for reading, but most of all, for the prayers and friendship. I love you guys so much.

The local Glory Girls Reading Group (Lolita and Andrea Jones, Evelyn McCallum; Felecia Audain, Marquita Williams, Jane Cornick, Yolanda Harris, Joyce and Rachel Campbell, Sonji Turner, Shirley Dotson, Shannon Warren, Frowanee Porter, Sis. Essex, and Sabrina Williams)

To all the readers—thank you for your support. You'll never know how much it means to be able to share with you. A special message to those who are in the midst of a trial—hold on and know that your trial is going to serve a purpose!

Blessings,

MaRita

CHAPTER 1

Sydney

I am my beloved's, and my beloved is mine.
Song of Solomon 6:3

The faint aroma from the floral arrangements, decorated with sprays of chrysanthemums, roses, and carnations, combined with the sterile smell of the funeral home, was enough to make her stomach churn. Sydney Ellington methodically opened her small pearl-embellished purse to retrieve her lace handkerchief, briefly holding it under her nose for a reprieve from the smell. Her thick pecan-colored hair, hanging just past her shouders, hid her face from the outside world until Mother Roberson, her church mother, mistakenly thought she was crying. She bent over, pulling Sydney to her by the shoulders in an embrace. "Honey, weepin' may endure for a night, but joy is comin' in the mornin'. You just hold to His hand, now." She then jerked her aged body as if she were young, indicating that the Spirit of the Lord had touched her.

"Thank you, Mother Roberson, but really, I'm fine," Sydney blankly responded, feeling further nauseated by Mother Roberson's perfume, no doubt bought from the dollar store she frequented. Even Mother Roberson's floral print, salmon and lime-green polyester dress that hugged her large frame seemed dizzying. She moved her legs under the chair so that the old woman's metal cane wouldn't hit her feet as she unsteadily made her way past Sydney.

Appreciative of the kind gesture but glad to return to her own thoughts, Sydney stared ahead at the ornate but tastefully decorated casket. The director of Wilson's Funeral Home, a dignified man who Sydney thought resembled the butler on the television show *Benson,* had explained to her in his quiet and solemn manner that the casket she had selected was one of the home's exclusive designs, making a point to let her know that the ivory-sculpted doves carved on the corners were handcrafted with the best craftsmanship available. Vance had always loved the finer things in life, and Sydney decided that she would spare no expense to lay him to rest in the most dignified way possible. In a strange way, having to attend to the details of Vance's wake and homegoing service had been a welcome distraction for Sydney since it kept her from thinking of her future without her husband.

At first, Sydney was disturbed that her church had allowed a guest church, Grace Tabernacle COGIC, to conduct their week's revival services culminating today, at her church due to its large capacity. This meant that having the wake at her home church, Great Deliverance Church of God in Christ, was not an option unless her father intervened. Instead, she elected to have the wake at the funeral home, which ultimately had been a better decision after all. Because of the space limitations at the funeral home, people were forced to pay their respects and leave.

Sydney surveyed the long processional of mourners who filed past slowly, either squeezing her hand or offering a nod of condolence as they departed. She braced herself, knowing that tomorrow at the homegoing she wouldn't so easily escape the finality and reality of Vance's death. Family, friends, and acquaintances wouldn't leave so quickly, affording her the opportunity to escape into her own thoughts.

From the moment Vance introduced himself to Sydney, she had been attracted to his deep walnut-colored skin, coarse jet-black hair which was always groomed meticulously, and tall stature—all physical characteristics she liked in a man. His unusually keen nose and coal-black eyes deep set against his black full eyebrows only added to his attractiveness.

However, Vance was made up of more than just good looks. With his charisma, charm, successful career, and easygoing nature, Vance attracted women like bees to honey. Sydney had initially tried to resist him, recognizing the attributes of a true player. However, there was a magnetic quality about him. The more she got to know him, the more she realized that there was a sincerity and realness about Vance that Sydney knew she couldn't resist. Convincing Sydney that his player days were long gone was no simple task for Vance, but in time she couldn't help but open her heart to him.

Sydney tried to avoid viewing the shell of a man she had shared the last seven years of her married life with, but now she was forced to deal with the reality of the situation as she sat, uncomfortable and rigid, in her chair. A week ago they had celebrated Valentine's Day, and Vance had given her the diamond "O" around her neck. She touched the necklace as her dark eyes moved anxiously across the room until they couldn't help but focus on her deceased husband. She then clutched her purse in her lap as if her life depended on it. Clinging to the purse helped her to fight back the well of tears reserved for moments of solitude.

Seated beside her, her mother, Darlene, whispered something unintelligible as Sydney struggled to avert her eyes from Vance's lifeless body. However, her eyes rested on him; she couldn't escape. His jet-black hair lay with perfection, just as Vance liked it, shiny waves neatly in place. His keen nose and dark skin with undertones of red from his grandmother's Indian heritage, showed no trace of his passing. He appeared to be in a deep sleep and Sydney thought it best to comfort herself with these thoughts, refusing to believe that he was gone. Instead, she reassured herself that Vance's gray pin-striped suit, accessorized with his favorite bluish-gray tie the color of a clear May sky, was the best choice. She had bought the tie last year, a gift for their anniversary.

Disbelief swelled in her like a tidal wave as she clung desperately to the hope that her husband, who lay so peaceful and handsome, would come back to life. Her heart refused to surrender to the life sentence she seemed to face. Surely, she thought, his muscular arms would cradle her once again. She had to believe that she would have at least one more prayer or "I love you" from him. Her life seemed void of meaning with the prospect of never having the gift of Vance's infectious smile.

Vance had a knack for making Sydney smile in even the most adverse circumstances. He used to give her his concerned look, staring into her eyes while placing his thick, strong hands on her neck to offer a brief massage. "Baby, this too shall pass. It's all gonna work out, and you're gonna make it, Syd. Just stick with the Lord and me. We got your back."

Although Sydney didn't always acknowledge her appreciation for Vance's support and comfort when she was troubled, she often marveled at how his strength and easygoing nature calmed her high-strung nature. When her faith wavered in a situation, she could count on Vance to stand in the gap for her. She silently thanked God for the tears that refused to fall but flooded her vision. Only then did her husband's body become unidentifiable, lifting the truth of his death from her mind if only for a second.

A high-pitched shriek jolted Sydney, causing the tiny hairs on her arms to stand at attention. The all-too-familiar voice of Vance's mother, Ruby, permeated the otherwise quiet room. The gut-wrenching wail echoed through the small funeral home as everyone froze.

"Oh, Lord, why? Why? Why, my baby?" Ruby wept, while her sisters from Alabama tried to comfort her.

Sydney had prayed for a calm, drama-free, dignified viewing and homegoing service, one designed to spare her releasing the emotional dam that was destined to overflow at some point. A tremor raced through her body at the despairing cry.

Her grief-stricken heart jumped in her throat when she heard the *thump* behind her. In a split second her mother-in-law collapsed and was sprawled on the floor. While the nurse from the funeral home and other concerned friends and family members swarmed like bees around the heavyset woman, Sydney winced, dazed, wondering if she should go to her. When she made an attempt to move, the lead in her legs let her know the answer. She covered her mouth with her handkerchief once again, only this time is was to retain her grief.

Sydney couldn't deny her conflicting emotions about Ruby's outburst. Part of her was upset and a little angry by her mother-in-law's behavior. Sydney's struggle to contain her emotions was more difficult with each passing moment and Ruby's outburst only made it that much more difficult. Although she yearned to weep in desperation and join her mother-in-law on the floor of the funeral home, Sydney knew that even in this trial, she was not supposed to grieve like those who didn't have hope. Her mind understood this. She was just waiting for her heart and spirit to get there.

Sydney silently prayed for the incident to subside until she felt the warm hand of her mother, Darlene, on her arm. Her mother whispered as she got up from the pew, "Honey, now don't you go frettin' 'bout Ruby." Darlene wrestled her hand into a deep pocket on the inside of her large purse which carried an array of necessities and pulled out a small vial.

"I knew that this would come in handy one day. Be right back. You just stay right here, honey." A faint smile came over Sydney's face as she remembered all the times she had teased her mother for carrying the smelling salts.

Before rushing over to Ruby, her mother seemed to read Sydney's thoughts, patting her on the shoulder. "Ruby's saved, and she knows God wouldn't put any more on her than she can bear—and that goes for you too. It's gonna be all right. You hear me, honey?"

Sydney nodded, thinking of how in the past she had loathed her mother's way of being composed because others sometimes took it for insensitivity. Despite Sydney's dislike of this trait in her mother, she knew that she herself had inherited it, although she felt unsure that she could uphold the façade of a bereaved but controlled widow.

Sydney's insides churned as she overheard her mother consoling Ruby. "We all got to lean on the Lord. Not to our own understanding, Ruby, 'cause it don't make no sense in the natural, honey."

The look Ruby gave her mother said what Sydney didn't have the heart to say. She, too, was tired of the endless scriptures people hurled at her as if it were going to make her feel better immediately, no matter how well-intentioned. Sydney wondered if she had some kind of moral obligation to make people feel better by agreeing with what they said when they tried to comfort her. But their "comforting" words couldn't fill the emptiness inside.

She didn't want to "get through this." At only thirty- three years old, her husband was gone. She was quite sure that her mama, for instance, wouldn't want to get through it if it were her daddy. Immediately ashamed and shocked at her own misdirected anger, she repented for her unkind thoughts toward her mother and others who loved her and were only trying to help. She just wanted people to stop acting like it was going to be okay. It *wasn't* okay, and she had to face the fact that it would never be again.

As the traditional gospel hymns recorded onto the funeral home's sound system played one after another, Sydney attempted to find solace in the soloist's words, "I'm goin' up to yonder. I'm going up to yonder. I'm going up to yonder to be with my Lord." The song always gave her so much hope at other people's homegoing services. They were words she had sung in the choir for other people's funerals since she was a child, but now the words only seemed to make the service more difficult to bear. Sydney didn't want Vance to be going anywhere forever without her, even if it was heaven.

Since Sydney's father had been her pastor all of her life, he had taught her well about the danger of not living saved and not being in the Lord's perfect will. She could not deny that the Lord had blessed her generously with Vance.

It was only a month ago that Vance had revealed his call to minister the gospel. He had served as a deacon and had served as Chairman of the Deacon Board for the last five years, and that had been challenging. While Vance had wholeheartedly embraced his new call to the ministry, Sydney had been less than enthused because she knew all too well what the responsibilities of a minister were. As it was, Vance's position as a deacon meant he was almost always the first to get to church and the last to leave. There were constant meetings that cut into Vance's already much-too-full schedule. With his position as the Vice President of Research and Development at Xerox, along with his church responsibilities, Vance's free time was scarce.

Vance hadn't even been afforded the opportunity to go before the church with the news. Sydney couldn't fathom why the Lord had called him to preach but had not allowed him to even begin the task. None of it made sense to her, but she knew that she should bless the Lord at all times, even when she didn't understand anything. She closed her eyes and whispered to herself, "Thank You for Your mercy, Lord. In spite of it all, thank You." It didn't matter that her heart didn't believe her words. She had been trained like an athlete trains for a marathon to do certain things out of obedience and habit. For her, speaking life and faith in dispiriting situations came as second nature.

Sydney could no longer hold back the hot tears that slid down her cocoa-colored cheek because her faith was being tested in ways that she had never thought possible.

Once the processional of mourners seemed to clear, Sydney stood up and walked over to Vance's body and touched his stiff left hand which exposed his wedding ring, a simply made gold band with three small diamonds adorning the center. Vance had told her when admiring his ring, "One diamond for the Father, one for the Son, and one for the Holy Ghost." She held her own hand out looking at her own much-too-lavish ring, at least according to her, and couldn't believe that their forever could be so short.

Sydney searched his body for clues, but there was no visible trace of the accident that had caused his death. To her, he only slept.

Within seconds, the smell of her father's inexpensive aftershave reached Sydney well before she felt his gentle touch on her shoulder. Her father cleared his throat in his customary way before whispering, "Sydney, are you okay, honey?" Samuel's raspy baritone voice faltered.

Sydney was surprised that her father, who had the habit of speaking to her and her sister like the pastor more than their father, sounded so much like the doting father he was at heart. Hearing his caring tone made Sydney wonder if she should disclose the events that had haunted her since her husband's passing.

She quickly decided against it when her father repeated, "You okay, Syd?"

"I just wanted to touch him, Daddy." Her fingers grazed lightly over the initials engraved on the gold cufflink of his shirt.

Samuel positioned his arm around his daughter's waist and gently led her back to her seat on the front row. Under his breath, Samuel whispered, "Only You know, Lord."

She sank back into the funeral home chair, emotionally exhausted. All of her life, Sydney's father had admonished his daughters, "Don't y'all let the sun go down on ya' anger. Ain't no blessin' in that at all." Sydney longed to tell her father about the argument she had had with Vance on the morning before his passing, but shame kept her from revealing the bitter confrontation.

She couldn't help but to think about what her father would think of her if he knew that she had not only let the sun go down on her anger, but also let it come back up again with it still coursing through her veins. She had treated Vance more horribly than she ever had the night before and morning of his death, and she was paying a dear penalty for it.

Vance had tried to end the argument that had begun the evening before, but Sydney wasn't ready for the conflict to end. She wanted change, and she wanted it immediately.

She had unleashed her frustration. "Vance, I'm so sick of everything and everybody being more important than me! You're never here and when you are, you're so tired and out of it that you only sleep!"

"Syd, like I told you last night, I've had a lot on me lately, but you're always important to me. Your happiness means everything to me. My schedule at work is going to slow down after the end of this month. Just hang tight and we'll take a cruise or do whatever you want to just get away." He had then tried to hug her, but she had pushed him away.

"I'm tired of the same old excuses, Vance. You're saying all of this now to shut me up, but your schedule will still stay the same old crazy way. Why does everyone else get more of you than I do?"

"Listen, Syd, that's simply not true. You know that you always have my heart."

Sydney remained unmoved and when Vance noticed, he continued, "You know I just got this promotion on my job. I told you from the beginning that it was going to be a lot of late nights and a little traveling for the first six months. Things are gonna get better."

"Do you think I'm going to believe that when you've already told Daddy that you've been called to the ministry? For the rest of our lives you're going to be busy, obligated, and tied down. I mean, I am simply not for having a baby with the kind of schedule you have."

Vance stopped her. "It's not just my schedule, Syd. You have a lot on your plate too."

She put her hand on her hip. "*My* schedule is nothing like yours. I'm prepared to totally adjust my life for a baby. As it is, we've waited probably too long. Do you realize that we've been married for seven years and, yes, our careers have taken off, just like we planned. We've helped Daddy to increase membership at the church. But look at our family. I mean, for all I know I may not even be able to have children." Sydney knew that this was the subject that affected Vance, since he had been trying to persuade her for the past two years that the time was right to have a baby. Sydney too, had, longed for a baby yet feared that she'd have to do most of the childrearing herself. She wanted her husband to be there.

Anguish spilled over Vance's face when he heard Sydney's words. He pleaded, "Syd, don't even speak that! You know that us having a baby is what I want more than just about anything right now. Don't penalize me for doing what the Lord has for me to do and for trying to provide the best life I can for you, Maya, and our future children."

Her voice dripping with sarcasm, Sydney responded, "Oh, yeah, I'm the one trying to prevent you from doing the Lord's work right? I'm also the one who doesn't even want you to work, right? It's just that you go overboard with everything. Don't forget, Vance, I grew up with my daddy working at the plant and being a pastor. Just like you, my father is a great man, and you're a great guy. Everyone loves him and wants him, but we needed him more than he was available for us. I don't want to subject our child to that! I have practically begged you to start saying no to some of the extra things you commit yourself to at work and at church, and what do you do? Even when Daddy asked for someone to head the men's fellowship group last week, what do you do? You volunteered, Vance!"

Vance looked down at the floor for a few seconds, unconsciously admitting his defeat by his lack of response.

"Exactly!" Sydney said as she folded her arms in disgust. Then, she dramatically threw her hands up. "Look at this grand house. We have this house, nice cars ... I mean, we have all of this, but I'll give it up for a baby and more of your time."

Looking injured and guilty, Vance still tried to convince her. "I'm not perfect, Syd. I've made mistakes, but it's time for us to start a family. A baby would mean so much to me, Syd. You gotta believe that my schedule will not be like this when we have a baby."

Sydney's nostrils flared as her anger unleashed itself without restraint. "If you think I'm going to have a baby with hopes that your schedule will change, you're out of your mind." She sauntered towards him, spewing out the words "You might think being a part-time father is okay for Maya, but I want a full-time father for our child."

When Sydney saw that Vance's calm demeanor was visibly shaken, just as swiftly as the fury had risen up in her, it suddenly replaced itself with quaking fear. Vance stormed towards her with both fists clenched tightly by his sides.

Her husband got so close to her that she felt his breath against her face and she backed up with apprehension.

"Mission accomplished, Sydney! I'm no more than a part-time father to Maya? So that's what you've been thinking all of this time? Don't act like I'm the one who has waited all these years to have children. If you recall, I've asked you several times during the past seven years and you've always been concerned about the impact it would have on your career. My father wasn't there for me, so the last thing I would do is be a part-time father to our child. The situation with my daughter is what it is. I can have Maya only when her mother allows and you know it. If I could have raised her myself, I would have gladly done that!"

Her eyes filled with tears because Sydney could count the times he had raised his voice, and he rarely had with her during their whole marriage. Yet, she couldn't bring herself to take back the stinging words she had slung his way so casually.

After waiting a minute or so for her response, Vance turned his icy glare from her, snatched his keys from the counter, and slammed the front door with such force that a small picture fell from the wall.

Sydney had surprised herself with the comment about Maya. Vance worked hard to be the best father he could be to Maya, considering that she didn't live with them. Although Sydney knew this, she had wanted to hurt him. Guilt rushed through her, but she consoled herself by remembering that she was justified to use any means necessary for the overall good. After all, she wouldn't be able or willing to have a baby at any age.

Reflecting back on the argument pained Sydney. Over and over, she said how sorry she was for the unkind words, how sorry she was for not being more understanding about his work and spiritual obligations, how sorry she was for not having a baby as soon as Vance wanted. Only there was no one to apologize to but the Lord. Just as her thoughts drifted to Maya, her stepdaughter, she prayed that the relationship wouldn't be severed due to Vance's death.

As if they could read her thoughts, Maya and her mother, Tiffany, appeared in front of her. Sydney squinted. In her delirium of grief, she imagined that it was Vance who stood before her for a split second. She had never seen the sixteen-year-old resemble her father as much as she did today. Her black wavy hair, cut in short, Halle Berry style mimicked her father's, and in spite of the fact that she had her mother's light complexion, her high cheekbones and tall stature mirrored Vance.

"Syd, are you okay?" Maya asked, with red eyes and a tear-streaked face. As she sat down on the pew next to Sydney, she struggled briefly to pull her short skirt down. Recently, Maya's choice in dress had been causing friction between Vance and his daughter. Sydney had tried to explain to him that it was a stage most teenagers go through. She had even reminded him of how difficult it was for a young girl as tall as she was to find trendy clothes.

Sydney laid her stepdaughter's head on her shoulder. "Honey, I'm gonna make it, but how are you?"

Maya's full lips trembled as she shook her head in disbelief and buried her head further into Sydney's chest. Tiffany stood over the two of them, covering her mouth with tissue to muffle her grief.

After Maya stood up, Tiffany sat by Sydney for a moment and the two embraced. There were no words between them, yet there was comfort.

Sydney's head pounded as Tiffany and Maya went back to their seats. Memories collided more quickly than she could sort, especially after seeing Maya again. She had seen Maya only once since Vance's passing, and she couldn't remember much about the visit. There were so many tears and expressions of sympathy from so many people, and Sydney handled them all gracefully with the exception of Maya. Maya's mourning made Sydney's loss more real, and she knew that, like herself, Maya's life would never be the same without her father.

As Sydney picked up one of the mortuary fans to cool herself, she silently prayed again that with Vance's absence, her relationship with Maya wouldn't change. She needed her stepdaughter more than ever, and Sydney imagined that Maya would continue to need her in the months and years to come—at least she hoped she would.

She studied the famous picture by Moneeta Sleet copied on the fan, which ironically showed Coretta Scott King, dressed in black mourning attire with her daughter Bernice hugging her at Martin Luther King Jr.'s funeral. Sydney couldn't count the number of times that she had seen this picture, yet it meant something different to her now on this day of her own mourning. She understood the faraway look Coretta's face held, and Maya, although years older than the young Bernice was at the time of her father's passing, had the same lost look. She wondered how Coretta really felt about having to share her husband with the world and if she had any regrets about that when her husband passed away so suddenly.

What would Maya, or anyone else for that matter, think if they knew that her final conversation with her husband had been filled with venomous words spewed out from her anger? Sydney knew that she was supposed to supply love, support, and understanding. She had never before made anything close to a disagreeable reference about Maya or the prospect of them having a baby, but Satan seemed to take ahold of her whole being and made her lash out in an uncharacteristic way.

Maya had recently begun to develop a tumultuous relationship with her mother and new stepfather. Sydney and her late husband had discussed Maya's noticeable changes with the effects of hormones, dating, and peer pressure. Although Sydney knew that these changes were typical teenager issues, losing a parent could only make things worse.

As Sydney observed Maya with her tall statuesque frame but childlike face, which seemed to be a carbon copy of her father's, still sobbing on her mother's chest, it pained Sydney to know what kind of impact the loss of her father would be at such a difficult and young age. Sydney renewed her determination to remain composed and strong, especially for Maya. She could not even dream of letting her stepdaughter see her fall apart under the strain of Vance's passing. Thinking of times she had witnessed to Maya about God's faithfulness and love for her, Sydney knew that she had to practice what she preached, even if it was difficult for her to understand how God could allow this to happen. She knew that God's will was for people to live, be healed, delivered, and set free. Still, He hadn't saved Vance from death. How this could work for their good was a mystery to her, but she had to somehow hold on to the Word.

When Sydney's mother, Darlene, returned to the pew with Sydney's father and sister, Sherese, Darlene held her eldest daughter's hand so tightly that Sydney's rings pinched her skin, reminding herself that this wasn't some terrible nightmare. Her father had spoken many times to them about everything working out for the good of them that love the Lord, but she couldn't see how Vance's death was working out for her good no matter how hard she tried.

Her father, positioned on the other side of her, sat stoically with his arm behind her. Since Sydney knew that her parents were upset and worried about her, she felt obligated to hold herself together.

Sydney reached up to smooth her hair, which was swept into a neat French roll, and straightened the skirt of her modest cream-colored suit. In her church, it was a tradition for church women to wear white when a saint passes on. As far a Sydney was concerned though, black would've been more appropriate since it would mirror her inner turmoil.

The program rested on her lap with words her mother insisted upon: A Homegoing Celebrating the Life of Vance Steven Ellington. Sydney resented using the word celebration but didn't want to appear as though she wasn't saved. Somehow a death just wasn't a celebration or a victory as far as she was concerned.

"Syd, isn't that Elliot Turner from high school?" her sister, Sherese, whispered from behind.

Without even turning to see who Sherese was talking about, Sydney answered in an annoyed tone, "I have no idea." Sydney couldn't help wondering why Sherese acted like they were at a basketball game or social event. Sydney whispered back, "Sher, it's the third time you've asked me who someone is. Please stop." Sydney didn't care who was in attendance, and her frown let Sherese know it.

"Sher, keep quiet, baby," Darelene scolded. "Honey, do you need some water or anything?" she whispered to Sydney.

"Thanks, Mama. I could use a glass." Sydney knew that her mother wanted to feel useful, and when she got in that mode, the best thing was to allow her to do something.

Whether it was sewing a dress or hemming a suit for someone, visiting the sick and shut-ins, or praying for the needs and desires of the church members and family, Sydney's mother was a true servant, always busy and willing to help. In fact, Darlene brought the phrase in the Bible, "pray without ceasing," to life. She had tried to impress upon her daughters the importance of helping others and sacrificing self.

While Darlene, wearing a white beaded suit and matching hat, returned with the glass of water, Sydney thought about how much her mother had grown to love Vance. Despite her mother's initial misgivings because of Vance's family background, his obligations to a daughter, and most importantly, his not being Pentecostal, Darlene was soon won over by Vance's faithful attendance at almost all of their services, not to mention his education, success, and natural charm. In no time, Darlene loved him as if he were the son she'd never had.

Sydney's father, Samuel, had been an entirely different story. Her father was set against the relationship between his daughter and Vance in the beginning and proved himself to be the most difficult to win over. Samuel thought that Vance was too slick and worldly for his down-to-earth, saved, and respectable daughter, and even more importantly, he questioned his future son-in-law's salvation. Vance's good looks, career, and charm were easy for Samuel to overlook. He was all too familiar with women falling for the wrong qualities in a man, only to end up sitting in his office crying about the collapse of a marriage. His daughter was much too good for that. He and his wife had always stressed the importance of marrying a saved, sanctified, and Holy Ghost-filled man. Apart from these characteristics, Samuel knew that he would never have the peace of knowing that his daughters would be protected and truly loved when he departed from this life.

In the beginning, Samuel didn't hide his disappointment by Sydney's choice in a husband and was equally dismayed at his wife's agreeable attitude toward Vance. Samuel remembered the hopeful look on Sydney's face when Vance first came to their home to meet them. He wasn't fazed by Vance's gift box of chocolates to his wife, along with a copy of "Shirley Caesar Live in Concert," one of his and his wife's favorite gospel artists. Even his conversation filled with "Yes, Ma'ams" and "No, Sirs" in appropriate places couldn't move him. At first, Samuel had refused to marry the two when Vance asked. Sydney was so hurt and angry that she decided to confront her father.

"Daddy, please just trust my judgment. Vance may not be Pentecostal, but he's saved. He wasn't blessed to be brought up in church, but he loves the Lord. He has been so faithful about coming to church with me. I can't even remember the last time he's been to his church," Sydney had wailed.

"What church is that?"

"You know, Daddy. I've told you several times now. He's a member of Hopewell Baptist on Clinton."

"You know, they believe that once saved, always saved. That might make him feel like it don't matter what he does or how he treats you with that type of thinkin'."

"Oh, Daddy, please stop with all the denominational stuff. He's saved. That's what matters."

"If it were only that simple. History has a way of repeatin' itself, and you done told me yourself that the boy's daddy left when he was young. What makes you think he knows how to have a family and be a real man?"

Tears of frustration filled her eyes. "You're just finding reasons not to like him, Daddy! Because his dad left him, he's resolved not to be like that!"

"Seem like a good time for him to prove himself would've been when he got that girl with child. That's when you find out what a real man is."

As the argument ensued for fifteen minutes or so, Sydney sat dabbing her nose until she searched her father's deep gray eyes and stated with assurance, "It's all because he wasn't raised in holiness, and that's just not fair! The requirements for being saved are in the Bible, cut and dried, Daddy, and Vance is saved for the last time."

"Watch yourself, daughter." Samuel had warned. "Seem like you're coming a tad too close to bein' disrespectful. You don't need to remind me what the Bible says about salvation. That boy needed to be thinkin' about salvation before he got that other girl pregnant with his baby."

Her father frowned and started to speak again, but Sydney interrupted, "Vance's little girl's name is Maya, and he takes really good care of her. He knows that what he did was sinful, but the baby is not the sin. She's innocent, and as far as I'm concerned, the Lord has forgiven Vance. I'm sorry, Daddy. I just need you to trust my judgment. You and Mama have raised me right, and I've prayed about this. I know that marrying Vance is the Lord's will for my life."

Several minutes of silence passed and then Sydney added, "I need and want your blessing."

All of Samuel Hightower's biblical training, decades of being a pastor, and many life experiences had not prepared him to let his daughter go. As he leaned back in his leather office chair, his stern countenance melted as he noticed his daughter's red and puffy eyes.

Darlene had informed Sydney that when her father had returned home to talk to his wife about the disagreement between the two, she had scolded, "Get over yourself, Samuel. Don't go blamin' the fact that you don't want Sydney to marry on account of Vance. There's nothing wrong with that boy. As a matter of fact, I think he's good for her. We both know what your real issue is."

"Excuse me, but just exactly what is my real issue? That boy knows nothin' about what livin' holy means! He can't possibly think that by joinin' the church and goin' to a few church services that makes you saved, sanctified, and filled with the Holy Ghost!" Samuel snapped.

"Don't you go raisin' your pressure. Just face it, Sam, you're just afraid to let your daughter go. That girl's gonna be fine, and what's more, we both know that Vance has been to plenty more services than most of those boys Sydney's age who grew up in holiness," Darlene answered in a nonchalant manner, undaunted by her husband as she continued scrubbing the kitchen counter. "And don't you go gettin' hung up on the fact that the boy grew up Baptist neither. There's one church. Saints got to remember that holiness is a lifestyle, not a denomination. Even we saved, sanctified, Holy Ghost-filled Saints got to remember that. We gotta get this thing right."

Samuel smoothed his thick mustache, a habit he'd acquired whenever he was upset, and asked his wife to come into his study.

He sank into his aged, leather chair, a gift from his wife and daughters at least eight years ago. As he studied the portrait of his daughters on his desk, he zeroed in on Sydney.

"Darlene, how old did you say Syd was in this picture? Was it seven or eight?"

Darlene stayed at the entrance of the door. "Eight. She was a sweet little thang, huh?"

"Sweet as she can be but too serious, don't you think?"

Darlene smiled. "Just like her father, I suppose."

"You're right. I just ain't ready to let go of my baby girl." He tossed his pen into his pen holder in frustration. "I guess there is something special about that boy and no matter how much I'm not ready for this whole marriage thing, I guess there's not too much wrong with him when you think about what could be wrong. When I think about it, he's a heap better than some of them boys Sherese tries to have us meet. I just hope the boy's for real saved."

His wife had smiled, but knowing that he had the gift of discernment, she had asked, "Now, Samuel, do you really have questions about the boy's salvation?"

Samuel let a grunt escape and he admitted, "Honey, I guess I believe he's saved, but I just plum don't like that he's got a child. That's gonna be a lot for Sydney."

When he realized that his wife wasn't going to respond, he added proudly, "Aside from that, I just don't think anybody is good enough for either one of my daughters."

Darlene untied her apron and folded it. "Now you're gettin' to the real root of it, Sam. It'll all work itself out as long as they stay saved and love one another."

Sydney's mother had made a point to reveal the conversation to Sydney so she could understand the depth of love that Samuel had for her. Darlene often feared that her daughters would take Samuel's actions at face value and misjudge his intentions. Sydney knew that her father felt there would be lots fewer visits from his daughter. Sydney had to accept that she wouldn't have as much time to call just to make sure he was eating right, and she wouldn't have as much time to keep him company while he did his gardening or help out with the youth at church. Sydney had to admit, if only to herself, that it was hard for her to let go too. She loved her father and often thought about the prayer her father had said to give her his blessing.

Samuel had looked up toward heaven and prayed, "Lord, forgive my selfishness and stubbornness. Please help me to no longer be a hindrance but to be supportive of my daughter's upcoming marriage. Help Vance to grow stronger in Your word and Your ways so that he will know how to lead his new family and love my daughter the way she deserves to be loved."

Her father married the two in an elegant ceremony with hundreds of guests at his church. In time, Samuel grew close to his son-in-law, and when he realized that Vance was committed to the Lord and Sydney, he also embraced him as the son he'd never had.

The remaining people lingered today, offered their condolences, and then filed out of the funeral home. Tomorrow, her father, who had performed her wedding almost seven years ago, would eulogize her thirty-five-year-old husband. Vance was too young and they were too happy for such a tragic ending. Sydney felt the nausea revisit her as her head spun.

Her sister, Sherese, had begun fanning her. "Syd? You okay?" Sydney didn't have the strength to answer, and her own questions were swirling around in her head. *Why Vance? Why now? Why?* She knew that she shouldn't think this way, but she just couldn't keep herself from wondering what she could have done so wrong for God to allow such a horrific thing to happen.

CHAPTER 2

Chanel

Whosoever shall compel thee to go a mile, go with him twain.

Matthew 5:41

Relieved to be home from the service, Chanel carelessly tossed her Coach bag onto the nearest end table, kicked off her winter-white stiletto heels, and flung her tired but restless body onto her plush ivory sofa. Out of habit, she groped for the remote to turn the television on, and when Jerry Springer appeared on the screen, she flicked it off in disgust. What she longed for was peace and quiet.

As she embraced a throw pillow, she wondered how her best friend was really doing. Chanel had agreed to leave Sydney at her parents' home only after Sydney had reassured her that she would be fine. Chanel told herself that Sydney seemed to be holding up pretty well considering the circumstances. Then again, Sydney was also the type of person who made it very difficult to tell exactly how she was feeling. Chanel yearned to be there for her friend, but this would be the first time in their over twenty-year friendship that she didn't have a clue as to what to say or what to do. In this situation, her sass and quick wit couldn't ease the tension or mask the devastating heartache of her best friend's loss. Vance really was gone.

She grabbed her rhinestone-studded cell phone from the outside pocket of her purse and dialed Sherese's cell number.

"Hello?"

"Hey, Sher, it's me. How you doin'?"

"Girl, I guess I'm okay. It's Syd I'm worried about though."

Chanel quickly sat upright with concern. "What? You need me to come back over to your parents' house? She is still there, isn't she?"

"Yeah, relax. Syd is talking to Beatrice and Albert Jones right now. They just heard so they were anxious to come by. You just get some rest. There's nothing nobody can do but pray, I guess. I just can't believe all this. I gotta admit, I have never seen Syd, Daddy, or Mama this shaken. Shoot, I don't know if I've ever been this messed up about anything myself. It just doesn't make any sense."

Chanel slumped back on the sofa. "Well, I guess that's to be expected. I can't believe it either, but God knows. Mmmmph mmmmph, mmmm. Tell Syd I'll call her later, and you definitely call me later on this evening. In the meantime, if you need something, just call. I can be over in twenty minutes."

"You know I will, Chanel. Oh, before I let you go, did you reach Tommy?"

"Not yet, but I don't even want to be bothered with his sorry self right now."

"All right then, I'll talk to you later."

"Yep, talk to you."

As tired as Chanel felt, she was met by the unwelcome spirit of restlessness that had been visiting her for the days since Vance's death. Her body felt like lead as she lifted herself from the sofa to the bathroom. After rummaging through her disheveled medicine cabinet, behind the Batman Band-Aids and small box of Q-tips, she found her prescribed sleeping pills. She quickly scanned the brown bottle for the expiration date and let out a small sigh of relief. The pills were still good even though they had been prescribed over a year ago by her primary physician for insomnia.

"Thank the Lord," she mumbled to herself as she popped two in her mouth, threw her head back, and swallowed them—a skill she had acquired at a young age.

Chanel started to leave the bathroom and then she remembered Sydney and Sherese's mother, who had witnessed her adeptness at gulping pills down without water. Darlene had scolded, "Child, what in the heavens are you tryin' to do? Put a hole in your stomach? You gotta drink water with pills."

When Darlene scolded her, Chanel found a strange pleasure in it since it showed that someone could truly care about even the little things. Recalling the words of the woman who had been almost like a mother to her, she filled the empty cup beside her toothbrush with water and drank.

She combed through her shoulder-length mane, appreciating the honey-gold highlights that Ta'Nisha, a new, young beautician at Diva Designs, had put in her hair a few days earlier. It didn't matter what was going on in Chanel's life, she religiously kept her hair appointments for two reasons: She didn't want to bother with her hair, and she never got to go to the beauty shop until she was an adult. Getting her hair done professionally became more symbolic for her as it made her feel that she had "arrived" and earned the privilege. Chanel always acted like Sydney's and Sherese's constant jokes about her always having her hair "laid" bothered her, but inside she beamed over the compliment. Still, no matter how good her hair looked, the dark gloomy circles under her hazel eyes revealed her mental state.

Even before Vance's passing, Chanel had been overworked and tired. Having her own business meant working long hours at the café, and taking care of her four-year-old son, Zachary, along with the stress in her marriage had put her on overload.

Chanel undressed slowly, reviewing her conversations with Sydney over the past several days. Her fear of saying something that might appear to be insensitive or inappropriate, an unfortunate trait she'd inherited from her mother, gripped her in an uncharacteristic way. Her usual sassiness suspended, her words were minimal. She had spent so many of the past several days with Sydney. Listening and helping her with the business that needed to be taken care of for the service consumed their time. Her wit, which had always proven to be an indispensable asset in times of duress, was now rendered useless. The only problem was that she wondered who she really was without it.

As she sank into the mattress, Chanel rationalized her loss of speech with her dearest friend. She had determined she would never become like her mother, Nyla, who had mastered the art of always saying the wrong thing. Long ago she adopted the policy that it was better to keep your mouth shut than to put your foot in it. She recited the scripture to herself. "A fool's mouth is his destruction, and his lips are the snare of his soul."

It reminded her to just be there for Sydney because she knew that words were less important than her presence now. Chanel was determined to use caution when interacting with Sydney, who was like a sister to her. She had learned all too well from her mother's lack of female friends that having a cutting tongue can be detrimental to relationships.

Although Chanel had been successful in restraining her tongue with Sydney, when it came to her husband, Tommy, she had become a loose cannon. Even though she could feel the Holy Spirit's small still voice prompting her to hold her peace and not argue with him, all too often she allowed her flesh to control her.

A few weeks ago, Chanel had told Sydney how angry she was with her husband. "He doesn't care about how hard I work. He's so selfish. What kind of man quits a dependable job to pursue some crazy dream."

"Chanel, you didn't think Tommy's dream of pursuing a career in music was crazy when you first met him, " Sydney had replied.

"Yeah, but that was when he was teaching. I never thought he'd actually quit."

"Well, I'll admit that he probably didn't pick the best time to do this, but the bottom line is, Tommy loves you. He's not so selfish, Chanel. He did get the green light from you before he started working on his recording, remember?"

Chanel had conceded that. She had told him it was okay, but things had changed. "I don't think if you love someone you make the kind of choices Tommy makes."

"He may not do everything you want him to do, but he does a lot. I don't know any man who is so involved with his child. Furthermore, that man drops everything when you need him. He's not as bad as you're making him out to be, Chanel. It really could be worse."

Chanel had quipped, "Easy for you to say, Syd. You're married to a darn near perfect man."

"Everything isn't always what it seems, Chanel. I'm just gonna leave it at that."

Lately, Chanel knew she had been sounding more and more like her mother which both alarmed and repulsed her, and she knew her words could cut Tommy sharper than any knife. Yet, she seemed unable to stop the criticisms when they started to flow.

Chanel decided to call her mother-in-law to check on Zachary. Tommy's mother loved Zachary dearly and jumped at the chance to spend time with her first and only grandson. When Chanel told her about Vance, Olivia had been eager to keep her son for the weekend.

"Hi, Olivia."

"Hey, how are you, honey?"

"I'm doin' okay. The question is, how are you doing with Zach?"

"Now, baby, you know that boy's busy as he wants to be, but he's the reason I'm gettin' younger instead of older so I'm good."

Even though Chanel wasn't supposed to get Zach until Friday, she said, "You know I can swing by and get him. The service is over and Chanel doesn't need me."

"No, now sweetie, you get you some rest. Me and Zach got some plans. I already promised him we was gonna go to the mall to the play area and get one of them hot cinnamon rolls. You wanna talk to him though?"

Chanel felt comfortable letting Zach stay when she knew Olivia wasn't overly tired and heard how happy her son was to stay with his grandmother. She yawned as she put her phone on the speaker so she could listen to her messages.

Her aunt had a habit of leaving her messages as if they were in mid-conversation. "You ain't never home, or is it you ain't got time for your old Aunt Ruthie? Listen, give me a call. Your Mama's was over here at the house yesterday and she ain't lookin' too hot. I know you all ain't talkin' still, but you need to give her some help. She took care of you all her life. Like I said, I know you don't need to see her. You can drop some change by me and I'd give it to her. Yep, get it right to her. Love you, baby. Call me."

Chanel put her head in her hands in frustration as she sat up on the edge of her bed. Her past made her feel like she wore ankle weights from which she couldn't break free. Ever since she had run into her Aunt Ruthie a few months ago at a gas station, an aunt she had barely seen as a child, she had been barraged with phone calls. Chanel had made the mistake of giving her money once after her aunt said she needed to go to the doctor for foot trouble. Now, Aunt Ruthie suddenly loved her and found every reason imaginable to call and ask for money. After asking around town, Chanel found out that her dear old Aunt Ruthie was a crack addict of the worst kind. Aunt Ruthie, her mother's half sister, was one of the many dysfunctional members of her mother's fragmented family. Long ago, Chanel had decided to forget about her broken heart and about not having a family like the Cosby's, but she was determined not be what she had seen in her mother.

Nyla spoke her mind with no regard for the feelings of others. As a child, Chanel grew to loathe bringing friends home because of Nyla's razor tongue. She never grew accustomed to the embarrassment that came from the cigarette hanging from her mother's discolored lips, the much–too-tight spandex pants that Nyla loved to wear, and the profanity-filled vocabulary she spat out at anyone who was in her way. Chanel's childhood memories haunted and shamed her.

By the age of thirteen, Chanel had grown tired of her mother's vulgarity and carefree lifestyle. Nyla's constant partying coupled with the countless men she brought into Chanel's life and her brother's life matured Chanel well beyond her years. She could never forget the argument that had catapulted her into early adulthood.

Forever etched in her memory was the shiver that ran down her spine and made her clench her teeth as she stood above her mother. Nyla sat on the dirty, rust-colored velvet sofa scorching yet another burn mark into it from smashing her cigarette into the aged fabric. The stench of alcohol, cigarette smoke, and the much-too-generous amount of Royal Crown hair grease on Nyla's unwashed hair seemed to almost burn the insides of Chanel's nostrils.

"Nyla, please. Can't you just try to sober yourself up a little?" Chanel never remembered calling her mother Mama. Although this bothered Chanel when she was younger, she realized that her mother didn't want men to know that she had two children. The older Chanel got, the happier she was about Nyla's insistence on her children calling her by her first name. Just as Nyla didn't want to acknowledge them as her children, Chanel didn't want to acknowledge her as her mother.

Nyla sucked in on the cigarette and blew the smoke back out, oblivious to her daughter's plea. Chanel's fear subsided and anger took its place. "You're embarrassin' me and Ramone. I feel like we're livin' in some kind of club or somethin'!"

Nyla, in her perpetually drunken state, raised up and swaggered over to Chanel, pointed her finger in her face, and with a nasty whisper, smelling of smoke and alcohol, said, "Listen up, you little goody-two-shoes. You think you better than me? Huh? Huh? You ain't—and your daddy ain't—and you never gonna amount to nothin'. I don't care how much you hang round that pastor's girl. You ain't her. You think you embarrassed? Girl, I'll show you embarrassed if you keep on."

Chanel cringed at her mother's hurtful words but remained silent, fuming on the inside. Chanel's nostrils flared with anger.

"What's more, little heifer, don't you be lookin' at me like that." She muttered, "Little narrow eyes like your daddy's. Smart mouth like his too." She took a swig of her cheap gin and seemed to swish it around in her mouth before continuing. "And you better not ever try to tell me how to live unless you intend on puttin' food in your own mouth and payin' your own light and gas bill!" Nyla hissed.

Her mother didn't work and Chanel couldn't figure out how or why she had collected disability for so many years, but she knew that the low-income housing development they were living in reminded her of the *Good Times* reruns she watched when their cable was on. She couldn't count the number of times their lights and gas had been shut off. So many times Chanel had dreamed of taking care of herself and Ramone and doing a much better job than her mother had ever done.

While Nyla's venomous words flowed without remorse, Chanel cut her eyes, crossed her arms, and said more with her look than any words could. Despite her mother's drunken state, Nyla seemed to feel the disrespect, anger, and disgust in her daughter's eyes.

Nyla rose up like a tornado on a killer rampage and drew her hand back and slapped Chanel with massive force. Chanel rocked but steadied herself, resolved not to let her mother see her wince or cry out.

When Nyla realized the battle of wills, she balled her hand into a fist and socked her in the mouth, determined to win. A splatter of blood speckled the rust sofa, and when Chanel crumpled to the floor in agony, she knocked a glass ashtray from the coffee table onto the floor.

Her younger brother, Ramone, rushed in and went to Chanel as she covered her bloody lip. "What's going on in here?"

"Boy, don't you start nothin' in here that ain't your business. Go on back to your room."

"Nyla! You plain crazy?" Before Ramone could say anything else, Nyla slammed her gin bottle onto the nearest table and began her assault on her son.

"You both gonna respect me! I done gave up everything for you ungrateful children."

As Nyla's rage continued, Chanel knew that Ramone could've retaliated, but he didn't. He took the abuse from his mother to defend her, and he showed her what love really meant that day.

From that day forward, Chanel put on an even tougher exterior, determined not to let her mother or anyone else tell her who she was or what she could become.

During this period of turmoil with Nyla, Chanel met Sydney one day in the school cafeteria. Chanel had always admired Sydney's neat pleated skirts, although other kids often made fun of them. Sydney admired Chanel's nonchalant attitude in the face of being picked on by peers.

Chanel had been sitting by herself, eating her lunch, when May Turner and her posse taunted her. May called in a singsong manner, "You enjoyin' your free lunch, Miss Goodwill?"

Chanel ate her lunch without even looking at May and her friends until May added, "Your mama need to go buy you some lotion at the Goodwill to put on them ashy elbows." Her friends laughed mercilessly.

Looking up from her lunch, Chanel got up, walked over to May and said, "When your daddy buys you a tooth to fill that big ole gap in your front teeth, that's when my mama will go to the Goodwill to buy me some lotion."

May and her friends stood speechless, and before Chanel turned to walk away, she added, "By the way, if you need to find your sorry daddy, you can probably find him over at my mama's house."

Sydney got up from where she was sitting and took her lunch to eat with Chanel, and their friendship blossomed from there.

Since Sydney often asked Chanel over to her house, Chanel could escape the troubled and chaotic atmosphere she was growing up in, even if it was only temporarily. This precious time Chanel spent at the Hightower home became a safe haven from the insults and drunken rages Nyla daily hurled her daughter's way.

Her brother's anger and loneliness manifested itself in gang activity and drugs, but still, Chanel's mother was so caught up in her own addictions and concerns, she didn't even notice her son's lifestyle was becoming destructive. When fifteen-year-old Ramone was killed in a shooting over a drug deal, Chanel's resentment toward her mother grew to total disgust.

Ramone's death spiraled Nyla's already self-destructive behavior into epic proportions. To Chanel, Ramone's death became yet another excuse for Nyla to abuse herself and refuse to accept accountability for her role in her son's demise. Chanel had decided that she didn't care what Nyla did to herself. Since Chanel had been unsuccessful at saving Ramone, she wasn't in the frame of mind to try to save a woman who should've been mothering her and her brother.

In spite of her lack of family support, Chanel always expressed her gratitude for the encouragement and love she had received from

Sydney, Sherese, and their parents. The Hightower family had treated her as a daughter when Sydney and Chanel became friends, picking her up for church services, taking her home after school activities she shared with Sydney, and providing love, spiritual training, and guidance to her. As a result, Chanel's teenage years often were filled with daydreaming that the Hightowers were her parents and sometimes secretly envying Sydney's and Sherese's loving upbringing.

Before drifting off to sleep Chanel listened to message after message. The last one was from Lena, her new assistant manager at the Anchored in the Rock Café.

"Mrs. Loughlin, I just wanted to let you know that the new shipment we've been waiting for is in. If you'd like me to, I can make a sign for the new orange mocha cappuccino. Oh yeah, also, Deborah Mannings called and she wanted to know if you needed any more mugs for the kiosk. Okay, well, you know I'll be here until nine thirty tonight, so call me if you have time. Talk to you soon."

Hiring Lena had been one of the best business decisions that Chanel had ever made. Chanel recognized that she needed more help than what her two part-time employees could give. And despite Chanel's misgivings about hiring an assistant, Lena fit what she wanted and needed for the business. Even though her new assistant was only twenty-two, her efficiency, energy, and willingness to learn made her an asset to the café. Vance was the one who had informed Chanel that one of his coworkers' daughters was looking for a job in restaurant management.

Vance had told her, "Chanel, if you want your business to grow, you have to take risks. Letting go a little will help you if you find the right person."

"That's the operative word, Vance—right. You don't even seem like you know a whole lot about her."

Vance had chuckled. "You are such a control freak, Chanel. It's all good, though. I guess that's what it takes, but the time will come when you need to trust somebody. You can't do it all by yourself."

As customer volume increased, Chanel caved to the pressure and agreed to interview the young woman. Chanel had been so impressed by Lena's drive and positive attitude that she was willing to take a chance and hire her on the spot. She had told Lena, "If you work hard and stay focused, there is no limit to what God can do for you."

On days like today especially, Chanel thanked the Lord for Vance's wisdom and guidance in hiring an assistant because it had made a difference. She had been able to spend a little more time with Zach and Tommy, as well as get ahead on some of the bookkeeping.

Chanel always wanted to give back to her community because she felt there were too many brothers and sisters who were just out for themselves. This was one of the reasons that she had decided to establish her business in her old neighborhood. Rochester, known for its brutal and long winters lasting from late October to April, seemed ideal for her café. Chanel knew that people in her community loved warm drinks on cold days just as much as anyone else in the city, but they couldn't afford three to four dollars for a cup of coffee.

Rochester, an established upstate New York city known for its thriving local businesses and restaurants along with its old money, was a city ripe for a new African-American business in an African-American community. Yet, it took a lot for African-American businesses to work there. Many people, black and white, were often skeptical of black-owned businesses.

People didn't hold back their opinions about her opening a business in her old neighborhood. Many felt that a business like hers couldn't possibly thrive in the "hood" in Rochester, especially the bank loan officers she'd approached with her business plan. However, when she finally got her loan approval, Chanel proved her skeptics wrong.

The first two years were challenging. Her café was in the same strip mall as the A&N Liquor Store, and the patrons of the liquor store would buy their liquor and then want to congregate at the tables of the café. They seemed to gravitate to the café in droves to sit in the warm and comfortable atmosphere. In time Chanel began to witness by playing gospel music over the stereo system and even placed little plaques on each table with scriptures such as "As for me and my house, we will serve the Lord." To Chanel's surprise, the patrons of the liquor store stopped frequenting her café without a word from Chanel.

In her third year of business, the boarded-up vacant office space next to the café was rented out to a local barber, Phil Jackson. In the first week of his barber shop's grand opening, he had let Chanel know, "Mrs. Loughlin, I gotta tell you, I always wanted to open up a barber shop, but I didn't know if it would work with all the crime in the area. Your café really made me feel like the shop could work."

Chanel was proud that she had inspired someone else to take a chance and invest something positive in the community. She had told the young owner, "Well, the Lord is good. All the glory belongs to Him."

The owner had smiled at her a bit uncomfortably, but she knew that he respected her. He had helped her by routinely trimming the small area of shrubs on the front side of the café, as well as helping her to keep debris from the storefronts.

In time, the Anchored in the Rock Café had established a solid customer base with a reputation for having the best and most reasonably priced coffee and pastries in the city, so much so that many claimed that Starbucks had nothing on it. Chanel knew that the success of the business had very little to do with the coffee and pastries or her. She knew that the Lord had blessed her and shown her favor by allowing her café to breathe a little life into such a depressed neighborhood.

The atmosphere in the small café was encouraging to the patrons, both saved and unsaved, because it made the customers feel peace, warmth, and love. Anchored in the Rock Café had been like her baby. She was intimately involved in every detail including the nutmeg-colored walls accented with other hues of browns and tans. Gospel jazz always played throughout the café and the smell of Mother Rivers' pecan pie, caramel cake, and sweet rolls gave the café its own signature taste in the community.

The city's only African-American newspaper, *Speakin' the News*, featured an article and review of the café. Chanel was so proud of the five stars the reviewer gave the café that she had the article framed in the entryway for everyone to see. She even highlighted the section that read: "The overall experience at the café leaves one not only feeling satisfied by the coffee and donuts, but also on a surprisingly refreshing spiritual high. From the music to the friendly staff, the Anchored in the Rock Café has a charm and sincerity that makes it sure to be an anchor in Rochester's south side."

Despite the glowing reviews, making and keeping her business successful wasn't without its challenges. For the first two-and-a-half years, every bit of the money Chanel made from the business had to be put right back into it to keep it afloat. She was so thankful during those times that after high school she had worked diligently for five years until she was an assistant manager at a local diner. Not only had Chanel gained the business savvy through school and practical experience but she was also able to save a little. Her financial discipline had paid off. God had blessed her.

———

Chanel dreamed about her father. Only it wasn't really her father. He looked like him and spoke like him, but he was there for her. In her dreams, she too looked like herself and spoke like herself, but she had peace. The air of confidence she possessed in her dreams came from knowing that Leonard wasn't the absent father he was when she was awake.

"*Daddy!*" *Chanel ran to greet her father on her high school graduation day.*

"*Hi, baby!*" *Leonard smiled with pride.*

"*I knew you'd come!*"

"*You know nothin' could stop me from seeing my daughter graduate.*" *The loose-fitting white linen shirt and matching pants her father wore accentuated his natural good looks as he smoothly slid his hand into his pocket to retrieve a small box for her.*

"*Daddy, you didn't have to get anything.*" *Chanel couldn't contain her excitement because even in her dreams her mother was still her mother and hadn't bought her a graduation present.*

Chanel took the small box he extended to her and opened it. In the velvet box lay a lovely gold charm bracelet with a charm that said "Daddy's Girl."

As Chanel embraced her father in the dream, she leaned on him with the weight of the world on her shoulders, only her father didn't collapse under the pressure. In fact, he held her tightly, holding her up with a strength Chanel had never experienced. And Chanel felt loved.

Chanel tossed and turned as her pleasant dreams of her father turned into a nightmare about her mother. She didn't know why having an absent father had been better in the deep recesses of her mind than a bad parent who was present, but it was. Maybe it was because her father always seemed so remorseful about his absence from Chanel's life. Maybe it was because her father was an admitted alcoholic but had gone as far as getting treatment. Maybe it was because she knew how impossible her mother was to live with. She just couldn't bring herself to reject the only close relative who seemed to want a relationship with her.

Anytime Chanel saw her father, he'd say, "Girl, if you don't look like your daddy, I don't know who does." Chanel always pretended not to know what he was talking about, but although she'd inherited her mother's deep caramel-colored skin and broad nose, her full lips and striking hazel eyes came from her father, signature Boudreaux traits. Her father had told her that almost every Boudreaux bore some semblance of their Creole heritage, and Chanel and her brother had proven true to his belief with their dark fine hair and exotic features. Chanel even admitted, if only to herself, that she had her father's exact build, short waist and long legs.

As much as she wanted to open her heart to her father, she only allowed him to come into her life on a very superficial level. She wanted her son, Zach, to have a grandfather yet she didn't want Leonard to hurt her son.

Leonard always made a point to tell Chanel about his Alcoholics Anonymous meetings, even encouraging her to come, but she always found a reason not to go. She could tell that some of his recovery treatment must have been to try to develop a relationship with her, so she tried to keep her sarcasm and bitterness aside, especially for the sake of Zachary.

In spite of her father's absence and her mother's abuse, Chanel had come out with a good measure of success. She knew it was all by the grace of God and through the help and prayers of the Hightower family. After high school, they had encouraged her to take several business classes at Monroe Community College and to pursue her dreams.

Pastor Hightower had told her often as a young woman, "Honey, the Bible says that without a vision, the people will perish. You just aim high." Mother Hightower was also an inspiration to her because she showed her how to be a mother by example. She had an air of class, integrity, and a dignified stature that Chanel tried to emulate. The Hightowers were her family.

The grief that Sydney suppressed was all too familiar to Chanel, because even though it had been years since Ramone's death, it felt like only yesterday. Vance's passing made her think about how much she missed her brother, how much her mother had hurt her, and how the Lord could allow her to go on without Ramone. The shadow that seemed to be looming over Chanel's life darkened with Vance's passing.

She wrestled in her leopard-print bedspread, trying to get her mind to cooperate with her body's tiredness. When she realized the futility of it, she picked up her large-print Bible and turned to the book of Proverbs. She liked the straightforward language and found it easy to understand, and although she was far from being a Bible scholar, she had memorized many Proverbs. As she read through Proverbs 14 (NIV), she stopped and lingered on verse 23 for a while. "All hard work brings a profit, but mere talk leads only to poverty." Chanel yawned again, still feeling the effects of the sleeping pill kick in as she continued to read, thinking that she needed to recite this verse to her unemployed husband. Before she knew it, she once again drifted off into a deep sleep.

———

Hours later, she dreamt that someone was ringing a bell. She turned over and sat up, only to realize that her phone was ringing.

Chanel picked it up and offered a raspy hello.

"Hello, baby," the masculine voice replied.

"Tommy?"

"Yeah, baby, it's me."

"Tommy, where have you been? I haven't seen you since the service. Why didn't you come by the Hightowers? You could've at least come home after the funeral, couldn't you?" Chanel groggily demanded.

"I'm sorry, but you know I don't do funerals well. It was hard enough to be there, let alone go to the house. I couldn't really handle interacting with everybody, you know?"

"No, I don't know, Tommy. Who do you know that *does* do funerals well? And what does any of that have to do with you coming home after you left the church?"

"Chanel, I figured you'd be at the Hightowers' house, not home."

"Well, you could've called to find out!"

Tommy raised his voice a notch. "That's what I'm doing now! Look I don't have time for this. I'm rehearsing with the guys now, but my schedule will be clear in about an hour."

"What kind of schedule do you have with no job?"

Tommy tended to get quiet when he got angry, but Chanel didn't care. His self-centered attitude annoyed her.

"That's a low blow, Chanel, but I'm gonna give you today. I know it's been a hard day for you."

Chanel mumbled, "You need to act like it then."

"Excuse me?" Tommy asked.

"Nothin', Tommy. I'll just see you later."

"Tell you what. You stick around there, and I can be home in thirty minutes, okay?"

Chanel didn't respond. Tommy repeated, "Okay?"

"Whatever, Tommy."

"I'm sorry, baby. Forgive me. Listen, let's go out to dinner."

Before Chanel hung up, she offered another, "Yeah, yeah, okay."

Each passing year of their six years of marriage had become increasingly more difficult for Chanel because of Tommy's behavior. Even though Tommy didn't ever get to know Vance well because he insisted that Sydney's husband was too "bougie" for him to hang out with, he was aware that Sydney and Sherese were the only real family Chanel could count on. His insensitivity never ceased to amaze her, but she didn't have the energy to argue with him this evening. Chanel agreed to meet him for dinner because she needed company now, even if it was with her self-centered husband.

As Chanel got up to shower, she tried to think about Mother Hightower's advice. She always told her, "Think on the good things, Chanel. Plenty of bad to focus on about anybody." She smiled as she remembered the first day she met Tommy Dubois. Chanel had been alone one slow Thursday evening at the café when the smooth ebony-complexioned man with dredlocks and deep dimples breezed in, carrying a flier that advertised a gig he was playing in a local club.

From the moment Tommy laid eyes on Chanel, he claimed he was in love. Although the then twenty-seven-year-old Chanel couldn't deny twenty-two-year-old Tommy's good looks, it wasn't so easy for her to ignore the age difference. However, Tommy convinced her to go out with him, and within no time, the age difference seemed minor. In reality, the age difference was not so minor as Chanel realized with each passing year.

Chanel did not understand how she could've been so willing to delve into a lifelong commitment with a man who, at almost thirty years old, still had aspirations of getting a recording contract with a major secular label. She had always known that Tommy was serious about his music, but Chanel had never imagined that he would consider doing it full-time. She had thought that with time, Tommy would play the keyboard and sing gospel music for the Lord since he was so gifted. She also envisioned Tommy's dream becoming less intense instead of the other way around.

Last year, Tommy had abruptly quit his job as a music teacher at Roosevelt Grade School because of a conflict with the principal. Chanel hadn't believed Tommy had even tried to get along with the principal, who had made it clear that the music department wasn't an area he felt was necessary in the public grade school system. Her husband's emotions had taken control, and because of it, the sole financial responsibility for their household lay on her shoulders.

As Tommy explained to her, "Chanel, I felt like he was disrespecting me. The black man has it so hard. How am I supposed to be teaching black children with a white boss who doesn't place any value in the whole music department! I can't put up with that type of mistreatment and racism toward the children and myself. I'd rather quit. Besides, I feel like God is telling me to go ahead and get my music together."

Chanel struggled for where to start with him because there were so many levels of disbelief and anger. How could the man who had never displayed much of an interest in the things of God now hear from God personally?

She put her hands on her hips and demanded, "Are you out of your mind, Tommy? What are your precious black children going to do now with you gone? Ever thought about that? And what about our bills and especially our health insurance? We have a son to raise, and you quit without thinking about us? I'm no saint, Tommy, but how in heaven are you gonna think God is tellin' you to play secular music? All of a sudden you're hearing from God? Don't you try to misrepresent God like that! Just say you did what you wanted to do!"

The mounting tension was impossible to disguise and all too evident to anyone who was in the couple's presence. Several weeks earlier, when Sydney and Vance invited them out for dinner, it had been a nightmare. Vance, who had come directly from work, was dressed in a suit and tie, looking polished and professional as he greeted Chanel.

Tommy and Chanel agreed to meet at the restaurant and as soon as she saw her husband sauntering through the double doors of the restaurant, Chanel felt her face warming from anger and embarrassment. Tommy had come to dinner looking like an overgrown thug. Although Chanel realized and accepted that Tommy wasn't her age, she wondered why he couldn't at least act his own. Without shame, Tommy wore his dreads gathered in a ponytail with a rubber band and much-too-baggy jeans and a FUBU shirt. Tommy didn't have a job, but Chanel wondered why he tried to *look* like he didn't have one. She had bought him many stylish and expensive clothes since they had been married, so she couldn't help feeling that Tommy was purposely dressing like a teenager to hurt her.

"Baby!" Tommy exclaimed while offering his wife a peck on the cheek. Chanel managed to mumble hello, but said to Vance in a voice dripping with sarcasm, "Vance, you look great, and you look like you worked really hard today! Make any big deals for Xerox?" Chanel cut her eyes and gave Tommy a spiteful look, intent on embarrassing her husband.

Vance's discomfort was visible as he loosened his tie while noticing that Sydney was coming in the door. Once they were seated and the waitress gave them the specials of the evening, the waitress took their drink orders: an unsweetened iced tea for Vance, two coffees for Sydney and Chanel, and a glass of the most expensive wine on the menu for Tommy. Tommy knew that Sydney despised any type of alcohol and that Vance had quit drinking altogether when he gave his life completely to the Lord. Chanel nudged her husband with force under the table, and he asked, "What in the world did you do that for?"

Chanel raised her eyebrows and pursed her lips together, eyeing Sydney as if to say, "I told you." Raising her glass of water up to her lips, Sydney looked away, attempting to think of something that would initiate a safe conversation for the four of them.

"So, how's my baby, Zachary?" Sydney asked enthusiastically.

"Yeah, how is our beautiful godbaby doing?" Vance added.

"Bro, he's growin' so fast. Yesterday I signed the little man up for piano lessons with this teacher who's supposed to be real good with little kids. Alexis Hughes, and…"

Chanel interrupted. "What did you just say, Tommy? You signed Zachary up without even asking me?"

Tommy took a deep breath in and muttered under his breath, "I thought you said you were cool with it. We just didn't say *when* we would do it."

"We didn't talk about that, and furthermore, I don't want that tramp whatever-her-name is to teach my child anything. You can just cancel that!" Chanel fumed.

Tommy tried to stay cool. "We can talk about it later, Chanel."

"You want your ex-girlfriend to teach my son how to play the piano, and that mess is not goin down with me whether we talk about it now or later! You need to try to take some of your free time to teach your son to play yourself."

"Ex-girlfriend? Where'd you get that from? You know me and Alexis go way back—all the way from grade school! Besides that, Chanel, the woman's married!" Tommy let out a sarcastic chuckle and looked toward Sydney and Vance. "Chanel thinks every woman I know is an ex!"

The waitress returned with the drinks to take the food order and once again, Sydney and Vance were grateful for the interruption. The solitude was only brief because after the ordering took place, the two were bickering again. Tommy had ordered the most expensive item on the menu, a lobster feast fit for a king, and Chanel couldn't take anymore.

"Syd, I know you and Vance wanted to take us to dinner, but don't think of taking care of the bill tonight. We'll get it this time. Obviously, Tommy is very hungry and has totally proven that he doesn't have an ounce of home training!" Chanel placed her napkin on her place setting and excused herself from the table.

Tommy added as she got up, "That would make two of us, now wouldn't that, Chanel?"

Sydney excused herself and followed briskly behind Chanel.

Vance had later told Chanel that Tommy confessed his frustration to him. Chanel found out that Tommy pulled his wallet out, left enough to pay for the entire dinner while avoiding making eye contact with Vance, and then left.

In the ladies' restroom, Sydney chided, "You are totally out of control, Chanel! How could you embarrass Tommy like that?"

Chanel remained composed, reapplying her lipstick in the mirror. "I can't help it, Syd. He shows up here dressed like a twelfth grader and orders from the menu like he's the president or something!"

"You've got to stop this, Chanel. I know you love him, so you really got to respect him. A man can only take so much."

· Chanel turned to face her friend, raising her voice. "A man can only take so much? You're kidding, right? What about me, Sydney?" She demanded. "What about me? How much do you think I can take?"

"It's just you don't want to kick a man when he's down. I know he's irritating, but you're the one saved in the church. You gotta show him that you know how to keep a lid on it. Besides, Tommy loves you. That's what is important. Can you just try to keep your cool and have a good time?"

Chanel folded her arms in silent resistance.

"For me? Please?" Sydney asked, while tapping her lightly on the arm.

Chanel gave her best friend a disgusted look, but reluctantly agreed. "I guess so." Chanel pulled her compact out and powdered her face, trying to regain her composure before returning to the table.

When they got to the table, they saw Vance sitting alone. At first, Chanel tried to act as if his departure didn't adversely affect her. Then, after an uncomfortable silence among the three, she did something she rarely allowed others to see. She burst into tears. "He left? I feel like I've made the biggest mistake of my life. I'm not in love with him anymore!"

Sydney reached across the table and touched her hand. "Sometimes it feels like that, but marriage is not about being in love all of the time. It's about the commitment the two of you made and the choice you two made to stick together through the ups and downs." Chanel rolled her eyes as if she's heard this speech numerous times, but it didn't faze Sydney. "Chanel, it's gonna all work out. You two just need some time together. Why don't you let us keep Zachary this weekend?" she asked, trying to console her.

Chanel nodded in agreement as Vance and Sydney counseled her over their uneaten dinners.

In the parking lot before they left, Vance asked Chanel before she got into her car, "Hey, Chanel? Mind if I pray for you?"

Chanel was in awe of Vance and often found herself, even in adulthood, longing for the life that Sydney had. She seemed to have it all while Chanel could barely get Tommy in the front door of a church, let alone say a prayer out loud.

Vance prayed, "Lord, we thank You for the friendship we have with Chanel. We thank You for blessing her, her husband, and son, God. We ask You for peace in the midst of this confusion. Please give Chanel godly wisdom and understanding. We believe that you're going to touch Tommy and draw him nearer to You. Help all of us to be a witness to him. We thank You in advance for deliverance, in Jesus' name."

———

As Chanel walked downstairs to put a cup of coffee on to perk herself up and shake the lethargy from the sleeping pill, she picked up one of Tommy's business cards, which had apparently fallen out his things onto the floor. It read: *Lil Tommy Productions (Keyboards, Writer, Vocals)*. When Chanel read: *It's All Big Time With Lil Tommy* under the address and phone number, she shook her head in frustration. She couldn't help noticing the dollar bills done in clip art on both sides of the card. Now that almost made her laugh. She couldn't believe that he was calling himself "little" at almost thirty years old.

He's unemployed, yet somehow he's "big time". The irony of it made her wince. She couldn't wait to tell Sydney this one.

While pulling the coffee filters out of the cabinet, Chanel wondered where it all went wrong. It hadn't always been that way though. When Tommy and Chanel met, she had been attracted to his six-foot-two-inch-tall frame, suave demeanor, and calming voice, but she was equally impressed by how he listened attentively to her, interested in finding out all he could about her. His honesty and humor struck her as refreshing, and the other men she had dated paled in comparison.

Tommy said he had been smitten by Chanel's sass, beauty, strength, and ambition. Now, the only thing she knew for sure Tommy still thought of her was that she was sassy-and not in a positive way.

When they decided to marry, Chanel felt sure that she was ready to spend her life with Tommy, although she had purposely avoided seeking Pastor Hightower's approval. She remembered the vows Pastor Hightower had given Sydney and Vance when they decided to marry, so Chanel decided not to consult Pastor Hightower at all even though he was the closest thing to a father that she had ever had. Deep down, she knew that he would disapprove of Tommy's nonchalant attitude toward the things of God. Tommy said he was saved but didn't believe you had to join a church, much less tithe or be involved in a ministry. In fact, Tommy felt he had done his duty if he watched *The Bobby Jones' Gospel Hour* on Sunday mornings.

As for Chanel, she hadn't been nearly as faithful in church since her business started flourishing. Ignoring the voice inside her that was telling her to slow down, she decided that the quickest and easiest route to happiness was for her and Tommy to take a trip to the courthouse for their marriage license.

Chanel knew that Tommy didn't care how they got married because he was so eager to have Chanel for his wife. Chanel also realized that Tommy's mother was less than thrilled by their pending union.

When Tommy told his mother that they were going to marry, Chanel sat with the giddiness of a young girl until she noticed the tears of sadness collect at the corners of Olivia Dubois' eyes. At first, Chanel thought surely the tears must've been tears of joy, but the downward turn of his mother's mouth told Chanel all she needed to know.

"Tommy, you're so young to have so much responsibility. Are you sure?" she asked with her eyes remaining fixed on her son.

"Mom, this can't come as a shock. I told you that I loved Chanel and that I intended on spending the rest of my life with her."

Olivia wrung her hands with fury as she searched her son's face for the seriousness of it all.

Tommy reached over, oblivious to his mother's drama, and grabbed Chanel's hand. "See, look at this ring, Mom. It came from the sweat of my brow too. Teaching and doing extra gigs bought this for my baby. It's not the biggest, but we'll have time to upgrade later."

When it was apparent that Olivia wasn't going to offer her congratulations to Tommy or her, Chanel politely pulled her hand from Tommy and refused to even look at his mother.

"Of course you were able to save up for the ring, Tommy, but that's only because you live here rent free."

"Now, Mom, hold up a minute. I been tryin' to get you to understand that I was planning on moving out any day now. You just didn't want to hear it. Besides, Chanel has her own house, and we're gonna live there at least for a while."

Olivia finally turned her attention toward Chanel to ask, "Dear, you're not pregnant, are you?"

Tommy protested and Chanel stood up. "Mom, please. You know Chanel's not pregnant."

When they left Olivia's, Chanel had started to take her anger out on Tommy for his mother's rude behavior, but she knew that's exactly what his mother wanted. Chanel had learned how to handle rejection and alienation of one sort or another from childhood, so her mother-in-law disliking her was not nearly as disheartening as Olivia would have hoped.

The two married without much fanfare with Sydney standing up for Chanel and Tommy's brother, Bryan, standing up with him. Afterwards, the two had a quaint reception in Vance and Sydney's backyard to kick off the beginning of their union. It was the happiest day of Chanel's life, with the exception of Tommy insisting that Outkast's "So Fresh and So Clean" be played at three different times during the reception.

Chanel was proud that she finally had a man in her life that she could depend on—one with a good job and one who gave her the emotional support and stability that she had craved so desperately all of her life.

Since their son Zachary's birth, much had changed. A few things changed for the better. They had the joy of their lives with the birth of Zachary, and her mother-in-law had warmed significantly with the birth of her grandson and she seemed to accept Chanel as a daughter.

They had worked hard to sell Chanel's tiny home to buy their modest but quaint home in Irondequoit, an established neighborhood in Rochester. She was determined to make sure that Zachary had financial security and stability. At thirty-three years old, Chanel was ready to be realistic about her future goals and desperately wanted Tommy to join her.

Tommy had stood defiantly before her and said cooly, as if he'd rehearsed this scene in his mind a million times, "You're the one who's always making the point that you make so much more money than I do. How many times have you pointed out what little money I bring home? According to you, my paychecks have been going into our savings accounts anyway!"

"You're just like all the other loser men in my life. So what now? You expect me to support you?"

Raising his voice, Tommy exclaimed, "I'm like what? I'm like what? Don't you *ever* refer to me as a loser! I'm not gonna be punked by you!" Tommy closed his eyes and bit his lower lip, trying to calm himself. "What I need from you is some patience and understanding. Have a little faith in me and know that I'm going to support us sooner than later. I just need a chance to make it. I just need you to trust me. Besides, just let me give my music career one last shot before I give it up," Tommy pleaded.

Chanel halfheartedly agreed to be the sole support of the family financially almost a year ago, but it was becoming increasingly more difficult to keep the bitterness and resentfulness at bay. The truth was, she felt Tommy had tricked her. When she met him, he had seemed so focused and responsible. She had been supporting Tommy's child-ish dream for a year with no results, and instead of him getting more realistic, he seemed to be even more engrossed in pursuing his dream.

She decided to bury her hostility, at least for the night anyway, as she finished getting ready for dinner. She went back to Mother Hightower's advice and ran Tommy's good points through her head. He didn't drink, smoke, or curse. He didn't cheat on her, at least to her knowledge, and then there was the main thing—she knew he loved her.

She opened her closet and pulled out the new camel-colored leather skirt and sweater set, a treat to herself for recently losing weight. Maintaining her workout regimen and healthy eating habits had been difficult but well worth it. The only drawback to her new size twelve physique had been that she had been receiving even more attention from her husband. Lately, she had found herself dodging intimacy with him. There seemed to be a disconnect with Tommy when it came to their physical relationship. He saw it as separate from his unemployment and overall selfishness. Chanel found it nearly impossible to be attracted to a healthy, able-bodied grown man who wasn't financially contributing much to the family and who had instead betrayed her trust.

Tonight, she didn't want to look good for anyone but herself. After getting dressed, Chanel surveyed her curvaceous body and whispered to herself, "Not bad." Her deep-set, exotic-looking eyes complimented her full heart-shaped lips and round face. Her golden-brown highlighted hair, layered and flipped up slightly in the latest style, shone as she spun around checking herself out from the back. After putting on her gold hoop earrings and bracelets, she applied her makeup flawlessly and left to meet her husband. All the while, she secretly wondered if Tommy would surprise her and love her forever, or if he would leave her as almost everyone else in her life had.

CHAPTER 3

Sherese

Let us search and try our ways, and turn again to the Lord.

Lamentations 3:40

"Sherese, now that's what I call a beautiful name, and it fits because you are just that," the attractive bartender flirted.

Offering a plastic smile, Sherese answered, "Thanks...Joe? Isn't that what you said your name was?" She shifted uncomfortably on the bar stool, flipping one of her microbraids. "Do you think you can get me another apple martini, please?"

"You really know how to play a brother, Miss Sherese. By the way, the name is Jack. Apple martini coming right up," he said, smiling while preparing her drink.

Sherese could feel his penetrating eyes roaming over her. Her eyes, the shade of brown closest to black, were warm, and according to her mother, Sherese could make her long lashes flutter like a butterfly. They perfectly accented her pecan-colored skin and small upturned nose.

Being an artist, Sherese loved splashes of vibrant colors, and the plunging neckline of her fuchsia-colored blouse seemed to catch and hold her suitor's attention.

Sherese rolled her eyes and with a half smile sarcastically added, "Oh, you think that I was tryin' to play you? Please! If I was playin' you, you wouldn't still have that silly grin on your face—believe that!"

His smile broadened after the comment, which signaled to Sherese that he liked feisty women. Jack silently prepared her drink. When Sherese attempted to pay for the drink, the bartender slid it politely in front of her and put his hand up in a halt motion and whispered, "It's on me, butterfly." Still smiling, he winked at her and then went to assist other patrons.

Although Sherese had purposely tried to make her eyes flutter, she had an almost eerie feeling about him calling her by her mother's pet name for her. Sherese watched Jack smile occasionally as he assisted the club patrons, relishing the idea that she had finally captured the man's attention after two months. In spite of his slightly receding hairline, his nearly bald head and baby face made him appear youthful. His shadow of a beard, along with the small scar that ran along his temple gave him a rugged look that intrigued her, and she guessed that he was a bodybuilder. His short sleeves exposed his massive muscles. Her little exchange with Jack had her more than a little interested.

Although Sherese was somewhat repulsed by the club called The Clique and what it stood for, she was equally drawn to its almost hypnotizing effect on her. She was spending more time than ever there since her friend, Danielle, moved to Florida because the guilty pleasure was simply too much for her to resist. The carefree crowd, blaring music, and apple martinis always managed to provide the temporary escape from reality that Sherese always yearned so desperately for, even if everyone referred to it as a meat market.

Sherese turned her attention to the bartender's muscular body once again, and his sable skin appeared to glisten as he grabbed a napkin to wipe the beads of sweat that collected above his upper lip and forehead. The bartender must have felt her glance, and for an instant their eyes met and locked. Embarrassed by her own obvious behavior, Sherese looked away and tipped her glass, gulping down the remainder of her drink.

Unlike other nights, tonight she had come into the club without as much as a thought of the man who had consumed her thoughts for weeks. She couldn't believe that tonight of all nights, the night of her sister's husband's funeral, the handsome bartender seemed to finally be taking notice of her.

As Sherese nodded her head to the pulsating rhythm of the neo-soul groove, she fought hard not to think of her brother-in-law's passing. But even the earsplitting music couldn't drown the grief that had taken residence in her heart for her sister's loss.

Sherese's relationship with her sister had been strained at times, but she still felt an unbearable heaviness for Sydney's pain. Since Sydney was seven years older, Sherese always looked up to her sister. Sydney had always been motherly and loving toward her younger sister until her teenage years when Sherese started to rebel. Sherese's nature drew her to throw caution to the wind. Her motto became, "You only live once." Sydney, on the other hand, had often said to her, "The choices you make today will affect your tomorrow." Their philosophies often butted heads despite the deep sisterly love they had for one another.

Tonight nothing seemed to lift the blanket of darkness surrounding her, not even the usual cure for her blues in the party atmosphere of The Clique.

A female bartender noticed her empty glass, and asked, "What can I get for you?"

Sherese didn't handle her liquor well, but she just wanted the pain to go away. Her mouth opened before her better judgment could stop her. "Another apple martini, please."

While the bartender prepared her drink, Sherese thought about how she had wanted to offer solace to her sister but felt unable. Sydney handled the visitation and funeral much like any other trial she experienced—with serenity and control. Sydney's habit of always being composed seemed to be acceptable with other troubles, but Sherese knew her sister had to be torn up inside. She just wished that Sydney felt she could lean on her.

After pulling a napkin from its holder, Sherese dabbed the tears that stung her eyes. She didn't want to burden her parents or Chanel because they, as almost everyone else she was close to, were grieving just as much as she was. Vance had died and it only exposed the difficulty she and her sister had communicating.

Sydney's habit of always belittling or being condescending to Sherese caused understandable resentment in Sherese. When they were younger, Sherese was silent against Sydney's harsh judgment of her. However, as an adult, Sydney's constant onslaught of questions usually revolved around Sherese's goals, finances, or personal life. A conversation with Sydney often amounted to her lecturing.

"Sherese, how can you go out to clubs and party when you don't even have your degree?" She would say, "Where are your priorities? I made it through school, and I'm not one bit smarter than you! You just need to apply yourself. You can't stay with Mama and Daddy forever. They're worried about you, and they want to see that you can take care of yourself. Your divorce was two years ago. Everybody has hard times. You just have to dust yourself off and move forward."

Most all of the time, Sherese would try desperately to respect her older sister. However, just days before Vance's death, Sydney had stopped by her parents' house and the two sisters had had a confrontation.

"Mama! Daddy! You all home?" Sydney called out after she let herself in the front door.

"Hey, it's me. Mama and Daddy are at the church. I think they had a meeting with the contractors about the new church building," Sherese answered.

Sydney walked in to find Sherese clad in old sweatpants and a T-shirt, surrounded by several *Essence* and *Ebony* magazines as she sat on the sofa eating ice cream while watching *The Oprah Show*. Sherese chuckled at something from the show, but she glanced at her sister who was dressed in a classic navy blue pin-striped suit with her hair swept up in a bun and said cheerfully, "Girl, you look so nice."

Sherese smoothed her hair down as she noticed the disgusted look on her older sister's face, remembering what her hair must look like.

"Okay, Syd, what gives? What's up with that crazy look on your face? Do I look that bad?"

Sydney winced. "How do you expect me to look at you, Sher? You haven't had a job in six months, and every single time I come over here, you're sitting in front of the television set. The least you could do is show Mama and Daddy some respect by going to church and trying to help them there."

Sherese was offended. "Why should I go when they always have you? By the way, why is it your business what I do here?" Sherese sarcastically replied as she placed her unfinished bowl of ice cream down firmly on the coffee table.

A look of disbelief came over Sydney's face. "My parents *are* my business, and especially since they've been paying your car payment for the last three months, sacrificing the little they have for you. Really, it's more like I'm paying for you to live here because I've been giving Mama something every month since you first got here." Sydney paused briefly while Sherese watched intently as her sister's nostrils flared like they always did when she was angry.

"What for?"

Sydney continued, "In case you haven't noticed, they're on a fixed income. So, I think it is my business what you're doing or not doing to get a job!"

Sherese stood up and planted her hands on her hips. "You know what? Mama and Daddy have never been ones to beat around the bush about anything, so don't try to act like I'm worryin' them. They tell me almost every day how much they like having me around here. Do you even know how much I do around here to help them? Syd, my life aspirations may not be as high as yours, but don't act like I'm some shiftless person who intends on mooching off of her parents forever!"

Sherese scooped up her magazines and bowl before storming out of the room, but she added quietly, "By the way, I had an interview today, and they offered me the job."

Sherese heard Sydney call after her, but she ignored her as she slammed the door to her room.

———

As the tempo of the music in the club slowed, Sherese was jolted back to reality when she heard a whisper from behind.

"Look at you, with your fine self. How about a dance?"

Sherese winced at the stench in the man's breath, which reeked of strong alcohol, cheap cigarettes, and a bad case of halitosis. Without even turning to look at her suitor, Sherese answered, "No, thanks."

Sherese ignored the profanity that escaped from the stranger's lips as she averted her attention to the couples flocking to the dance floor. As much as Sherese longed for companionship, she couldn't risk getting involved too deeply with anyone. She would never allow herself to be hurt the way she was with D'Andre.

Not long after their elopement, she realized that her marriage to D'Andre had been a mistake. She still hadn't recovered all she had lost from her relationship with him, and Sherese was determined not to allow any man, woman, or child deprive her of happiness again.

As one slow song played after another, Sydney took a swallow of her drink as her head swam with painful memories. She often wondered how she had ended up with a loser like D'Andre. The only conclusion she could come to was that he made her feel special, like she fit in, at least at first. She had never felt like she fit in as a child. Sherese never easily conformed to meet her parents' expectations as Sydney had, but when she had met D'Andre, she felt like she had found her place.

As a child, Sherese's seeds of discontent with her home life grew so much so that by the time she was a teenager she began to rebel in ways Sydney had never done, and their parents couldn't understand it. Ever since Sherese could remember, she didn't like the church she had always been made to attend and didn't appreciate the members who invaded her parents' lives and took their time away from her. She despised being made to cater to the church members when they unexpectedly dropped by for dinner or called in the middle of the night. She hated the fact that she and Sydney had to often wear church members' children's clothes or clothes from the thrift shop because their parents had most of their money tied up with church expenses. Forever etched in Sherese's memory was the day one of the girls at church pointed at her said, "You got on that ugly shirt my grandmama got me last year!"

Probably more than anything, she hated being held to a higher standard just because she was the pastor's daughter. Sherese often wanted to tell people that she wasn't the one called to pastor or have a church; her parents were. When people lied about her or other kids picked on her, Sherese's parents always made her apologize first. She got the worst spanking of her life because she pushed a girl from the church who consequently fell onto the floor, causing a bump on her head. The girl, LaShay Howard, had been calling Sherese names for months, but when she tripped Sherese, she could no longer contain her anger.

In front of the church members, her mother, Darlene, calmly gave Sherese the look, which her daughters knew all too well meant trouble. Darlene took Sherese home and whipped her mercilessly with a switch that Sherese had to pick from a tree in the backyard.

She was to never even think about retaliating again, especially with church members. The message Sherese received was that her mama was choosing the church members over her.

One event from Sherese's childhood still simmered on low boil and prevented her from forgiving her parents or the church. On her eleventh birthday begging her parents for two years, her parents had finally saved enough and cleared the church calendar to take a family trip to Disneyland. Her mother and father scrimped and saved for those years to make Sherese's childhood dream come true. For two whole weeks before the trip, every night she knelt on her knees, praying that nobody from the church would call with a catastrophe. Just when Sherese thought the Lord had answered her prayer, the night before the trip the phone rang in the middle of the night. Jolted out of her sleep by the sound of the ringing phone, Sherese held her breath, praying that someone from the church hadn't become seriously ill or worse. She knew that it was probably the only thing that could make her daddy cancel the trip.

Sherese's heart sank as she heard her father say, "Now, Sister Meadows, don't you cry. I'll be right over. Yes, he was a good man and he's with the Lord now. You're not bothering me, now. That's what I'm here for." Sister Meadows was one of the first members and a pillar of the church, and Sherese knew all too well that her father would not abandon her in her hour of need.

Since it was too late to get a refund for the tickets, her father had insisted that they go without him. She felt her parents' disappointment, but Sherese never understood how someone who was dead could be more important than a trip they had been planning for two years. To add insult to injury, the trip had ended up horribly since Sydney ended up with chicken pox.

She became convinced that a loving God would not allow her parents to struggle and sacrifice as they had with no benefits as far as Sherese could see. Furthermore, God never seemed to answer her prayers. Convinced that she would never live a life like her parents when she got on her own, Sherese slowly began her emotional withdrawal from her family.

Throughout her teenage years, Sherese hung out with girls who had a reputation for being fast, skipping school, staying out late, and even stealing. No pleading, praying, demanding, or threatening seemed to work. The more her parents tried to restrict her, the more she rebelled. Even as her parents forced Sherese to the altar to pray and tarry with her, the breakthroughs only proved to be temporary. Sherese took her mother's, "I rebuke you, Satan, in the name of the Lord," as a personal rebuke of herself.

Sherese had always kept a journal, and even when re-reading it a short time ago, she was surprised to count the number of times she had supposedly gotten saved. She totaled eleven times that she had gone to the altar throughout her teenage years, claiming salvation. Although she always remembered being sincere at the moment, she never seemed to be able to let go of her hostility.

Finally, after barely graduating from high school, her parents were forced to give her an ultimatum. Sherese had overheard her parents as they talked about her. Her father seemed resistant at first, but Darlene had convinced him to try tough love tactics with their daughter.

Darlene had pleaded, "Samuel, I love that girl as much as you do, but if we don't force her to live with the consequences of her actions, we are hurting her. She'll never be responsible and more importantly, she'll never truly get saved."

"That's my baby girl, Darlene, and I just don't want to be too hard on her. Everybody's different and we shouldn't penalize her because she's not like Sydney."

"Comparin' Sherese to Sydney is not a thought in my mind. Right is right, and wrong is wrong. Sherese has been wrong, and she refuses to abide by our rules. The best thing we can do for her is to let that girl go. She thinks it's so bad here with us, so let's just allow her to be out there. I hate it as much as you do, but she's got to grow up now. That girl has such a gift to draw and paint and won't even go to art school. It's a shame."

When her parents sat her down and told her that she either had to abide by the rules of the house and go to community college or she had to leave, she had told her parents as respectfully as she could that she would move. She had enough money saved up to get a studio apartment on the south side of town, and even though her parents didn't agree with her decision, they helped her by buying her some inexpensive furniture.

While working for a temporary agency, she was placed at Boulder Construction as an office aide. The work was easy enough, and she enjoyed the attention she received as one of the only two women at the company. She had gone out with a couple of the guys who worked construction, but when D'Andre Bryant shoved the office door open so hard that it hit the back wall, Sherese knew that he was someone she wanted to know better. His light brown eyes, which equally matched hers in intensity, had initially flashed in anger but seemed to soften slightly as he rested them on the new beauty in the office.

"May I help you, sir?" Sherese asked coyly.

Temporarily forgetting what he had gone into the office for, D'Andre tried to gather his thoughts together, shifting his weight from one foot to the other uncomfortably.

Sherese smiled warmly. "Cat got your tongue?"

"Well, I guess I need to file a complaint," D'Andre responded, now looking slightly embarrassed.

As Sherese turned to get the paperwork for him to fill out, he asked, "You must be new. I haven't seen you around here before."

"I started here about a month ago. I'm Sherese, by the way."

"Sherese, I'm D'Andre. Nice to meet you." He took the paperwork from her as he looked her over, impressed.

To Sherese's surprise, he turned to leave without another word. Sherese couldn't help feeling disappointed. She turned to the fifty-year-old office manager, MaryAnn, and tried not to sound too interested. "So, what's up with that guy? Do you know if he's married?"

MaryAnn wasn't fooled by Sherese's tone because she knew by the look on the young girl's face that she was attracted to D'Andre. "Word to the wise, Sherese; stay away from him. He's bad news. He's been nothin' but trouble since he came here about a year ago. The boss is tryin' to give people with past records a shot at making an honest living, and he's in that crowd."

"A record? What'd he do?" Sherese asked, trying not to seem overly curious.

"I know it wasn't anything like murder or rape, but it was enough of an offence that he was in for at least a few months."

"Well, it couldn't have been that bad. Besides, bad boys intrigue me."

"I'm sure you bring your parents sheer joy," MaryAnn quipped sarcastically.

"So, come on, MaryAnn, is he married or not?"

"Nobody listens to me." MaryAnn pushed her file cabinet drawer shut and pulled her glasses down to the tip of her nose so she could make eye contact with the impressionable girl. "He's not married to my knowledge, but I like you, Sherese. I think you're much too good for any of these roughnecks around here. I've been around here a long time, and I'm a pretty good judge of character. You need to— "

Before MaryAnn could respond, D'Andre sauntered back into the office with his paperwork in a roll, hitting it lightly against his pant leg.

Sherese smiled and walked back toward the counter to greet him. *What did MaryAnn know?*

With a deep baritone voice, D'Andre asked, "Sherese, ummmm, I don't know if you like rap, but there's a little concert tomorrow night downtown. We could go if you want. The rapper is just a local artist, but my partners said he was real good."

"Are you kidding? I'd love to go." She jotted down her number and handed it to him. For the first time, Sherese got a glimpse of his gleaming white teeth and broad smile, a stark contrast to his dark skin and overall rugged appearance.

Sherese went over excitedly to talk to MaryAnn, but the office manager just shook her head in frustration and asked Sherese to make copies for her.

In a few short months, Sherese and D'Andre eloped because her family had made it crystal clear to her that they didn't approve of him. Her mother, who could generally always find redeeming qualities in even the most unseemly person, couldn't find one positive thing to say about him except, "The Lord can save him too."

Sherese knew that he didn't go to church, but she didn't know about his drinking binges, marijuana smoking, or chronic jobless-ness. Still, Sherese tried to make the relationship work, even if it was just to prove that people weren't right about her husband.

After time though, she had to admit to herself that she had only been attracted to D'Andre physically. He had no depth, no apprecia-tion of her artistic gifts, and no respect for her family and friends.

He had been so protective of her those first few months of their relationship. He had admitted when their relationship started to get serious that he did spend some time in jail because the police mistak-enly thought he was selling drugs. Sherese knew that he smoked and drank some, but she had never seen him drunk or high.

When Sherese discovered that he had been fired from his job, she rationalized that he had just been dealt a bad hand in life. She knew that D'Andre never had the love and support he needed as a child. While she had secured a permanent job at the phone company, D'Andre refused to look for work.

She couldn't share her fears about the future of her marriage with her family, but she had confessed to Chanel. "It seems like the more I put up with, the more D'Andre puts on me. He's staying out all night and hanging out with shady men. I mean, it's become a daily thing."

"Sugar, men will do what you let them do to you. You're really gonna have to put your foot down. Nothin' worse than an unemployed Negro."

Once Sherese got the encouragement she needed to confront her husband, she approached him in what she thought was a reasonable way.

"D'Andre, I'm really unhappy with your behavior. You haven't been looking for work, and what's worse, you're disrespecting me by staying out all night, bringing all kinds of riffraff in our home. Something's gotta give."

D'Andre's eyes remained fixed on the television set, but the way he gripped the sides of the armchair tightly let Sherese know that he had heard every word and was angry. "You need to shut your yapping mouth, Sherese!"

Fire rose up in Sherese. "You don't tell me to shut up! Who do you think you are?"

Before she could rise from the couch, he had her by the throat. Sherese froze in fear as she gasped for air until she noticed the crystal candy jar beside her. She struggled to reach the top and hit him in the face with it. He loosened his grip just enough for her to break free.

She had run to the bathroom and locked the door to escape him. Her body quaked with fear as she heard him cursing. Only when she heard him get his keys and leave did she sob wildly, staring at the red handprints on her neck.

When she felt safe, she ran out of the bathroom and called Sydney, who had consoled her without one single "I told you so." At the time, it didn't matter that everyone else was right about her doomed marriage. Sydney and Vance had rushed over to help and advised her to call the police, but Sherese refused. She just wanted out.

About a month after she divorced him, she found out that he had been arrested and would serve time for selling drugs and drug possession. Devastated by the failed and violent marriage, Sherese turned to her parents, who offered their unconditional assistance and love.

Her mother had counseled her often, telling her, "Just trust in the Lord, Sherese. This, too, shall pass."

Her father, as spiritual as he was, made his advice short and sweet. "God hates divorce, but just ask Him for forgiveness. Cut your losses and move on. He wasn't strong enough for you no way."

Sherese had been living with her parents since the divorce and had been so wrapped up in her problems that she rarely thought about Sydney's. Her older sister always appeared to have it all under control. Now all she could think about was how trivial her past and current problems were in comparison to Sydney's tragedy. She also battled the guilt of the argument she had had with Sydney just a few days before Vance's passing.

She picked up her glass and whispered, "Cheers!" to herself as she emptied it in one last gulp.

By her third drink, she was light-headed and disoriented when Jack came from behind the bar and whispered in her ear, "How about we go outside to get some air?" His minty breath was cool, sweet, and inviting.

Sherese didn't answer but put her coat on the best she could. With his arm around her waist, carrying her jacket and purse, Jack guided Sherese outside as she giggled carelessly.

———

Sherese's head throbbed as she attempted to pull a pillow over her head to keep the sunlight that crept into the room from her face. As she let out a little moan from the pain in her head combined with the nausea, she was startled by the deep voice that offered a pleasant, "Hey, sleepyhead." With that, he pulled the pillow off her face and leaned over, kissing her lightly on the cheek.

Sherese sat up feeling confused and used. She struggled to remember what happened. Unable to disguise the horrified look on her face, she gasped, "Oh, God, help me!" she said. Sherese had done her share of flirting at clubs, but she had never slept around. The thought of it made her stomach ache. She tried again to get up, but this time, she carefully wrapped the sheet around herself.

Jack, who had just been lighthearted, suddenly became silent. Sherese couldn't believe her lack of discretion, and Jack's sympathetic look both humiliated and sickened her. Apparently he had been up and dressed for a while because she noticed that he was freshly shaven and had Levis and a T-shirt on, which only further embarrassed her.

"Sherese, look, please don't feel—"

Sherese cut him off and tried to clear her hoarse throat. "Where's your bathroom, please?" She scanned the room to discover her clothes neatly folded on an armchair by the door.

He smiled uneasily, attempting to mask her discomfort. "Down the hall and to the left, and when you come out, I fixed some coffee. That'll help with your hangover. Heaven knows, it's helped mine."

"Yeah, okay." Sherese grabbed her clothes and raced to the bathroom. She noticed the artwork that lined the walls. *The creep has decent taste,* she thought, admiring the African-American church scenes although she couldn't believe that he would have the audacity to display Christian-themed artwork with his apparent lack of morality. Not only was he a bartender, but he had also taken advantage of her in the worst way.

She rushed into the bathroom, decorated in masculine shades of gray and black, and locked the door behind her. When she took one look at her bloodshot eyes and disheveled braids, she burst into tears. Sherese couldn't believe that she didn't remember anything beyond walking out of the club with him.

She flung open the linen closet to find a washcloth and ran some cold water, placing the cloth on her face as she tried to relieve the pounding in her head. Her head spun as she tried to think of a quick way to get out of the situation. She figured that this brother must've been happy as a schoolboy having his way with her, so she would just tell him the truth—that she had to hurry to get home to take care of some business. Besides, she knew that her parents must be wondering where she was.

After she got dressed, Sherese attempted to creep out of the bathroom unnoticed, but Jack startled her by standing propped against the wall next to the bathroom holding a steaming cup of coffee for her. She searched for words as she accepted the cup but put it down on the dresser in his bedroom. "Listen, Jack. I really need to get home to…to…well, I just need to go."

"You're in no shape to go home yet. Besides, I wanted to get to know you better, so please stay awhile," Jack pleaded.

"Didn't you already get to know me well enough last night?" she snapped.

"What? Are you upset? Please don't feel badly." He seemed genuinely surprised.

"Am I upset? No, I'm not one bit upset that I was taken advantage of by a man I don't know." Sherese ignored his extended hand holding a mug of coffee.

"You were the one making all of the advances toward me!" he said, trying to defend his honor, which broke his calm demeanor.

"You call yourself a bartender, and you can't identify a woman who's sloppy drunk?" Sherese snapped.

"I knew you were tipsy, but you said you had wanted me for months or I wouldn't never—" Jack said as he lowered his head and placed his cup of coffee down firmly, splashing the liquid on the dresser as he searched her face for answers.

"You never would've what? Anyway, you got what you wanted, but now I have to get out of here." Sherese slipped her heels on and snatched her keys off of the dresser. "I have no idea what I said to you last night, but I made a mistake. I'm sorry that this happened, but I do need to go."

Jack bit his lower lip and Sherese noticed that he seemed genuinely puzzled and agitated about the outcome of their night together, but she didn't care. She got as far as the hall and Jack called out, "Hold up. Let me get my shoes on because I have to take you back to the club to get your car."

Sherese's cheeks warmed in embarrassment. She had totally forgotten that she didn't drive last night. She desperately fought to regain her cool in the midst of her embarrassment. She knew that it wasn't Jack's fault that she got drunk and that they slept together as a result. But seeing his pleasant disposition totally wither away gave her a twinge of satisfaction as they left to get her car.

CHAPTER 4

Sydney

My tears have been my meat day and night,
while they continually say unto me, Where is thy God?

Psalm 42:3

"Who's there?" Mother Houston called out.

"It's me, Sydney," she answered as she stepped with hesitation through the front door.

When Sydney made her way to the living room, she found Mother Houston, whom she fondly referred to as Auntie, doing needlepoint while listening to a sermon on the radio. The elderly woman who had been her mother's best friend for nearly forty years had graciously stayed at the house for her to receive condolences, food, and flowers from friends and family. When Sydney's tired and fragile body appeared, Mother Houston set her needlepoint down and warmly embraced her goddaughter.

Sydney returned the embrace. "Hi, Auntie. Thank you so much for everything. I just couldn't come home until I got myself a little more together. Thank you for getting Vance's clothes to the funeral and—"

Mother Houston interrupted her as the frown between her eyes deepened. "Now you not going to even think about all that. I ain't done nothin' at all but what I wanted to do, baby." She kissed her firmly and fell back onto the chair.

Sydney let out a sigh as she sat down on the sofa and noticed her godmother rubbing her knees. "How are you, Auntie? Has your arthritis been bothering you?"

Mother Houston's soft voice quivered slightly but was sympathetic. "Look at you with your sweet self, tryin' to ask about me. I'm doing all right, but how you doin'?"

Sydney purposely avoided eye contact with Auntie. "I'm gonna be okay. I'm just tired, and I have so much to do. "

"You need me to do somethin'? I can help you get some things together upstairs. I'll be glad to."

"Thank you, but I just need to do some things myself. I'm going to be fine, I promise," Sydney said trying to convince herself more than her aunt.

"Ain't no use in you tryin' to do it all, Syd. You ought to let me or your mama help you," Mother Houston said wistfully, while pushing her glasses up on her nose.

"I just went through all of this with Mama and Daddy, so Auntie, please don't make me go through it again, okay?" Sydney pleaded.

"Well, good enough, honey. You just know you can call me day or night." Auntie pulled up one of her knee-highs, which had slipped down. "I'm gonna be gettin' on home, but you call me when you need me. My bag's already in the car."

"Why don't you let me take you home?" Sydney stood up.

"Honey, what keeps me young is doin' for myself." As Mother Houston put her sweater on, she explained, "So many folks brought cards, plants, flowers, and food, I just had to make a list on the notepad next to the phone in the kitchen. Ain't no way I could've remembered who brought all that stuff." She paused. "He was some kind of special, that Vance, but the Lord knows," she said as her voice trailed off. Mother Houston slowly walked toward the front door. "I'll call to check on you in the morning, sugar."

Sydney hugged her godmother one last time, letting her head rest gently on Auntie's shoulder, taking in the smell of the warm scent of lavender on her sweater. "Thank you so much, Auntie. I love you."

"Love you, too, baby." Mother Houston ambled down the sidewalk, swinging her pocketbook by her side.

Sydney waited until her godmother's Buick Century was far down the street to shut the door, but just as soon as she turned the deadbolt, the *click* seemed to echo unusually loud in her large home. Fear seized her. She was alone and had to face the empty space that she had once shared with her late husband. For days she had opted to stay with her parents, dreading to face the reality of Vance's absence. Staying with her parents had been a welcome reprieve from this. Her mother busied herself by seeing to Sydney's every need, and her father was just as intense in his focus on his eldest daughter. Even she and Sherese had spent time alone together, something they hadn't done in years.

Sydney sat on the bottom step of the spiral staircase and hugged her knees to her chest. In a week she would have to return to work, so she needed to try to get some measure of solace in her own home. She didn't know what her new life would be like. Just a few short weeks ago, she'd worried about having a baby with her husband. Now she wondered how she could go on.

Should she stay in the expansive 4,000-square-foot dream house they had built or choose to get a smaller house or condo? Her thoughts ran rampant. Sydney knew a little about their insurance policies, stocks, and investments, but for the first time, she was beginning to realize that Vance made a lot more preparations than she had ever thought. While she took care of the day-to-day expenses, Vance had their financial plans well mapped out. He had taken so many precautionary measures for her and Maya's future in the event of his death that Sydney had an eerie feeling. Sydney wondered if he sensed that something might happen to him before they grew old together.

She took a deep breath, remembering that she had to call their accountant tomorrow. He had been calling every other day for her, but she had avoided his phone calls.

Sydney wandered almost aimlessly into the kitchen and turned on the light to her counter lined with two sweet potato pies, buckets of fried chicken, honey-baked ham, a caramel cake, and a host of other side dishes brought by family and friends. The saints made sure that she had enough food for an army.

She reached for a knife to try a piece of the caramel cake that she knew Mother Rivers had made. In spite of the fact that she had lost her appetite for almost everything, the caramel cake actually made her mouth water. She savored the moist, rich cake smothered in smooth, brown caramel icing that had been her absolute favorite dessert since childhood. Every birthday, Sydney's mother paid Mother Rivers to make one of her caramel cakes to celebrate. It didn't matter what gifts she received because the caramel cake was always the highlight for Sydney. Mother Rivers didn't have the reputation throughout the city for her caramel cakes for nothing.

Sydney delved into the cake. For the first time since Vance's death, she experienced a fleeting moment of satisfaction. Despite all the changes in her life that had taken place over the last several days, the cake remained the same, unchanged.

After finishing her cake, she anxiously began her ascent up the spiral staircase to prepare for bed. She hadn't been to their bedroom alone since Vance's passing, so Sydney took each step with careful deliberation. How had she and Vance left things? She couldn't remember. Why were her palms sweaty when this space had been her home for years?

She lingered outside of the entrance to the room, sucked in a deep breath, and swung open the bedroom door. Like a baby, Sydney took her first feeble steps into their sanctuary. Startled by Vance's smell permeating the room, Sydney felt as if someone had punched her in the stomach.

He was actually living here with me, here, alive, just days ago. I can still smell him. How can he be gone?

Their bed was unmade as she had left it, and their monogrammed robes, a Christmas gift from her sister, were thrown on top. Sydney made a beeline for the bathroom to undress for her shower, determined not to break down. Many items in the room proved that he had been there not too long ago, but the noiseless space that she grappled with made it evident that he would never return.

In the bathroom she couldn't help noticing Vance's side of the vanity, cluttered as it always was with shaving cream, razors, cologne, and lotion. Sydney picked up his hairbrush and examined it closely, wondering how his black hair could still be clinging to the brush bristles but yet never brush his hair again. She ran her hand across the bristles, and returned the brush to the vanity, careful to put it back exactly where Vance had left it. She didn't want to disturb anything that would erase him from her existence.

It hadn't been easy, but Sydney had thwarted all of her mother's attempts to come to her house to clean or help go through Vance's things. Vance's mother had been more difficult to dissuade, but Sydney was determined not to do anything or let anyone disturb Vance's things before she was ready.

Even her mother's remark before she left the house wouldn't convince her to do anything before she felt she could let go.

"It's simply not healthy for you to go to that house by yourself with all of Vance's things there like that," she had said. "You should at least let me come to stay the night with you."

"Mama, this is something I need to do *by* myself and *for* myself," she had said with conviction. "I've been with you and Daddy long enough. I'll see to Vance's things and I'll be more than okay tonight. Like I said earlier, I'll call you and Daddy first thing in the morning."

Sydney refused to be swayed by her mother's hurt look and the wringing of her hands. Sydney assured herself that no one understood her relationship with Vance. Nobody really knew how she felt. She wanted time to herself to pretend that he was still here, at least for a while.

She showered and pulled Vance's favorite Alabama A&M University T-shirt over her head to wear to bed. When she turned the gold-embellished comforter back, she noticed crumbs and a chocolate chip cookie on Vance's nightstand. Vance's habit of eating cookies in bed always irritated Sydney, but she stared regretfully at the empty glass his lips had touched and the one cookie left on the plate.

The words, "I really never cared about the crumbs in the bed," escaped from her lips in a whisper.

At the thought, violent sobs quaked through her small frame as she dropped to her knees. "Why? Why? What am I gonna do, Lord?"

She clung in desperation to the comforter they had shared and buried her head in the pillow, trying to muffle her weeping. Everyone described her as strong, but she also defined herself that way. Sydney cried harder as asked herself who this woman was who couldn't accept reality and pull herself together.

Long ago she made a vow not to let others see her break as she viewed it as a sign of weakness. Sydney's refusal to cry as a child, even during a spanking, marked her indelibly as tough. Her family often teased her about this as a child. Her sister and cousins often tried to find ways to make her cry by doing things such as playing the dozens. Now, the joke seemed to be on her.

Sydney tried to pray and thank God for something, but at the moment, she went blank. How could people tell her that she would be able to help somebody else by going through this? God surely didn't allow her husband to be taken away so she could help somebody. She didn't want to help anyone. She just wanted the pain and the incredible ache in the core of her to cease. Unable to stop the well of tears from flowing, Sydney wept until her throat was raw. Her swollen, bloodshot eyes stung as one tear after another fell.

From childhood Sydney had dreamed of marrying a man who was not only saved but also well-educated, and Vance fit her criteria with ease. After attending Alabama A&M University to get his undergraduate degree and MBA, he moved back to Rochester where he landed a job at Xerox. In no time, he worked his way up in the corporate world to become one of the youngest and few African Americans to have a position in upper management for Xerox.

Sydney had attended undergraduate and graduate school at the University of Rochester, also majoring in business. While in graduate school, she landed an internship at Kodak as an accountant in the department of human resources. She discovered that despite her success as a student and blossoming career, her suitors dwindled to almost none. The men who did approach her seemed to be threatened in some way by her intelligence and business savvy, and she had become weary of the whole dating scene. On occasion, when she had dated men who were successful, she found that even they felt like they had to compete with her in some way.

Long ago, Sydney had decided that regardless of how lonely she was, she would never settle for less than what she knew the Lord could provide her with in a man. She understood the struggles faced by the black man, but she wanted a black man who was secure and knew she wasn't the enemy.

In Vance, Sydney had found the confidence and security she yearned for in a mate. He had been her anchor, her one sure thing. His strong faith strengthened hers. Sydney would always tell Vance, "Honey, just in case my prayers are hitting the ceiling, can you pray for me?" Vance would chuckle, but he would stop what he was doing to pray for her on the spot.

Without warning, once again she caught the lump in her throat that she had become so accustomed to and rushed to the bathroom

to get a sip of water to force it down. Barely able to swallow the water, Sydney choked. As she gasped for air, she grabbed the phone, wanting to call someone to come to her aid, only she couldn't think of who to call. Her mind raced. Her mother and father would worry. Chanel wouldn't know what to say. Sherese, well, Sherese would probably just cry with her, and that was the last thing she wanted right now.

She wanted Vance. She needed Vance. So she cried for the blank slate that lay before her, a future without him. She dug her hands into the comforter angrily and buried her face, weeping inconsolably.

When her cries subsided, she listened for the Lord's answers to her questions. *Why? Why? How could You let this happen, Lord?* Her daddy had always taught her to listen for the Lord's answer. He felt that too many people prayed for answers but didn't have the sense to listen to what He was saying. So she waited. And she waited. Just as it had been every day since Vance's death, there was not a whisper in her ear, an impression on her spirit, a scripture that leapt off the pages of the Bible to give her insight, and not even a word from an enlightened saint that helped. The silence suffocated her.

Instead of climbing into their king-sized bed on her side, she got in on Vance's side, not bothering to brush away the crumbs, and curled her body like a kitten into the space where he had slept every night since they had married. For that moment, she almost felt Vance cradling her and this helped her to fall into the deepest sleep she had had since his passing.

"Excuse me, Mrs. Ellington. I apologize for interrupting, but you have an important call on line two."

"Cynthia, I thought I asked you to hold all calls. I've got to work on these numbers for Mr. Neal. He's expecting them before noon," Sydney replied, annoyed. Her eyes stayed glued to her computer, not even bothering to look up.

"I understand, Mrs. Ellington, but it's a police officer. It seems like it may be important."

"What?" Sydney picked up the phone. "Yes, officer, this is Sydney Ellington. What is it?"

"Mrs. Ellington, is it correct that your husband is Mr. Vance Ellington?"

Sydney's heart pounded furiously as she answered, "Yes, why? Is he okay? What's wrong?"

"I'm sorry to inform you that he's been in an accident. I don't know the details, but he's being transported to Strong Memorial. Would you like an officer to assist you?"

"What do you mean? Is he okay? Never mind. No...I'll be right there."

Sydney dropped the phone and ran out of the office to her car as fast as she could. While driving through the city, she found her cell phone, wanting to reach her parents. She couldn't remember their number or anybody's number and had never taken the time to program the numbers in. She couldn't calm herself down enough to think clearly. *This couldn't be real* was all she could think as her shaking hands clasped the steering wheel tightly. Then, she remembered. **Pray, Sydney, pray hard,** she thought.

"God, please don't let—God, I'm sorry for everything. Just let him be okay!"

After she raced to the hospital, she ran frantically into the emergency room where two police officers and a doctor met her.

"I'm Vance Ellington's wife. Where is he? Is he okay?"

The doctor looked at her with sympathy. "Mrs. Ellington, is there someone you can call to be with you?"

"For what? No! No! What do you mean? For what?"

"Mrs. Ellington," the doctor stated apologetically while looking into her frightened eyes. "Your husband didn't make it. His internal injuries were far too severe."

One police officer interjected, "Mrs. Ellington, he was hit head-on by a semi. We've begun investigating the scene and will give you the details as soon as they are made known to us."

She searched each of the three faces and saw that they meant what she thought they meant. She shook her head and whispered, "No—No—No! That's impossible! I just saw him. I just saw him less than two hours ago."

"Mrs. Ellington, please let us call someone," the officer repeated.

"I want to see him now!"

An African-American nurse went to her and put her arms around Sydney. "Honey, his injuries were quite severe, and it's probably best to wait until a family member or friend can go in with you. Why don't you give me a number to call a family member to go with you?"

Sydney trembled uncontrollably and broke out in a cold sweat. She yanked herself from the hold of the kind nurse and then quickly tried to gain her composure.

"Okay, I just need to call my Mama and Daddy." She didn't want to alarm her mother, but instead, called her father at the church. Her father would be strong for her.

When her father's gaze met her as he walked through the sliding glass doors of the emergency room, Sydney ran to him. He embraced his daughter, and she hadn't even noticed the tears that fell from his eyes as she wept uncontrollably.

"Daddy, Daddy!" she groaned.

For the first time in her life, Sydney woke up crying. Vance's damp T-shirt clung to her body from perspiration and was close to being as drenched as her pillowcase. She wiped her tear-streaked face so she could focus in on her alarm clock. At almost 4:30 A.M., she was surprised that she had slept for most of the night. The same endless replay of that dreadful morning tormented her in her dreams every night. Her only reprieve this time was that her dream ended with her crying in her father's arms. Previously, her dreams had ended with Sydney unable to contact her parents or anyone else.

Although nothing in her life had been routine lately, she reached for her Bible to do her daily morning devotions as she had faithfully done for years. The text for the day came from Psalm 27:5 and read, "For in the time of trouble he shall hide me in his pavilion: in the secret of his tabernacle shall he hide me; he shall set me up upon a rock." Although she had read the verse many times before, it now meant more than it ever had before. She needed the Lord to hide her and give her the peace she so desperately yearned for.

One of her favorite verses in the Bible came from this psalm, so she read the psalm over and over again. She had committed the verse to memory. "I had fainted, unless I had believed to see the goodness of the LORD in the land of the living" (v. 13). She couldn't count the times that she had comforted others going through trials with this verse. Now, she couldn't believe that reciting these same words just seemed hollow. The words didn't comfort Sydney as they seemed to comfort others. Maybe she had been wrong to direct people to this scripture in their grief. She could not fathom goodness coming to her in this life anymore. Without her husband, her life felt meaningless. She had testified numerous times about how the Lord was first in her life, but now she knew the terrible truth. Deep in her heart, she may have put Vance ahead of God. In the recesses of her mind, Sydney couldn't help wondering if this was why the Lord had allowed Vance to be taken away.

Anguish and spiritual unrest rose up in her like a tidal wave swelling at its crest. She couldn't quiet the haunting voice, whispering, "God doesn't hear you. You're wasting your time. You've committed your life to a useless cause." A deep depression filled with hopelessness and desperation blanketed her whole being as the morning sunlight crept into the otherwise dark bedroom. Sydney closed her Bible.

CHAPTER 5

Chanel

I will not leave you comfortless: I will come to you.

John 14:18

Agitated, Chanel slammed the phone down. She had been trying to call Sydney for hours with no luck.

"Tommy! Tommy! Can you get Zach, please? Now!" she yelled as her son laughed, attempting to do figure eights through his mother's legs.

"Stop, Zachary. You're too doggone big!" Chanel fussed at her son.

"Relax, baby." Tommy rubbed Chanel's shoulders briefly before scooping Zachary up. "Come on, boy, before your mama strangles both of us." Tommy lifted his son up playfully in the air.

Chanel rolled her eyes and let out a deep breath, saying, "I don't understand why Sydney won't answer the phone. I'm going over there."

"Hey, now, I thought we already talked about this, Chanel. It's only been a few weeks since Vance passed. I still think you need to give the girl space. I know that you're best friends, but this here is something she may need to handle alone for a while."

Chanel could barely understand Tommy's words with Zachary's boisterous laughter. "Tommy, I can hardly hear you. Please stop throwing that boy up in the air. He'll be sick. Anyway, you don't know Sydney like I do. Besides, her mama called me upset this morning and said that Sydney called her to let her know she was okay, but that she still didn't want to see anybody. That can't be a good sign. She won't even pick up the phone when I call."

A look of further exasperation overtook Chanel's face as she dialed Sydney's number one last time. "I need to check on Sydney, so I'm gonna leave Zach here with you."

"Chanel, don't play. You know I'm supposed to meet B.J. at the studio at 10 A.M. I told you that yesterday."

Chanel did remember that he had mentioned something about going to the studio, but every day he found some reason to shirk his responsibilities. She needed help with her son. How did he expect her to run a business, take total responsibility for Zachary, and take care of the house?

"Don't play? Do I look like I'm playin'?" Chanel asked sarcastically. "You stayed out until almost three this morning, and you still can't manage to spend some time with your son? Look, I'm talking about helping my friend whose husband just died, and you're talking about hanging out with that raggedy B.J.? You need to get your priorities straight. Isn't it enough that I am the one supporting you financially? Do I have to be the daddy too?"

Zachary pounded on Chanel's leg. "Mommy. I wanna watch *Spongebob!* Mommy!"

"Stop it, Zach," Chanel angrily said until she looked down at her curly-headed son. Her heart softened, and she rubbed his head to apologize.

Tommy snatched Zachary up. "You are really trippin', Chanel. How can I forget that you're the one payin' the bills? Seems like you remind me every day. Is there anything I do right anymore? I stayed out until three this morning so that I can get this CD project together. You know this! I'm tryin' to start supporting you and Zachary again, but I guess you just can't understand a man tryin' to do the right thing. You're so used to somebody doin' you wrong, you're gonna find it in me no matter what I do. And what's more, ain't nobody Zachary's daddy but me! I don't care what you're payin', Chanel. I'm the man of this household!" Tommy yelled.

Chanel couldn't ignore Zachary's cries as her son reached for her from Tommy's arms. She didn't care how angry Tommy got today. She wasn't going to let Tommy shirk his responsibilities any longer. He would spend time with his son today. She had things to do. She bet Antonio, a man she had met and been conversing with recently, wouldn't treat her like this.

Chanel marched to the kitchen cabinet and grabbed a bag of fruit snacks to give to Zachary and kissed him on the the forehead.

"Thank you, Mommy," Zachary beamed.

She silently prayed that the Lord would help her to shut her mouth. But she couldn't let Tommy have the last word. When Zachary was away from earshot, Chanel snapped, "Tommy, if you have to tell me you're the man of the house, just what do you think that says about you? I'm so sick of you tryin' to play like you're a husband and daddy. Grow up!" Feeling victorious, she hurriedly grabbed her keys, slamming the door behind her before Tommy could respond.

Pangs of guilt swept over her as she backed her silver Four Runner out of the driveway. She hadn't meant for things to get out of hand, especially in front of Zachary. Long ago Chanel promised herself to never allow her son to grow up in the chaos that she had grown up in, which meant no arguing in front of Zachary. Tommy always knew how to push the right buttons. Although she felt bad for leaving the house with Zachary crying for her, Tommy needed to realize what he was doing to their family.

She almost hoped he would leave. If it weren't for Zachary, she convinced herself that she probably would leave.

There was too much for her to think about right now. As she popped in one of Karen Clark Sheard's old CDs, she pushed number two and listened to her favorite song, "Nothing Without You," and she tried to meditate on the words and calm herself. Chanel knew that in spite of all her successes and failures, she was nothing without the Lord. Just acknowledging this seemed to calm her down as she sped off down the street to check on Sydney.

Chanel had always been able to count on Sydney, so she wanted to let Sydney know that she was here for her. She knew that Sydney had to be in bad shape not to accept her phone calls and could kick herself for letting Tommy convince her that what Sydney needed was time alone. She whispered a prayer saying, "Lord, I know I don't come to You except when I need something most of the time, but I just pray that Sydney's okay. Please let her be all right."

Despite Chanel's nervousness about the condition of her friend, she parked and walked briskly to the door. As she started to ring the doorbell, the door slowly opened. There stood Sydney, looking much cheerier than Chanel expected.

"Come on in, girl," Sydney said, trying to sound as if she were glad to see Chanel, but she looked anxious.

Talking as normally as she could, Chanel asked, "Syd, what's up? You could call a sister and let her know you're okay!" She added as Sydney motioned for her to come in, "I've been calling and calling."

"I'm sorry, but I'm fine. I've just been trying to get things together, you know?" she explained while offering to take Chanel's jacket.

Immediately, Chanel noticed that Sydney was still in her robe and it was almost noon. For her, staying in a robe on a day off was typical, but Sydney had never stayed in a robe past seven or eight in the morning in all the years Chanel had known her.

"You want something to drink or eat?" Sydney offered.

Chanel searched her friend's face for anything that would signal that she was anything less than okay. "No, Syd, but I came by to see if you wanted to hang out with me today. I have to drop back by my house to get Zachary in a little while, but I figured we could go shopping or something."

"Chanel, I'm fine. I just need some time to myself."

Chanel, pretending to be looking at one of her newly manicured nails, eyed her friend. "That's all you've been doing, right? Besides, I won't take no for an answer."

Chanel was satisfied when Sydney reluctantly agreed to go with her.

While Chanel waited for Sydney to get ready, she sat in the spacious living room, decorated in rich plums and golds. Her eyes fixed on the picture above the ornate fireplace mantle that Sherese had painted of Sydney, Vance, and Maya. Chanel was in awe of Sherese's talent. The painting captured the essence of the three of them. She had always remarked to the family about how lively they looked in the portrait. In the past, when she had admired the picture, she had always secretly envied the life that Sydney had. Now, she just felt ashamed that she had had those thoughts and felt painfully sorry for her best friend.

After a short while, Sydney came down the steps looking a little more refreshed, wearing her tailored black slacks and a loose-fitting tan blouse. She caught her friend admiring the painting. "Sherese is really talented, huh?"

"That would be an understatement, Syd. She's phenomenal. How is she, by the way? I talked to her yesterday, but only briefly since I had an appointment when she called."

"She got a new job at the local newspaper as an artist. They were really impressed by her raw talent, but they want her to go to school. They've even agreed to pay her tuition. That girl doesn't know how blessed she is. Some of us pray for just a small bit of that kind of God-given gift."

"Syd, what are you talkin' about? You have so many gifts. I don't see how you can even say that."

"Girl, the Lord has blessed me in *spite* of, not *because* of."

"That applies to everyone. Really, Sydney, you don't see all that others see in you. You've already done more than most people do in a lifetime."

Chanel's countenance lightened as she joked, "I also feel like there may be a Missionary Ellington somewhere in this house."

Acting as if she were looking behind her, Sydney teased back. "Ain't no Missionary Ellington nowhere round these parts. You remember when Daddy put me up to do that ten minute sermonette on a Friday night a few years ago?"

"How could I forget? You did a good job, Syd!"

"You must be crazy, and you know as well as I do that flattery is sin. I got up and defied all Daddy's rules for people when they speak. First, I sang a song, tryin' to use up some of my minutes. Then, I gave my testimony, and you know how Daddy can't stand that when you're supposed to be givin' the message. Then, I read the longest scripture I could find."

"Everybody's gotta start somewhere, Syd."

Sydney placed her hand on her hip. "If that's the case, Sister-girl, when are you gonna start? Don't think Daddy's not aware of how you conveniently take Zachary out to the nursery on Friday nights when he calls people up to speak."

"Anyway, this is not about me. Let's go, girl." Chanel said, pleased that Sydney could still find something to joke about.

———

While the two were on their way to Chanel's to pick up Zachary, Sydney asked her friend, "You remember how giddy I was when I first met Vance?"

"Do I remember? Who could forget? I think we hardly talked during that time period. Vance had you so wrapped you forgot all about your friends."

Sydney smiled and raised her eyebrows.

"Correction." She pointed to Chanel and said, "I had *him* wrapped."

After a lighthearted chuckle, Chanel added, "You were both wrapped. It gave me hope about men when I didn't have one."

Sydney stared out of the car window, admiring the many lilac bushes now in season, which adorned the front yards of the neighborhood houses. "The lilacs are so full this year. Have you noticed? I can even faintly smell them in the air."

"Yeah, they're so pretty, but I have to admit that I always think they kinda stink."

"They remind me of the Lilac Festival. Vance and I never missed a year going," she reminisced.

She and Vance had made going to Highland Park in the spring a tradition. They loved seeing the world's largest display of lilacs, and no matter how many times they saw the hues of lavender, violet, and royal purples spread over fifteen acres, the couple always acted as if it were the first time they had seen it.

Chanel knew that it would be difficult for Sydney to make it through this season without him. Instead of spring marking rebirth and renewal, Chanel grieved for Sydney knowing that all she could probably think about was loss and death. Chanel wondered if it was better for Sydney to discuss Vance or if it would be better to just avoid the topic of her late husband.

Ignoring her hesitation, Chanel asked, "Hey, Syd. Go ahead. Tell me where you and Vance met again? Was it at school or church?"

Sydney smiled, "No, remember, we met at Wal-Mart, of all places."

Sydney had been a struggling graduate student in a local supermarket bargain shopping with her calculator in hand when the stately man approached her. Vance always made a point of telling family and friends that he had been in awe when he saw the attractive twenty-two-year-old young woman clad in a pink Nike sweat suit, reaching to get a can down from a top shelf. Gladly offering his assistance, Vance was immediately smitten by Sydney's petite athletic build, long chestnut hair pulled into a ponytail, and striking doe-like eyes. Her flawless complexion, showing no hint of make-up, exposed what she often referred to as an unattractive mole. Vance, on the other hand, insisted that it was not a mole but a beauty mark, and its position, on the right side of her upper lip, was attractive and made her his "black Marilyn Monroe." His way of turning negatives into positives was one of the many reasons she fell in love with him.

Sydney took a deep breath and kept her eyes glued out the passenger side window, but she began to talk about Vance. "He was wearing a pair of loose-fitting black linen slacks and a matching black silk shirt. He was so fine that day, girl. His cologne was intoxicating. I remember the smell as if it were yesterday. Anyway, he offered the can to me while sliding one of his business cards into my hand and said real smoothly, 'Give me a call sometime.'" Sydney had deepened her voice in an attempt to sound like him.

She continued, "Girl, I very politely but firmly returned the card to him and responded, 'I don't call men.' As I turned to push my cart away, I added, '—first, anyway. Thanks again for your help.'"

"I know Vance was trippin' over your reaction to him," Chanel said, enjoying Sydney's reaction at recalling the memory.

"With a stunned look on his face, I left that boy standing right there in the center of the aisle. I just kept on even though it was so hard to turn him down. The thing about it was that brothers need to understand that there's a proper way to approach a sister."

"You're not jokin'. They need to recognize," Chanel joked.

"I'm thankful for how Mama and Daddy raised Sherese and me. It was traditional, and you know how people were always teasin' us and hating us for it. Now, I'm thankful. You know how Mama and Daddy have been married for almost thirty-eight years?"

"Mmmm hhmm," Chanel nodded.

"Well, to this day, Daddy still opens doors for Mama and treats her with every courtesy. Daddy has always told us how a man should court and pursue a woman. He used to tell me and Sher, 'Girls, if a man really loves y'all, he'll walk out in the rain, snow, or sleet for hours to do for you. Nothing's too hard when a man loves a woman.'"

Chanel knew firsthand that chivalry was alive in the Hightower household, and as long as she had known Sydney, Chanel had been determined not to buckle under the pressure by relaxing her standards for society, friends, or a man.

As Sydney continued her story, she explained how she had been pleasantly surprised to see the attractive man sitting on a bench close to the exit when she checked out. She went on, "He ran to catch me in the parking lot with a pleading look and boyish charm, asking, 'Excuse me, I was…wondering if you would you allow me to have your phone number?'"

Sydney recounted her late husband's full lips that exposed a wide smile flashing his white teeth. She described how even the generous gap between his two front teeth provided him with a unique magnetism, making it simply too much for Sydney to resist.

"Vance told me he was astonished at his own level of discomfort and insecurity at this first encounter with me, feelings he really never had had before when approaching women. I didn't know I would marry him, but I can say that after the first couple of dates with him, I knew he was somebody really special."

Their year-and-a-half long courtship had been wonderful, filled with walks in the park, attending church services, watching movies, and having late dinners after Vance was off from work and she was finished with her classes for the day. Sydney made a point of always planning their time together in the midst of other people for the most part because she was resolved to be celibate until marriage. Chanel knew that the few real relationships that Sydney did have always broke up because of this.

Although Chanel knew that Vance hadn't warmly embraced her insistence on waiting for marriage until engaging in a sexual relationship, he loved her enough to wait. Sydney knew about Vance's checkered past with women, so she counted it a blessing that Vance respected her enough to wait and was thankful for his patience, because she was all too aware of his meandering ways before they got together.

Vance had told Chanel that although Sydney wasn't as glamorous as some of his ex-girlfriends, Sydney's natural beauty, low-maintenance lifestyle, and amazing focus in her life were refreshing for him. He had become bored with superficial women who offered him no intellectual conversation and who were infatuated only by his career and material possessions. Before Vance and Sydney's marriage, conversations with Vance let Chanel know that while he didn't consider himself a necessarily spiritual person, he believed in the Lord and recognized that finding Sydney was a true blessing.

"You two were really beautiful together," Chanel said, but when Sydney didn't respond, Chanel knew she was immersed in her thoughts.

When the two got to Chanel's house, an uncomfortable silence was present until Zachary walked in.

"Zachary! How's Auntie's baby boy," Sydney beamed.

"Auntie!" Zachary exclaimed as he climbed into her lap.

Chanel put her hand on her hip. "Girl, I don't know why you insist on making him a baby. That boy is already almost your size."

"You know you better hush that nonsense. He's gonna be Auntie's baby forever, right, Zachary?"

Zachary smiled, nodding his head.

"Zachary! Zachary! Where are you?" Tommy called from upstairs.

"Right down here, Daddy," Zachary yelled back.

"Come here, now!"

As Zachary ran upstairs, Sydney surprised Chanel by saying, "I always thought we would have children."

Chanel couldn't fill the space between them. Anything she could think to say didn't seem appropriate.

"I just didn't consider that Vance and I *wouldn't* have a family one day, even though I wasn't ready now. Chanel, it was a horrible mistake."

Chanel silently prayed that the Lord would give her the right words to say. She gently squeezed Sydney's arm. "Please don't beat yourself up about that. I mean…I know it's hard to think about." She looked away, feeling her response wasn't right and inadequate.

"I'll make it. I just have my moments." Sydney stood up and asked, changing the subject, "Hey, how about a snack. I'm a little hungry for some reason."

"Could it be that you never eat anything. Lord knows, I hope one day you realize that you are not a bird."

By the time Chanel was ready to leave for their shopping spree, Sydney looked more like her old self but was still quiet until she noticed Chanel's boots.

Sydney broke the silence by changing the subject. "Okay, girl, where in the world did you find hot pink cowboy boots? They're actually kind of cute on you!"

"Kinda cute? Hmph!" Chanel smiled. A running joke between them was Sydney's conservative style in contrast to Chanel's flamboyance. "You know I'll get you a pair," Chanel teased.

Sydney adopted a Texas drawl and answered, "I believe I'll decline, but thank you kindly."

"You remember when I went to that hair show last year? Well, they had this fashion show afterwards and these were calling my name!"

Sydney shook her head.

"What? Who says a black woman can't wear some cowboy boots out!" Chanel continued, lifting one leg in the air for display.

"Well, just check out those rhinestones running up the back and sides. They're you," Sydney added.

Chanel noticed the wide and genuine smile on her friend's face and felt much better than she had, knowing that Sydney could still smile.

"How about we hit Salina's Boutique first? They're supposed to be having a mad sale."

"That's fine; whatever you want to do."

Chanel then changed her mind, remembering that Sydney wasn't a big fan of the flashy styles at Salina's.

"You know what? I have a feeling Ann Taylor would put you in a better mood than Salina's."

"Yeah, you're probably right. Hey, I was thinking that Maya might like to come along if you don't mind. Besides you know how much she loves watching Zachary, so it'll help too."

"Girl, yes; it's a blessing to have a brainy friend."

After they finished shopping and dropped Maya back at her mother's house, they went back to Chanel's where she put Zachary to bed.

"I thought that boy would never go to sleep," Chanel commented as she looked across her cluttered counter tops.

"Seems like there's not enough time in the day, and Tommy doesn't seem to be helping."

Twinges of embarrassment came and left as Chanel began wiping down the cluttered countertops, which were the complete opposite of Sydney's elegant marble countertops. As much as Chanel liked the finer things in life, she was far more into accessorizing their existing house than buying a new one. The small, quaint house on the Northeast side was in the heart of the city's hardworking middle class, but Chanel had worked hard to fill her home to capacity with Ethan

Allen leather embossed furniture in the front room, a stunning cherry dining table with matching curio cabinet, as well as other expensive furniture and artwork throughout. Chanel had immediately fallen in love with the quiet neighborhood, glad that people stayed out of her business, and she quite naturally stayed out of theirs.

However, in recent months, the white aluminum siding had begun to peel. In addition, the rusty pipes, old water heater, and crumbling cement in the old driveway were causing her to reconsider how deep her love for the house and neighborhood really was. She also could no longer ignore how cramped things had become since Zachary was getting bigger, and she knew she would either have to put out some serious money for maintenance and remodeling or sell.

The truth was, though, that Chanel had trouble parting with things she had become accustomed to. There had been so much instability in her life as a child that she clung to the familiar house, in spite of the fact that she had more than enough money stashed away to easily move into a larger home.

As she joined her friend at the kitchen table, Chanel could tell from Sydney's faraway look that she was absorbed in her thoughts. She chose her words carefully, as she didn't want to upset her friend. "Syd, I gotta tell you. I'm worried about you, and I'm not quite sure what to say or not say. I just want to know how you're really doing."

Sydney tried to sound sincere. "*Really,* girl, I'm okay. The Lord's gonna see me through this."

"You must be forgetting who you're talking to. I know you still trust in the Lord and all, but you're still human. I just want to help, and the way I see it, the only thing I can do is to listen to how you're feeling," Chanel responded, eyeing Sydney carefully.

Sydney tried to say as nonchalantly as she could, "The guy who…well,…the guy's name is Brian O'Leary and his blood alcohol level was three times over the legal limit. His trial is going to begin in a few weeks. Vance has been gone for three months, and I'm just glad that this creep is finally going to have to face what he's done."

Chanel struggled to control her emotions and find the right words to say. "I knew it. I just knew the way the accident happened that it had to be something like this." She tried to make eye contact with her friend, whose eyes remained fixed outside the window.

"He's been out of the hospital for about a month, according to the public defender. He's probably been with his family recovering," Sydney said in a low but monotone voice.

"Syd, I'm so sorry, honey, but doesn't this make it a little better to know that justice may be served?" Chanel suggested.

Sydney finally turned to look at her friend and said in a mocking tone, "Justice? There's no justice for losing Vance. I mean, even if they put this guy in the electric chair, there's still no justice."

Chanel dropped her head down. "I'm sorry. I just—." The phone rang, giving her an easy escape from the difficult conversation as she moved swiftly to get it.

"Hello." Chanel's greeting wasn't received by anything but silence, so once again, she said, *"Hello?"*

As she listened to the raspy cough on the other end, her stomach tightened with fear.

It couldn't be her. What did she want? Chanel wondered.

She listened quietly for the voice to clear.

"I guess you don't wanna talk to me."

Chanel stood there, paralyzed by the voice on the other end.

"I know can't none of us on this side of Rochester do you no good with your coffeehouse and all, but I was just callin'."

"Nyla, what is it? You need something?" Chanel demanded, wanting to kick herself for asking the woman who *always* needed something if she needed anything.

"Naw, well, if you got some cigarette—naw, I was jus callin'." Nyla sounded like she was coughing up phlegm, which both sickened and disgusted Chanel, but she was determined to get to the bottom of the phone call.

"How's the boy doin'?" her mother asked as though she really didn't want to know.

"You talkin' about Zachary, your grandson?"

"Mmmm hmmm." She coughed some more.

She had forgotten for a moment that Sydney was there until she tapped her from behind, mouthing, "Is it your mama?"

Chanel nodded and asked, "Nyla, what is it that you want?"

"Never mind, girl. Sorry to bother you," she said gently, and Chanel heard the call disconnect.

Her mother had hung up on her. Chanel desperately wanted to be the one to do that to her. She couldn't help being upset that Nyla could still somehow control things with her.

"What did she say, girl?" Sydney asked with her hands on her hips, waiting impatiently.

"You got me. She's gonna try to tell me that she was just calling, acting like she didn't want anything. Do you believe that craziness?"

Sydney's face softened, and she settled down on the sofa. "Maybe she was, Chanel. Maybe she just wanted to see if you were doing okay. I mean, it has to really get under her skin to know that she hasn't even seen Zachary—ever!"

"Ohhh no, don't tell me you're fallin' for one of Nyla's tricks!" Chanel plopped down beside her.

"You haven't talked to the woman in years, Chanel. Why don't you pray about talking to her? It can't hurt. Nyla's just as human as anybody else. She can change."

"You are just too optimistic for me. If she's feelin' bad, that's good enough for her. She deserves some sleepless nights as far as I'm concerned."

"Well, you know we can't agree when it comes to your mother, so I'll drop it, but hey, I just thought of something. Don't think I forgot about your telling me about that guy Antonio you met the other day. Please tell me you haven't been conversing with him?"

Chanel was relieved that the conversation had moved. She had been treading in unfamiliar territory and found herself utterly unequipped to deal with Sydney's tragedy and certainly not with her mother.

With a sigh, Chanel looked around uneasily and lowered her voice, unable to mask the grin on her face. "Well, actually the fine brother did call me on my cell yesterday. He wants to take me on a friendly lunch date. Before you start to trip, he knows I'm married." Chanel's smile faded as she noticed Sydney's disapproval.

"I'm sure he does," Sydney added sarcastically with raised eyebrows and a no-nonsense attitude. "But you did set him straight though about not going on a date with him, didn't you?"

Pleased that this topic seemed to bring back the Sydney she knew and loved, Chanel eagerly responded, "Now you know I did, girl."

She could tell that Sydney's intent stare was searching her face for any hints of dishonesty. Because of the number of years they had been friends, it was easy for Sydney to make her feel convicted about something when no one else could. Chanel couldn't stand that quality about Sydney sometimes, but she always ended up appreciating it somehow in the end.

Despite Chanel's best efforts to change the subject, Sydney remained silent, which signaled to Chanel that she didn't believe a word she was saying. Chanel felt badly about telling her friend a lie, but she wasn't in the mood for lectures. There seemed to be so many bad things happening around her, and Antonio had given her, quite unexpectedly, something to get excited about. She and Tommy hadn't been getting along for months, and she had even started sleeping in their guest room. In addition, she was having a more difficult time dealing with Vance's death than she had expected, and her business at the café was slowing down for no apparent reason. The one bright spot in her life, with the exception of Zachary, seemed to be her meeting Antonio.

Her lunch date with Antonio was set for tomorrow at one thirty, and she made sure that Lena could cover for her. She wanted to make sure that she had plenty of time to get herself together before meeting him. Their phone conversation had been brief, but she did find out that he was an account executive for a local radio station. He had told her how anxious he was to see her again, and although Chanel didn't say it, she too was excited about the lunch date.

Sydney continued to eye Chanel suspiciously as she questioned her. "Now how did you meet Antonio again?"

"You remember I told you that Tommy and I were supposed to be taking Zachary to see *Sesame Street Live* the other day, right?" At Sydney's nod, she continued, "Of course, he cancelled at the last minute, talking about how he had to go to do this gig somewhere. I was so mad, but I knew that I wasn't about to let Tommy ruin my plans again. So I just decided to go without him."

"Yeah, girl, I remember all that. Just get to the meeting," Sydney demanded.

"Okay, okay. This cute little girl came up to Zachary while we were waiting in line during intermission and said she liked the lights on his tennis shoes. Well, I look over to see who is coming to get the cute baby, and it's this fine man. Did you hear me when I said *man*? He introduced himself to me very politely, and when he picked the baby up, she just started screaming. I felt so bad for him that I asked if I could try to settle her down."

Sydney looked in total disbelief. "You are just not the one to be bothered with kids other than your own, so I know he must've been fine."

Chanel chuckled as she continued. "Well, in all seriousness, he's not a brother most sisters would take a second look at based on looks alone, but he's very well-dressed. I mean, sharp as a tack from head to toe and smells good too. He's real dark chocolate, extremely muscular with a round, bald shaved head." Chanel made the hand gestures of a perfect ball. "His eyes are dark and really deep set with a nice strong nose, and when he smiled at me…girl. And when he told me he was divorced, I was just too mad that I couldn't say the same."

"You're awful, Chanel," Sydney said, shaking her head in disbelief.

"Well, somebody's gotta be. It's sure not gonna be you!" she joked. "Anyway, he's from Buffalo and only recently moved to Rochester. Apparently, he gets his daughter on every other weekend, and he doesn't really know too many people."

"Mmmmm hmmmm," Sydney answered in a melodious yet condescending manner.

"Really. He just wants the kids to get together sometime since they're the same age." Chanel couldn't even keep her face straight because she didn't even really believe what she was saying.

"What about him asking you on a lunch date then?"

"Oh, well, since he's an account executive for a radio station and I told him I owned a small café, he said he wanted to talk to me about advertising on the station. He said it really didn't cost as much as I might think."

Sydney admonished, "Well, he sounds like he could be tempting, especially for an unmarried, unsaved woman. But you now, you just watch your step. I know you and Tommy have your challenges, but you know the grass is always greener…" Sydney's voice trailed off until she said abruptly, "Things are getting better for you and Tommy, aren't they?"

"Are you serious? We can't agree about anything. We can't even agree on what time Zachary should go to bed, let alone the big issues," she sighed. "I'm just tired."

As Chanel talked about some of the problems in her marriage, she noticed that Sydney began to get the same disconnected look that Chanel had seen throughout the day. Chanel immediately apologized. "I'm sorry, Syd. You know sometimes I can be so insensitive."

"There's nothing insensitive about airing your feelings. It's all gonna work out between you and Tommy. I see the way he looks at you. You two love one another. That's the most important thing."

"It takes more than love to make a marriage work though."

"Take it from me, love is the main thing. Everything can work out if you both want it to."

Chanel nodded. "Maybe that's what I need to be praying about."

Sydney got up to put her cup in the sink. "I know you, Chanel. You want your marriage. Just don't complicate things by bringing someone else into the picture."

"Yeah, I know, I know," Chanel said, trying to convince herself more than Sydney.

"Well, I should head home before it gets too late." Sydney gave Chanel a quick embrace. "Just don't sweat the small stuff, Chanel. Be thankful that the Lord is giving you two another day to share."

Feeling guilty that she had been so self-absorbed, Chanel was a little embarrassed as she went to get the now sleeping Zachary so she could take Sydney home.

CHAPTER 6

Sherese

*Carry each other's burdens, and in this way
you will fulfill the law of Christ.*

Galatians 6:2 NIV

Sherese marveled in admiration at having her very own office as she spun around in her swivel chair, proud that she had completed her first week of work as a graphic artist for *The Rochester Times*. Even though technically her space was considered a cubicle, it was hers, and for the first time in her life she really felt like she was making a contribution toward something important. The tropical plant that Sydney gave her for a gift of congratulations really added warmth to her space, along with the small painting of her mother, Darlene, she had done herself several years ago. She was feeling optimistic about her future. Her parents and Sydney had surprised Sherese by giving her an intimate dinner to celebrate her new job, and it seemed that her new position gave everyone permission, if only for a moment, to be happy. It didn't matter that the position was an entry-level one because Sherese realized that this job was the beginning of a career unlike her previous jobs, ones that just paid the bills.

She had even been able to push the incident with Jack to the background, especially since he finally seemed to get the message by her unreturned calls. She couldn't even remember why she had given him her parents' real number along with her cell phone number anyway.

Her mama had left her at least several notes daily to let her know that Jack had called.

"Now, Sher, this Jack seems like a nice fella. Why don't you wanna talk to him again? Where did you say you met him?"

"Mama, I told you a hundred times. I am not interested in him, so there's no point in even talking about him."

Her mother had muttered, "Well, it must've been something for you to give the boy your number."

In his last message on her cell phone he had said, "Sherese, this is Jack again. I just wanted to tell you how very sorry I am for everything. Uhh hmmm. I had seen you before, and I finally got the courage to talk to you. Anyway, I'd like to take you to dinner so you can really get to know the kind of guy I am. I didn't mean to take advantage of you."

Neither Jack's profuse apologies nor her sincere regret would erase the awful events of that night. She couldn't bear to see him again, and as for The Clique or any other club, she vowed that she would never step foot in them again. Her shame and humiliation had deep roots that she didn't have time to weed out. It was simply a mistake that she had made and her resolve to never go that low again would have to suffice.

While Sherese knew that she wasn't living for the Lord, her upbringing wouldn't allow her to wallow in sin either. In the innermost parts of her being, she knew there could be no straddling the fence spiritually. Sherese was either right or wrong, and although she knew she was on the wrong side, she didn't feel totally ready to give her all to the Lord. She was not prepared for a life of sacrifice and self-neglect, a life she watched her parents live with no visible rewards. Sherese wanted prosperity, fun, and a carefree lifestyle.

Avoiding spiritual matters was paramount for her even as she sat in the church pew Sunday after Sunday listening to her father preaching the gospel. Sherese would often be in another world in her thoughts as her father would suck in air, sounding like he was on the brink of collapse, heaving, "Ya' think ya' not makin' a decision about getting' saved, huh?"

He would heave some more, clear his throat, wipe the sweat which poured down his temples, and say as if his life depended on it, "Church, ya' makin' a decision when you don't decide. Holiness or hell! Ya' can be hot or cold cause if ya' lukewarrrrrrrm, he'll spew ya' right out!"

Her daddy would do a half turn and loosen the collar on his purple robe and Sherese would hear the other elders and ministers and missionaries say, "Yes, sir!" Every now and then, a missionary would get excited and call out, "Say that, Pastor!"

Sherese would often observe Minister Bailey, the minister of music, trying to slyly creep back into the service from downstairs. He could never resist getting an early taste of the fried chicken the church mothers were preparing to sell after service, and although he could slide in on the organ seat to play some chords to back up her father when he got tuned up, everyone joked that it had to be the greasiest organ in Upstate New York as much as Minister Bailey ate. In spite of the slippery organ, Minister Bailey got around on it just fine. He knew how to hit all the right notes to get the saints shouting. Sister Desmond, always the liveliest and the loudest in the congregation, would start to spin in circles around the church, and she had no shame in letting her dress fly up as she spun, exposing her knee-highs to the congregation. Everything seemed to move on her, with the exception of her hair, which seemed to always be frozen and filled with rhinestones in the latest updo.

Then, Lil' Bubba Bailey, Minister Bailey's son, would really get folks going, driving the drum beats faster and faster. Even though her daddy was adamant that saints should dress in a respectful way to show reverence to God, he let Lil' Bubba wear the do-rag that he refused to take off. When her daddy confronted him, he didn't come to church for months. Even Pastor Hightower had to admit that the services weren't the same without Lil' Bubba, so he decided that the saints would do better tolerating the raggedy do-rag he insisted on wearing than to do without his flawless drumbeats.

Then, when Brother Lightfoot would pick up that saxophone and blow like he was playing to get paid or something, all the women that hadn't stood before would stand, shouting and praising God, until even her Mama, first lady of the church, would get up, dropping her tambourine to do a Holy Ghost dance, and shout, "Thank Ya, Lord!" When Mama got going real good in her shout, Sherese's daddy would grab the microphone and put it real close to his lips and hold one arm out, singing, "Let the church say yesssss. Yessss." The tempo to the music would slow way down and get softer and there would be a call and response in singing. "Yes, Lord. Yes, Lord. Yes, Lord. Yessss. Yesss. Yessss." Her dad would start singing the "Yes, Lord" song when her mother began to slow her dance down. Her daddy had never been one to quench the Spirit, but without a doubt, when the congregation heard the "Yes, Lord" song, they knew it was time to calm down and get back in order.

Sherese knew that her parents were sincere, but there was just too much she knew about the people in the church for her to want to be around them any more than on Sundays. Sherese didn't need or want the people who were hungry for position, power, recognition, or sympathy from the church. She felt like the world gave her enough of that, but she couldn't justify or explain the ache deep inside of her. It was an emptiness that could not be filled, and she had a suspicion that it had nothing to do with church people.

She left her memories and glanced at the clock. It was time for her to clock out from work, so she gathered her things, ready to meet her mother to go apartment hunting. As she was leaving, a security guard stationed outside the main entrance smiled and asked, "You're new here, aren't you?"

Purposely not returning his smile, she added, "Yes," and hurried past him. He called out, "Hey, I just wanted to tell you that I think you're pretty."

Sherese pretended that she didn't hear him and hopped into her car as fast as she could. She had agonized about whether to wear her favorite short black skirt since the last thing she wanted was some man coming on to her. As much as her mama and daddy wanted her to settle down with a "nice" guy, Sherese was determined to get her life together once and for all. A man simply wasn't part of her plans right now.

When she pulled her Honda up in front of her parents' house, her father was up on a ladder cleaning the gutters of the large, but worn, brick home.

"Hey, how's my working girl?" Her father beamed as beads of sweat clung to his aged and weathered dark-brown face.

"Daddy," Sherese said in a scolding manner. She put her hands on her hips and asked, "Mama know you're up there? Besides, I thought Tommy was gonna clean those gutters out for you this weekend? It's not good for you to be up there with your arthritis."

"It ain't too bad out here, and ya' know I'm not gonna wait on that boy to get over here. Besides, I like to be out here. It's not good for me to be cooped up inside."

"Okay, just holler if you need something." Sherese opened the squeaky front door, but not before calling out, "Hey, you still didn't say if Mama knows you're up there."

"Don't you go worryin' her. She's been callin' people all day about apartments for you. Ain't no need for you to move from here, but if you must, you need to see what she found out for ya'."

"Well, I'm gonna let you slide this time, Daddy, but you really don't need to be up there."

"Who's the parent, young lady?" he added, smiling while removing his cap to scratch his coarse salt–and-pepper hair.

Sherese smiled and opened the door to the welcoming smell of her mama's chicken and dumplings. Darlene's face lit up when she noticed her daughter had entered. She motioned for Sherese to come sit down and said into the phone, "Let me call you back this evening. My daughter just walked in. Okay, you just hang in there. I'll call you later. Bye, now."

"Hey, Mama. How are you today?"

"Just talkin' to my friend, Louise. She just ain't been the same since Harry Jr. got locked up." Darlene gazed out of the kitchen window deep in thought. "The question is, how are you doin', baby?"

Darlene gave her daughter's arm a quick squeeze in recognition as Sherese twirled one of her braids through her fingers. "I had a great day. I think I'm really going to like my job."

"Sherese, you just make sure that you thank the Lord for blessing you. Don't take nothin' for granted, you hear?"

She hoped her mother wouldn't start preaching to her. She quipped a quick, "Yes, Ma'am," and changed the subject. "You found a lot of apartments for me to look at?"

Her mother pulled out one of the heavy oak chairs to sit down next to Sherese. who was examining the apartment ads that her mother had circled in the paper. "Yeah, they have a good amount."

"So, Mama, you ready to go check some of these out with me?"

"That's what I wanted to talk to you about." The look of concern that covered her mother's face made Sherese put the paper down.

"I spoke to Sydney earlier, and you know I think it's a shame that she's in that big house all by herself."

Sherese I took a deep breath. "Mama, are you gonna suggest that I move in with her?"

"Well, yes, as a matter of fact, that's exactly what I was gettin' ready to say." Her mother rubbed her hands together, something she did when she was anxious.

"Before you go any further, does Sydney want me to move in?"

"Of course she wants you to move in. I wouldn't bring it up if she didn't."

"Okay, let me rephrase my question. Did Sydney suggest that I move in with her first or did you?"

Her mother fidgeted in her seat a little, pretending to smooth her apron out, before saying, "Now, what does it matter who suggested it?"

Sherese studied her mother's wrinkle-free face, despite her sixty years of age. By almost all accounts, her mother's outward beauty paralleled her inner beauty. Although Sydney had inherited more of her mother's looks than Sherese had, as her mother spoke Sherese saw her own long eyelashes, copper brown-colored skin, and petite frame. At times, it bothered her, especially since Sydney had the same flawless complexion with the exact mole over her upper lip that her mother had. Sherese, on the other hand, was prone to occasional breakouts and felt she needed makeup to stand out.

Sherese placed the newspaper down firmly before stating deliberately, "Mama, I don't even really want to discuss going over there if you had to talk her into it."

"For goodness sake, Sherese, I did not have to talk her into anything. That girl hasn't been able to think straight about much since Vance passed. I wouldn't expect her to think like that, and you shouldn't either. You wouldn't have to pay rent, and besides, you could save up to go to school."

Leaning against the counter, Sherese pleaded, "I'm ready to be on my own again, Mama. I've been staying with you and Daddy the past couple of years, and I'm grateful. Now, I'm ready to stand on my own and support myself. Please don't press this issue. I just can't right now."

Her mother picked up a dishtowel and started wiping the spotless table, signaling to Sherese that she was upset. "You know all you've just said is 'I.' This is not just about helping you out. I'm worried about Sydney. Even though she seems okay, I know she needs somebody around her, whether she thinks she does or not."

Everyone knew how much Sydney and her mama were alike. Her mother and Sydney prided themselves in being in control of their emotions, while Sherese often carried her feelings on her sleeve.

When Darlene noticed that Sherese remained firm in her stance not to offer to stay with Sydney, she continued, "How can you be okay with Sydney staying in that big house all by herself? I talked to your daddy about us goin' over there, but you know how he is. He wants to be here and he says it's okay for me to go, but you know he won't take his medicine and eat right if I'm not right here."

"Mama, please don't make me feel bad," Sherese pleaded.

Her mother pursed her lips together tightly. "It certainly doesn't make a lick of sense for you to pay rent in an apartment when your sister is alone going through the worst time in her life. Don't be selfish when the Lord has blessed you so, Sherese." With that said, her mother slowly walked out of the room, leaving Sherese to stew over her final words.

Why her mama had to try to make her feel guilty about getting what she wanted was beyond her understanding, but conversations with her mother almost never resorted to arguments. Darlene stayed too prayed up to really argue about much of anything, and she was the type of woman who said what she had to say and that was it. The lack of discussion made Sherese feel like things were often left unresolved. However, her mother appeared oblivious to the tension between the two.

"Mama?" Sherese walked down the hall until she heard the noise of the television.

Her mother was in the living room, listening to an evangelist on TBN while folding clothes on the sofa.

Darlene didn't look up from her task to acknowledge her daughter who sat down next to her. "Mama, I really want to finish this discussion with you," she began. "You know that I can totally get on Sydney's nerves, and I don't want to make a bad situation worse. I'm messy, she's a total neat freak. I stay up late, she goes to bed early. I love to talk on the phone, she can't stand it. That's not to mention that she corrects everything I say and do." Her mother kept folding and Sherese continued, "I could go on but I won't. I love Syd more than anything, but moving in with her could be a catastrophe waiting to happen. I can probably do more good for her from a distance."

"There *are* things you could do, Sher. For instance, it wouldn't do you no harm to be a bit more tidy."

Sherese fell back on the sofa in frustration and said in a defeated voice, "She absolutely can't stand it when I sleep half of the day away on Saturdays."

"Now, chile, you know you have no business sleepin' your life—." Her mother stopped short for a second and started again. Her mother cracked a smile. "Some stuff Sydney will just have to get over. She knows she can't control you."

"Mama, she detests when I come home late. She'll worry herself sick." Sherese knew her mother's victory was imminent.

"You don't need to stay out too late anyway." She began to fold clothes with a fury that Sherese had never seen. "People are crazy, Sherese. You're not too grown for something to happen to you. What's out in the world for a church girl like yourself? You need to get saved. That's what you need to do."

In a childlike voice, Sherese whined, "Mama, she would get upset about me doing something she didn't like, and it would be over."

Sherese knew her mother wouldn't argue, but she also knew that her mother admired her tenacity. Sherese always made her think and kept her on her toes unlike Sydney, who almost always succumbed to whatever her mother said.

"Why even say somethin' like that? I know my daughters well enough to know that they can get along fine if they really want to. That's all I have to say about it. The rest is up to you."

No matter what her mother said, Sherese had to do what was really best for herself. She returned to the kitchen to pick the paper up to call some apartment complexes.

After mapping out which apartments were closest to her job and her parents' home, Sherese decided she would get started on Friday after the work week. Her boss had asked that she critique one of the graphic artist's work in tonight's paper, so she was curious to take a look. Hearing the front door open, Sherese called out, "Daddy, could you bring me the evening paper off the porch?" As the footsteps drew nearer from behind, Sherese said, "You want me to fix you a plate before you and Mama go to church?"

The door slammed shut and Sydney asked, "What's up, Sher?"

She hid her surprise. "Oh, hi, Syd, I thought you were Daddy."

Sydney tossed the paper on her younger sister's lap. "You know, I don't think I'd mind having a plate though. What's for dinner?"

Sherese got up and took the lids off of the two pots simmering on the stove. "Mama made some chicken and dumplings, greens, and corn bread. I think there's even some peach cobbler left from last night."

"Great," Sydney replied enthusiastically.

Looking at her sister doubtfully, Sherese asked, "Since when did you start eating chicken and dumplings? You used to almost be in tears when Mama fixed them cause you always hated them."

"Well, some things you have to acquire a taste for."

The two sisters chuckled lightheartedly, and Sydney added, "Whatever! You can't joke me too hard cause you were broke down when Mama cooked liver and onions."

Sherese shook her head as she remembered. "Girl, remember when Mama and Daddy made me sit in front of those liver and onions for dinner for two days? I was so mad and hungry that I called Retha from across the street and paid her to sneak me some homemade donuts from her daddy's store."

Sydney tried to catch her breath as she said through tears of laughter, "That silly girl came to the door and said, 'Good evening, Mrs. Hightower. I just wanna know if you can give these donuts to Sherese, and she owe me $1.25 by Saturday cause my Daddy say he just can't give folks donuts for free cause they don't like what they Mama cooked.' Mama got you good for that one!"

Sherese stood up, lightly slapping Sydney on the shoulder. "Girl, I had forgotten all about that!"

The small creak in the floor let them know Darlene was coming into the kitchen. "What in the world is so funny with y'all tonight?"

The two young women looked at each other and burst out into laughter again, so their mother just shook her head and checked on the food.

Sherese inwardly thanked the Lord that they had found something in common so entertaining. Sherese wondered if losing Vance had opened Sydney up to the possibility of really getting to know some of the good things about her.

Just then, their father walked in, "What y'all doin in here, causin' a big commotion?"

"Hi, Daddy," Sydney said, greeting her father with a light kiss on the cheek.

"Hey there, sweetie. You makin' out okay?" her father asked.

"I'm doing fine," she replied. "Where in the world have you been?" Sydney asked, noticing his dirty overalls.

"I must've missed you since I went in the backyard to work. By the way, you need to make sure that you eat. You're gettin' too thin, which is somethin' the Hightower women don't never seem to do." Then he added under his breath, "Shoot, your mama's family don't have that problem neither. Everybody 'cept her got them big bones and big—"

"Speak for your own family, Samuel," Darlene quipped, never missing a beat.

Samuel grinned. "Yep, I'm gonna get washed up and changed for supper, Darlene."

"I laid some clean clothes and linens on the bed for you," Darlene added.

Her father grunted, "Why thank you, baby doll," as he left the room.

Before anyone could say anything, Samuel called, "Honey, where is my gray T-shirt?"

"Lord knows, you're father can't find nothin' without me. You two watch the dinner for me," Darlene directed, wiping her hands off on a dish towel.

As her mother departed, the sisters stayed in an uncomfortable silence.

Sherese could see that Sydney appeared to be struggling about something, but since she figured it must be something about Vance, she didn't question her. She wasn't accustomed to silence with Sydney. She would always harangue her with questions about her job, apartment hunting, or finances. This time the only thing was, as the minutes seemed to tick away slowly, Sydney didn't speak.

After five minutes or so, Sherese finally began to ask Sydney a question, but they simultaneously began to speak.

"You first, Sher."

"No, Syd, you go ahead," Sherese insisted.

Sydney blew a breath out slowly. "Okay, I just wanted to tell you that I'm really proud of you getting a new job and everything. I know I've been kind of hard on you these past couple of years."

"Syd, you don't have to say that, but thanks." Sherese couldn't suppress the smile on her face.

"No, really, Sher, I'm sorry about the blowout we had a couple of months ago. You're just so talented with your art, and I just wanted to see you use what God has given you. Anyhow, I'm really happy for your success."

"I don't know what to say," Sherese said.

"Well, you don't have to say anything, but I do want to talk to you about one more thing."

"What's that?" Sherese went over to stir the pots on the stove while Sydney talked.

"You know I've been trying to decide what I'm going to do with the house. Without Vance the house just seems too big, but I don't know if I'm ready to sell it, you know?"

Sherese nodded.

"Mama and I talked a little and she thought it might be a good idea if you thought about moving in with me for a little while."

Sherese turned and sat back down at the table to face her sister. "Mama talked to me too, but I think it's time for me to do for myself now, Syd. You've said that to me so many times, and now I'm ready. Mama means well, but I know you need your space, and quite frankly, I do too."

Sydney bit her bottom lip. "Well, the thing is, I'm asking you if you'll do it for me."

Sherese looked at her sister with skepticism. "Why would you want me to come stay with you? You don't think I can make it on my own, do you?"

"It's nothing like that. It's just that I thought that you could have the whole basement to do your painting and drawing. Vance has the new computer he just bought, so you could even do your work there."

Sherese tapped her fingers across the table. "I don't know, Syd."

Sydney reached over and put her hand over her sister's. "I need some company. I've been having trouble sleeping, and to tell you the truth, sometimes I feel so lonely," Sydney said as her eyes began to fill with tears.

When Sherese saw her sister's eyes cloud, her own filled instantly. "Don't cry. I just want to make sure you know what you're getting yourself into. The last thing I want to do is to get on your nerves or get in the way."

Sydney stood up and Sherese could tell that she was trying to shake the emotional toll the conversation was having on her. "I don't mean to pressure you. I know you're ready to get on with your life. I just want you to know that if you're considering it, you wouldn't have to pay rent. You'd have privacy, and you'd be a little bit closer to your job than you are right now."

Initially, Sherese had formed her lips to tell her sister that it wouldn't be possible, but the more she searched Sydney's face, listening intently as she explained, she realized that Sydney was serious. For the first time, Sydney seemed to be reaching out to Sherese, and Sherese was momentarily stunned.

She went to the refrigerator to pull out the lettuce to make a salad. Instead of responding to her sister's request, she asked her, "What kind of dressing do you want for your salad?"

Sydney went to the counter to assist her sister with the salad preparation. As Sherese handed Sydney a tomato to slice, she studied her older sister's face, whose smooth skin was unusually dark under her eyes. "Sydney, I gotta be honest with you. When Mama mentioned me moving in with you, all I could think about was a train wreck. I mean, we're sisters, but we're total opposites," Sherese admitted.

"I understand, Sherese. You don't have to explain. It was a long shot asking, anyway," Sherese said.

"Wait a minute, Syd, let me finish. We're different, but I think it can work if we can respect each other's differences. I know you don't agree with some of my choices, but I,'" Sherese took a deep breath. "I think it could work since we'll both have our separate space."

Sydney sliced the tomato with precision, slid the pieces into the salad bowl, and wiped her hands on a dish towel, clearly trying to repress her excitement. "You can absolutely have your own space. The guest room and bathroom is yours, and the entire basement is yours. Just knowing that you're there will help me."

Sherese smiled at her sister as she began thinking of all the perks that would come from staying with her sister. "I guess it would give me a chance to save up for a house instead of renting."

Sydney shook her head in agreement and hugged her sister.

"Are you *sure* you can put up with me for a while, Syd?" Sherese asked.

"I think you need to reverse that question." Sherese couldn't help noticing that her sister seemed to be relieved, but Sydney's eyes seemed to be watery again. "You okay, Syd?"

"I'm good now," Sydney replied. "Maybe we could start moving stuff tomorrow after work if your schedule is free."

"I'll keep a lot of my stuff in storage, so it won't be that difficult," Sherese responded.

"Actually, I've been working on selling Vance's vintage car in the garage, and when that gets sold, you can just move all of your things there. Also, there's quite a bit of storage room in the basement that's free. You're welcome to use as much of that space as you can," Sydney offered.

As Sydney placed the finished salad on the table and Sherese filled the glasses with ice, her parents walked in together. Her father commented, "You girls being here together like this reminds me of how things used to be around here."

"You know your father would like nothing better than if y'all just moved back in here for the rest of our lives," Darlene said, smiling.

"Sometimes I wish I could just go back to the way things were when we were little," Sydney said in a soft whisper.

While her mother put the food on the table, she told her daughter, "Everything must change; that's what they say, at least."

Everyone got quiet until her father said, "Darlene, honey, why don't you turn that television down. We're gonna pray and bless the food."

After his wife turned the television down, Samuel reached for the bottle of anointing oil on the top shelf of the pantry and began to anoint each member of his family's head as he began to pray, "Hallelujah, thank You, Jesus. We love You tonight, heavenly Father, and we bless Your name. You've blessed us so, Jesus. We're forever grateful. Tonight we're asking a special blessing upon my daughters. Lord, look on our precious Sydney. Comfort her and put Your loving arms around her. Give her peace and understanding. Help us to be a help to her, Lord. We also ask You to bless our wonderful daughter Sherese. Guide her, fill her with Your Holy Ghost, and cover her with Your blood. Give her a mind to serve You with her whole heart, soul, and mind. Finally, Lord, bless my wife. Help me to be the husband You would have me to be for her. Give us wisdom and direction. Strengthen us for Your service. Now, Lord, we ask You to sanctify this food, purify it for the nourishment of our bodies. We'll forever bless Your Holy name. Thank God, Amen."

Sherese ate heartily, feeling that for once, she could help her sister and start her new career and life on the right track.

CHAPTER 7

Sydney

O God, do not keep silent; be not quiet, O God, be not still.

Psalm 83:1 NIV

Memories tumbled from all directions like the fall leaves swirling aimlessly in the autumn wind. As Sydney drove home, she remembered last fall. In some ways it seemed like it was only yesterday, but then again, it seemed like eons ago.

They had gone away for the week, like they did every year in the fall. Neither one of them liked to ski, but they loved Vail, Colorado. The snow-capped mountains made them feel like they were insulated from the cares of life, and the snow and cold became their reason to stay inside.

After twenty minutes, Vance finally got the fireplace going. Sydney had worn her pink angora sweater and was sitting comfortably on the sofa with a quilt thrown over her legs.

"It's about time. I didn't think you'd ever get that thing started," Sydney had joked.

Vance put the poker down. "Oh, ye of little faith," Vance had said as he snuggled up next to his wife. "I used to have to start our wood-burning stove and fireplace during the winter. You can take a man outta Alabama, but you can't take Alabama outta the man."

Sydney massaged his hand in hers. "That's what they say but I was getting worried watching you struggle with that fire."

Vance began to hum the old standard, "The Autumn Leaves" as he softly kissed her neck. Sydney joined him, humming in harmony to the song that they both loved. She stopped humming for a moment, looking into his eyes, lost in the depth of them. "We're both becoming quite flaky as we mature."

Vance lightly touched her lips with his. "Girl, I plan on a lifetime of being flaky with you. There's no place I'd rather be."

Sydney smiled, relishing the tranquil and intimate moment with her husband. They both closed their eyes, lips meeting. She inhaled the woodsy scent of his cologne and felt the warm breath of his urgency to have her near, only matched by her longing to keep him close. She saw the future stretched out before them into endless tomorrows until their hair was gray and their skin wrinkled.

They held each other so closely that they were one until the fire crackled, startling them both, and they laughed.

Burnt orange, yellowish-red, and nutmeg-brown colored leaves were strewn on the well-manicured lawn and its long winding driveway, creating a colorful picturesque mosaic. As Sydney pulled up in her white Mercedes, a gift from Vance several years ago, she noticed Sherese in front of the garage painting a picture of the leaves on her canvas which was propped up on an easel. She stopped just short of the garage and greeted her younger sister.

"Hey, Sher."

"Hey, what's up?" Sherese answered before placing the paintbrush between her teeth to wipe a smudge from the canvas.

After examining the only partially completed landscape, Sydney complimented, "It's just not fair that you got all the talent. That looks great."

"Are you kidding? I'd give my right arm to have just half of your brains. I was thinking, if this turns out, it'd be great in your sitting room because it looks like the colors would match perfectly."

"That's really thoughtful, Sher. I think that would really add elegance to the room." After watching her sister paint for few minutes, Sydney yawned, "Well, I'm going to try to unwind." She frowned, looking at Sherese's paints and brushes strewn carelessly on the yard and driveway. "Just make sure you clean all of that up before you come inside."

Sydney sincerely admired her sister's artistic gifts, but she wished Sherese would be more ambitious. Growing up, Sydney had worked hard for everything she got, whether it was good grades or in extracurricular activities. Sherese, on the other hand, didn't ever seem to try particulary hard at anything, yet she had an awesome gift in drawing and painting.

Sherese bit her bottom lip, clearly aggravated. As talented as Sherese was, her habit of not totally cleaning up after herself was beginning to take its toll. Sydney disregarded the offended look on her sister's face and went inside. Once she made her way into the house, she nearly tripped over two pairs of Sherese's shoes. When Sydney walked through the kitchen, she noticed empty glasses and a plate with traces of food left on the counter by the sink. She sighed in frustration as she went upstairs to change her clothes, unable to ignore Sherese's denim jacket, hanging on the knob to the staircase.

Upstairs after changing her clothes, Sydney went to the window and glanced down at her sister who was still working on her paint-ing. In spite of the light breeze that seemed to blow, the leaves looked as if they were posing, waiting for Sherese to paint them. Things just seemed to happen naturally for Sherese. She didn't have to try so hard to be good at anything. Sherese's carefree nature and easygoing personality drew people to her like a magnet, and her talent put many in awe of her.

In high school, Sherese had barely studied but got average grades all the way through. After graduation, Sherese managed to get offered a partial scholarship to art school which she politely declined, to her parents' and Sydney's chagrin. In high school she also earned the title as Most Artistic and Friendliest Student. As a teenager, Sydney had to pray hard not to let envy creep into their relationship. Her mother would tell Sydney, "Your sister just breezes through life with no thought for tomorrow, but you take the whole world on your shoulders. Don't take yourself so doggone serious, girl."

What her mother didn't know was that Sydney wanted so badly to know what the Lord had given her. Sherese had a God-given gift, something Sydney took as a clear purpose for her in life. Sydney, too, longed for some visible, clear sign that would let her know what her purpose was. When she married Vance, Sydney just knew that she had discovered her purpose. She was not just going to be a good accountant, but she would be a wife to Vance and one day a mother to his children. Now she was left behind, wondering what God wanted her to do with the rest of her life.

Once again loneliness blanketed her with darkness. The falling temperatures signaled yet another change of seasons, which reminded her of another period of time without Vance. She had made it through the spring and summer without him, but in another month or two, Rochester's premature first snow would come, reminding Sydney of when Vance asked her to marry him.

On one of Upstate New York's customary blustery, cold, snowy days in December, Vance showed up unannounced to pick her up from her part-time job as the assistant manager of a photography studio to take her to their favorite spot on campus, The Book Bungalow. She often studied in the bookstore between her graduate classes, and Vance had grown to love the ambiance as much as she did.

As she got into the warm car, she brushed her lips across his clean-shaven cheek. "Why, Vance Ellington! I have to admit that I'm surprised that a Southern boy like yourself wants to be out on a snowy day like this, but you know I'm always game for the book-store," she commented. Sydney often teased him about his Southern upbringing and ways since he and his family had relocated to New York from Alabama during his freshman year in high school. Conversely, he often teased her about being raised in the North.

"Baby, you know when Southern boys get cold, we know all the best ways to get warm quick!" They both chuckled and he added, "Hey, how about we head up to grab a couple of caramel cappuccinos from the café. Besides, I heard Cornell West's new book is out, and I want to grab a copy," Vance added.

Sydney smiled, relishing the moment. She took nothing the Lord had blessed her with for granted. She thanked God every day that she had a man with whom she could drink coffee and also discuss relevant issues and events. In the past, guys she had dated had inferred that she was too stiff and serious. With Vance, it was different. He accepted and loved her as she was.

When they held hands as they walked into the cozy bookstore, crammed with books shelved in almost every open space, Sydney let out a satisfied, "Mmmmmm," as she smelled the delightful aroma from flavored coffees and pastries. She found one of her favorite over-sized reading chairs in one of the corners of the quaint bookstore, humming to John Coltrane's smooth jazz playing over the intercom system in the store.

Sydney positioned herself in front of one of the large picture windows so that she could watch the falling snow while Vance went to get their cappuccinos, and she thanked God for the happiness and sheer joy she had felt since the beginning of their relationship.

Although she had been in only a few relationships, they hadn't been serious. She knew that her relationship with Vance was something special. The other men she had dated had seemed so immature and intent on sex. In fact, she had shied away from most of the black men in the graduate program because she found out that they labeled her frigid, giving her the nickname, Ice Queen. She didn't care what they said about her as long as her reputation didn't include being labeled as loose or immoral.

When Vance returned with their cappuccinos, he leaned over her shoulder, placed the warm cup in her hand, and softly brushed his rugged cheek across hers, lightly kissing her neck while putting his hands on both sides of her hips on the chair.

"Syd, there ought to be a law against a woman looking this fine in jeans. I don't think I can wait much longer for you, girl. You sure you can't stay with me tonight?" he suggestively asked.

Sydney's smile faded and she pulled away, slightly joking at first. "Now I understand why Mama and Daddy never would let us wear jeans." Then, her tone turned serious. "Come on now, Vance. We've been over this. You know how much I love you, but I just—"

Vance threw his hand up in a halt motion. With a devilish grin, he interrupted, "Now, don't go getting yourself all worked up, Syd. You can't blame a guy for trying. I just love you so much and you know how much you turn me on, baby. I respect your position about not wanting to be intimate with me since we're not married, so I think—" He stopped and started again carefully. "I think that you should put some serious thought into marrying me."

Sydney chuckled, "Yeah, okay, now I know you are out of your mind, really, Vance. I think you'll be old and gray before you get married. You're not the type."

"What? How can you say that, girl? I'm only twenty-five! What's up with that?"

Sydney searched Vance's face for a hint of insincerity. "I can't help that you just don't strike me as the kind of guy who will get married in the near future."

Noticing the serious and slightly hurt look on Vance's face as he pulled up a chair close to her, she eyed him carefully as he reached into his leather briefcase and handed her a package, beautifully wrapped in gold foil paper. Sydney's stomach tingled with nervousness and anticipation about Vance's sudden change in mood and the mysterious package.

"What's this? Let's see. It's not my birthday, and Christmas is a week and a half away. Have you done something you feel guilty about?" Sydney playfully asked as she accepted the package, trying to lighten up the seriousness of the moment.

Small beads of perspiration appeared on Vance's face as he continued, "You're crazy, baby, but that's why I love you." He gazed into Sydney's eyes intently. "As for me not being the marrying type, well, honestly, I thought it would be a long time from now, but you are just my type, and I don't intend on letting you get away," he explained while kneeling down in front of her as she unwrapped the small package.

Still a little unsure of his sincerity, Sydney tore open the package to reveal a small, purple velvet box. She gasped and put a hand over her mouth as she stared in disbelief and amazement at the dazzling and crystal-clear, two-carat princess-cut diamond.

"Syd, I want to spend the rest of my life showing you how much I love you. Will you marry me, baby?" Vance asked, holding her hand.

"Oh, Vance," she cried, "yes, baby!"

Overcome with emotion, the two shared a heartfelt embrace, and as Sydney wept tears of joy, she noticed a tear or two rolling down Vance's face as well, also basking in the glow of the moment. When they finally let go of each other, they were startled to find a small group of patrons and the cashier applauding their new engagement.

In the midst of the congratulations and excitement, Sydney was amazed at the inner peace that flooded her whole being. She always knew this was a sign the Lord gave her to let her know that she was going in the right direction. Everything would be all right.

Their plan to focus on their careers and ministries had worked nearly perfectly. Vance's advancements at Xerox had come almost annually, but with that came more responsibility, which meant more time at work, something Sydney hadn't planned for even with her penchant for meticulous scheduling and deadlines. The years had flown by, and their plan to have children after five years had been thrown off by Sydney's stubborn refusal to accept her husband's work and church schedule. It pained her to know that she was the reason why they hadn't had a child. Now there would be no symbol of their love together.

Ironically, just last week The Book Bungalow, was torn down due to the city's effort to renovate the downtown area. Now, her life was torn apart as well, and she didn't know how she could rebuild it. Sydney had called Maya twice last week and asked for her to come over, but Maya had explained, "I want to see you, but Mom says I should wait so I don't upset you so much."

Sydney had quickly tried to reassure her. "It's okay. We're gonna be upset for a while, sweetheart, but it's okay. I'm okay."

"Can we wait just a little while, Syd? I mean, what about next Thursday or Friday?"

Sydney had been hurt but she understood how emotional Maya felt. Her emotions, too, were raw. Still, she wanted a part of Vance with her, but signs of Vance's presence seemed to be disappearing before her. Her desperation to grasp at anything that kept his presence near scared her. It had been months since his death, and she still refused to touch his belongings, even when it came to small things like the pair of shoes that he had slipped off and left on the doormat in the garage. Moving them meant she had to accept that he would not return.

This time, she thought, she would pray through this attack of the enemy as he assaulted her mind. She recited Psalm 23 and knelt down by her bedside and whispered, "Lord, You know what I'm going through. Please help me and let me know You're here." She choked a bit. "Help me to understand why You've allowed this to happen in my life. Please help me to understand why." Then, she recalled a message she had heard earlier on Christian radio by T.D. Jakes. He had reminded her of the importance of thanking God in prayer, so she decided to shift her thoughts toward the things she was thankful for.

"Lord, I thank You. I thank You for…" Her mind grew hazy. *What did she have to be truly thankful for?* She tried to think of things to be thankful for, but she always seemed to have a counterpoint to everything she mentioned. She continued, "Thank You for my life and my health," but in her heart she thought, *Why couldn't it have been me who died? What is my life without Vance?* She mumbled, "Thank You for my family," but she knew that her family didn't have a clue as to what she was going through.

In frustration, she stopped praying for the afternoon, deciding that the Lord knew her heart anyway. She knew that the Lord understood she wasn't thankful for much right now. All she could muster up was, "Lord, create a clean heart and a right spirit within me." As she stood up, the Lord brought the name "Maya" to her lips. The creases in her forehead relaxed a little as she realized that the Lord could search her heart and know that, yes, it was Maya she was thankful for.

She held the phone for a moment, hesitating before dialing since she had called Maya last week. However, she knew it was Friday and maybe their meeting would help Maya too. Sydney tapped the phone against her leg lightly and bit her bottom lip. She wondered if she was really ready to spend time with Maya today, admitting to herself that she did have a slight sense of dread about seeing her stepdaughter. Sydney didn't want to be the basket case she had been by herself with anyone, and especially not with Maya. When Sydney thought about how much Maya looked and acted like Vance, she fought against her fears to see her and dialed her number.

When Sydney called, Tiffany answered. After they exchanged pleasantries, Tiffany said, "Oh, let me give you Maya's cell phone number."

"Cell phone number?" Sydney remembered that Tiffany didn't want Maya to have one, but Vance had wanted her to have one.

Tiffany chuckled. "Girl, call me a sucker. Her dad wanted her to have one so badly, so with all that's happened, the least I could do was honor his wish."

"That's really nice of you, and I'm sure Maya is happy now."

"Happy is not the word, Syd. This cell phone stuff is out of control. Can you believe these kids have Blackberry's in high school? Sydney's friend, Madison, has had a cell phone for years."

"You've got to be kidding!"

"I could go on and on about kids these days, but I know you didn't call for that. Maya's at school. She had a preseason basketball practice, but you should be able to catch her there."

After Sydney asked if it would be okay to pick Maya up from school, she asked Tiffany, "Do me a favor, Tiffany?"

"Sure, what do you need?" Tiffany asked sincerely.

"Please send me Maya's monthly bill."

"No, Sydney, I couldn't possibly do that. Besides, that girl is old enough to pay for her own bill. She makes a good amount babysitting, you know."

"Yeah, I know, but Vance would've done it. I just want to do some things for her that I know he would have done. He was so crazy about her getting the latest laptop, computer software, and Ipod."

"That's a sweet gesture, Sydney, but it's really okay. It's just a blessing that Vance had prepared for Maya's college tuition. I must have cried for an hour when I got the paperwork." Tiffany's voice seemed to falter a little. "I've never told you this, but thank you for always being so kind to Maya and loving her. I mean…this might sound weird, but I always knew if something ever happened to me that you would be a wonderful mother to my daughter."

Sydney's eyes welled up with tears. "Thank you for trusting me with her over the years. As for the cell phone bill, please send it to me. It will make me feel good too—I need to feel like I'm still doing something useful."

Sydney remembered how her heart sank when Vance first told her that he had a child. They had gone to eat French cuisine at Phillips and over the crème brûlée he had told her that he had a six-year-old daughter.

Sydney had gone out with Vance despite his Methodist upbringing. Dating a man outside the Pentecostal denomination was taboo enough for her and her parents, but she had never even considered dating, let alone marrying, a man with a child.

Despite her initial shock, Sydney appreciated Vance's honesty about his previous relationship with Tiffany, explaining that he and Tiffany weren't saved at the time and had been on-again, off-again high school sweethearts. Their relationship had become even more troubled and sporadic when Vance left for college at Alabama A&M University to study business and Tiffany stayed in Rochester to go to school to study speech pathology.

Vance had explained, "Syd, I can't tell you how much I regret my immaturity, and more than anything, I regret not being saved. I knew that the Lord was calling me, but I was so into having a good time. I just didn't think about consequences."

During a summer vacation when Vance came home to Rochester, Tiffany informed him that she was pregnant. Since they both decided that they weren't ready for marriage, they agreed that the best thing for the baby would be for Vance to go back to finish his studies in Alabama so he could get his degree to support them.

Vance had confided to Sydney that while he was away at school studying business, he was miserable. He worked two part-time jobs so he could send Tiffany money for Maya while going to school full-time, and he came home every opportunity he could. Tiffany, on the other hand, was able to continue her education and care for Maya with help from her parents and Ruby.

After Vance graduated, he headed back to Rochester with hopes of rekindling his strained relationship with Tiffany, and more importantly, to be near his daughter. In spite of the perks of his new position at Xerox including his salary and close proximity to Maya and Tiffany, it was soon evident that the relationship between Vance and Tiffany wouldn't work. The distance between the two was far more than the miles were between Huntsville, Alabama, and Rochester. Still, Vance did all he could do for Maya, seeing her faithfully every chance he could on weekdays and at least every other weekend. Sydney knew that Vance had done all he could do to ensure that Tiffany had what she needed to care for Maya, but he often felt guilty about Tiffany bearing most of the weight in raising Maya.

As much as Sydney adored Maya, in the beginning of Vance and Sydney's marriage, there were times when Sydney struggled with feelings of jealousy, caused by Vance's relationship with his then six-year-old daughter. He doted on Maya and was unable to disguise his giddiness on the days he got to spend with his daughter.

During a lunch with her sister, Sherese, and best friend, Chanel, Sydney had revealed her feelings about Maya.

"She's a cute girl and all, but I just don't think there's room for two women in Vance's life."

Chanel had nearly dropped her fork on the plate. "You are such a trip, Syd. You meet a fine brother who's got an MBA to match yours, worked himself up the ranks from a clerk to a VP, who wants to give you the doggone world on a silver platter, and all you can think about is that he has a daughter he loves, provides for, and spends time with, and that puts a cramp in your style. Now who's the one with the problem?"

Sherese had grinned with satisfaction, always ready to take Chanel's side. Sydney was well aware of the fact that Sherese gloated when Chanel said things that Sherese wanted to say but wouldn't for fear of repercussions. "She does have a point. Shoot, any woman in Rochester would jump at the opportunity to even date someone like Vance. He worked his way up the honest way. No drug dealing, no two-timing, and nothin' seems to be on the down low about him. The man has no debt that you've ever mentioned, pays his child support, and—."

"Okay, okay, I get the point, but it's not as easy as you all are making it sound," Sydney interrupted.

"You're just gonna have to have to realize that everyone can't be perfect like you, Syd. Besides, I believe the man's heart is big enough to love you and his daughter. I'm not tryin' to be mean but, girlfriend, you really gotta stop being spoiled. Stuff happens in life, despite your Pollyanna perspective," Chanel added before slurping up the last of her frappacino. Sherese had chuckled and Sydney sulked, aggravated by Sherese and Chanel's comments. She hadn't wanted to share Vance with anyone, even if it was his daughter.

Sydney had realized that Chanel was right. Vance's heart really was big enough to love both of them, and to Sydney's astonishment, she discovered that her heart, too, had been big enough to love her stepdaughter as a daughter. Even Maya's mother warmed toward Sydney at the beginning of their marriage because of Maya's affection for Sydney. Tiffany had joked to Sydney at one of their initial meetings, "Girl, if I didn't have a wonderful relationship with my daughter, I might be jealous of you."

Sydney felt Tiffany's smile and empathy over the phone. Before she called Maya, she thought about what a kind person Tiffany seemed to be. Although they never had ill feelings toward each other as far as Sydney knew, they had never really talked too often. She couldn't help wondering why it had taken such a tragedy for them to do so.

———

As Sydney turned into Stone Bridge High School, her sweaty palm slid around the steering wheel. She had no explanation for her nervousness, but her heart raced and she pulled in front where Maya stood talking to a friend. When Maya noticed Sydney's car, she waved goodbye to the girl she was talking to and opened the car door.

Maya tossed her practice bag and backpack into the backseat. "Hi, Syd!" she said and gave her a brief hug.

"Hey, Maya, how are you?"

"Good. What about you?"

Sydney felt her anxiety ease as she asked Maya about basketball practice. "Coach makes us do so many laps before practice, shoot, I can barely make a basket afterwards. I keep tellin' him I've been playin' varsity basketball since I was a freshman and I don't need to keep doing the fundamental stuff."

"I don't know a lot about basketball, but I do know that sharpening your basic skills in anything can only help you down the line."

"Now, you sound like Dad."

"No, actually you sound like your dad." Sydney remembered Vance's stubborn refusal to read directions whenever he put anything together. One day he had decided that he would mount shelves in their garage, but he didn't bother to read the directions. When Sydney noticed the instability of them, she had offered, "Vance, honey, please read the directions. I can read them to you because it looks like something is missing; they're too wobbly."

He had told her firmly, "I don't need to read the directions. Do you know how many times I've mounted shelves?"

Sydney crossed her arms while she shook her head no.

Vance breathed hard as he struggled with the shelves. "Too many times to count."

Sydney knew that when Vance had made his mind up about something, that was it. She couldn't convince him to do much of anything when he felt the task was too elementary. *Maya got that trait honest from her dad,* Sydney thought.

While the two talked on the way to the restaurant, Sydney glanced occasionally at the profile that resembled her late husband's in an uncanny way. Maya's dark eyes were as pentrating and deeply set as her father's. Her pointed nose and glistening jet-black hair overwhelmed Sydney with the remembrance of Vance, so much so, that as Maya continued talking, she discreetly wiped the tear that had fallen down her face.

———

After dinner with Maya, Sydney thought about how well their brief outing had gone. Sydney could see a little of the spark returning to Maya that she had lost since Vance's passing. She, however, still felt like she had lost herself.

She and Vance had worked so diligently to have the best of things. He had given in to her every whim in decorating the house with an English style. Sydney especially loved the large cherry wood columns that seemed so warm and inviting when entering the front door. Now, nothing seemed inviting or warm. The luxurious home, expensive cars, and good job didn't mean anything without Vance to share in them.

Still, family and friends were getting back into their normal routines, but her mind clouded more and more. Others' lives seemed to adjust to Vance's absence. For her, the more time went by, the more intensely she felt his absence. For instance, anytime she passed a mother with a baby or saw Zachary, she was reminded of the child she would never share with Vance. And when she went to bed at night, the utter silence that permeated her whole being left her empty and scared. The "big things" were difficult, but it was the "small things" that were unbearable. When her back itched after getting undressed, Vance wasn't there to scratch it. Pulling the heavy garbage can to the curb was distressing because it was one of the reminders of the emptiness she felt without him. Every time she made coffee for one instead of two, she felt the reality of his death hit her like a cement block. She settled herself for another long night.

The blaring sound of a car horn interrupted her sleep. She got up, unable to remember falling asleep the previous night. She glanced at the clock, shocked to discover that it was almost eleven o'clock. After throwing the covers off, she ran to scan through her closet to find an appropriate suit for work until it hit her: It was Saturday. She sighed heavily and flicked off the light in the closet.

Remembering the honk of the horn, she went to look out the window to find Chanel's car parked in the driveway. Sherese, who apparently had decided to continue her painting outside, appeared to be deep in conversation with Chanel. *Had Sydney forgotten that she and Chanel were supposed to do something together?*

Before Sydney went downstairs to greet her friend, she checked her appearance in the mirror. She attempted to pat powder on her worn face to cover the dark circles under her eyes, but to no avail. *How could I still have circles under my eyes after sleeping for ten hours?*

After quickly brushing her teeth and washing her face, she tucked her white t-shirt in her jeans and pulled her long, coarse hair into a ponytail, hoping Chanel wouldn't comment on her haggard appearance. However, when she opened her door to Chanel, her friend immediately gasped, bringing in the scent of perfume that she doused herself with her. "Girl, look at you! You okay?"

With exasperation, Sydney replied, "If there's one sin you don't even think of engaging in, it's flattery. Look, I'm fine. What brings you over this way? Did I forget that we were supposed to do something?"

"No, I just wanted to drop by to see how you were doing."

Sherese walked in behind her, smiling broadly. Sydney could tell that Sherese was happy to have Chanel over, but Sydney didn't think kindly on drop-ins, even if it was her best friend.

"Chanel, do you see how that girl, Rhonda, did my braids the other day? She hooked a sister up!" Sherese twirled her long microbraids though her fingers playfully.

"You know how they do it at The Diva Salon. I told you them girls ain't no joke," Chanel remarked. Then, she pointed toward Sydney, pretending to be inconspicuous. "Somebody we know and love could use a little TLC at Diva too."

Sydney did not find her friend humorous, commenting quietly, "I don't feel like listening to a bunch of gossip. Besides, I don't think I look *that* bad."

The smile faded from Chanel's face and she walked closer to Sydney, resting her hand on her arm. "Now you know I was just teasin' you, girl. No need to get so serious. With the grade of hair you got, you don't need to go to the salon. I just thought it might make you feel better to get your hair out of that ponytail and pamper your-self a bit."

"Yeah, I know," Sydney sullenly responded, embarrassed by her inability to take a little light-hearted fun.

"What in the world are we all standing in the foyer for? Let's go to the living room," Sherese commented, trying to sound cheerful.

"Anybody want a drink?" Sydney asked, trying to recover from her irritable mood.

"No, Syd. Just have a seat. Sherese and I want to talk to you."

"Why am I starting to feel like I've been set up or something?" Sydney offered.

Sherese politely guided Sydney to the sofa. "Come on, Syd. We just want to talk," she said as she pulled an envelope out from the jacket in her pocket. "I called Chanel because when I got the mail yesterday, a letter came for you." Sherese stopped talking for a second and started again as Sydney looked at her questioningly. "It looks like…It looks like it's from—" she paused.

"From who?" Sydney demanded impatiently.

Chanel interjected, "From Brian O'Leary, Syd."

Sherese held the letter out for her sister who yanked it from her with force. "How could you screen my mail, Sher?"

"Hey, I resent that. I wasn't. I was just trying to see if there was anything for me," Sherese explained.

"That's really not fair, Sydney," Chanel said stately.

"What do you have to do with it anyway, Chanel? I mean, what business is it of yours?" Sydney said in a heightened voice.

"First of all, your sister asked me to be here. And, second, I care about you." Chanel looked as if she were trying not to let Sydney's response hurt her feelings.

"This is between me and my sister, Chanel." Sydney's voice was uncharacteristically cold.

With that said, Chanel sauntered out making eye contact with Sherese to make sure that she was okay. Sherese gave her a look that signaled she could go, but Chanel stayed.

"Why are you treating me like I'm a child, Sherese? *You* are the one staying here with *me!* Going through my mail is one thing, but screening it is unacceptable. Then, you have the nerve to get backup?"

"Sydney, you're totally taking this out of proportion. I just wanted to prepare you for hearing from the guy. See, Chanel, this is exactly why I find it difficult to talk to Sydney. She can act so crazy about stuff."

"Really, Sydney, this is a bit irrational. She didn't open your mail."

"Chanel, you can go ahead and side with Sherese, but she's out of line even discussing with you or anyone else who I've gotten mail from!"

Sherese rolled her eyes, keeping her attention focused on Chanel. "I'm so tired of tiptoeing around her."

Before Sydney could respond, Chanel raised her voice. "Okay, both of you hold up! Sydney, please know that the only reason Sherese told me is because she was concerned. Just calm down, please."

"Calm down? Do you think that this is the first correspondence I've received from him? Huh?" Sydney yelled, standing up.

"Sydney, I'm sorry! You do need to calm down. You're scaring me" Sherese said.

"This letter will go with all the other ones he's sent—in the trash," she said as she ripped the letter in two, getting ready to take it upstairs to the trash. "Stay out of my mail and my life, Sherese!" She stomped up the stairs even though she knew how childish it must have seemed to her sister and friend.

She couldn't believe the nerve of Sherese or Chanel. *What did they think she was going to do? What did they think they could do to help her?* When Sydney got to her room, her eyes fixed once again in the gold-trimmed wastebasket beside her bed. She crumbled the latest unopened letter from the man who had ruined her life and tossed it in with the others.

CHAPTER 8

Sydney

Turn to me and have mercy on me;
grant your strength to your servant.

Psalm 86:16 NIV

It had been almost six months since Vance's death, and with the exception of an occasional blurb on the news about the trial proceedings of the drunk driver who had been charged with vehicular homicide, Sydney did not hear anything about the accident. She carried on almost mechanically with her newly established routine consisting of work, church, and an occasional outing with Maya, Chanel and Zachary, or her parents. Although it was obvious to those closest to Sydney that she wasn't coping well, any attempts to confront her with this fact fell on deaf ears.

Sydney felt that hiding her true feelings from her family not only kept her family from worrying, but she also prided herself on maintaining at least the outward appearance that she had the faith she had professed so many times. She didn't want them to feel let down by her grief, desperation, and lack of faith. The truth was, her faith was at an all-time low, despite her faithfulness in church services and activities.

A certain measure of comfort came with Sherese's move into the house, but the two still hadn't connected in any considerable way.

Sydney kept to herself, wallowing in grief, knowing that her sister wasn't happy in her home. Sherese was uncharisterically quiet in the house. Sydney noticed how carefully Sherese moved about the house, not knowing what could potentially set Sydney off. Yet Sydney could not make herself open up to her sister. Sherese would come in around one or two in the morning, causing Sydney to stay up worrying until she heard her turn the key in the front door.

One night, Sydney had stayed up like the parent of a high schooler, sitting in the dark living room, lying in wait. Sherese breezed in without taking her shoes off, one of Sydney's pet peeves, and gasped, "Oh, Syd, you scared the life out of me."

Sydney had scolded, "Where have you been? Do you know it's two o'clock in the morning? I was scared that you had either been abducted or were at the side of the road somewhere. The least you could've done is call!"

Sherese didn't say it, but Sydney could see, "I told you so," written all over her face. Sherese grimaced and said, "I'm an adult. I may be living here with you as you requested, but I don't have a curfew."

Insulted, Sydney stood up. "Simple consideration is the only thing I'm asking for. Considering what I've been through, I think you should've at least done me the respect of letting me know you wouldn't be home until the morning." By the look on Sherese's face, Sydney could tell that her sister felt guilty.

Sydney had confessed to Chanel over coffee at the Anchored in the Rock Café, "I don't know why she gets on my nerves so much lately."

"I don't know. I hardly find the fact that she likes to sleep late and forgets to rinse off a dish or two to be worthy of this level off disapproval. Chill out, girlfriend," Chanel had advised. "You gotta remember you wanted her to be there."

"I know. I just wish she were a little more motivated. She could really do something great with the talent she has," Sydney said.

"You know, Sydney, if you ask me, this isn't about Sherese. You take stuff out on her just because you can. She's gonna move out if you don't stop being so doggone picky and snooty with her. You act like it's your moral obligation to fix Sherese. Try concentrating on her good points."

Sydney knew Chanel was right. Sherese was helping her out, after all. Even so, Sherese's late nights and inclination toward messiness bothered Sydney, but what bothered Sydney the most was Sherese's ability to roll with life's punches more gracefully than she could. When Sherese divorced, she quickly went to her parents and to Sydney and Vance to ask for help. Although Sherese wasn't saved, she openly admitted that she wasn't able to make the commitment as much as it worried her family. Sydney, on the other hand, professed God's goodness and had witnessed to her sister numerous times, questioning her, "How could you deny the Lord's presence in your life, Sher? He's been too good and too faithful for you not to give Him your all."

Now, Sydney's reflection on those words stung. She had spoken with so much convinction and authority, and now she feared being exposed. It had been her father who had been her spiritual crutch until she and Vance married. Afterward, her husband had become her spiritual crutch and her shining pillar of faith, and she hadn't even realized it until his death. Sherese's truthfulness about who she was and where she was spiritually proved to be a painful reminder of Sydney's own shortcomings.

On the day that Sydney received the last check from the insurance company since Vance's death, Sherese came home to find her older sister holding the letter and check that accompanied it, huddled in Vance's black leather La-Z-Boy chair crying.

"Syd?" Sherese stood waiting for a response as Sydney sat motion-less. "What's that in your hand?"

"Nothing, I'm fine," Sydney managed to say through her sniffles.

Sherese detected her sister's defensive tone and asked, "You're fine?" Throwing her hands up in the air in frustration, Sherese continued, "That's all you ever say, 'I'm fine,' but I come in here and you're crying." Her face softened as she kneeled down in front of Sydney. "What's up with that? Don't you feel like you can talk to me?"

"There's nothing anyone can do to help me. I just have to have some time to regroup, you know, figure out how I'm gonna make things work."

"Yeah, I understand, but I just thought it would be a little easier if you talked about your feelings more."

Sydney's body stiffened as she wiped her face, sat up, and brushed past her sister, leaving abruptly. Sydney retreated to her bedroom and slid down the wall to rest in a sitting position on the floor. Dropping her head in defeat, Sydney didn't know how her sister could help during her time of need, and she could tell that Sherese was growing tired of her.

Questions swirled around in her mind. *How can she help me? How can anybody in my family help me? No one's been through what I'm going through, so how can they help? What would they do if they knew that I really want to fall apart?*

Sydney couldn't help but notice the hurtful look her sister had, yet she didn't want Sherese to be disappointed by her weaknesses, which seemed to intensify as the months dragged on. Sydney knew that as much as Sherese didn't appreciate her sister's advice and opinions, she did respect her. Sydney needed that respect. Without the admiration from her family, especially Sherese, Sydney really wouldn't know who she was.

At the sound of the light tapping outside the door, Sydney quickly wiped her face.

"Can I come in, Syd?" Sherese asked softly.

When Sydney opened the door, she looked startled. "What's wrong, Sher?"

"Syd, how about you let me in?"

"You are in."

"I'm not talking about your room. I'm talking about what's going on with you."

She peeked around Sydney's shoulder at her room.

"Okay, well, for starters, you're always riding me about cleanliness and look at your room. I mean, why don't you clean some of these things in here or at least dust them? I can help."

Sydney raised up. "No! Don't you touch anything in here. Can you please tell me why you and Mama are so anxious to want to get rid of Vance's stuff? It doesn't have anything to do with you or anybody else for that matter!"

Sherese looked at her sister questioningly. "Syd, you're really making me wonder if you need some outside help. I mean, the other night you bit my head off for getting a bar of soap from your bathroom. I can't believe that you got mad because I suggested moving Vance's toiletries to the cabinet instead of out on the sink." Sherese scanned the room. "I can tell you haven't moved one thing of his in here. You've got to start to go on living your life."

"Don't even think about getting me to see a shrink. I'm not crazy, I'm just a woman who loved her husband. When the love of your life dies tragically, then you can give me some advice, how about that?" Sherese paused, and when her sister didn't respond, she continued, "Can you explain 'go on'? You stayed with Mama and Daddy for two whole years after your divorce. It's only been six months since Vance passed away which, in my opinion, merits a little more time to 'go on' than a divorce."

Sherese raised her hands up in a surrender motion. "All right, Syd. You win. I give up. I was only trying to help, but I'm outta here."

After her sister slowly shut the door, Sydney gazed over her bedroom and bathroom. All of Vance's toiletries looked as if they had been left exactly where they were when he left the house on the day of the accident. His messy can of shaving cream surrounded by several loose and used razors were left out, not to mention a cologne bottle that had not been opened for six months. The only real indication that Vance wasn't coming home was the thick layer of dust that covered his belongings. Sydney wondered if she really did think that this would bring him back. She had to admit to herself that the atmosphere was beginning to feel more like a mausoleum, and Sherese's presence felt more like one of an intruder. She had to have Sherese out, but she was just waiting for the right time to break it to her.

Anger, not sadness, was the overwhelming feeling Sydney grappled with on a daily basis. It seemed to find her no matter what situation she was in. One day after returning home from the grocery store, Sydney discovered that she was missing several bags of groceries so she called the store, only to find out that the bag boy had apparently put them into another customer's cart by accident. Despite the store manager's apology, Sydney lashed out furiously. "What do you mean you're sorry? Do you realize that I now have to travel at least twenty minutes to get back to the store because of the incompetence of your employee?"

The store manager tried to apologize. "We are truly sorry for the inconvenience. We just hired the new bag boy, and—"

"I'm sure you are!" She slammed down the phone violently.

Whether it was scolding the clerk at the dry cleaners about a missing button or laying on her car horn if a driver cut in front or back of her car a little too closely, Sydney seemed to always be prepared with an overzealous and angry reaction to the smallest of infractions.

Unfortunately, Sydney's outbursts weren't limited to just strangers. For years she had been directing The Sunshine Band, the children's choir at the church, and her father and parents praised her for her patience and rapport with the youth. However, several weeks ago an older boy in the choir broke a cardinal rule by chewing gum and then refusing to spit it out. Instead of Sydney speaking to the boy's parents, she chastised him harshly in front of the other children, telling him,

"I don't know who you think you are, but you need to get out of my choir loft this instant! Until you learn some home training, don't you even think about coming back!"

The boy promptly told his mother, who reported it to Pastor Hightower. When her father was told about the incident, the pastor decided to have a meeting with his eldest daughter. Sydney had persisted vehemently, "I'm so sick of kids being disobedient and defiant, Dad. We really are in the last days. You need to do something about the unruly parents too. They don't even make their kids mind. Why should I have to be the babysitter?"

"I understand that the child's behavior was wrong, but your response was a little more severe than I think it should have been." Her father's chastisement hurt her and made her angry. Her father's insistence on taking the church members' side was wearing her thin, but she listened respectfully.

"Just make sure that all you do and say is out of love when inter-acting with the children."

"Yes, Daddy." Sydney was humiliated because she had never been reprimanded in any way from her father concerning any of her involvement in church leadership.

"Sydney, I want to pray with you before you leave. You've had so much to handle in so little time, but do you believe God is able?" His daughter nodded. "Do you believe that He can handle every burden?"

Her eyes flooded with tears as she nodded in affirmation. Samuel got a dab of anointing oil from the bottle on his desktop and laid his hand across her forehead. Sydney closed her eyes as her father prayed.

As Sydney lingered in the empty sanctuary, leaving her father alone in his study, she studied the mural of Jesus that Sherese had painted on the wall years ago. His outstretched hands were massive and inviting and the beam of light around his head made her long for His presence. For some reason though, He seemed far off. Even as her father had prayed intensely, she had felt nothing. Somehow she knew He was there, but she couldn't feel Him. She left from the side door of the church wondering if she would ever feel His presence again.

Sydney's erratic behavior had even carried over to her job. She displayed unwarranted hostility toward several of her subordinates and lately she knew that people were talking behind her back. While she was outside of the break room, Sydney overheard a conversation about her. Sal, also an accountant, was talking to another employee.

"I understand that she lost her husband, but that doesn't excuse her for being a witch. It's like she's bent on making everyone suffer since she's suffering. It's getting real old, and somebody needs to tell her about herself."

His words hurt her deeply, but as much as Sydney hated hearing this, she knew that something had to change. She just didn't know how. The downward spiral her life seemed to be taking was unstoppable. The same sinking feeling she experienced when they closed the casket at Vance's homegoing service hit her with massive force.

Every day she was riddled with the same questions. *Is this it? Is my life supposed to just go on like he never existed? Why him? Why now?* She wanted to shout from the rooftops and let people know how wonderful he was, only she couldn't because then she would have to say "he was," not "he is." Referring to him in the past tense was still impossible for her. Sydney resented life going on with almost everyone acting as if he hadn't even existed, and she could no longer fight the nagging guilt she had about their argument before Vance's death.

Since his death, Sydney had come to realize the depth of his love for her through his business decisions concerning her and Maya. He had insurance policies that she didn't even know existed so that she and Maya would be taken care of if anything were ever to happen to him. Their attorney explained that with the money she had in investments, bank accounts, and death benefits, she could live in the house for the rest of her life if she wanted and would never have to work if she didn't want to. Furthermore, Maya's college tuition would be totally paid for. Sydney had always dreamed of retiring by the age of fifty, which was something she could actually do now, but it would be a nightmare without Vance to share it.

Recently, she had started doing her daily devotions and prayer in the morning, but they proved to be nothing more than a ritual because her heart was hurt, tired, and angry. She couldn't resist feeling like God had done this to her although her father had explained that the Lord didn't make it happen; He just allowed it to. It didn't matter though because whether God made it or allowed it to happen, it was all the same in the end. Vance was gone. She continued to pray for strength and understanding, but to Sydney, there could be no greater good to accomplish as a result of her husband's death. She flatly refused to accept that this was a reason for his passing.

Sydney stared intently at the unopened letter on her lap from Brian O'Leary, the man who had killed her husband. In spite of the fact that the return address read, "New York State Prison," Sydney had decided long ago that she would never give him the opportunity to make himself feel better by even acknowledging anything he had to say. Sydney hadn't even gone to the trial.

O'Leary had been sentenced to seven years in prison, but with good behavior, he would be eligible for parole in just four years because it was his first offense. After that, he had months of community service obligations to fulfill, but he would be free to continue on with his life. The man who had robbed her of the love of her life along with her sense of stability, purpose, and fulfillment, would still be able to continue to spend time with his family and friends.

She had told Chanel and Sherese, "There is nothing that that man, Brian O'Leary, could say to me that would make a difference. On the morning he decided to drink and drive, he changed my life forever, and I have no plans on consoling him." O'Leary had been the one to carry out the act, and she was resolved that the letter would join the other letters that remained in the trash basket beside her bed. Despite her intentions to never open the letters, she couldn't bring herself to take them to the trash can in the garage. It was almost as if she could direct her bitterness and anger toward the unopened letters, and it almost seemed to help her feel a bit better, at least for a while.

When she grew weary of thinking, she fell into a deep, dark sleep and dreamt of her husband.

Dancing on the deck of the ship, they moved fluidly as if in sync with each ebb and flow of the ocean. Her feet barely touched the floor as the ballroom music kept them in time. She laughed as Vance twirled her effortlessly. Back and away. Back and away. He whispered while he had her close, "My black Marilyn Monroe." The moonlight cast its shadow over them as her strapless white dress flowed in the night breeze.

Without warning, a disturbing voice bellowed from the opposite side of the ship. "Vance! Vance!"

The music stopped, and Vance abruptly let go of Sydney.

"No, don't let go," Sydney called with her arm outstretched.

Vance darted toward the voice that beckoned. Without warning, the side of the ship Vance walked toward began to sink. No time to reach him. Sydney screamed. People were drowning. She clung to the ship desperately trying to understand. No sign of Vance.

A tiny leak was in the corner on the side of the ship she was in. She had to find a plug for the hole. Nothing worked except for her finger, which fit perfectly. Unknowingly, she fell asleep in her dream, and when she awoke, she realized that she was soaked. The side of the ship she was in was now sinking. In horror, she realized that she, too, would drown.

Sydney tossed and turned furiously until she sprang up gasping for air, awakening from her disturbing dream. She had been plagued with all sorts of dreams where she couldn't save Vance's life and barely escaped with her own. Brian O'Leary may have been the one in the actual prison building, but in many ways, she felt like the real prisoner. She couldn't escape the pain, not even in her sleep.

Groggily, Sydney smoothed down her hair and dialed Chanel's number as fast as she could. After her dream, she needed the company of her friend. When she didn't answer at home, Sydney decided to try the café on her personal line.

"Chanel, it's me. You busy now?"

"I have a few customers but, girl, it's after seven. You know how things start to slow down. Besides, Lena's got it under control. Hiring that girl has been one great decision. Do you know that yesterday she took Zachary to Tommy for me? Tommy was all the way downtown at Precision Studio on Main. That girl offered to take Zach. She's a jack-of-all trades. I mean, nothin' I ask her to do is too much. I'm sorry for going on and on, Syd. What's up?"

"I was thinking that it's been so long since we've done something fun with Zachary. You wanna take him to Chuck E. Cheese or something tonight?"

"Girl, I would've liked that, but my baby's not feeling great today. He's coming down with a cold so Tommy's at home with him."

"Poor thing," Sydney said knowing that this would mean Chanel would need to be home this evening. Disappointed, she made small talk with Chanel, promising to call tomorrow after work.

Picking up the phone again, she decided to call Maya. Maybe spending time with her would lift her spirits, she thought.

Pleased that Maya's mother didn't mind her spending the night, Sydney picked her up and the two went to see a movie together. Afterwards, they went to dinner at Maya's favorite burger place and chatted at length about Maya's school happenings, clothes, and boys.

As Maya sipped her strawberry milkshake, Sydney told her about her high school days. Maya seemed unusually lighthearted at the moment, which proved to be infectious for Sydney.

"Ummmm. Syd, this may be a stupid question, but I was wondering about something."

"What's that?"

"You seem okay, but I just wanna know if you miss my dad as much as I do?" Maya asked innocently while staring down at her milkshake.

Sydney's brow furrowed, and she responded softly, "Baby, I miss him so much. I'm trying just like you." The two were silent momentarily until Sydney broke it by saying, "I'm just glad to have a part of him here."

Maya beamed and said, "See now, that would make two of us. I just can't seem to concentrate on my schoolwork like I used to, and it's hard to talk to my friends anymore cause they just don't understand that all that stuff they want to talk about is stupid and not important. It's like they were all sad for me, even my teachers, for a little while, but no one even asks anymore besides my mom and you. Grandma Ruby calls every now and then, but she can't talk long cause all she does is cry when she talks about Dad. One time I asked her to tell me about his childhood, and you know what she said to me?"

"What?" Sydney asked.

"She said it made her too sad to talk about her only son. That really tripped me out. I said, 'But Grandma, you mean you don't even want to talk about my dad?' She just kept right on doing what she was doing. Don't get me wrong, I know it's hard, but how am I supposed to get better when everybody acts like he didn't exist or else they act like I'm supposed to be over it?"

Sydney gazed directly into her eyes. "Maya, you can always talk about your father with me. People have a hard time with death. They think that they're doing what's best for you by not talking about it. Your grandma is just doing what she had to, trying to deal with her pain the best she can. But I'm here for you though. Anytime, day or night, you can call me. I haven't lost my father, but I think I understand some of what you're feeling."

Exposing a mere hint of uneasiness, Maya asked carefully, "What do you think about me coming to live with you?"

Sydney was stunned, but kept her cool. Maya's mother had called her several times since Vance's death, explaining to Sydney that she was worried about her daughter. Just last week Tiffany had called and said, "Sydney, I just don't know what to do to get through to Maya. She used to be so sweet, but she's just been so rebellious lately. I know she's trying to cope with her dad's passing, but she's gonna have to deal with it in a way that's doesn't disrespect me. She doesn't want to abide by my rules, and I just won't have it."

"What exactly is Maya doing?" Sydney asked with concern.

Tiffany explained that Maya refused to listen to Richard about anything, and how the other day she had told him to shut up. Tiffany continued to tell her that it just wasn't like Maya to show so much aggression toward Richard. Sydney couldn't believe that Maya had gone as far as telling her stepfather that he would never be able to take her father's place.

"All Richard wants is to be what he's been all along, which is her stepfather. She wants to stay out with her friends or stay holed up in her room when she's home. She acts like I'm torturing her when I tell her she still has chores she has to do. I could go on, but I won't." Tiffany sighed. "I'm sorry for calling about this. I know you have a lot on your plate, but I just don't what to do for her," she finished.

As Maya sat in front of her, Sydney knew that her stepdaughter was just trying to deal with the grief and anger. Maya explained, "Don't get me wrong. I love my mom and Richard, but they just don't understand what I'm going through now. Richard tries to tell me what to do, and he's not my dad. Mom says I'm being evil to him, but I'm the way I've always been with him. I think they just expect me to act like he's a replacement for my dad or something." She shook her head. "He's not though, and he *never* will be, so they might as well hang that up," Maya said with attitude.

Sydney gently touched Maya's sleeve across the table. "I understand, Maya, but let me tell you something. I'm not really sure about a lot of things, but I do know that your dad would never want you to break your mother's heart. The older you get, the more you'll understand your mom. She is just trying to do the best she can."

Maya looked upset, but hung her head, mumbling, "Yeah, I know."

"Maya, your mother may not understand all that you are going through, but she did care deeply about your father. She's grieving too, especially for you. Just give her room to make a few mistakes. You are always welcome to come with me, and you already know that. But do you remember a few years ago when you wanted to come to live with us? As soon as your dad talked to your mother, he said he couldn't allow you to come unless she agreed. Your mom wants and needs you. Just hold tight. You're almost out of high school anyway. Why don't we just agree to spend much more time together?"

Although Maya was visibly crushed at the realization that living with Sydney was not an option, she seemed to understand what Sydney was trying to get across to her. When Sydney saw the disappointment cross Maya's face, she felt the familiar lump rise in her throat as she fought back tears. She, too, would love to have Maya with her all of the time, because it would be the next best thing to having Vance there.

Maya agreed that they would spend more time together, but asked Sydney, "Why does everything have to be so hard?"

"It'll get better. Trust me, it really will. We just have to trust in the Lord. He's going to get us through this." Sydney hoped that Maya couldn't sense the doubt lying just behind the surface of her confident words.

CHAPTER 9

Chanel

Blessed is the man that endureth temptation:
for when he is tried, he shall receive the crown of life,
which the Lord hath promised to them that love him.

James 1:12

Chanel still hadn't finished all she had to do at the café even though it was almost ten o'clock. As much as she tried to keep her mind focused on the café, Zachary, and her troubled marriage, her thoughts seemed to drift to her new secret friend, Antonio. While she was dating, she probably wouldn't have given someone like Antonio the time of day. She would've thought he was much too "starchy" and uptight for her.

Before, she had been attracted to a more carefree type and loved men with a little bit of a rebellious streak, which perfectly described what she had been so attracted to in her husband. She had loved Tommy's ability to take risks and be different. He even had a motorcycle, which at the time intrigued Chanel, and the first time she saw him play and sing, she knew the heavens had opened up before her. Now, things had changed. His motorcycle had become impractical. It had also become a dangerous toy.

Having her own successful business and a son had matured Chanel, only Tommy seemed to be regressing. While he was teaching school, Chanel could always admire how hard he worked and what a dedicated teacher he seemed to be. Even though Chanel knew he was frustrated by his conflict with the principal and his lack of time to devote to his dream of becoming a full-time musician, Chanel had prided herself on marrying an educated and responsible man. He would come home from work, and as tired as she was, she would shower him with praise, and he basked in the attention she gave him.

She remembered when he came home from school and had been nominated for Teacher of the Year at his school. Chanel had told him, "Tommy, you just don't know what it means to me to have a life like this with you. I don't have one man in my family that I can think of who has done as well as you. I feel like we're breaking the curse that the men in my family have had. You're such a role model to so many of those kids. I'm so happy with you."

Tommy had loosened his tie, smiling seductively at his wife. "Girl, you know how to make a man feel good, don't you?" He had thrown his jacket on the nearest chair and pulled her to him with one strong arm around her waist. He nuzzled her ear and whispered, "You don't know what it means to *me* to share my life with someone as sweet, loving, smart, and sexy as you."

She remembered the tingle that went through her body as her husband made her feel like she was the only one in the whole world. But that was years ago, and now it was Antonio who consumed her thoughts, not her husband.

From their first in-depth conversation, Chanel could tell that Antonio was a no nonsense person who definitely appreciated setting realistic goals and achieving them. Chanel had declined his dinner date, but when he asked to make a playdate with the two kids, Chanel agreed. They had met at a fast-food restaurant with a play area and talked about the children for most of the time. When the conversation turned to work, he had told Chanel about his job as manager of a local radio station. He had worked his way up from very humble beginnings just like Chanel. He told her, "My moms didn't have the money for me to continue to get my bachelor's degree, and I didn't have the sense to know that I could actually get financial aid to finish, so I just read a lot of books and started doing some serious cold calling. I had a degree in general education, but since I had always wanted to work in radio or television, I read everything I could get my hands on about T.V. and radio professions. I'm tellin' you, I must've sent out fifty resumes before Channel 8 News called me for an interview as a part-time administrative assistant to the general manager. The pay was terrible, but I jumped at the opportunity. I worked doing a little bit of everything for everybody, and with a little politicing, I worked my way up, and voila, I am the GM."

Chanel understood what determination it took when you didn't have anyone to pave the way for you. She knew what it meant to be the first one in the family to attend any postsecondary school. She had told Antonio, "I know your mom must be very proud."

He had gazed off into the distance, then turned to look at her. "Actually, my mother hasn't taken too well to my so-called success. Because I won't give her money constantly, she thinks I'm quote, 'too big for my britches.' We don't have too much of a relationship right now."

Chanel couldn't believe their similarities and even revealed a bit of her troubled relationship with her mother in the past few days on one of their secret phone conversations. He had been pressing her to meet for dinner, and it had been getting more difficult to deny his requests.

As she mopped the floor, she heard a light tapping on the front glass door. Before reaching the door, she noticed Antonio Black smiling, with a pink rose between his teeth. She wondered why he would come in the café with a romantic gesture in such a public place. She hurredly unlocked the door, signaling for him to come in, "You are so crazy. What are you doing on this side of town?"

"I can't tell a lie, Chanel, mon cheri. I was hoping that you'd still be here," Antonio said while handing her the rose.

Chanel shook her head. "So the brother speaks French, huh?" She felt a stirring in her that she hadn't felt in a long time. Chanel allowed him to hold the rose for a few seconds before accepting it. "You gotta stop doing stuff like this, Antonio. I keep tellin' you, I'm married."

The deep lines that creased his dark chocolate face let her know he was disappointed, but it didn't break his stride. He slowly walked toward her. "I don't like to think about that, and I don't think you should either, at least not right now anyway."

Then, he bent over and whispered sweet words in her ear softly as his breath tickled her throughout her body. She tried to turn away slightly, but she wanted more. She thought about how Tommy didn't do special things for her anymore, so she was drawn even more toward this new man.

When she felt his soft lips urgently pressing against hers, she hadn't realized her eyes had even closed until she opened them and felt the room spin. As the tingles swept through every pore of her body, she forced herself to come to her senses. "The rose was sweet but the kiss was too much, really, Antonio. I can't do this. I'm not that kind of woman. I have a husband and a child. I love my family. I love the Lord," she said as she moved away.

Chanel busied herself by collecting magazines and newspapers strewn over the the tables and front desk.

Instead of Antonio retreating, he pursued her smoothly and slipped behind her, holding her generous hips lightly. "The Lord wants you to be happy, Chanel. You deserve the best that life has to offer."

Chanel fought to force herself to be irked by his blatant disregard of her words, but she knew that Antonio could read her body much better. She closed her eyes as he stroked her sides.

"You are a real jewel, Chanel. If you were mine—"

Chanel interrupted by quickly turning toward him and placing her finger up to his lips to hush him. She glanced toward the door to make sure that no one was there and reciprocated by putting her arms around his neck. "Thanks for being sweet."

He tightened his hold on her slightly and Chanel closed her eyes, delighting in the security and warmth of his strong embrace until the phone rang.

"Don't get it, Chanel," Antonio pleaded.

She wiggled impatiently from his arms. "It's my private line. It could be about Zachary or something."

She ran over to the phone and picked it up while surveying Antonio's physique. His light cashmere sweater hugged his body in all the right places. When Chanel heard her husband's voice, her mind blanked with panic. "Chanel, earth to Chanel," Tommy called.

"Oh, yeah, what's up?" she asked, clearly uncomfortable.

"The question *is* what's up with you? You busy or something?" he asked.

"No, I'm just thinking about something."

"Hey, I just wanted let you know that Mama picked up Zachary from the daycare. If you didn't have any plans for this evening—" Chanel rolled her eyes as she listened to Tommy and then interrupted, "I know, I know. You need to go to the studio, right?"

"Yeah, is that cool? I'll be home by midnight if you can pick up Zachary."

Chanel rolled her eyes. "I thought you had already picked him up hours ago! Can I count on you to do anything you say you're going to do anymore?"

"Before you go off, Chanel, I got tied up here."

"You get tied up every day, and the problem is, there's never anything to show for it."

"All right, Chanel. I can't deal with this now. Just pick up Zach. He's at my mom's. I gotta bounce. Peace out."

Chanel turned her phone off and whispered under her breath, *I gotta bounce? Peace out?* Even his vocabulary annoyed her. How she had gotten past his dress and vocabulary in the beginning was a mystery to her.

For an instant, Chanel forgot that Antonio was there until he asked, "Hey, you okay?"

She turned toward him with a noticeable change in her disposition. "Yes, I'm fine," Chanel answered as she began to collect money from the cash register.

Chanel felt Antonio's eyes canvassing her body, and she tried to decide if she was sorry she had decided to wear her snugly fitting embroidered jeans.

She glanced at him half scoldingly and half flirtatiously. "Brother, you need to chill out on that."

"Sorry, I just can't help myself around beautiful women."

The remark infuriated Chanel since it made her feel like she could be any woman. She wasn't special to Antonio. Antonio's presence now crowded her.

Noticing her reaction, he tried to smooth things over. "I just can't control myself around you. You are just what I need," he whispered.

What had sounded so sexy before was gone. His words reminded her of a hissing snake and she jerked away. Chanel adopted her business sounding voice as she tried to distance herself. "Well, I've got a lot to do, but thanks for stopping by. I just need to be alone right now so I can finish things up," she mumbled, slamming the register shut.

He waited for a few seconds, but took a deep breath, letting her know he was upset.

Still, she couldn't help being relieved when she heard, "See ya' later," as the door shut behind him. Then, it was her turn to take a deep breath as she closed her eyes and said, "Thank You, Jesus," once again grateful that she had narrowly escaped the temptation. She knew that the Lord always made a way of escape, but resisting his charms had been getting more and more difficult, especially since Tommy seemed so unaware of her needs and desires.

Each time Chanel remembered the evening she had called and met with Antonio after a terrible disagreement with Tommy, her emotions conflicted. Most of the time, Chanel felt ashamed of the fact that she had initiated her emotional affair with Antonio out of anger and disgust with Tommy, but at other times, she felt a sense of satisfaction, believing that she was only getting justice. She told herself that her friendship with Antonio would never get physical, despite her attraction to him. Recently though, it had become more and more difficult to categorize her relationship with him as simply friendly. Since the two had kissed, Chanel could sense Antonio's expectations for the relationship going to a much more intimate level. Although her body wanted to forge ahead aimlessly, she couldn't ignore the small still voice of the Holy Spirit inside, telling her he was trouble and that she was wrong.

She had argued with Sydney when her friend reminded her that a virtuous woman was more precious than rubies. Chanel had snapped, "Proverbs also says that a husband will praise her." Tommy rarely seemed to appreciate anything Chanel did, but she knew that her decisions would impact Zachary's life drastically. Regardless of how horribly she and Tommy were getting along, she had to think about her son and his best interest. Chanel wasn't a silly woman, but she knew that her actions were becoming more and more reckless.

Chanel locked up the café and decided that she would pick up a pizza before getting Zachary from her mother-in-law's. As she walked to her car briskly, attempting to avoid the chilly Rochester night air, Chanel was startled to see that Lena was in a car parked in the lot. Chanel tried to get her attention without alarming her, only Lena had seen her coming and rolled down the window to greet her.

"Hey," she said uncomfortably, avoiding eye contact with Chanel.

"Lena, what in the world are you out here in the parking lot for?" Chanel asked, hoping Lena hadn't seen her and Antonio.

As the young girl rummaged through her purse, she stammered out, "I think I left my house keys inside."

Lena still avoided making eye contact with her, but Chanel offered, "Let's run back in the shop and we can see if you left them, okay?" Although she couldn't be exactly sure what Lena saw, she knew it must have been something since she was acting so strangely. *Had she seen the embrace between the two?* If Lena had seen something, she was sure that it must have looked worse than it really was. Chanel decided that she had to act as normally as she could in spite of Lena's behavior. She would have to clear her head before she figured out how to handle this.

After Chanel unlocked the café, Lena went straight back to the break room which doubled as a utility room and retrieved her keys from beside the phone. As soon as Lena got them, she rushed to the door and murmured, "Thanks," as she left the café.

Chanel slid quickly into her car, closed her eyes and placed her head on the steering wheel. The last thing she needed was someone trying to wreck her marriage by spreading nasty rumors. *Why had she told Antonio where she worked? Why had he shown up unannounced like that? Why had she been silly enough to hug him? Why had she been stupid enough to kiss him like that?*

She would have to have a serious talk with Antonio, and tomorrow she would talk to Lena and try to clear the air. As for tonight, she just wanted to get her son. She wanted to hold him and reassure him that his mommy wouldn't be the cause of the breakup of their family.

"Mommy! Mommy!" Zachary yelled as he leapt up into his mother's arms.

"How's my boy?" Chanel asked.

She thanked her mother-in-law, "How was he today?"

"Since when does Grandma need a thank you for watching her grandbaby?" Olivia asked.

"You've really been a lifesaver lately. I've been so busy today with customers and getting ready for the audit next month. You would think Tommy would try just a little bit to help, but…he just doesn't understand." Chanel had always made a point to avoid discussing her marital problems with her mother-in-law, but she needed to vent.

Olivia interrupted, "Honey, no need to tell me about what Tommy's doin'. I've been tryin' to talk some sense into that boy." She struggled to zip Zachary's coat up as she continued, "Unfortunately, I don't think I made a big secret about how I felt about you at first. It was hard to let go of Tommy, and I thought the age difference was just too much. But, honey, once you two got married and I saw how good you were to my son, I knew I'd made a mistake about you. You're good for my Tommy."

Chanel smiled faintly, glad that Olivia saw her redeeming qualities in spite of what Tommy may have told her.

"He needs to go and get himself a real job and stop livin' in the clouds like his daddy. The boys' daddy almost had us filin' bankruptcy, tryin' to start one business after another. He just never could settle on one thing and focus. Finally, I just had to put my foot down. That's what you gonna' have to do with my son. He needs to go back and teach." She shook her head in frustration. "All that college for nothin'."

Olivia pulled Zachary's hat on and hugged her grandson tightly.

"Thanks for saying that I'm good for Tommy, but I'm not so sure anymore. I love him, but I'm tired."

"I can tell you been frustrated. You just got to find a way to let him know he's got to be realistic without shatterin' his spirit. He means to do right by you and Zachary, honey. He might just need the Lord to show him exactly how he needs to do it. Ask the Lord to give you the words to say."

It was easy for Olivia to say. All the way home, she thought about what her mother-in-law had said to her. Chanel had always respected Tommy's mother even though Olivia hadn't liked her. When Chanel got pregnant, Olivia changed dramatically. She had shown her acceptance and respect for Chanel, which was more than she had hoped for.

Since Tommy was the last of four boys, Chanel could understand Olivia's protectiveness, especially since she was now a mother. She could feel Olivia's genuine love for her, and Chanel felt the same way about her. Zachary adored his grandmother. She didn't know how she would ever repay her for the peace of mind she had knowing Olivia was watching Zachary almost every day after preschool so she could be at the café. Chanel was forever grateful that her son had the family she never had.

As she headed toward home, Olivia's words rang in her ears. Her mother-in-law's concern about Tommy having his spirit shattered was noble, but she wondered who on earth was concerned about shattering *her* spirit?

Chanel opened the door to find Tommy in the kitchen. As she eyed the massive bowl of pasta on the counter and the large chrome pot simmering on the stove, Chanel surmised that he had cooked spaghetti and cleaned up his mess, which Chanel was grateful for but didn't acknowledge.

"Hey, baby! I guess we're gonna have the spaghetti I cooked *and* pizza. We both had Italian in mind, huh?" Tommy greeted her happily, eyeing the pizza box in her hand.

"Tommy, I wish you would've called to tell me that you cooked," Chanel replied, with a sigh.

"Chanel, I was trying to surprise you. The guy who owns the studio had an emergency so I couldn't record tonight."

"You know what? A great surprise would've been you picking up Zachary and letting me know that you cooked, so I wouldn't have made the stop."

Tommy took the pizza box from her hand and offered, "Why don't you get washed up so we can eat together tonight?"

Chanel was floored. *Was he serious? Since when did they sit down to eat dinner together at the table?* The norm around their house was dinner in front of the television, and they rarely did that together. Chanel knew that Tommy must be up to something. She didn't have any idea what it was, but she was sure it would only be a matter of time.

Chanel bathed and started to pull out her regular flannel pajama pants and a T-shirt and changed her mind. She dug until she found her long mint-green silk gown and slipped it on. She pulled the matching bathrobe from the back of the closet and put a splash of body spray on. She thought it might help if she did something out of the ordinary as well.

When she came into the kitchen, Tommy, wearing oven mitts, took the pizza out of the oven, and did a double take when he saw his wife. "I think I see an angel."

Chanel tried to cover her embarrassment. "Tommy, please."

He pulled the oven mitts off and went to her, holding both of her hands. Then, he spun her around in a dance-like motion. Chanel couldn't help smiling.

He held her face in his hands. "You are the most beautiful woman in the world. You don't have to have a stitch of makeup on, and you're simply ravishing. How about we skip dinner?"

Chanel pushed him back playfully. "Skipping dinner is *not* an option for me. This is one hungry sister right here." She went to the freezer to put ice in their glasses. "Now after dinner, we'll have to see what happens."

Tommy beamed with excitement. "This is gonna be the absolute fastest dinner on record." He looked at his son, yawning while he ate his pizza. "Son, eat while you can, cause Dad is puttin' you in the bed."

After Chanel bathed Zachary and put him to bed, she joined her husband in the kitchen where she helped him dry the last of the dinner dishes.

"Zachary went to sleep, huh?"

"Yeah, thank the Lord."

"Did I tell you how good you look tonight?"

"As a matter of fact, I think you have." Chanel felt her guard beginning to drop, and calm came over her. She couldn't believe that he was doing dishes. For the first time in months, she allowed herself to relax and enjoy the moment. When Tommy slowly pulled the dishtowel from Chanel's grasp and held her closely, she responded. Her hug from Antonio paled in comparison to the intimate embrace she shared with her husband. Tommy knew her like no man could ever know her, and the trust and familiarity of her husband was romantic.

Chanel rested her head on her husband's broad shoulders and felt the tension of the day release. "Tommy, I wish we could just stay like this forever."

"I think I can get that worked out, baby. Just leave it to me." He brushed his lips softly across hers, rubbing her back until the doorbell rang, disturbing the moment. Profanity escaped from Tommy's lips as he heard the bell ring again and again.

"That foul language has got to go," she suddenly reprimanded. "But who could that be at this time of the night?"

"Sorry," Tommy said without real remorse as he ran to answer the door.

Chanel leaned against the kitchen counter, disgusted as she heard Tommy greet some of his musician friends.

"Baby, guess who's here?" Tommy asked as he came through the kitchen door happily.

Chanel folded her arms and gritted her teeth. "Let me guess, Tommy. It wouldn't be some of your hoodlum friends, would it?"

"Come on now, Chanel, we can't be rude."

"*Rude?* What's rude is coming over here unannounced at eleven o'clock at night. Who is it anyway?"

"Roderick and Steve, and they brought their girlfriends. I know it's bad timing, but they won't stay long. Please come on and at least say hi!" Tommy pleaded after giving her a quick kiss on the cheek.

"You know what? Have fun because I'm going to bed." Chanel turned to walk upstairs.

Tommy's smile dissolved. "Chanel! Chanel! Don't be like that! I don't believe you," he whispered harshly as Chanel marched up the stairs.

Chanel checked on Zachary who slept peacefully and climbed into bed. After an hour of watching QVC and the Food Network, she yawned and decided to try to get some sleep. She groped for her earplugs from the nightstand drawer to drown the bass that reverberated through the house from the music downstairs. This time, though, she wouldn't go to the basement and interrupt them by notifying them that the loud music was disturbing her. Tonight, she would fight fire with fire. She reached for her cell phone and dialed Antonio's number. He would understand.

The phone only rang once and he answered.

Chanel whispered, "Hey, it's me."

"I know, and I'm glad you called, lovely."

Sensing his smile through the phone, Chanel beamed at the term of endearment.

"Well, I can't really talk...he's here. I mean...my husband is downstairs with his friends." She fought through her silliness and guilt. She wondered what she must look like making a call to him with her husband downstairs. It was bad enough that she was even talking to him at all.

The rhythmic beats from the music amplified, so she spoke without whispering, braver than she had been. What did she care if Tommy heard her? Why should she feel guilty? Tommy certainly wasn't respecting or caring about her, so why should she stop talking to Antonio? *It wasn't like she was having an affair,* Chanel thought.

"Don't say a word, precious. Just let me talk to you," Antonio said in the most incredibly sexy way she had ever heard a man talk to her. His deep voice was smoother than Barry White's and as soothing as a warm bath after a tired day. He continued to amuse her with his conversation, consisting of relaying his day to her, interjecting tidbits of humor. The brother had even thought to ask her about her day at work and then wait to hear her detailed response. Antonio seemed too good to be true.

When she heard the music abruptly stop, Chanel interrupted and whispered, "Hey, I better go. I think my husband's coming up."

Just as she went to turn her phone off, she heard a faint, "Bye, sweetness," as she closed her eyes to go to sleep. Her sleep would be sound tonight with thoughts of Antonio.

The door to the bedroom opened, but she kept her eyes shut. She could tell that Tommy turned on the lights. He began talking to her as if he knew she were up.

"Chanel? Chanel? You asleep already?" When she didn't respond, he gently shook her, hoping to rouse her.

She could tell he was frustrated by his loud movements throughout the room. She peeped in a crack between the pillows to see what he was doing. He pulled his dreds back with a rubber band and began unbuttoning his shirt. Then, he went into the walk-in closet and slammed the door behind him.

Infuriated that he could be so rude, Chanel jumped out from under the covers and grabbed her pillow, heading straight for their guest bedroom. Tommy trailed behind her until she slammed the door between them. She heard him yell, "Remember, that's my room not yours!" Tommy had been sleeping in the guest room off and on, depending on Chanel's mood to tolerate him.

Chanel ignored his sarcasm and angrily kicked her feet under the blankets to get to sleep. She had a busy day tomorrow. It wasn't too long ago when the slightest disagreement with Tommy would prevent her from getting to sleep. But now the arguments and disagreements had become so frequent that she could sleep soundly after them.

Figuring out what to do about Tommy was something she'd just have to think about later. This night, Chanel was just enjoying the reprieve that Antonio gave her, assuring her that her dreams would be sweet.

CHAPTER 10

Sherese

*If my people, which are called by my name, shall humble themselves,
and pray, and seek my face, and turn from their wicked ways;
then will I hear from heaven, ...and will heal their land.*

2 Chronicles 7:14

Sherese put the final touches on a painting of her parents that she had been working on for months to go in the new church building. Her contributions to the church had been almost nonexistent with the exception of the painting, and Sydney had made no attempt to hide her disdain about it. However, Sherese had long ago decided that she would not allow guilt to dictate her attendance or involvement in her father's church. Her parents had chosen their path, and she would choose her own.

Why did she have to go to church to get to heaven? Besides, some of the most unscrupulous characters she knew were in the church. She knew the role some of the most devout members tried to portray at church was a far cry from what they actually lived at home. For instance, every single Sunday, all of her life, Sister Desmond shouted and ran around the church like she had a corner on getting the Holy Ghost. But throughout the week, she stayed on the phone gossiping and lying about mostly innocent members like there was no tomorrow. It seemed the more reprimands and counseling Sister Desmond received from the pastor, the more mess she seemed to kick up.

Another member, Deacon Charlie Pritchard, got up and, as usual, testified about how much he loved the Lord and how much he cherished his wife of thirty years, but he was known to be one of the biggest cheaters in the city. She couldn't understand how her parents could choose to live a life dedicated to such a hypocritical group of people.

Sherese prided herself on keeping it real with others and herself because deep down she knew the Lord knew her heart anyway. She was convinced that the Lord didn't give any extra brownie points for someone just because they sat in service three or four times a week. *What did a chicken dinner sale have to do with salvation anyway?*

Thankfully, her parents had stopped pressuring her about attending. They seemed to be content that she was at least still faithful about coming to Sunday morning services. Living her life in a fishbowl wasn't something Sherese desired, even if all of her other family members were content to do so.

After placing her brush down on the edge of the easel, she stepped back, folding her arms while admiring the painting. She thought that she had really captured her father's charisma and mother's beauty. Still, something was missing, and for some time she couldn't figure it out until she picked up the original photograph her mother had given her. As she studied the picture and examined her painting, she knew exactly what it was. Her painting hadn't captured the essence of her parents because it lacked the warmth in their eyes. Although her parents could work her nerves on occasion, they were warm people. Sherese picked her brush up and went back to work.

Two hours later, her frustration had grown to epic proportions as she stepped back once again to view her work. Each time she noticed that her parents' eyes looked different than she had painted them before, but still not warm. She decided to forego her usual perfectionism in her artwork and thought that no one would probably notice but her anyway. She painted her small signature on the bottom corner with mild satisfaction.

As she cleaned her brushes, she remembered that her parents had wanted to talk to her, and she could just imagine what Sydney had complained about to them. Hopefully her parents would understand that Sydney was being totally irrational and nitpicky. Sydney had actually resorted to posting notes for her around the house. On the door that went into the house from the garage, there was a note that read: *Kindly remove your* shoes *please.* On the door to the refrigerator another one read: *Please wash dishes immediately after use.* Sydney even had the nerve to place a note on her bathroom sink, one her sister never used, imploring her to clean the bathroom weekly. Sherese thought the notes were silly and didn't even bother to confront her sister about them. She was, however, getting her departure plan ready because Sherese had "helped" all she could.

Since it was Saturday night and she wanted to get out of the house, she called her girlfriend, Margo. They agreed to go to a new Mexican restaurant because they had a live band on Saturday nights.

Sherese decided to get dressed so she wouldn't have to come back home when she left her parents' house. After showering, she hummed as she selected her colorful poncho, tight jeans, and heels. As she put her last earring on, her cell phone vibrated. She saw Chanel's name and number and picked up.

"Hey, girl, what's up?"

"Same ole stuff here, I didn't want anything. Just tryin' to kill some time until Lena gets here. I'm at the café and mostly everything I'm gonna do for the day is done. So, what you got up for tonight?"

"Actually I'm going over to Mama and Daddy's. They want to talk to me. I think your girl has complained about me to them."

"Sher, you're always thinking the worst. What if they want to talk to you about the way Sydney's been acting lately?"

"Yeah, I guess you're right. It probably is about Syd, now that you mention it. Well, I guess I better go because I'm gonna try to talk to Syd for a minute before I go."

"Okay, call me tomorrow."

Sherese really valued her relationship with Chanel. She showed her concern for her but never imposed her opinions and judgments on her like her sister did.

Sherese realized that she was the happiest she'd been in a long time. Usually, she regarded her happiness in terms of the guy she dated. But she found out that she didn't need a relationship to be content. Her job was going well and she had been saving her money. She had even been talking to a realtor about the prospect of buying a small home or condo. It was hard for her to believe that only a few short months ago, she didn't even have a job. Things were looking up.

After she sprayed on a few squirts of her favorite perfume, she left to lightly tap on her sister's office door.

"Syd? Syd?" she called.

When there was no response, Sherese gently opened the door to find the room empty. She called and searched throughout the house. When she looked in the garage to see if her car was there, she was surprised to find it wasn't there. Sydney hadn't even mentioned she was leaving, but she had been keeping to herself so much lately.

The only ones who seemed to be able to convince Sydney to get out once in a while were Chanel and Maya. Sherese was losing patience with Sydney's cold and hostile attitude toward her. She couldn't wait to unload on her parents about Sydney's behavior, and Sherese couldn't help wondering if Sydney needed some professional grief counseling.

As Sherese pulled up to her parents' home, she was more than a little disappointed to find Sydney's car in the driveway. Her parents must not have expected Syd, and now Sherese knew that she couldn't have that talk with her parents she was so prepared for.

Sherese found her parents sitting in the family room with Sydney. When she walked into the family room, an unusual quietness came over the room. Her mother was always bustling about, finding it difficult to sit still while her father almost always had the television or radio on and turned up loud, since he was developing a hearing problem. However, tonight was different. There was no television on. No radio was blaring. Her mother was still, and all eyes were glued to Sherese as she greeted them in a jovial manner, "Hey, what's up, everybody?"

The room was so quiet that Sherese could hear the small wooden clock that sat on one of the end tables ticking. Someone had died. Sherese was convinced.

"Hi, baby," her mother finally responded, attempting to sound normal.

"Hey, what's up, Sher?" Sydney asked, a little too jovially.

Her father simply held a warm but uneasy smile and said, "Grab you a seat, daughter."

"What's wrong with you all? Is somebody sick or something?" Sherese questioned.

"No, honey. We just want to talk to you and Sydney about something really important."

Sherese was confused. It became apparent to her that they didn't want to talk about Sydney by the looks on their faces when she entered the room. Slowly, she pulled the heavy but rickety piano bench out and sat facing her family. Her father's heavy breathing made her nervous as he cleared his throat while tightly gripping the remote. Sherese even thought she saw her mother's knees trembling a little, but she couldn't be sure. She searched Sydney's face, but her sister looked as clueless as she did.

Her mother pulled her glasses off her face and began to speak first.

"Me and your daddy love you girls more than our lives. You know that, don't you?"

Sherese nodded somewhat nervously and Sydney stated emphatically, attempting to reassure her, "We know that, Mama."

"Well, there's somethin' we've kept from you." She looked at Samuel for help.

Their father cleared his throat again and continued, "We wanted to tell you, Sherese. It's just never been the right time. It's still not the right time, but—,"

Her mother chimed in. "But if we don't tell you now, we may never tell you."

The right time for what? Things began to move in slow motion for Sherese. She couldn't believe she was going to hear a secret concerning her. She held the sides of the piano bench tightly in expectation.

"What is it, Mama?" Sherese managed to ask.

Sherese searched her mother's eyes for a clue as to what was coming, but her mother took a deep breath and continued. "You both remember my sister Rosa from Mississippi?"

They both nodded. Even though they had met her only once a long time ago when they were young, they remembered Rosa. She was an alcoholic and an embarrassment to the long line of staunch COGIC descendants. Although Sherese and Sydney couldn't remember exactly how she looked, there had been many stories circulating in the family about Rosa. They knew as children that they weren't supposed to know about her unscrupulous behavior, but they overheard their mother and other families make reference to her. She was one of the only "loose cannons" in the family.

Often when the girls were children, if one got mad enough at the other, they would secretly call one another Rosa, the ultimate insult.

All eight of her mother's sisters' black-and-white photographs decorated the top of the piano, with the exception of Rosa's. The girls never seemed to miss out on their Aunt Rosa since they had so many aunts to dote on them, but Rosa was a mysterious family member whom Sherese's mother was never eager to talk about.

Her mother carefully chose her words and went on. "Rosa's my baby sister as you both know. She always had her own way of goin' about things and this got her in a heap of trouble. That girl couldn't stand playin' by the rules at all. She said she'd never marry, and she didn't as far as I know. She said a man would never tell her what to do. Anyway, Mama and Daddy didn't know what to do with her, and she rebelled like the dickens. Anyway, seemed like the older she got, the more angry she got at my parents for tryin' to control her."

Sherese couldn't stand how long it was taking for her mother to get to the point. *What did any of this have to do with her?*

Her daddy interjected, "What your mama's tryin' to say is that Rosa ended up expectin' when she was a teenager."

Sherese frowned until Sydney asked, "You mean pregnant, Daddy?"

"Uh, yeah," he answered as he shifted in his seat uncomfortably.

Darlene began to wring her hands, but continued on. "Sher, there's no easy way to say this. We should've told you years ago, but we were scared. Please forgive us."

The room spun and Sherese braced herself for what she feared was coming.

Darlene's lip trembled. "Sher, my sister gave you life, but you've always been mine. You've always been mine and your daddy's."

Sydney sat up straight, placing her hands over her mouth in disbelief.

Her parents got on either side of Sherese and put their arms around her as she sat stunned and momentarily speechless.

"What did you say? I don't understand?" Sherese asked finally in a state of bewilderment, trying to find some hint of a cruel joke in either of her parents' faces.

Tiny beads of perspiration collected on her mother's forehead. "My sister wanted to take care of you, but she was just not capable. She couldn't even support herself. She knew I wanted another baby but couldn't have one, so we thanked the Lord for blessing us with you."

Her mother rambled on inextricably while tears fell down her father's brown rosy cheeks.

Darlene started again. "You weren't but three weeks old when we went down to Mississippi to bring you home. At first, we said we would tell you as soon as you were old enough to understand, but I never wanted you to feel like there was a difference between you and Sydney. I didn't want you to be burdened with grown-up issues so young. Then...then when you became a teenager, you were having a hard time. We knew it would make it worse. Before we knew it, you got married and when things didn't work out, well, it was just never the right time. But we know it's not fair to keep this from you as an adult, and we have just found out that Rosa's sick. We just couldn't keep it from you anymore."

Sherese hadn't seen her mother shed a tear even during Vance's funeral and yet she knew how much Darlene loved him. Now, her mother began to weep, pulling Sherese's unresponsive and limp body to her. Sherese could faintly hear her mother and father telling her how sorry they were for not telling her sooner and to please forgive them, but echoes of their conversation were all she heard.

Sherese felt as if she were suspended in mid-air, thrown carelessly to the wind. Even as Sherese heard her sister's soft cry and felt her delicate kisses on her forehead, she could not feel the full impact of the blow. She had been tricked and misled all her life.

When she came to herself a bit, the only words that managed to escape from her lips were, "My father?"

At those words, she heard her father say, "Help us, Lord Jesus." Samuel held his wife's hand tightly. Darlene backed up a distance from Sydney and let out the last bit of information that she'd been holding all of those years.

Before answering, Samuel let go of his wife's hand and held Sherese's face in his hands gently. "I am your father, always have been and always will. Do you hear me?"

Sherese sank lower on the seat, staring down at her hands in her lap while her mother began.

"Rosa doesn't know who he is—at least that's what she's told us."

Feeling as if she'd been slapped, Sherese felt the massive sting throughout her body as she grabbed her purse and jacket and ran out the front door. She heard the violent patter of footsteps racing behind her, but she escaped. As she sped down the dark road, she headed toward The Clique.

Propped against the wall inside of the club was the only way Sherese felt able to stand. She heard the familiar deafening sound of the laughter, music, and conversation and noticed some familiar faces in the dimly lit party atmosphere with only the strobe lighting to illuminate the darkness. Yet, the club looked different. Everything was different now.

Sherese hadn't had a drink, yet her steps were unsteady as she walked to the cramped, dirty restroom. A woman reapplying her heavy eye-liner stopped when Sherese walked in.

"You okay?" she asked with concern and a heavy tongue.

Sherese stared at the fortyish-looking woman who was dressed like a twenty-year-old. "Yeah, thanks."

As soon as the woman tried to leave the bathroom, she pushed the door to open it, only to realize she had to pull it open. She giggled, "Silly me. Have a good time, sweetie."

Sherese made a dash for the nearest stall and vomited. Her sickness had nothing to do with alcohol. Her whole body shook as she struggled to make sense of what had just happened. Could it be possible that she wasn't her parents' daughter?

She wiped her mouth with a paper towel and examined herself in the mirror. Wasn't her nose just like Samuel's? People had always told her she looked like a good mixture of both of her parents. Suddenly, she didn't know who she looked like.

Sherese always felt differently than Sydney about church and her parents' rules, but she never would have attributed that to being adopted. She and Sydney didn't look alike, yet she knew many siblings who didn't resemble one another.

She was shocked, horrified, and angry. *Why didn't they tell me?* She couldn't understand why they had waited so long. But if they had to wait, she wondered why they would tell her now when things had *finally* taken an upswing in her life.

As soon as she opened the door, the loud music seemed to help a little bit to stifle her thoughts. A sudden determination rose up in her to find Jack tonight. Sherese figured it was just as safe for her to be with a virtual stranger than with her parents.

Once seated on a stool, she scanned behind the bar and then the dance floor for him. When Sherese didn't see him after twenty minutes or so, she yelled over the music to the female bartender on duty, "Do you know if Jack's working tonight?"

"You talkin' about Jack Simmons?" she responded without looking up from the drink she was preparing.

Sherese didn't remember his last name but figured that it must be the same Jack.

"Uhhh, yeah."

"Jack resigned a few months ago," she stated simply and then turned to help other patrons.

She hadn't even considered that Jack wouldn't be here. As she sipped on her Cosmo, a tall, slender, light-complexioned man with acne covering his cheeks slid onto the nearest stool. Wearing a dated Kangol hat, a tan rayon shirt and pants set, and alligator shoes, the stranger began speaking in drunken unintelligible words. When he leaned toward her, she pushed her drink aside. Suddenly, the atmosphere of the club was making her feel worse, something she didn't think was possible. With that, she left her drink and decided that The

Clique wasn't such a good idea after all. She had no tolerance for drunk, unruly men tonight.

She felt slightly better when the cold night air hit her face. In the quietness of the night, she felt the Lord's presence, beckoning her to come to Him. She dismissed the thought when she began to wonder why God would allow so many "godly" people to let her down in such a devastating way.

As she started up her car engine, she sat trying to figure out what her next move would be. Sherese knew that staying at Sydney's would be out of the question. She needed to go get some clothes from the house, but she decided against it. There was no way she could risk Sydney being there. She couldn't deal with her family now. As she drove past a Wal-Mart, she decided to run in and grab some night-clothes and sweats for the next several days because she knew she would need them at the hotel she'd be staying at.

CHAPTER 11

Sydney

I reckon that the sufferings of this present time are not worthy
to be compared with the glory which shall be revealed in us.

Romans 8:18

Sydney sat with Chanel at her favorite table next to the front window of the café. She loved how the large poplar tree shaded that corner of the café and gave the table a unique coziness. As she talked to Chanel, Sydney could read that her friend was stunned. She knew Chanel was trying to grasp the depth of what Sydney had told her but struggled to act like the news about Sherese wasn't as mind-blowing as it really was. Often, Chanel had wondered why the Lord allowed her to be born into such a dysfunctional family, but the older she got, the more she realized that every family had their share of drama, even ones that looked as picture-perfect on the outside as the Hightowers.

Sydney leaned in toward her friend who sat across from her at the table. "You think Mama and Daddy were wrong not to tell Sherese that Aunt Rosa's her birth mother?"

Somehow, as bad as the whole situation was with Sherese and her parents, Chanel couldn't help noticing that Sydney was somehow more engaged and normal than she had been since Vance's passing. Aside from the dark circles that remained under her eyes, she was actually beginning to look more like herself.

"Syd, you know, it's hard to say. How can you even start to make a call like that unless you've been in their shoes? I can't do it. All I can say is that whatever your parents did, I'm sure they had Sherese's best interest at heart."

"Oh, yeah, I know that. It's just that she's so hurt. On the other hand, Mama and Daddy are hurting so much. I know they were trying to do what was best, but I gotta admit that I don't know how I'd feel if it were me, you know?"

Chanel nodded as she fingered her hoop earrings, deep in thought.

"How do you think *you* would feel, Chanel?" Sydney searched her girlfriend's face for a reaction, but Chanel picked up her cup of steaming coffee and even bit off a nibble of her protein bar before answering, seemingly considering her own feelings about the subject.

"Well, you know my situation. Yeah, I know who my mother is and all, but Nyla hasn't been much of a mother to me. My father, well, I've only gotten to know him recently. So, my perspective is a little different. I love your parents as if they were my own, and they aren't my biological parents. After the shock wears off, your sister will see the light. They did what was best. Come on, Syd. You know as well as I do, that Sherese would've grown up feeling like an outsider. She already feels like she's living in your shadow. Now if she really thinks about it, she'll think about the fact that your parents so desperately loved her and wanted her to feel accepted that they didn't tell her. They knew Sherese better than I think she knows herself at this point."

"Maybe you're right. I just think—," Sydney said while warming her hands on the sides of her cup.

Chanel held her hand up in a stop motion. "Bottom line, Syd. When it all comes down to it, we all just want to be loved. The biological part has very little to do with it. Trust me, Sherese will get over this hurdle. God always lets us go through trials to strengthen us, and ultimately He will get the glory if we trust Him through it."

Sydney was always in awe of Chanel's ability to react so calmly in adverse situations. Her friend could get heated and overreact from minor injustices and trivial matters, but when it really counted, when the really big things happened, Chanel's level head and open mind were real assets. She hadn't reacted to the news of Sherese's adoption like it was anywhere near the catastrophe that Sydney thought it was. Sure, Sydney generally stayed calm and composed on the outside, but on the inside, she worried and had trouble letting things go.

"Chanel, I know that I haven't said too much since Vance has passed. It's been really hard." Sydney looked down and paused for a second. "But I just wanted to tell you that you mean so much to me. Your friendship, I mean. From the moment you heard about Vance, you've been trying to stick to me like glue, and it's really aggravated me at times." The two friends smiled, and Sydney made eye contact with Chanel.

"The thing is, Chanel, you've been there for me and Sherese. Being with you has really made me realize that it doesn't matter so much what family you were born into. It's the family that's in your heart. You're a sister to me." Sydney swallowed hard and added, "I just want to say thank you for everything."

Chanel's hazel eyes clouded and she grabbed the napkin under her cup to dap her eyes before reaching for her friend's hand across the table and holding it tightly. "Don't thank me for anything. I love you and your family. You know that. You and Sherese are gonna be fine. You two are going through some heavy stuff by anyone's standards, but just keep trustin' in the Lord. It's just a season. Shoot, girl, you know as well as I do how your daddy's been tellin' the congregation for years, 'We all got our cross to bear.'"

Although she knew what Chanel said was right, she also knew that unless her sister knew the Lord as her Savior, her situation would seem totally hopeless. Sherese needed to know more than just that the Lord exists. She needed to be in fellowship with Him and trust Him totally in order to find her way.

Chanel reached for her purse and pulled out her wallet. "When Ramone died, I thought that was it for me. He was really all I had. He loved me unconditionally. Like I've told you other times, meeting you and your family gave me an idea of what the love of God can do for you. I realized that Ramone was gone, but the Lord really carried me through the darkness until I could see light. I realized that God still has work for me to fulfill His purpose for me."

She opened her wallet and displayed a picture of Ramone to Chanel. She ran her fingers across her brother's face. "I was cleaning out my desk drawer, and I hadn't seen this picture in years. It used to hurt too badly to see pictures or even talk about him, but now I just want to remember the good things. I want to do better, do more with the time I have left. It sounds all cheesy, and I know I keep sayin' it, but I do want to fulfill God's purpose for my life."

Sydney bit her bottom lip, deep in thought. She took Chanel's wallet and stared at Ramone. "You two looked so much alike."

Chanel took her wallet back and put it in her purse. "Yeah, I know. Everybody used to say that. I miss him, but things get a little bit better with time."

As Sydney warmed her hands around her cup, she said, "I thought I knew my purpose until Vance passed. I thought I had it all, and now it just feels like somebody pulled the rug from under my feet and I can't get up."

"Stop tryin' to jump up, Syd. Get up slowly."

"I just don't know how. I depended on him for everything, and I'm only just now realizing that my trust should've been in the Lord." Sydney stood up, wanting to avoid the painful conversation, and stared at the blowing branches of the poplar tree. She added wistfully, "Now I don't know how to do anything by myself."

"Syd, I learned a long time ago that it's all good to have expecta- tions, but you always have to know that your life is in His hands. We can put a certain amount of trust in people, but we have to totally trust that God is sovereign, no matter what it looks like. When you get derailed, your choices are to stay stuck or get back on and try again. I know it may seem harsh, but just trust God and press through this."

"Press? I thought I understood what press meant, but you know what, girl?" Sydney suddenly sat back down, making sure no one else in the café could hear her. "You don't know what that word means until you face some serious trials, heartache, and pain. I *have* been pressing, but I can't forget Vance and just go on even though I know the scripture says something about forgetting the things in the past. I'm not ready to put Vance in my past."

Chanel could hear the defensive tone rising in Sydney but she remained calm. "I would never in a million years suggest that you forget Vance. Even if I'd be crazy enough to say something like that, you couldn't. I think we need to forget the negative stuff. We need to leave the pain, guilt, despair of the situation, regardless of what it is and focus on the mark, which is Christ and all He stands for and wants us to be. The Lord knows your pain, Syd. He knows what you and Sher can bear. He knows how heavy the load is, but He allowed you to carry it for a purpose."

Lena suddenly appeared and interrupted, "Sorry to bother you, but can I get you two anything else?"

When Sydney and Chanel told her they didn't need anything, Chanel whispered, "I promise, that girl's gettin' to be a little too helpful."

Sydney whispered back, "You're so hard on folks sometimes."

"I hope you don't think I'm being hard on you. As I was saying though, some things—no, a lot of things—are a press because your flesh wants you to give in, throw in the towel, forget everybody and everything. You gotta resist that urge and press toward the mark for the prize of the high calling of God in Christ Jesus. Go forward. It's not the life you expected, but it's yours. No one can live or fulfill your purpose but you."

Now Sydney sat tearily nodding but surprised by her friend's godly wisdom. She never knew that Chanel had such depth in her spiritual life. Sydney realized that she may have always been too busy giving advice to listen. She was always the one who preached to Sherese and Chanel, but now it was Sydney's turn to receive the truth from her friend, and the impact of Chanel's words was great.

While Sydney sat, thoughtfully attempting to absorb Chanel's words, Chanel's countenance seemed peaceful as she sipped some more of her latte. "Girl, are you gonna drink your latte or what?"

Sydney didn't smile, but spoke instead. "Chanel, I just can't stop thinking about the whole situation with Sherese. There's just this one time I remember that this lady came to the house. I don't know if it was my Aunt Rosa or not, but the whole encounter was a little weird. I must have been ten or eleven and Sherese was three or four. It was a weekday, but Mama put on our Sunday dresses and pressed our hair and everything, because she told us we were going to have a visitor. Well, this lady came in the house and I could tell she was sort of pretty underneath all the makeup. I couldn't help staring at her lips because they were ruby red and the lipstick was sort of outside of the natural lines of her lips, making her look kind of comical."

Sydney closed her eyes for a moment as if it would help her remember more.

"The only other thing that I can remember is that her pantyhose were sort of twisted down by her ankles, and she seemed to shake a lot when I gave her a hug. Something keeps tellin' me that was Aunt Rosa, but I can't be sure."

"So you never saw her again?"

"Never." Sydney looked off in the distance, deep in thought. "Chanel, do you think I should ask Mama about that or you think I should just leave it alone?"

"Girl, that's gotta be your call. I can't see where it would make anything worse or better."

"Well, just keep us in your prayers. I better get back to work," Sydney said as she glanced at her watch and began to put her coat on.

"That goes without saying." Chanel noticed she was ready to go and slid her half empty cup toward her to take it behind the counter.

Sydney folded her arms and frowned. "Chanel, this conversation has revealed something to me."

"What's that? Don't order a latte at my café because you'll waste it?" Chanel joked as she pointed to Sydney's drink.

"No, sorry about that though," she said with a small smile. "Seriously though, girl, it's really let me know that I need to pray, consecrate, and fast more."

"Don't we all," Chanel nodded, taking the cups to the back.

Sydney called to her friend, "Thanks for letting me vent, but I gotta go. I'll talk to you tomorrow."

Chanel hollered back, "We'll talk later. Love you."

When Sydney returned to the office, she tried to ignore the sympathetic looks that seemed to assault her in most every coworker's face since Vance's passing. She knew everyone meant well, but she didn't want or need anyone's sympathy. She felt violated by the constant questions about her personal life. She almost wished that people at work didn't know, but at the same time, she knew that she had been given a lot more leeway because of it.

As Sydney walked into her office, she couldn't believe the harrowing task that stood before her. Droves of papers were stacked up in her "To Do" tray as never before, although she knew that her boss, Ed Neal, had been giving her an extra light load in the months since Vance's death. Although Mr. Neal had tried to convince Sydney to take a leave of absence with her many extra vacation days, she had thanked him for his understanding but quite adamantly rejected his offer. She was convinced that work would take her mind off of things and that she could stay focused. Today, however, as she picked up her rapidly blinking phone to retrieve her numerous messages, she said aloud, "I can't do this."

Sydney decided that she would try to work from home for the rest of the week if Mr. Neal approved it because she knew that her productivity would improve, not having to worry about what others were thinking of her. Besides, she could also try to catch up with her sister since she remembered it was her day off from the newspaper.

"Mr. Neal can see you in a few minutes, Sydney. He's taking a call right now," Barbara, her boss's secretary, explained.

"Thanks, Barb." Sydney seated herself in the lobby and got on her Blackberry.

After a few minutes, Mr. Neal came out and greeted Sydney with a welcoming smile. When Sydney saw that he not only wore his usual shirt and tie, but also had on a suit, she was pleased that she had worn her winter-white suit and heels.

"Why, Sydney Ellington, please come on in and have a seat."

Mr. Neal, just fifty with a head full of thick, gray hair, had a youthful face and athletic body, giving him a mature and distinguished look. By all accounts, he was well-liked by many in his division. Sydney was thankful to have him for a boss. He had carved out extra time in his hectic schedule for Sydney early on in her career to help her understand how the accounting department operates at KODAK because he always felt that Sydney was going places. Her drive and ambition reminded him of when he was younger and he knew that a little mentoring could go a long way with the right individual. Sydney had a lot of promise and Mr. Neal had put a great deal of confidence in his employee.

"Sydney, how are you?"

Sydney sat erect, almost on the edge of her seat. "I'm fine, Mr. Neal. How are you?"

"I'm well." After loosening his tie around his neck a bit, Mr. Neal sat in his chair and leaned back, putting his hands behind his head in a casual manner. "I had a business meeting with the government people today, and the worst part is this tie."

Sydney smiled but wasn't comfortable with the small talk.

"What brings you here today?"

Sydney took a deep breath. "Well, I just wanted you to know that I'm working on the numbers for the Imaging Division and I expect to have those complete for you by next week. Other than that, I wanted to see if it would be okay to work from home for the rest of the week. I am so much more productive there lately."

"That would be fine, but do you think there's anything we can do to enhance your productivity here at the office?"

Sydney hadn't anticipated this. "Well, uh. No, I don't think so. I guess it's just me. I find it better to work alone, I guess."

Mr. Neal took his hands from the back of his head and pushed himself up to the desk. "I understand that you're going through a great deal and we value your work, Sydney. I'm willing to do all I can to help, but I just want you to understand that while much of what you do is done alone, you are part of a whole department. You're a part of a team, and some of your team members—well, let's just say that they have expressed some concerns about your behavior toward them. When I heard that you wanted to meet with me, quite frankly you beat me to the punch."

Sydney swallowed and her cheeks warmed as she struggled to find the right response. "There have been complaints about me?"

She couldn't mistake the sincerity in his voice. "I'm sorry to say that you've had quite a few."

"Why?" she asked, unable to conceal her despair even though deep down she had a good idea about why.

"You know I'm a straight shooter, Sydney," he said with a professional tone. "Some have felt that you have been harsh and abrasive, something I know is quite uncharacteristic of what I know about you."

Embarrassed, Sydney answered, "I'm so sorry, Mr. Neal. I will make every effort to be more aware of my interactions with others."

Mr. Neal seemed to sense Sydney's pain and didn't want to prolong her humiliation, but he added, "I know that you have a great deal on your plate, so my offer still stands. Think about using some of your leave to take some time for yourself."

"I will give it some thought, Mr. Neal. I'm deeply sorry about my behavior, and thank you so much for allowing me to work from home."

"No problem, Sydney. Let me know if I can do anything else," Mr. Neal said as he lightly tapped his pen on the desk. He then stood up and shook her hand, "You take care of yourself." He patted her hand, "I really mean it. Let me know if I can do anything for you."

"Thank you so much for everything," Sydney said as she left his office.

Humiliated, Sydney gathered her files and laptop, leaving the office in utter dismay. She had never been reprimanded at work for her behavior or performance.

As Sydney drove down the interstate in silence, she began to think about her life. She considered her friend's conversation over lunch. Had she really ever had to press? And weren't good things supposed to happen to you as long as you did what was right?

At work, she had always been organized and professional. She completed tasks before the deadline. Everyone could count on her to pull more than her share of the load, and she had always been a good team member. Now her reputation at work was at stake because she couldn't keep her personal struggles separate from her career.

At church, people looked up to her because of her dedication to the Lord, the church, and church members. If Sydney spearheaded a meeting or committee, the event was certain to be successful. Her gift of rallying people together, keeping them focused, and encouraging them until the completion of the project made her one of the church's greatest workers. Most recently, she had been responsible for raising the most money for the building fund. She had single-handedly taken the children's choir from six or seven members to close to forty children. Being so involved meant Sydney often had to make sacrifices, but she always felt like there was a reward for her diligence and dedication.

With a pang of guilt, she thought about how much of *her* time had been spent with work and church activities, just like her husband's had. She had always thought of Vance's schedule as the culprit, but actually, she had been just as busy. Sydney had believed that she could circumvent pitfalls in life by being obedient to what the Lord wanted her to do, and she had thought that surely the Lord would be pleased with her good works.

However, all of her accomplishments in the church along with the countless services she had attended somehow didn't amount to much anymore. Although she knew intellectually that it rained on the just and unjust, she had always felt that she would somehow be exempt from tragedy. Her good works were supposed to exempt *her*. Now, she was coming to grips with her own shortcomings and weaknesses. She was beginning to realize that she wasn't on some higher plain spiritually because of her faithfulness at church or because her father was a pastor—or even because her late husband was a deacon. She also found herself examining her motives for doing work in the church, which should've always been out of her pure love for God, nothing else.

She needed greater faith, strength, and power to make it through this period of her life. This, she knew. Sydney just didn't know to do it. What had worked in the past wouldn't get her through this time. Sydney had to face the fact that she needed some deliverance, and she needed it now.

CHAPTER 12

Chanel

I press toward the mark for the prize of
the high calling of God in Christ Jesus.

Philippians 3:14

Her two closest friends had heavy loads to bear, and Chanel felt the weight of their burdens. She silently prayed for the Lord's will to be done in their lives. Reflecting on her conversation with Sydney, Chanel didn't really even know how she had found the right things to say. But then again, she did. She knew that the Lord had empowered her to speak with authority, but she didn't understand *why* He did. Chanel hadn't exactly been living a life above reproach. Her marriage was falling apart before her eyes, and Antonio was getting harder and harder for her to resist. Why or how could the Lord speak through her? Or maybe it was just in spite of her.

As she drove around the sharp curves in the park, Chanel tried not to think about doing the right thing anymore since she knew that meeting Antonio would be the highlight of her day and week. Her meetings with Antonio had been restricted to sitting together and talking—until yesterday. Chanel had sensed all along that Antonio wanted her, and she couldn't deny that she was attracted to him too. If only she couldn't hear that quiet voice telling her that it was dangerous. He had placed his hand on her chin, pulling her gently to him for a much too long kiss.

She carefully groped in her purse until she found her lipstick. While maneuvering the car with one hand, she reapplied her lipstick with the other. After spraying a few squirts of her small bottle of perfume, she proceeded slowly through the park to find Antonio. She spotted him before he saw her, waiting in his car patiently. Lightly, she tapped on her horn to signal to him that she was there. He smiled warmly and got out of his car, walking toward her.

"Hi, beautiful!"

Chanel blushed as she greeted him, noticing the crisply starched white button-down shirt. The candy cane striped tie, with shades of black and a sliver of gold, gave him a polished and professional appearance. "Antonio, you really know how to put it on thick."

"Oh, that's nothing compared to what's to come," he suggestively teased as he got into the passenger's seat.

She turned toward him. "Don't do that."

"Do what?" he asked.

"Don't go too far." Chanel noticed how his bald, shiny head looked and decided she didn't like it as much as she thought she had.

"Chanel, I think about you all of the time. I can't focus on anything or anyone else but you. I can't help saying the things that I do."

Chanel pretended to be distracted, looking in her purse. "I'm just not ready for that. I know that I'm developing feelings for you, but I know how wrong it is."

"It's not wrong. If your husband were giving you the time and attention you deserve, you wouldn't be here. You're a good person and any guy would thank his lucky stars for having you to come home to. I just can't believe that that joker doesn't even have a real job."

Chanel rolled her eyes. She didn't appreciate anyone else putting Tommy down. She knew that he wasn't intentionally hurting her. Tommy was an intelligent man, and he had been working hard at his music. She felt like she had made a mistake confiding in Antonio.

"Chanel, " he whispered, while stroking her arm.

She had never noticed the length of his fingernails before. They seemed to be longer than her own short nails. It turned her way off. To her, a man having nails longer than hers meant he didn't work hard. Tommy knew how to work. Her husband's calloused hands showed that he knew how to fix broken things. She just didn't like the unpaid work he had been focusing on. "Oh, I'm sorry. I was just thinking." Chanel leaned her forehead onto the steering wheel.

"I know you're in the church and stuff, but God understands. When you get married, the man is supposed to support his family and treat his wife like a queen."

"You gotta Bible verse for that?" Chanel asked sarcastically.

"Naw," he chuckled. "But I just *know* that God would want that."

Chanel laughed inside. This brother had no clue about what God wanted or he wouldn't be here. That thought lead her to ask herself, *Why am I here?* She broke her silence. "Hey, let's not talk about my life anymore. I still don't know terribly much about *you.*"

"Not too much to tell, but what do you want to know?"

Chanel thought for a quick second. "Well, I'm curious to know why your marriage broke up if you supported the family and treated your wife like a queen."

"My ex-wife was a trip when we were married." Antonio shook his head, "She had problems with trust. I know you're going to find this hard to believe considering the circumstance we're in, but in all honesty, I never cheated. She accused me constantly of it though."

"Constantly? What made her do that?" Chanel asked with skepticism. A red flag went up when someone blamed a failed marriage totally on the other person.

"I have no idea. I guess she was just an insecure woman. Of course, I tried my best to compliment her and make her feel good about herself and our relationship, but nothing worked. I couldn't take it anymore."

"So *you* divorced *her?*" Chanel couldn't believe that this was getting worse by the minute.

"Yes, I divorced her, but she agreed to it. Neither one of us was happy. There's no point staying in a marriage if you're not going to be happy. You know what I'm saying?"

Antonio was beginning to look extremely unattractive to her, especially the way his eyes squinted. Chanel guessed that he most certainly had cheated on his wife and had probably never given her the satisfaction of the truth. She felt like the Lord was revealing things to her about herself. She thought about how badly she felt about blaming Tommy for all of their problems. She hadn't been an angel, after all. After being silent for a couple of seconds she said, "No, I don't know what you're saying. Did your vows say that you should stay married only as long as you were happy?"

Antonio rolled his eyes dramatically. "Give me a break, Chanel. You know yourself that as unhappy as you are right now—" Antonio stopped.

"What?" Chanel demanded.

"I was just going to say that I'm sure you can't imagine being as miserable for the rest of your life as you are right now."

She recanted, "I never said I was miserable. A little unhappy maybe, but not miserable."

Antonio's glare seemed to penetrate right through her as he asked, "Then, sweetheart, why in the world are you here with me?"

Chanel turned the key in the ignition to start the car. She thought again about her conversation with Sydney. She, too, needed to press through the difficulties in her marriage. She knew the Lord was speaking to her through her conversation with Sydney and now through this whole episode with Antonio. Again she asked herself, *why in the world am I here with him?* "Antonio Black, you are correct. I have absolutely no reason to be here with you. You see, I have problems in my marriage, but all I'm doing is making them worse by being with you. I'm sorry for involving you. I really think it would be best for us to stop this now. I won't be accepting or making anymore phone calls, and I hope that you'll respect my request for you to stop. As for seeing one another, that's done too."

Antonio looked perplexed by Chanel's sudden change in behavior. "Let's talk about what just happened because I'm lost."

"Yeah, I know," Chanel whispered, staring ahead while waiting for Antonio to get out of the car. When he realized that she had nothing further to say and wouldn't even look at him, he became infuriated and slammed her car door as hard as he could, but not before profanities escaped from his lips.

As Chanel put the car in drive to pick up Zachary, she said to herself, "Chanel, get ready to press toward the mark, girl."

When Chanel really thought about it, it had been way too long since she had been to Tuesday night prayer and Bible study, at least with any consistency, and it showed in the condition of her marriage. She knew that if she were going to make it in her press toward the mark, she would need strength from having the Word hidden in her heart and her mind focused on spiritual things. There would be no more listening to or engaging in the idle chatter that came too close to gossip in the café. She was going to have to pray like never before to defeat the enemy's attack on her marriage. There was so much to pray about.

When Chanel pulled into the church parking lot, she was glad that she had arrived early since Elder Hightower's car was the only car in the parking lot. This meant that she might be able spend a few minutes alone with him, which was rare. Although Chanel knew that Elder Hightower's teaching was old-fashioned by many people's standards, she deeply appreciated his straightforward delivery of the unadulterated Word of God. Her pastor lived the life he preached about. He was truly a living testimony and being able to observe that alone was life changing for Chanel. Pastor Hightower's sermons always seemed refreshing and heartfelt, and it didn't matter that he didn't use props in his sermons or have big projector screens, or even a television or radio ministry. What Chanel needed, she always found in the teaching and preaching of the Word at Great Deliverance COGIC.

Chanel was only ashamed that she wasn't responding as she knew she should in her marriage. She shuddered to think about where she would be without the love of Christ and the love of those who shared His love with her.

As Chanel carried Zachary while he slept soundly, she walked with effort through the double doors of the sanctuary. There, she found Elder Hightower bending on his knees to pray. When he heard one of the doors swing open, he got up and greeted Chanel.

"Hey, there, daughter! It's good to see you and the baby." He patted her and took Zachary from her arms. The Hightowers refused to see Zachary in any other way but as a baby, and it made Chanel feel like Zachary was really their grandchild.

"Pastor, it's so good to see you. Is Zachary heavy enough for you?"

"Wouldn't be too good if he was light; no good for a boy to be too light," he chuckled heartily. Then gently laid him on one of the pews.

"You were going to pray? Because I don't want to disturb you."

"We can go to my office to talk if you like, or you're welcome to pray with me?"

"Oh, sure," Chanel answered as she placed her coat under Zachary's head and walked up to the altar.

He reached from behind the podium to remove his bottle of anointing oil. As she raised her hands, he asked as he anointed her head, "Do you have anything special you'd like to pray about?"

After taking a couple of seconds to gather her thoughts, she confessed, "Well, I'm confused about my marriage right now, and I just need wisdom to know how to handle it. You know the same prayer I've prayed for years, Pastor. I want Tommy to fellowship here with me and Zachary."

Before he knelt down with her at the altar, he asked, "Ya' know that Satan comes to steal and destroy?" She nodded. "Ya' know that God is not the author of confusion?" She nodded again. He placed one hand on her shoulder and closed his eyes, which Chanel knew meant he had a Word from the Lord for her.

She shut her eyes and let her pastor prophesy to her. "Ya' resisted that temptation, but your work is just beginnin'." Chanel's stomach dropped. She had resisted Antonio, and she thanked the Lord for that.

He continued, "Ya' got to forgive and recognize that we all need the grace and mercy of God. You can't be set free unless you forgive. All the pain, all the hurt, all the loss." He paused for a moment and tears began to roll down Chanel's face. She had resisted the temptation, but she hadn't come close to forgiving. "God knows. He cares for you, daughter. Forgive and you'll be set free from the bondage you've been in for much of your life."

Chanel knew exactly what the Lord wanted. It wasn't just Tommy that she needed to forgive either. With her eyes shut tightly, she could see her mother's face. She knew that she had to find a way to forgive, but she didn't know how to begin to open the wound that had been bandaged so long.

CHAPTER 13

Sherese

Have I not commanded thee? Be strong and of a
good courage; be not afraid, neither be thou dismayed:
for the Lord thy God is with thee withersoever thou goest.

Joshua 1:9

Seven…eight…nine. Nothing was working. Fourteen…fifteen…
sixteen. Not moving out of Sydney's into her own new apartment.
Twenty-one…twenty-two…twenty-three. Not avoiding her parents.
Twenty-nine…thirty…thirty-one. Not avoiding Sydney or Sherese. Not
eating, not sleeping, not clubbing, not working, and not even exer-
cising. Sherese sat up, exhausted, not able to do anymore than thirty-
one sit-ups.

There were times that she was grateful for her naturally slender
body, and this was one of them she thought while she wiped the
sweat as it rolled down her neck and gulped down the bottled water,
thirsty and drained. Exercise was an activity Sherese despised, but
she would try just about anything to feel like herself again instead of
like a stranger.

She picked up her phone and braced herself to listen to today's
message from her mother.

"Sher, this is Mama. I know how upset you must be, but I'm gonna
keep callin' till you pick up. Your sister says she spoke to you briefly

yesterday and that you're okay, but I need to see or talk to you myself." There was a brief pause. "I've been over to your new apartment since the first day Sydney gave me your address. I thought I heard the television on yesterday, but I don't figure you'd let me and your daddy wait out in the hall while you were in there. Well, Mama and Daddy love you, honey. Call us. Please."

Sherese slammed the phone down into its base. Sydney had a lot of nerve giving her the phone number and address. What did she want from her anyway? Her mother had already ruined her life as far as Sherese was concerned.

After she showered and changed, she logged on to her computer as she had been doing for the last several days and stared nervously at the name. ROSA HARRISON, 3481 PINEVIEW AVE, NATCHEZ, MISSISSIPPI 39401 / UNLISTED PHONE NUMBER. Sherese just wanted to see the face that had given her away because she was too drunk, drugged, or just plain selfish to care for her.

The only thing holding her back was money. She hadn't been on her job long enough to build up any substantial savings, especially since she had moved into her own place. Sherese had even thought about selling something, but the only asset that she had worth anything was her car, which wasn't an option since she would need it to make the twenty-hour trip to Mississippi. Sydney had money, and she would almost certainly let her borrow some. Sherese just couldn't stand asking Sydney for anything because then Sydney felt like she had the right to control the situation. Then it hit her. She would ask Chanel.

Although Chanel hadn't mentioned anything about it to Sherese, she knew that Sydney pretty much told her everything. In addition, she always had money—maybe not quite as much as Sydney, but she was doing well financially even with her husband's unemployment.

Sherese dialed Chanel's café without hesitation.

Chanel answered, "Anchored in the Rock Café, may I help you?"

"Chanel, it's me, Sher."

"Hold on one quick second, Sher." Sherese could hear Chanel giving Lena instructions. "Lena, hold down the front. I'm going in the back so I can hear. Just let me know if you need me."

Sherese hadn't spoken to her since she found out about the adoption, so she knew Chanel was anxious to talk to her.

"What's up, Sher? Girl, I've been so worried about you." Chanel went to the back room for silence.

"Well, I know Syd told you about all the drama," Sherese said, trying to sound as nonchalant as she could.

"Yeah, I know it's kind of rough knowing that things aren't exactly what they appeared to be but, baby, let me tell you this, nothin' ever is. I've been calling to let you know just that." Chanel sighed. "You know I'm here for you."

"I know that. You've always treated me like a little sister, and I'm thankful for your friendship. As far as the adoption, the whole thing has got me questioning everything about myself and my family."

"What do you mean?" Chanel said with genuine concern.

"It's gonna sound crazy, I guess, but questions like, Who am I? Why am I here? Why did my mom give me up? Why didn't my parents tell me about the whole adoption thing, you know?"

"Yeah, I see what you're saying."

Sherese continued, "I mean, it's got me asking myself who does really love me and have my best interest at heart? All these years of my parents riding me about this and that—for what? They can't even be honest with me? Then, it's not even mentioning the whole deal about who my biological father is. Did Syd tell you that apparently Aunt Rosa doesn't even know? "

"I'm living proof that you can still come out okay even if the parents who gave you birth drop the ball. I'm not sayin' you weren't dealt a big one, Sherese, but from where I'm standing, being adopted by an aunt and uncle who love you more than life is no small blessing. No matter how out of control everything may seem right now, just know that the Lord is still in control." Chanel paused for a moment and continued. "You're a beautiful person, Sher, inside and out, but you need to get saved. It takes that and then some. Like your daddy says—"

Sherese interrupted, "I *know*, I *know*, 'Lot of good folk gonna bust hell wide open.'" She started to smile until she really thought about how real and devastating the situation she was in was.

"So, you wanna get together for dinner or something?" Chanel asked.

"No, but thanks. Actually, I was calling because I need a favor."

"Sure, anything."

"Well, it's a little awkward for me to ask, but I wanted to see if I can get a small loan. I wanna see my biological mother."

"Okay," Chanel responded deliberately, encouraging Sherese to continue.

"The thing is, she lives in Natchez, Mississippi. If it wouldn't be too much to ask, I just need a couple of hundred dollars in cash to carry. I have my credit card for gas and hotels."

"Girl, of course. You know I got you covered, but why in the world are you driving? Isn't that a day or two away in a car?"

"I know all that. I'll be fine."

"Why don't you let me get you a plane ticket?" Chanel asked.

"No, but thanks. I'm sort of looking forward to the drive to clear my head. Besides, I'm going to break it up by staying overnight at least two nights on the way there and two nights on the way back at a hotel. The drive will be good for me."

"What about work? What about Sydney and your mama and daddy? Do they know you're intending on doing this?"

"As far as work goes, I can take off and make up the time when I get back. I just don't get paid when I don't work. About my parents, no, they don't know, and I don't want them to right now. Please don't tell Sydney, because if you tell her, she'll never keep it from them."

"You're makin' it hard on a sister, Sher. When are you leaving? And remember to travel on the best routes. Don't try to take a shorter route and be off in some no man's land," Chanel worried.

"Hold up, Chanel. I know you're worried, but please don't be. I'm calm, rational, and I'll be safe. I have the trip all mapped out, and I've even made reservations for my hotel stays."

"All right, so when are you leaving?"

"Tomorrow?"

"Tomorrow?" Chanel asked in disbelief.

"If tomorrow is a problem for you—"

Chanel interrupted, "That's not the issue. I can give you the money right now. I just didn't know it was so soon."

"Yeah, I've been giving everything a lot of thought," she sighed. "Rosa doesn't know I'm coming, but I want to take her off guard. My life is upside down, and all because that woman gave me up. How could anything be more important than your child?" She waited for a few seconds for a response from Chanel, but she stayed quiet.

Sherese continued, "I can almost understand my mama and daddy's position, but what Rosa has done is just unforgivable. Why should I suffer while she has no consequences for her actions? I want her to at least look me straight in my eyes and explain to me why."

"Trust me, Sher, I know you probably don't want to hear this, but the adoption really could've been the best thing for you. You don't know what your mother's life was or is like. I know I had many days as a child when I wished my mother would've taken us to somebody else to raise. She probably would have, but there was nobody. Besides, it probably made her feel better to torture me and Ramone."

"It's weird because I've always felt so bad about what you've been through and about your relationship with your mother, not knowing I had no relationship with my own mother."

"Wait one minute, Sher. You may not have a relationship with your biological mother, but honey, your real mother is Darlene Hightower. She's the one who deserves the title of mother. Remember how I told you that I've never called Nyla Mom?"

"Yeah."

"You know the reason. That woman did very little mothering with me. I can safely say that your mother, Darlene, has done a lot more mothering than Nyla ever has."

Tears filled Sherese's eyes. "I just feel like they lied to me. I mean, it was a lie of omission."

"Your parents are human, Sherese. I don't know all of their reasons for not telling you, but love was the motivation. You can't just look at the bottom line all the time. Sometimes you have to look at the intentions. You can forgive things a lot better when you know there were never bad intentions."

"Yeah, I guess you've given me a lot to think about. Right now, I just need time to absorb all this." Chanel's worth to Sherese was immeasurable because she had a way of telling her like it was without being condescending toward Sherese as Sydney often seemed to be.

"You take your time to think about everything, but let me add, the negative consequences of being raised by your biological mother are endless. My brother is dead because my *biological* mother opted to keep us. Girl, I know you think nobody understands what you're going through, but just look at my brother as a possibility of what could've happened."

Through her sobs, she said, "You're right, Chanel."

"I'm not tryin' to be right, Sher. I just want to give you another side, you know, somethin' to think about. Now, when do you want the money?"

"How about I drop by your house in the morning?"

"That's fine. Do you think five hundred dollars will be enough?"

"That's way too much. I was just thinking of maybe three hundred."

"That settles it, five hundred it is."

She smiled again. "Love you, Chanel."

"Chin up, Sher. Love ya' too," Chanel answered as she hung up.

Reaching under her bed, Sherese pulled out her suitcase and began packing for the longest trip she'd ever taken alone so she could come face-to-face with her mother.

CHAPTER 14

Sydney

Whereas ye know not what shall be on the morrow.
For what is your life? It is even a vapour, that appeareth
for a little time, and then vanisheth away.

James 4:14

After Sydney brushed around the headstone that marked where Vance's body lay, the familiar feelings of indignation swept over her whole being as it did every day when Sydney visited the cemetery. How could a life with such promise and meaning dwindle to nothing but this? Sydney smoothed her petite hands across the cold gray granite that his name was engraved upon as if she were touching him.

She kneeled on the grass crisp from winter's frost and placed a live red rose on top of the headstone. Intellectually, Sydney knew that her husband wasn't there, but she needed something to hold on to that signified his life. She often found herself fighting not to think about the decaying corpse that the grave held. The thoughts assaulted her violently and without warning. Yet, she would not stop coming to Yorkshire Cemetery. The rest of the world seemed to be going on as if Vance had never even existed, but Sydney's life was turned completely and totally upside down. She wanted things to stop or at least not take on any sort of normalcy.

While even Vance's loved ones were beginning to be able to get together and reminisce about their experiences and special times with Vance, Sydney could not. She wasn't ready to talk about him in the past tense. There was too much unfinished business he had left behind. There were still too many whys left, and it seemed the more she cried out to God for answers, the more silent His voice became. She was spiritually bankrupt but too ashamed to admit it to anyone.

After lightly kissing the headstone and whispering, "I love you, baby," Sydney headed for home.

Since Sherese had moved out, Mother Houston came by so often that Sydney had given her a key. She was a widow too and knew that whether Sydney liked it or not, right now she needed to be surrounded by people who really knew what she was going through. Mother Houston's husband had passed away after nearly thirty-four years of marriage, and she understood that losing a spouse was something that could make you lose your mind, faith, or both.

As Sydney pulled into the driveway, she noticed Mother Houston's Cavalier and an old station wagon, which was unfamiliar to Sydney. When she walked in the house through the garage door, Mother Houston and a Caucasian woman, looking to be in her mid-to-late forties, greeted her while drinking tea at the kitchen table.

"Oh, baby, how are you today?" Without giving Sydney a chance to respond, Mother Houston warmly embraced her. "I know how much you like my spicy beef stew. I was just over here to bring that when you got a visitor."

"Thanks," Sydney answered as she eyed the woman who she figured must have been selling something. She couldn't stand people who tried to take advantage of the elderly, so Sydney was thankful that she had arrived when she did.

Sydney greeted the woman and Mother Houston said, "Baby, this is Ann O'Leary. She needs to talk with you about something important. I'm gonna scoot on outta here so you can get acquainted." She placed her cup and saucer in the sink and grabbed her coat and purse as fast as Sydney had ever seen her do. Sydney walked her to the door, looking puzzled at Mother Houston's reaction, but kissed her lightly on the cheek as she left.

Ann O'Leary? Her mind raced. Why did that name sound familiar? Then, she remembered. *God, no, please.* She prayed that this wasn't something to do with the Brian O'Leary who had murdered Vance. She couldn't face that today, not now.

Ann O'Leary stood up tentatively and extended a visibly shaking hand toward Sydney as she walked back into the kitchen. "Hello. I'm sorry for stopping by your home like this unannounced, but I just had to meet you. Mrs. Houston said it would be okay to come in because she figured you'd be home any minute."

Sydney looked at Mrs. O'Leary's extended hand but didn't shake it, instead asking, "Who are you?"

Mrs. O'Leary put her hand back down at her side, and answered somberly. "I am Brian O'Leary's wife."

She was dumbfounded. How could the woman have the nerve to come to her home at all, let alone without calling? She stood for a long moment before the other woman spoke.

"Mrs. Ellington, I wanted to tell you how sorry I am about your husband," she said carefully.

Sydney was immediately insulted. She acted like he had had a sudden heart attack or something, not as if her husband had murdered Vance. "Yes, I'm sorry too," Sydney spat out venomously.

"Brian's in prison or he would be here."

"Mrs. O'Leary, I don't want to be rude, but as far as I'm concerned, your husband should be underneath the prison. Furthermore, I really don't think it's a good idea for you to be here." Sydney felt her body shaking with anger.

Mrs. O'Leary hastily grabbed her worn coat on the back of the chair. "I'm sorry I came, and I can certainly understand your feelings."

As Mrs. O'Leary gathered her belongings together, Sydney examined the woman's ruddy pink skin, disheveled dirty blonde hair, and chipped nail polish. Her faded pink floral shirt didn't match her turquoise polyester pants. Obviously, she didn't have much money, but in spite of her dress, Mrs. O'Leary was rich. Mrs. O'Leary had everything because she had a living, breathing husband. She would exchange the house, the cars, and anything else to have Vance alive.

Sydney examined Mrs. O'Leary's eyes. She wanted to know what this woman wanted, yet she was afraid to know. Her eyes were riveting. Although Mrs. O'Leary's eyes were ice blue and Sydney's were brown, there was something in the woman's eyes that was familiar, reminding her of her own. She couldn't figure out what it was about their eyes that were similar, but it made her stop the woman from leaving.

Sydney's face softened a little. "What is it that brought you here, Mrs. O'Leary?"

"Ann. Please call me Ann," she said as she clung to her large vinyl handbag and jacket. "There are no words we can say to make anything better, but Brian wants you, no, *needs* you to know how very sorry he is. Mrs. Ellington, he keeps talkin' 'bout killin' himself. He says he'll never forgive himself for what he's done." She shifted her weight from one leg to the other and waited for Sydney to speak. When Sydney didn't say anything, Mrs. O'Leary continued. "You see, we have seven kids—two boys and five girls. They need him, but nothin' I say to him seems to convince him of that."

Sydney glared at her. "What is it that you want from me? You want my forgiveness. Because if you do, I'm sorry, I can't help you. I can't help him, and quite frankly, I can't even help myself." She raised her voice, and even though it quivered in anger, Sydney kept on. "You see, Mrs. O'Leary, you have your family intact while Vance and I will never get the chance to have children. I mean, can you tell me how I'm supposed to feel about a man who was so selfish that he drank until he was sloppy drunk and had the nerve to get in a semi and kill the man who meant everything to me?"

Mrs. O'Leary started to cry softly as she listened to Sydney's stinging words. While watching the grief-stricken woman gasp for air, it came to her. Sydney realized what it was about Mrs. O'Leary's eyes that reminded her of her own. Sydney saw the same kind of despair, the same kind of suffering, and the same kind of burdensome weight in the depth of Mrs. O'Leary's eyes that she saw in her reflection in the mirror every day.

"Brian has been an alcoholic since our son died when he was two years old. He drowned in the bathtub while Brian was home alone with the kids. He ran to see about one of the other kids who was crying and took longer than he meant to. When he came back, Richie was blue. He called the paramedics and did CPR and the whole bit. Nothin' worked though."

She wiped her nose with a napkin, and took a deep breath before starting again. "Brian done a terrible thing that most people would find unforgivable, but I just had to take a chance and come here. He said he had written you a lot of letters, but you never answer. He just wants you to know he's sorry, Mrs. Ellington. I'm sorry too. He was so torn up he couldn't even make any apologies or anything at the trial. He had to be medicated just to be able to sit up straight. I guess I just want you to know that Brian is not a monster. Other than his drinking, he's been a good husband and father. Like I said, he made a horrible decision to drink and to get in his semi that morning. His life will never be the same because of your husband's death." Mrs. O'Leary grabbed another napkin from the holder on the table and wiped her raw eyes and red nose.

"I don't know what to say, Ann. I can't pretend that I forgive him when I don't, but I am deeply sorry about the loss of your son."

"Thanks for hearin' me out. I'm sorry for gettin' you upset. God bless you, Mrs. Ellington."

God bless you? Sydney wondered if she was a Christian. Guilt seemed to come over her like a wave as Sydney listened to Mrs. O'Leary's attempts to start her old station wagon, until she finally she heard the engine start up. A heavy sigh escaped from her lips as relief was finally there. She was gone.

Anger raged through her—so much so that she slammed the teapot into the sink with force. She didn't want to change her mind about the monster that so carelessly killed her husband. She felt like she really couldn't make sense of Vance's death if it was an accident caused by a grieving and remorseful man. Now, who would be the enemy if she allowed herself to feel compassion for the O'Leary family? She had heard stories about people who displayed incredible acts of forgiveness over similar acts, but Sydney didn't care if she didn't meet their standard. She didn't want to forgive and she hadn't all these months. Brian O'Leary had become inhuman—a man without a heart. To Sydney, he had no real feelings, no story. It had been easy for Sydney to throw the letters away. Because of Ann O'Leary's visit, Sydney now had to attach a heart and family to him. Athough she couldn't go back to thinking of him the way that she had, she wasn't prepared to forgive either.

When she reached her bedroom, she reached inside her waste-basket to count the six letters that he had sent. Over the months, Sydney could never bring herself to use the wastebasket for anything but the letters from Brian O'Leary. She also found herself unable to empty the wastebasket filled with his unopened letters. She gathered them together, and after taping two of them together, she organized them by date, starting with the first letter.

"Lord, help me," she muttered aloud as she began reading.

Mrs. Ellington,

I know you must think I'm crazy for writing this letter, and I guess I am. I've done something that I'm ashamed of and deserve to be killed myself. Only they didn't kill me like I wanted. They took my wife and children into consideration. They took the fact that I had no prior convictions into consideration. That was funny since it was just the first time I had gotten caught drinking and driving. I had gotten away with it for so long, I guess I thought I was above the law. I thought I had it under control.

I read the article about your husband in the paper. Someone like that—I guess I don't know why I didn't die instead of him. I know you must be wondering that too. I have a high school degree and seven kids and a wife. We live in a trailer. Your husband, from what I hear, sounded like one of the movers and shakers in the city.

After I read the article in the paper about your husband, they put me on a suicide watch after I tried to cut my wrist with a plastic dinner fork. (I'm not telling you this for sympathy, but just because I want you to know the truth,) The prison therapist I'm working with said that I should write you so that I can tell you how I feel about what I've done. I'm also in a recovery program even though I know I'll never put a drink to my lips again (in or out of jail). Unlike other alcoholics, I've never said that before.

Mrs. Ellington, there are no words to say how bad I feel for what I've done. If you can't forgive me, please just know that I am truly sorry.

Sincerely,
Brian O'Leary

Sydney read all the letters he had written to her over the previous months and all were very similar in content to the first one. Although she felt a measure of pity for the man, she didn't feel like justice was served. She didn't want him to commit suicide, and yet she didn't want him to live either. Feelings she never knew she could have overtook her. Hate, rage, and even jealousy plagued her. She hated what O'Leary had done.

Sydney prayed that night for the Lord to comfort and give her peace. She also prayed that Brian O'Leary would not take his life. Although she wanted him to feel the depth of her pain, she never wanted him to die. If anything, she wanted him to suffer as she was, but it wasn't as satisfying as she had imagined. Still, she wrestled because no matter how many letters he wrote, and no matter how sorry he was, her life would never be the same as a result of the one bad decision he made. As Sydney nestled once again into Vance's side of the bed as she had every night since his death, she tried to drift off to sleep—but Ann O'Leary's grief-stricken eyes haunted her mercilessly.

CHAPTER 15

Chanel

And why beholdest thou the mote that is in thy brother's eye,
but perceivest not the beam that is in thine own eye?

Luke 6:41

Chanel was empowered by the Holy Ghost, and she knew that her strength to overcome things was nothing she could do alone. She had tried too many times in the past. Tommy had been at the studio every evening for the past week and didn't come home until two in the morning, yet Chanel was peaceful. There were no attacks and no unkind words slung his way. Even when Zachary had thrown his tantrum in the grocery store after a hard day's work, Chanel had stayed cool and was able to resist "snapping off" on him. After she got home, fed Zachary and put him to bed, Chanel turned gospel jazz on. She slipped off her shoes and sank into her overstuffed leather chair, relishing the stillness.

The phone rang and she started not to answer, but she still felt prepared to take on whatever curveballs of life the evening held until she realized it was her mother.

There was no hello. Chanel picked up the phone, only to hear, "How's my grandchile doin'?"

"Hello?" Chanel asked sarcastically, recognizing her mother's drunken voice.

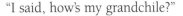

"I said, how's my grandchile?"

"Zachary is fine."

"You gettin' sassy, girl?"

Chanel took a deep breath, trying to let some of the exasperation she held in out as she answered, "What are you talkin' about?"

Instead of a simple response from her mother, she snarled, "You ain't got no problems, so don't go actin' like you can't respect me. No matter what you think of me, I am still your mama."

"Zachary is fine. Is there something else?"

"As a matter of fact, there is. We ain't got no money to pay the rent."

"Who is we?"

"Me and Charles."

"Charles?"

"He's my man." With no warning, Chanel heard a dial tone. She slammed the phone down. Chanel didn't understand why Nyla couldn't just leave her totally alone.

She went to turn off all of the lights so she could meditate, listening to the relaxing music, only when she sat back down, she noticed the small beam of light from under the office door. Chanel figured she must have left the light on. Then again, she couldn't remember the last time she had been in the office. She decided her irresponsible husband had probably left it on.

When she opened the creaky door, Chanel jumped, surprised to find Tommy on the computer. She hadn't seen his car parked in the driveway, and he hadn't made a peep for the past forty- five minutes that she had been home.

"Oh, Tommy! You scared the daylights outta me!" she said as she placed her hand on her chest and took a deep breath.

Tommy glanced up for a moment and gave Chanel a menacing look without a word spoken.

Chanel had never seen Tommy look so angry and mean. "Tommy, what's wrong?"

He refused to look at her again, while his eyes were transfixed on the computer screen.

Chanel wondered why he was tripping. She marched over toward him until fear stopped her dead in her tracks. Suddenly, she remembered her carelessness. Then, she crept closer until she stood beside him. Her heart dropped when she saw that he was reading e-mails sent between her and Antonio.

He angrily flipped his baseball cap, which had been backwards, to the front and read to her from the computer screen, "I don't see why you waste your time with a man who doesn't appreciate your inner and outer beauty. What good is he to you if he's not being a real man and supporting you? Sweetheart, you're all I can think about and I can't wait to see you tonight." Tommy fumed. "I can't wait to see you tonight?" He looked at her, demanding a response.

Immediately, Chanel backed up a distance from him. "I know it sounds bad, but nothing really happened. That was weeks ago."

Tommy angrily held up the e-mails he had apparently printed out, crumpled in his fist. He gritted his teeth. "It's right here in black-and-white, Chanel!"

Chanel couldn't stop her knees from the slight tremor that had abruptly started from nervousness. "Tommy, please let me explain. He was nothing—nobody—"

Tommy tossed the crumpled papers in her direction. "Don't play me like I'm dumb, and don't act like a victim."

Chanel had never seen Tommy this angry. She struggled to find the right words to calm him down. "Tommy, just listen for a minute. Nothing happened. He was interested in me, and I guess I just enjoyed the attention."

"*Apparently.*" Tommy shot up from his chair and pointed his finger in her face. "I'm sick of this crap, Chanel. You gonna try to play me like that? I've never even looked hard at another woman since the day we met! That chick Lena's been comin' on to me for months, and I've been struggling for a way to tell you that your little prodigy has the hots for me. I didn't so much as give her a hint that I was unhappy." He slammed his fist down on the desk and Chanel jumped. "You think it's been easy for me? Every time I turn around, you're throwin' off at me, tryin' to make me feel like less than a man. Then, you go and bring in another man?"

Chanel stood helpless and in a panic as Tommy inhaled and blew air out through his mouth noisily. "Who is he? And did you sleep with him, cause I'm almost positive you have."

Without warning, he pulled the whole computer off of the desk and violently wrestled the cords from the outlet and threw it across the room.

"Tommy! Tommy, stop! I didn't sleep with him!" She grabbed at his sleeve, and he yanked it away from her forcefully.

Before leaving the room, he hollered at her, "You're so saved, yet you don't know the first thing about the Bible. Aren't you supposed to know that sleepin' with other men when you're married is a sin? I may not be the man you want, but I've always been the man you needed. You've always just been too blind to see it!"

"Tommy! Tommy! You're right. He's nothing to me! I'm sorry!" she screamed, running to stop him. As she caught hold of his shirt again, he flung her off.

Seeing the pathetic look he gave her shamed Chanel and she bowed her head.

"Please believe me, Tommy. I didn't sleep with him," she whispered as he walked out the front door.

"Oh, God, how can this be happening?" she muttered as she held her face in her hands, crying. She sat in a stupor, not knowing what to do. *I love my husband. I love Tommy.* Until Tommy had begun reading the e-mails, she hadn't realized how much she did love him and how much she did want her marriage to work. She had spent months berating him because she hadn't agreed with his choice to pursue his music. Before she knew it, she had let her anger about one thing spiral into a lot of other unimportant things.

All at once, the important things were clear. Tommy loved her. Tommy *had* loved her, anyway. He loved Zach. He wanted them to be happy. Even with his dream of pursuing music, he had often told her, "This is for you and Zach, baby. All the days and late nights at the studio are eventually going to pay off. I'm gonna get you the biggest diamond you can imagine, and we're gonna get a nice pretty house with a housekeeper, all for you." Chanel had always looked at it as negative, but now she realized that his dreams weren't all rooted in selfishness. Like she had told Sherese, she, too, had to focus on intentions. He had never intended to hurt her by pursuing his dream. He had never meant to alienate her and make her feel that she was handling everything all alone.

Her mind raced with Tommy's redeeming qualities. He was so patient with her, so protective of her and their son. And he always thought the best of her, even when she had shown him the worst.

She had jeopardized their whole relationship for nothing. Before, she had only wanted it to work because she knew that it was the right thing to do. Now, however, she wanted it to work because she realized that there was nobody made for her as perfectly as Tommy.

It didn't matter how Chanel tried to explain. It didn't matter that she hadn't slept with Antonio. The fact was that she had lusted for another man. She told another man Tommy's flaws in an attempt to get someone on her side. Quite purposely, she had left out all of the times she had been sick and Tommy was at her beck and call. She had left out how much Tommy had done to remodel the café, diligently working to make her business look professional and upscale, despite the deteriorating neighborhood it was in. Chanel had also left out that Tommy constantly asked her if it was okay that he was pursuing his dream. She had always been agreeable and never *totally* honest with him about how much it was driving her away. There was so much more than that Chanel left out, so many wonderful things that she never told Antonio, or anyone else for that matter.

Chanel called her mother-in-law to see if she minded keeping Zachary for several days. She was relieved when Olivia told her, "Honey, you know you don't ever have to ask when it comes to me keepin' my grandchild."

She just needed to clear her head, she thought as she pulled her suitcase out to pack some things.

Chanel had rung Sherese's buzzer at least several times before she finally answered.

"Sher, what were you doing and exactly how long did you plan on makin' a sista wait?"

"Sorry, I was thinking you were Mama and Daddy at first. Sorry I didn't come by yesterday. I couldn't pack my things as quickly as I thought I could."

"Just let me in," Chanel said, agitated.

As Sherese opened the door, she looked questioningly at Chanel's suitcase and two small bags.

"Hey, what's up with the luggage?"

"How about some company for the ride to Mississippi?"

Sherese was stunned. "You're jokin, right?"

"As a matter of fact, I'm not. Olivia's cool with keeping Zachary for a few days. I already ran by there and dropped his clothes off and told him goodbye. Girl, that boy didn't even act like he cared. He loves being over there. As for work, Lena's got the café under control, and I'm free for at least several days."

"Please tell me you didn't say anything to Syd?" Sherese asked skeptically.

"No way, girl. Sydney's in another one of her 'leave me alone' moods, so I haven't talked to her in a few days. So, you up for me goin' or what?"

Chanel could tell that Sherese hadn't even considered anyone going with her. When Sherese didn't immediately respond to her, Chanel said, "Look, I know it's probably not a good idea. I know it's a very personal thing, but I was worried about you."

"Please don't. I *told* you that I'll be fine."

Chanel leaned on the counter, disappointed that she wasn't needed for the trip.

Sherese blurted out, "I want you to go after all. I just don't want you to put yourself out because the money is more than enough to help."

Chanel cheered up. She was glad that Sherese had changed her mind. It would be safer anyway. "Well, what time do we leave?"

"Now is as good a time as any," Sherese answered, as she tidied up before leaving. While they packed the car up, Sherese asked, "Do you think Sydney will be okay without us for a few days?"

"I was thinking about the same thing," Chanel admitted.

"Tell me the truth, Chanel. Do you think I should tell her?"

"Well, there is always that chance that she'll tell your parents, but I think that Sydney will understand and respect your wishes."

"So tell her then?"

"I guess my gut feeling is, yeah. Sydney needs to know so that she can at least tell your parents not to worry."

"I guess we're gonna make a quick trip to my sister's then."

On the way to Sydney's, Chanel's mind was racing with thoughts of Tommy. She hoped that Sherese hadn't noticed, but she realized that her unhappiness was evident when Sherese asked, "Chanel, you and Tommy okay?"

"You've got enough to worry about without dealing with the mess me and Tommy are always kicking up."

"What's going on?"

Chanel tried to sound like the problem between her and her husband was trivial because she didn't want to add any stress to her friend. "In a nutshell, I made a stupid mistake and got busted. Just pray for us, girl." Chanel changed the subject. "So, you got any prospects for a man in your life?"

"No and I'm not looking. I've got enough drama right now. Don't need no more!" Sherese shook her head vehemently as she turned the volume up on the radio, letting J Moss' new song blast as they sang along with the chorus.

Before they knew it, the two were at Sydney's. Sherese braced herself for her sister's opposition to the plan, but it didn't matter what anyone said, she was headed for Mississippi.

A light snow began to fall, signaling that the shift from fall to winter was complete as Sherese and Chanel walked to Sydney's front door.

"Hey, what are you two doing here?" Sydney was instantly suspicious because she wasn't up for another confrontation about the way she was handling Vance's death.

"Are you gonna let us in, or what?" Chanel asked.

"Sorry, of course, come in."

"Are you busy, Syd?" Sherese questioned.

"And if I were?" Sydney had her hands on her hips.

Chanel interrupted, "If you were, that's too bad!" Chanel pulled off her shoes and sat as if she were challenging Sydney for a fight.

Sydney's face held a Mona Lisa-like smile. "Well, fortunate for you, Chanel, I don't happen to be busy. I just don't get why nobody seems to call first. No respect, I tell you."

As Sherese took her shoes off, she thanked God for Chanel since she could be the buffer she often was between the two sisters. "I'm sorry I didn't call. I just wanted to talk to you for a few minutes."

"So, shoot," Sydney offered while they entered the living room to sit with Chanel.

"I'm not asking for your approval, Syd. I just want to clarify that first, but I did feel that I should tell you what my plans are."

"What plans?" Sydney's eyebrows were raised, and Chanel could tell by her tone that she was offended.

Noticing the look on Sydney's face, Sherese tried to start again. "What I'm saying is that I'm going to Mississippi, and you can't stop me. I gotta get my head straightened out, and I want to meet Rosa, I mean Aunt Rosa."

"Okay." Sydney answered plainly.

"Okay?"

"Okay. I figured you might need to do that. Listen, Sher, I don't know what I'd do if I were in your position, but I was thinking that I'd probably need to meet her."

Chanel smiled knowingly, nodding her head at Sydney's approval of the trip.

"When are you leaving?" Sydney asked.

"Chanel and I are about to get on the road now."

"Chanel? You're going? Today?"

Chanel could tell that Sydney's feelings were hurt. She knew that Sydney was probably wondering how Sherese could ask Chanel before her.

Chanel tried to clear the air. "Sherese mentioned she was leaving and I thought, 'Why not go with her?' I imposed myself on your dear sister, but I just need a little break. So, why don't you come too? It'll be just like old times except now, instead of Sherese tagging along with us, we'll be tagging along with her."

Sherese's eyes widened at the tease as she looked at Chanel. "You two realize that this is not a vacation I'm going on, don't you?"

"Of course, we do, Sher. What time does your flight leave?" Sydney asked.

"We're driving. The car is ready to go, and we're all packed. I just wanted to let you know that we were leaving because, as you know, I haven't spoken to Mama and Daddy yet. I'm not ready for that, but I don't want them to worry about me either."

"Since you're driving, I guess I really could tag along. Mr. Neal's wanted me to take time off, and I'm sure that I can get Sister Gilmore to conduct choir rehearsal for me. That is, if it's okay if I go. Are you sure you don't mind me coming?"

Chanel noticed that Sherese's heart seemed to sink. Chanel also knew that Sherese didn't want or feel that she needed Sydney's company, but Chanel felt that Sydney should come although she didn't exactly know why.

With a defeated attitude, Sherese finally responded. "Come on, Syd. We'll wait while you pack."

Before Sydney went upstairs, she remembered, "Oh, Sher, you and Chanel will be back for the dedication of the new building on the Sunday after next, won't you? Daddy would be crushed if we didn't make it."

When Chanel realized that Sherese was at a loss for words, she answered for her. "Girl, you know we wouldn't miss it! Let me see, today is Tuesday, so we'll be in Mississippi by Thursday and stay several days—that's plenty of time to make it back and rest some. Now hurry up, girl! We don't have all day!"

"Oh, one more thing!" Sydney added.

"What on earth could that be?" Sherese asked with sarcasm.

"I'm gonna call this hotel I remember in Natchez. It's on the water, and it's so pretty. Don't worry about the rooms, guys—my treat."

A surge of excitement seemed to stir in Sydney as she dashed upstairs to get her belongings packed.

Sherese rolled her eyes. "Fantastic."

"Don't be like that," Chanel corrected.

"How could you?" Sherese fumed.

"How could I what?"

"I wasn't even gonna tell Syd. Now you gonna ask her to come? You knew that wasn't cool with me!"

"Maybe I felt led," Chanel said softly.

"Led by who?" Sherese demanded.

"Led by the Holy Ghost, Sher, who else?"

Chanel knew that Sherese couldn't stand the way her family members often excused their behavior by saying that God, Jesus, or the Holy Ghost made them do it. Sherese thought it was as bad as saying, "The devil made me do it."

Sherese sulked and mumbled, "We'll see about that."

"Yes, we will see it. We'll all see it," Chanel knew in her spirit that the trip they were about to embark upon together was no accident. She knew that God had ordained this journey even though she didn't know how or why.

CHAPTER 16

Sherese

Thou knowest my downsitting and mine uprising, thou
understandest my thought afar off. Thou compassest my path
and my lying down, and art acquainted with all my ways.

Psalm 139:2,3

"It's old, but it's good, girl."

"Mmmmm. Mmmmm. Mmmmm. Juanita Bynum is just too anointed. It don't make a bit of sense," Chanel chuckled as she ejected the "No More Sheets" cassette, whose tattered sticker revealed its old age.

"It doesn't matter how many times I hear it, it's new every time," Sydney said.

Sherese, who was at the wheel, rolled her eyes, aggravated that Sydney and Chanel had taken control over the sound system in her car and her trip. She had planned on listening to her Destiny's Child CD, but Sydney had brought most of her enormous collection of sermons and gospel music.

Although they had asked her if she minded them playing a couple of sermons, Sherese had reluctantly agreed since she knew that they would vehemently oppose her R&B.

Juanita Bynum's message had been more difficult to ignore than some of the other messages she had heard in the last five hours. Guilt had overwhelmed her about her night with Jack as she listened to Bynum's message of salvation, purity, and deliverance. Sherese knew that she was being convicted, and she didn't want to be turned to a reprobate mind. However, she wasn't compelled to repent for all of her sins either. God already knew her heart, so there was no use, as far as she was concerned, lying to herself and God.

Sydney interrupted Sherese's thoughts, "Hey, get off on that exit. I can't hold it anymore."

After moving over to the right lane, Sherese pulled onto the exit, entering the nearest gas station. "This is a good point to stop cause we're gonna be getting off on 271 in a few," Sherese said, as she tried to examine her MapQuest directions.

Chanel snatched the directions. "Are you outta your natural mind tryin' to read these things while you're drivin?"

Sherese gave a scowl but didn't reply. All she thought about was what a mistake it was for them to come with her. *The trip would have been so much better without them,* she thought while pulling into an empty space.

"You can go ahead. I'm gonna wait here." Sherese said as she sat sulking.

"I'll just be a minute, and I can take the wheel when I get back," Sydney offered.

"Naw, that's okay." The last thing that Sherese needed was to have either one of them controlling the wheel, although she knew she couldn't drive forever.

Ejecting the Bishop G.E. Patterson CD was the first thing Sherese did after they left, relieved for the welcome silence. She had heard enough sermons to last her for the rest of her life. Not only were her childhood memories filled with countless Sunday morning sermons, but she also could never forget the preaching at Young People's Willing Workers on Sunday evenings right before Sunday night service. Forever etched in her brain were the Bible studies every

Tuesday night, choir rehearsals on Thursday night, and more preaching again at Friday night services. The older Sherese got, the more convinced she was that the people in her dad's church were weak. That was the only way she could justify people needing that much church.

She could also never understand how Sydney could love church as much as she did. Although Sherese did view most of the church members as needy, she didn't see her parents or Sydney that way. She just didn't understand her sister's need to be so immersed in church all of the time. Sherese had told herself more than once that if she had the brain her sister had, there would be no limits to where she would go in her career. She would never let church activities interfere with her future.

The only thing was that Sherese didn't have the 4.0 transcripts her sister had to back her up. Graduating with a low C grade average and several jobs on her résumé was now a source of frustration for her. She had often secretly wondered if her parents had expected less of her than Sydney. Now, things were different. Knowing that she was adopted made sense. Maybe Sherese had struggled with school and church because of her genes. Had Sydney gotten the best of the Hightower and Harrison genes, while she was left with Rosa's genes and those of some man no one even knew?

Thinking about who her biological father was, was something Sherese tried to steer clear of but she couldn't avoid thinking about the father she had known all of her life. An evening conversation with her father when she was eight years old came to Sherese's mind as she thought about the man she admired more than any man in the world.

"When's takeoff, Sher?" her father teased.

"Daddy, stop." He always joked that his daughters were going to fly away when their hair stood up and needed to be combed.

"We got church tonight, and we got to drive; no flyin' tonight."

Sherese giggled.

As her father got her brush and smoothed down her coarse hair, Sherese asked him, "Daddy, why we always gotta go to church?"

"Because God made us to worship and serve Him. That's what we do by goin' to church. That's why the good Lord created us," he answered as he concentrated on smoothing the coarse dark hair framing her face.

"I get tired of bein' in church all the time. Can't we serve the Lord without goin' to church sometimes?"

"I reckon we can, but the Lord's given me a job to do at the church. You're my daughter, and I need you to be there to support me. You understand?"

Sherese hadn't understood, but she nodded anyway.

The words "You're my daughter" echoed in her head over and over again. Her saved, sanctified, Holy Ghost-filled father had lied, hadn't he? She really wasn't his daughter. But who was her real father? Sherese didn't know if she would ever get the answers she so desperately needed to try to make some semblance of order in her life, but if she prayed for anything, she prayed that she would find out. A hot tear ran down her face.

Spending the last few weeks longing for the events of that terrible day in her parents' living room to rewind wouldn't make things go back to where they were. Now she had the answer to why she was so different; but now, she also had so many more difficult questions looming over her. It felt too heavy a burden.

The light tapping on Sherese's window startled her as she tried to put her game face back on, ready to deal with Sydney and Chanel and their deluge of sermons.

"We're freezing!" Chanel called from outside the car as Sherese unlocked the car, dreading their hasty return.

"It's not supposed to be this cold yet. I can't wait to get to Mississippi. It's still gonna be pretty nice there."

Before Chanel buckled herself in, she asked, "You sure you don't want one of us to drive?"

Sherese started to say no, but she changed her mind when she thought that trying to get some sleep could drown the sermons out. "I guess I could use a little sleep." Sherese slid out of the driver's seat and went to the backseat.

Chanel happily took the driver's seat and pulled back onto the interstate.

Sydney raised her voice. "Girl, we gotta stop at that Waffle House. I need to get some of those hash browns—covered, smothered, and melted—or whatever they call 'em."

"That does sound better than these pork rinds," Chanel answered, holding up her bag of half-eaten pork skins. She pulled off at the exit to turn around.

"Oh, Sher, I'm sorry. You don't mind, do you?" Sydney asked.

"Why should I mind?" Sherese answered as she slumped lower in her seat.

Catching Sherese's disapproval, Sydney turned toward Chanel and quietly told her, "It's okay. We don't have to stop here. I can just get something later. We need to go ahead and get on the road anyway."

"Listen, I'm already here, and I ain't gettin' ready to go back now. Sherese, just chill out. We gotta eat or else we won't be any good when we get there."

Exasperated even more, Sherese managed to stammer out, "I'm straight."

As they entered the small restaurant, the heavy aroma of cigarette smoke met them and followed them to the no smoking area. The black-and-white checkered tile that boldly decorated the back and side walls of the restaurant made it look cheap to Sherese, and to make matters worse, she was freezing.

When they sat at the booth, Sherese asked irritably, "Is the air conditioning on in here or what?"

Chanel and Sydney silently agreed to ignore Sherese's complaints as they browsed the laminated menu stuck between the napkin holder and the salt and pepper shakers. In minutes, a middle-aged woman with striking strawberry-blonde, bouffant hair and blue eyes greeted them. "Heya, girls. What'll you have today?"

Sherese and Chanel ordered without hesitation, both anxious to get back on the road. While Sydney browsed the menu, Chanel interjected. "Syd, why are you even looking at the menu? I thought you knew what you wanted."

"I know, but it's just like when you go to McDonald's, you still want to look at the menu." She looked up to the waitress. "I'll have hash browns, covered and smothered. I'll also have coffee with two creams and three sugars."

"Did you see that blue eye shadow that lady had on?" Sherese asked, talking about the waitress.

Without warning, tears began to well up in Sydney's eyes.

"What's wrong, Syd?" Sherese asked, afraid that her complaints had pushed Sydney to her limit.

Sydney nodded, but Sherese was afraid because she could count the times she had seen her sister cry, even including when Vance died.

"Are you okay, sweetie?" Chanel asked, handing her a tissue from her purse.

In broken speech, Sydney tried to explain her outburst of emotion. "It's just that Vance and I made stopping at the Waffle House one of our little traditions whenever we traveled. He always ordered the same thing and always put two creams and three sugars in his coffee." She sniffed, looking down toward her lap. "Everything is so different now. I feel out of place everywhere without him."

As Sydney wiped her nose, Sherese also tried not to cry for her sister because she finally felt like she could relate, at least a little, to how her sister was feeling.

Sydney continued, "I felt so bad because I couldn't remember the sound of his voice yesterday. I kept trying to hear it in my mind, but I was struggling, you know?" Chanel and Sherese nodded but remained silent.

Sydney continued, "But, just now when I placed my order, which was what Vance always ordered, I heard his voice in my head, you know? And it was with total clarity." She forced a smile. "I know I'm crying, but it's not all bad. I'm just relieved that I still remember that deep, calming voice of his." She took a deep breath and whispered, "I don't ever want to forget it." She covered her face with her napkin as she quietly allowed a few more tears to escape before gaining her composure.

Chanel tried to ease the tension of the moment and blurted out, "Boy, I can't believe that brotha actually ate at the Waffle House. With all those monogrammed sleeves, sterling cufflinks, and starchy suits, I just can't see Vance coming into a place that's more me and Tommy's speed!"

Sydney uncovered her tear-streaked face and stared at Chanel. Then, Sydney couldn't help but to return the smile that Chanel offered as the tension lifted.

After the waitress gave them their orders, Chanel prayed, "Father, we thank You for Your presence in our lives. We know that You know what we need even before we ask for it. Move by Your power and by Your Spirit on this trip, Lord. Strengthen us. Encourage our hearts where we feel faint. Help, Lord, as only You can. Now, bless and sanctify our food for the nourishment of our bodies, in Jesus' mighty name. Thank God. Amen."

Back in the car, Sherese thought she would surely explode if her sister and Chanel kept listening to sermons and gospel music for the remainder of the trip. As much as they irritated her, something wouldn't let her say anything to Sydney or Chanel since they would surely perceive her as Satan himself. Instead, she continued to pout, still trying to tune out the Bishop Patterson sermons and spiritual conversation.

Staring at the open fields with an occasional worn barn or animals decorating the otherwise blank fields, Sherese wished she could paint. She pulled her sketchbook out and began to try to draw some of what she saw, but her mind was too crowded and disturbed to do a decent job.

"Shoot." She ripped the partly sketched-on piece of paper and crumbled it into a ball.

Sydney crunched her ice loudly and said with a mouthful, "For goodness sake, Sher, you might as well cuss if you're gonna say that. What's wrong with you anyway?"

"Nothing except for that annoying crunching you're doing."

Sydney frowned but ignored her sister as she continued her engaging conversation with Chanel.

Sherese couldn't help replaying the nightmarish scene with her parents over and over again. Her mind kept repeating the same images of her parents' anguished faces and the words they had said that changed her whole perception of who she was. A faint, but familiar haunting stirred in her soul and overwhelmed her. She remembered having the same feeling when she and D'Andre separated, but now it took hold of her with a grip of such force, it scared her.

How could she make sense of her life or anything for that matter? Pretending as if she were okay wasn't an option anymore. As sorry as she felt for Sydney's loss, Sherese couldn't begin to help her while she was drowning in a sea of grief herself.

With the exception of Evangelist Joyce Rogers' preaching, silence enveloped the car as night fell. The darkness paralleled her dark emotional desperation. The pain was too much for her to bear, and now, she didn't want to meet Rosa. Who Rosa was and why she had given her away was not important anymore. Nothing in her life had any real purpose or meaning.

Sherese had clung desperately to the hope that her new job and apartment would bring her peace and comfort within herself. She had even thought that getting married in the future to a good man and having kids was something that would complete her. But what could she offer to a potential husband or children? How could she offer anything to anyone when she didn't even know who she really was? She *needed* to know who her mother was. Maybe she would never know who her father was, but she had to have questions answered from her mother. Sydney was so much like her mother—maybe Sherese was like hers. Sherese needed to know if she looked like her, talked like her, or maybe even walked like her. For years, she had wondered what it was that was missing from her life. Her parents had always told her it was the Lord that was missing, but now she knew the truth—it was her mother.

"Sher, you all right back there?" Sydney asked, clearly wondering about the quiet. "Sher? Sher?"

Chanel turned the CD player off and glanced back at Sherese. When Chanel also noticed that something was terribly wrong with Sherese, she asked, "Hey, what's up back there?"

"I wanna go back. Turn around," Sherese demanded as she stared out of the rear window. Sherese knew she was being irrational, but the fear of meeting her mother, a woman who had given her up, overwhelmed her. While thinking in the car, she began to consider what she would do or say if Rosa still didn't want anything to do with her. She didn't know how she could handle that kind of rejection.

"What do you mean you want to turn back?" Sydney asked in disbelief.

"Girl, did I miss something? What happened?" Chanel glanced at Sydney while trying to stay focused on the road.

"You both heard what I said. This is all one big mistake. First, the trip was supposed to be alone, and second, I changed my mind, which wouldn't have been a problem if neither one of you would've forced your way in my plans!"

Sydney opened her mouth to respond, but Chanel reached over and lightly tapped her as if to say, 'Don't say anything to her.'

"I don't know what's wrong with you, Sherese, but we're not turning around."

When Sherese realized that Sydney and Chanel weren't going to take the bait to engage in an argument with her, she leaned her head on the seat back, closed her eyes, and said, "Pull over at the next rest stop. I wanna drive again."

CHAPTER 17

Sydney

When I said, My foot slippeth; thy mercy, O Lord, held me up.

Psalm 94:18

Once Sydney and Chanel were sure that Sherese was asleep soundly in their hotel suite, they agreed to meet in the sitting area in the hotel lobby to discuss Sherese's sudden desire to go back to Rochester.

"I thought she would never go to sleep," Chanel said as they walked to the elevator.

"I guess I just can't believe it was that difficult to talk her into staying overnight in a hotel. We've been driving all day and most of this evening." Sydney yawned and continued, "She's always been headstrong, but tonight she was unbearable. I keep trying to put myself in her position, but I just can't. I don't know what I would do if it were me."

As Chanel pushed the lobby button once they got into the elevator, she responded, "Well, I have tried to put myself in her shoes, and I don't think it's as bad as it seems. It's not like she was given up to strangers. She was given to her aunt and uncle, her blood. Girl, if Sherese's biological mother is anything like Nyla, she should be thanking the good Lord for His protection."

As the elevator stopped and the little buzz sounded, letting them know it was all right to go out, Sydney said, "Yeah, I guess I never thought about it exactly in that way, but I'm still stuck on the fact that Mama and Daddy kept it from her for so long. It's almost like they should've just left things the way they were."

Sydney seated herself on one of the floral paisley-patterned chairs. "I guess it's just the shock of it all. When Mama and I spoke last, she said that she and Daddy actually agreed at one time that they would never tell Sherese. Only a few family members know in Mississippi, so I guess they never really thought it might get out. I guess they changed their mind when they found out Rosa was sick. Mama said she'll be coming to Natchez next month, so whatever it is that's wrong with Rosa must be pretty bad."

"I guess we'll find out when Sherese meets her, huh?"

Chanel watched the hotel patrons walk up and down the halls while she talked. "I don't see how anyone could have better parents than you and Sherese. The thing is, when the shock of the whole thing wears off, Sherese will be happy that she's had the life she's had. Trust me on that one."

Sydney smiled uneasily. She knew her parents were the best parents in the world, but she wasn't so sure how the whole thing would turn out with Sherese. Usually, Sydney was so sure about herself and things concerning Sherese. Now, she searched for help from her dearest friend. "Do you think we should try to get her to go on to Mississippi?"

"Honey, I really don't think that Sherese is going to get some kind of understanding of things if she doesn't try to find her biological mother. I know she's sayin' she wants to go back to Rochester, but she's just afraid. I think she'll feel better when she meets Rosa."

"You know, Chanel, I think she'll get a measure of peace of some sort meeting Rosa, but I've known for a long time that Sherese has been running from the Lord. Daddy and Mama have always said that she has a special anointing on her life. I really don't know why that girl has so much anger towards the saints, but I think she's misdirected her feelings towards the Lord too."

Chanel chimed in. "Lord knows that some of them folks in church ain't saints."

"Yeah, you're right, but it seems like Sherese can't get ahold of that. She's always taken things to heart. I'm just sorry that she's allowed it to hinder her relationship with the Lord. I mean, I don't want to judge her, but I just think that if she ever needed that relationship before, she needs it now."

"The best thing we can do is to pray for her. God has a way of allowing trials to open up our understanding of who He is. He's in control. As much as we may hurt for Sher, we just need to pray that this whole experience will draw her closer to Him, not further away."

Sydney knew this was true not only in Sherese's situation, but in her own as well. Her cries, pleas, and questions to the Lord for understanding seemed to go unanswered, but Sydney knew deep inside that the Lord was still there, caring for her despite her lack of understanding. Even in the midst of this ordeal with Sherese, the Lord seemed to be calling her out of the deep pit of despair to clarify her purpose.

"I can't let Sher allow Satan to get the victory in this, as bad as it all may seem. He's really trying to destroy us."

Chanel raised her eyebrows. "He can try all he wants, but you just remember that the devil can only do what God allows him to do. He's stronger than the world that's against us. We just have to trust that—" Her cell phone rang, interrupting her sentence. "Hold on, girl. It's Tommy."

Sydney strolled the lobby, admiring the prints of Monet and Renoir that lined the walls. Whenever she saw beautiful paintings, she couldn't help thinking of how gifted her sister was. She knew that Sherese was just as gifted as many renowned artists, but Sydney only wished that her sister thought so. When she glanced over in Chanel's direction to see if she was off of the phone, she saw Chanel's hands covering her face.

Walking toward her carefully, Sydney asked, "Everything okay?"

Chanel lightly massaged her temples. "Things are as okay as they're gonna be, for right now at least. Tommy and I just need some space."

"What do you mean by space? What's going on? You're not still talking to that guy Antonio, are you?" Sydney eyed her suspiciously.

Chanel's looked away, visibly embarrassed. "Syd, I totally cut it off with him. It was crazy for me to even think that I could have a friendship with him instead of just facing the issues in my relationship with Tommy."

"It was just friendship wasn't it? Chanel, right?"

Chanel made eye contact with Sydney. "I have to admit that we got closer than I should've but nothing much happened." She sucked in a deep breath and continued, "Well, I can't say nothing happened because we kissed, but that was it."

Sydney couldn't disguise the disappointment. She whispered as if someone might overhear her, "You kissed? What do you mean kiss? What kind of kiss?"

"Well, let's just say it's over now, thank the Lord. I just don't know if my marriage will be able to withstand my mistake."

A small gasp escaped from Sydney's lips. "What do you mean? Tommy knows?"

Chanel tried to sound as nonchalant about it as she could, but Sydney knew when her friend was trying too hard to sound like something wasn't a big deal. "He found e-mails between us yesterday. I know he thinks that we slept together, but we didn't even get close to that. I still have some sense."

"Girl, you got a whole lot of sense. That's why I know that you two have to get this straightened out." Indignation swept over Sydney's countenance and was evident in her tone.

"He wouldn't listen to anything I said," she said quietly. "I thought he was gonna go crazy. I mean, I didn't even know that he cared like that."

"Come on now, Chanel. You had to know that Tommy loves you. Over the years, I've watched how he dotes on you. He's always looked at you like you're the only woman in the world. I know he's not perfect, but who is? Furthermore, what's up with you not even being right for the sake of Zachary?"

Chanel sighed heavily and explained, "Yeah, I guess I know, but in a way, I think I've pushed him away. It's almost been more comfortable to have tension between the two of us because it keeps me from being close. Growing up with my mother and feeling rejection from my dad hasn't left me too positive on the love tip, if you know what I mean. I guess I've been pushing him away. "

"Now that you know better, I guess you have to do better."

"Thanks for the encouragement, Syd."

"I don't mean to backtrack, but what did Antonio say in the e-mails?"

"It was just real superficial stuff. He was just telling me how beautiful he thinks I am and, you know, stuff like that."

"What did your e-mails to him say?" Sydney knew Chanel's evasiveness was due to her friend's shame, but she didn't care. Chanel needed someone to be held accountable to other than the Lord.

"I didn't really say anything much except that I enjoyed his company."

"You don't consider that much? Are you out of your mind? What else?" Sydney knew that when Chanel averted her eyes, there was more to the story.

"The only other thing I can remember saying that was really about anything was that I sort of complained about Tommy."

Sydney closed her eyes with her head pointed up towards heaven. "Jesus, help her, please."

"Let me say it since you wanna hear it." Chanel continued. "I told him that the bills were really starting to pile up and that Tommy seemed totally clueless about the pressure I was under. I also told him that I thought Tommy was selfish and immature."

Sydney looked at Chanel with attitude before she asked in a patronizing tone, "What in the world were you thinking? I mean, why couldn't you just vent with me or Sherese? Better yet, why didn't you just tell Jesus?"

"I don't know, girl. It's bad, isn't it?"

"It's bad because you can't go making a man feel like less of a man, especially to another man! You *know* this, Chanel. What did he just say?"

With each response, the volume of Chanel's voice seemed to lower, almost making it difficult for Sydney to understand her clearly. "He just wanted to know where I was. I think he may have been thinking that I was with Antonio or something."

Sydney knew that she was beginning to speak out of pure emotion, and she didn't want to say the wrong thing to Chanel, so she stood up and ended her discussion by telling her, "You, my dear, need to hightail it on home. I'll get you a ticket and you can be home tomorrow morning."

"Thanks for the offer, but I'm not ready to confront him again. He's too angry, and I'm sorry...but—"

Sydney finished her sentence for her. "Not sorry enough, right?"

"No, I am really sorry, but we have so many issues we need to get straight. Right now, I just need the Lord to give me some peace and direction. I've been so busy with the café, Zachary, and the bills. Sometimes it seems like I can't even think straight."

Chanel rubbed her temples in frustration and continued, "While he's off in somebody's studio chasing his childhood dream, I'm standin' on my feet most of the day at the café. Then, I end up feeling so guilty about neglecting my baby, so I end up wearin' myself out to spend as much time with him as I can. In the meantime, that Negro is chillin' out constantly at the studio, maybe getting an occasional gig. How many times do you think he's come to the café to help me? I can actually count the times."

Sydney knew that Chanel was being honest, but she didn't want Chanel to jeopardize her relationship. "I think Tommy has good intentions. He's just been really focused because I think he probably feels like this is his last chance to make it."

"Well, in the process, he's been pushing me and Zachary away."

Sydney knew it was pointless to go any further with Chanel. "I'm going to pray for you all."

"Thanks. We need that more than anything." Chanel stood up, ready to head back to the room for sleep.

As Sydney got ready for bed, she thought about her conversation with Chanel. Even though she acted like she didn't understand how Chanel's frustration with Tommy could lead her to develop a relationship with Antonio, she understood all too well. She wasn't a risk taker like her friend and probably never would've talked to another man, but her own marriage had its share of frustrations.

Sydney knew that having Vance had been a blessing, but she had had many lonely days and nights with his hectic schedule. One night, early in their marriage, she had finally gotten the courage up to confront him about it.

Vance paced the floor. "How in God's green earth can you say you're lonely, Syd?"

"Vance, just because we're in the same room doesn't mean that I can't be lonely."

"I don't get it. I just don't get it. I'm tryin' my best to make the best life I can for us, and it seems like you just find something wrong."

"We're in church at least three or four evenings out of the week. And don't let it be a revival or state meeting. Yep, you're right. We're sitting in the same sanctuary, but we're apart. Even when you do get the opportunity to sit next to me, it's not like we're talking or anything."

"What is it that you want me to do, Syd? I can't resign from my job. I gotta work. So, what is it? You want me to quit being a deacon?"

Sydney, overwhelmed with guilt, couldn't think of exactly what she wanted Vance to quit. She appreciated his dedication to the Lord, her father, and the church. She appreciated his dedication to her, but she was still lonely. She had bowed her head down. "No, I don't want you to quit being a deacon. Could we just maybe not be quite so involved in everything that goes on at church?"

"Don't even try that, Syd, because every time I give in and we don't go to church on a night we have service, you don't have a good time. You always feel guilty and wonder how things are going without us there."

Sydney knew her husband was right, and she didn't have a solution for it. The only thing she was sure about was that she was not going to bring a baby into the picture without her husband being home more.

As she wrapped her head up in a scarf for bed, she regretted the complaints she had made to Vance. Just as she had advised Chanel to think about Tommy's intentions, she wished that she had focused on her late husband's intentions instead of the feelings that she had had at the moment. Vance had only wanted to please the Lord, her, Maya, his boss, and even her father. She couldn't help thinking about the unnecessary pressure she had put on him. When she got in the bed, she thought to herself, *Girl, you had no idea what real loneliness is.*

She prayed that Chanel could appreciate and think on the good things about her husband before it was too late.

CHAPTER 18

Chanel

I reckon that the sufferings of this present time are not worthy
to be compared with the glory which shall be revealed in us.

Romans 8:18

Chanel quickly covered her mouth with her hands as she attempted to muffle her outburst from her throbbing toe. She had misjudged where the edge of the bed was in the dark and unfamiliar hotel room, stubbing her toe. At 5:32 A.M., she was in no mood to have any obstacles as she prepared to do her devotions and to try to clear her mind before they got back on the road. When the pain in her toe ceased to subside, she almost did a u-turn back to the bed but decided that Satan would be too happy if she gave in so easily. Instead, she eased slowly into the bathroom, careful not to make any noise that might wake Sydney or Sherese.

After she gently closed the heavy bathroom door, Chanel positioned herself in the most comfortable way she could on her knees. Silently, she repented for her sins and prayed for Sherese, Sydney, and her marriage. The Proverb "Every wise woman buildeth her house: but the foolish plucketh it down with her hands" came to her mind with clarity as she knelt, waiting to hear from the Lord. The scripture seemed like a swift punch in the stomach because she knew she had been foolish. Over and over again, she remembered things that she had said and done over the past months to contribute to the demise of her marriage.

She knew that Satan used shame and guilt to make people believe that they weren't worthy to repent and come to Christ. Logically, she knew that Jesus paid the penalty for sin by the cross, and she also knew that she was saved by grace, and not works. However, her own feelings of unworthiness kept her from being totally free. Constant thoughts of Nyla's insults and condemnation were also lurking beneath the surface, waiting for an opportunity like now to rear their ugly heads. She was being assaulted with thoughts of not being wanted by either of her parents, Ramone's death, and her failing marriage. More than anything, she had always dreamed of a family and she desperately wanted to be everything that her mother hadn't been. Now, it was all on the line.

Chanel was overwhelmed with the weight of her depressing thoughts, but she remembered that through Christ she was more than a conqueror. While she opened her Bible, she whispered, not wanting to wake Sydney and Sherese, "Satan, the Lord rebuke you for coming into my mind."

Pastor Hightower often taught about how important it was to speak aloud and to speak life into desperate situations. She decided to put this into action as she began reading Ephesians 6:11-13 in an authoritative manner. "Put on the whole armour of God, that ye may be able to stand against the wiles of the devil. For we wrestle not against flesh and blood, but against principalities, against powers, against the rulers of the darkness of this world, against spiritual wickedness in high places. Wherefore take unto you the whole armour of God, that ye may be able to withstand in the evil day, and having done all, to stand." She continued to read the remainder of the sixth chapter of Ephesians, and when she finished, she read it over again and prayed. By the time she had read, meditated on the Word, and prayed, she knew that the Holy Spirit had given her the deliverance, comfort, and strength she needed to go on.

As Chanel rose up from her knees, she said, "Thank You, Jesus," feeling as if she had finally cracked some secret code. She didn't need to be in church or have the elders lay hands on her to really experience the presence of God. So often, she had thought that the "real" spiritual experiences could happen only at church, but for the first time, she had ushered in the Spirit of Lord without the organ playing, other saints praying, and the whole atmosphere of church. It seemed simple, but it felt huge. God would be right there helping, directing, and comforting her if she only allowed Him.

When she quietly walked out of the bathroom, she noticed that Sherese was gone, but Sydney was still sleeping. It struck Chanel as odd since she hadn't heard Sherese leave, but she attributed it to the intensity of her devotions.

"Hey, girl. What time is it?" Sydney asked with her eyes, which still showed traces of smudged mascara, only half opened.

After glancing at the digital clock on the nightstand, Chanel answered, "Probably too early to be up. It's about a quarter after six."

Chanel sat up on the other bed and looked towards Sherese's empty sofa bed. "Where's your sister, and how did she manage to get up and out of here without me hearing her?"

After rubbing her eyes, Sydney sat up with a puzzled look. "You haven't seen her?"

"Nope. When I came out of the bathroom, she was gone. I didn't hear her leave."

"You think she went to get something to eat?"

Chanel shrugged her shoulders. "That's your sister."

Sydney got up and grabbed her cell phone, deciding to try to reach her.

"Hey, Sher, where are you?" Sydney then said defensively, "I'm sorry. No, absolutely not. I was just making sure you were all right."

After Sydney hung up, Chanel saw that Sydney looked upset. "Where is she?"

"She said getting some air, but it ticks me off that she was getting smart with me. That girl had the nerve to ask me if I thought I was her mother. I know what she's going through, but I'm gonna end up going off on her."

"Naw, you can't do that. She's got so much to deal with, you know? Guess we're gonna have an exercise in patience on this trip."

"Yeah, yeah, yeah," Sydney said as she sat back down and turned the television on.

While Chanel was showering, Sydney tapped on the bathroom door. "Chanel, sorry to bother you, but Tommy's on the phone."

"Why is he calling me this early? It's eight-thirty in the morning. Tell him I'll call him back when I get out" Chanel called.

"He says it's important. Come out now, please."

"Here I come." She wrapped a towel around herself and reached outside the door for the phone.

"Tommy?"

"Chanel, I think Zachary's really sick. I've been up all night with him. He's been vomiting, and now he's got a fever."

"What? Why didn't you call me?" Without waiting for an answer, she continued. "What's his temperature?"

"It's 103, but I just gave him some more children's Tylenol. It's probably a virus, but do you think I should call Dr. Hatcher?"

"Definitely. Listen, I'm gonna come home, but it's gonna take me some time to get there."

"I think he'll be okay. I called Mom, and she's on her way over. I just thought you should know. Where are you anyway, Chanel?" Tommy sounded aggravated.

"I told you last night that I was on my way to Mississippi with Sherese and Sydney. Sydney answered my cell phone when you called, so I hope you believe me now."

"I really don't know what to think right now."

"I'm going to catch the next flight out. We're right outside of Nashville, so we can't be too terribly far from the airport. I'll call you when I find out the details. In the meantime, please get the olive oil from the top shelf in my closet and anoint him. I'll be there as soon as I can."

"Anoint him? I think I need to wait for the sanctified wife to get back to do a job like that," Tommy said with attitude.

"We don't have time for this foolishness. Our son is sick."

"I'm the one who called you. You're the one who's gone."

"Don't be childish, Tommy. I'll see you soon. Kiss my angel."

"Later," he quipped before she disconnected.

When Chanel got off of the phone, she realized that Sherese had made it back and both of the sisters were looking at her with concern.

"What's wrong with Zachary? I overheard you saying he was sick," Sydney asked.

"He's going to be fine. Tommy says he thinks he just has a virus, but you know I won't feel right if I don't get home as quickly as I can."

Sherese nodded, and pulled her laptop out. "I can get on the Internet and check to see when the next flight leaves from Nashville International."

"I'm getting your ticket, so I don't want any protests from you. I wouldn't have it any other way," Sydney said as she got up to shower and dress.

Chanel raced down the lengthy corridors of the hospital, trying to remain calm. "Can you please tell me Zachary Dubois' room number?" she asked with a slight tremble in her voice as an attendant at the nurses' station pointed her in the right direction. She couldn't believe that what she thought was a little virus had brought her son to the hospital. Her mother-in-law had called her in a near panic. Zach's fever kept going up and he was listless. She told her Tommy had rushed him to the emergency room.

When she found Room 276, she took a deep breath and entered to find Tommy sitting beside Zachary, who seemed to be sleeping soundly.

Tommy stood up when he noticed his wife's presence. "Chanel. So, Mom did get ahold of you."

Although she answered, her eyes stayed focused on her son. "Yeah, she told me that you were taking him to the emergency room, but why have they admitted my baby? Is he okay? What's wrong?" Chanel asked as she fought to keep her emotions under control upon seeing her listless son hooked up to an IV.

Tommy, too, stood over Zachary as he tried to console Chanel. "Don't go getting yourself all worked up. The doctors don't know for sure what's wrong, but they want to make sure that his fever stays under control and that he doesn't get dehydrated. They're running some tests, but the doctor thinks it may be food poisoning or a virus or something."

Chanel leaned over the bed, lightly kissing her son's dark curls once and then on his forehead. She then placed the back of her hand to feel his warm and flushed cheeks. "What's his temperature?" Before waiting for an answer, she asked anxiously, "Food poisoning? Where on earth could that have happened?"

"I don't know where he couldn't gotten it, but they don't even know for sure what it is. I don't really think that's what it is. We've eaten almost everything the same. His temperature is fluctuating, but when I brought him in, it was 104." Tommy paused for a second or two, shaking his head in disbelief. "I can't lie, Chanel, that boy had me scared. He just got totally limp."

Tears began to stream down Chanel's cheeks as she imagined her son that sick. She closed her eyes, looked up towards heaven and whispered, "Jesus."

Chanel carefully walked toward Tommy until they were standing face-to-face. "Oh, Tommy, I shouldn't have gone. It's my fault. I shouldn't have left him. I just got so caught up with everything and everybody else."

Tommy put his hands deep into the front pockets of his jeans, bit his bottom lip, and his eyes finally met his wife's eyes. However, he made no immediate moves to comfort his wife.

Through her small cry, she managed to whisper, "I'm so sorry about everything. I mean, I'm really sorry."

Tommy said nothing, but he offered a gesture of comfort to his wife as he reached to caress her back gently for a few seconds. "He's gonna be okay. We're both praying, right?"

She was surprised that Tommy was the first to mention praying in order to try to comfort her. "Yes, we are praying," Chanel answered as she attempted to get her emotions under control.

Tommy's mention of prayer reminded Chanel of the experience in her morning devotions. She recognized that this was an example of the warfare Paul was referring to in Ephesians. Her prayers had not been in vain. She was determined to exercise her faith. The Holy Ghost had empowered her to face this battle with her son, and she intended on taking the whole armor of the Lord with her to give her some sense of security in the midst of this mysterious illness of her son.

As the nurse came in to check on Zachary's IV, Chanel and Tommy heard a knock on the hospital door.

A look of relief came over Chanel and Tommy as they greeted Pastor Hightower and the first lady of the church. "How did you find out? I thought you both had to attend the revival in Buffalo tonight?" Chanel asked.

First Lady Hightower's Estee Lauder fragrance met Chanel far before the brisk and anxious hug did. The first lady's eyes were fixed on the young child who was like a grandson to her. "Oh, look at that sweet baby," she said sympathetically, in no hurry to answer Chanel's question.

As First Lady Hightower pulled the covers up closer to Zachary's neck and smoothed the blankets around him in an attempt to find something helpful to do, she answered, "Your mother called us, Tommy. She was so upset, and she wanted us to pray. Of course, we've been doin' that and we'll continue, but we had to see him for ourselves."

The pastor cleared his throat as he stood looking at the child who could always talk him out of candy from his office candy jar. "You don't even think about that revival. Them folks down in Buffalo like to have church til all hours of the night. They'll keep praise and worship going for a good while anyway. Besides, this is more important."

Everyone in the room could feel Tommy's discomfort at the pastor and first lady's presence. Ever since Tommy's first visit to Great Deliverance COGIC, he had let Chanel know that although he loved the Hightowers, he felt that the church was a little too "old school" for his taste. Anytime he visited his wife's church, Tommy thought that the choir sang too many traditional songs, and he couldn't help poking fun at the minister of music's loud and colorful suits. More importantly, he felt that the church's stance on many issues was much too strict and confining. He knew that Pastor Hightower firmly believed in the saints being accountable to God and also accountable to him. This was all a little too intrusive for a man like Tommy who wanted to go to church only when he wanted to go.

"So, Tommy, how things goin' at New Life Christian Center, isn't it?" the Pastor asked before putting a mint in his mouth.

Chanel could see that Tommy's discomfort was turning to misery because he didn't want to discuss his church, especially with Pastor Hightower. He knew that Pastor Hightower didn't agree with co-pastors because he felt like there couldn't be two heads to anything. New Life had husband and wife co-pastors. Pastor Hightower also didn't agree with husbands and wives attending at two places of worship. He had made no secret that the family should worship together.

"It's going well. Thanks for asking," he answered, avoiding eye contact with the pastor.

"You be sure to tell Pastor Walker and his lovely wife that I said hello."

Tommy halfheartedly nodded, trying to be polite since the church was so large that he had barely ever even spoken to either one of them.

"You know, Tommy, Pastor Walker and I go way back. He was a COGIC minister years ago. That's how a lot of these mega-nonde-nominational churches got started, right in the good ole Church of God in Christ."

Darlene interrupted, "Oh, Samuel, enough now. They can't think about that right now."

Pastor Hightower stood up from his chair and said, "You're right, honey. Forgive me. What would I do without my helpmeet? That woman keeps me in line, don't she?" He looked at Darlene with pride.

Chanel noticed that Tommy's face temporarily clouded, letting Chanel know that he must have been thinking about what his life would be without her.

He put his arm around his wife. "You kids just keep your chins up and stick together. Trust me, that's a tough boy you got there. He'll be fine," Pastor Hightower stated with assurance.

The pastor cleared his throat and put the palm of his hand on Zachary's head and began to pray while Darlene touched his arm in agreement. Tommy and Chanel moved in closer to the bed as they joined in the prayer for their son.

After the powerful prayer, Chanel felt much more at ease and she could tell by how Tommy's face had relaxed a bit that he, too, felt better. Before Darlene left, she advised Chanel, "Just be sure to be very calm when he wakes. He's bound to be really fussy and clingy. You just gotta act like it's all okay even though I know you're worried. You don't want to scare him, dear."

Chanel assured Darlene before they left that she wouldn't alarm Zachary. She loved Darlene as much as she loved Pastor Hightower and it was evident because she was one of the few people on earth who could even begin to tell her how to handle situations with Zachary. Giving others a piece of her mind was something Chanel could easily do, but she respected Darlene and knew that she and Pastor Hightower had godly wisdom, which she embraced whole-heartedly since it was so rare these days.

When the nurse came in to check Zachary's temperature, it awakened him from his sleep. Before Zachary could let his first listless groan escape from his lips, Chanel and Tommy were at his bedside.

Between his faint moans, Chanel heard Zachary's cry of "Mommy!"

"It's okay, baby, Mommy and Daddy are right here. You're just fine. The doctor's gonna check you out."

Zachary reached his arms out toward Chanel with as much strength as he could muster, but his weak body wouldn't even let him sit up, which sent a cold shiver down Chanel's spine.

"Hey, Mommy's little man. Just relax, baby. You're gonna be outta here soon." She wrapped her arms around him as much as she could without lifting him up, not wanting to pull his IV out. She softly caressed his face and arms to try to ease at least some of the anxiety and tension in her son.

Tommy looked on helplessly until Dr. Ramsey, the attending physician, came in to check Zachary's vitals. Once Zachary had drifted back to sleep, he asked Chanel and Tommy to follow him to the waiting area.

"Can I get anyone a cup of coffee?" Dr. Ramsey offered as he pulled his fingers through his stringy auburn hair.

Once Tommy and Chanel declined his offer, Dr. Ramsey got straight to the point. "Mr. and Mrs. Dubois, as you know, we did tests on his blood as a precaution, but your son's symptoms seem to indicate that he may have meningitis, which could be bacterial. This is a very serious problem if, in fact, this is what it is. So with your go-ahead, we can do a spinal tap. But let me again say it's only an educated guess at this point."

Chanel gasped. "Spinal tap? Meningitis?"

"What exactly does that mean?" Tommy asked with his brow furrowed.

"It just means that we'll draw some fluid from his spine to diagnose him. We just want to be sure that's what it is, and if it is, we will be able to identify what type of meningitis it is so we can treat it more effectively."

"I've heard of meningitis. I heard it was contagious and that a person can die from it." Chanel folded her arms across her chest in an attempt to warm the coldness that she felt as fear began to once again take hold of her emotions.

"What's really important is for us to act quickly."

"Yes, Dr. Ramsey, please do whatever you need to do to help him. Can I just ask one quick question?" Tommy asked.

"Of course."

"You didn't really address whether it really can be fatal or not."

"While it is true that there are a small number of cases that result in death, I don't want to get you overly anxious without cause. We'll get him prepped for the spinal now unless you have any objections. He's in good hands." He looked at the couple for their approval and when he saw their nods he said, "All righty then." He put his pen in his jacket pocket and tucked his clipboard under his arm as he briskly left the family standing in disbelief.

CHAPTER 19

Sherese

When I was a child, I spake as a child, I understood as a child,
I thought as a child: but when I became a man,
I put away childish things.

1 Corinthians 13:11

Sherese couldn't believe that what was supposed to be such a private and life- altering journey was turning into such an utter disaster. She was tired of the guilt she felt at being so miserable in her sister's presence. Focusing only on herself and her problems was impossible when Sydney was present and had endured the loss of her husband. Still, she couldn't help thinking that at least Sydney knew who she was and who her parents were. Because of that, Sydney was self-assured, confident, and grounded while she floundered aimlessly and without direction.

Although initially Sherese had been adamant about going back to New York, especially when Chanel had to leave, Sydney had convinced her to persevere. Sherese found that she didn't have the energy to debate with her sister anymore and finally agreed to continue on with the trip as planned.

In spite of Sherese's serious reservations about confronting the woman who had given her up as a baby, she agreed to press forward with the trip to meet her biological mother. She figured it couldn't get any worse. That was, until her sister insisted on trying to engage her in conversation as they traveled.

"You know, Sher. I'm kinda glad to get to spend some time with you."

Sherese didn't even try to hide the sarcasm in her grunt.

"Well, I know I haven't always acted like it, but I guess I've just always felt responsible for you, being your sister and all, I mean."

After waiting several seconds for a response from Sherese, Sydney tightly gripped the steering wheel and continued, "You must resent me for acting like Mama at times, and I admit, I can be bossy and overbearing. Vance used to say it all of the time." She glanced over at Sherese, but her thoughts seemed to be elsewhere as she stared out of the passenger side window.

"I just want you to know that I'm here for you. I can't even pretend to know what you're going through, but I know it's tough."

"Syd."

Sherese knew that Sydney was glad that she was finally ready to respond. "Yeah?" Sydney answered.

Sherese picked up her sister's purse off of the floor next to her leg. "Your phone is vibrating."

As she groped for her phone, Sydney's disappointment was evident. "Hello?"

"Hi, Mama. How are you? What? Zachary's been admitted into the hospital? What's wrong?"

Hearing that Zachary was in the hospital forced Sherese, at least temporarily, to come out of her mood, but she stayed quiet. Her mother was the last person she wanted to talk to.

"Mama, you think I should come home? Yes, I'm out of town. No, I didn't tell you. It's not a trip for my job. I'm glad you and Daddy were able to go up to see him. Are you sure that you don't think I need to come home now? I'll try to call her. Well, I know you've been worried about her, but don't. She's fine. I'll her about Zachary. Yes,

Mama. I'll tell her to call you. Yes, we're together. We'll be back as soon as we can. Call me if you find out anything about Zachary. I love you too."

Sydney lightly tossed her phone back into her purse as she drove, while her sister sat fuming.

"Please tell me that Mama doesn't know we're going to Mississippi."

"She asked, Sher. You know I couldn't lie to her."

"I didn't want her to know anything or be involved. For that matter, I didn't want any of you involved."

"That's not fair," Sydney complained.

"Fair? Don't even try to talk to me about fair. You know who your parents are!"

"Yes, you're right, but you can't punish them forever. Can't you just try to put yourself in Mama and Daddy's position? Their intention wasn't to hurt you. They love you."

Sherese lowered her voice. "I know they do, but it doesn't change the fact that they lied to me. I just need to focus on me. I just can't handle how they feel too."

"They didn't lie to you. They just didn't tell you."

"That's a lie of omission, and you know it!"

"Yes, but they did it so you wouldn't feel differently. I talked to Mama in depth."

Sherese folded her arms but she couldn't mask her curiosity about the conversation. "What did *she* say?"

"Very unlike Mama, she cried a lot. I asked her point-blank why she and Daddy waited so long to tell you. She paced back and forth until I couldn't take it anymore. I told her, 'Mama, you've got to relax.' It was only then that she sat down and took a deep breath and explained."

"*Okay,* go ahead," Sherese said impatiently.

"She said, 'We had a lot of reasons for not telling Sherese and you. Some were selfish—I mean, we wanted her to be ours totally. Most of the reasons, though, weren't selfish at all. We truly did what we thought was best. As far as we knew, Rosa was totally strung out. She wouldn't have been no kind of way good for Sherese. Kind of personality your sister has—it just wouldn't have been good for her, that kind of rejection. Sherese has always had a mind of her own, a very independent thinker, from the day we got her. But there's a gentleness and a fragile thing in her that we just didn't want to disturb. It never seemed to be the right time, you know?' I had nodded. Mama said, 'When I got a phone call from Mississippi saying that Rosa had done takin' real ill, your daddy and I tried not to panic. Instead, we prayed hard about what to do. We both felt like Sherese deserved to know the truth now. We felt like she had matured with all that she had been through. We also prayed that maybe this could be a turning point for her.' She said that there was nothing more important to her and Daddy than for us both to be saved. She said, 'I don't know if my sister has a long time here on earth or a short time, but I do know that we felt like the time was now to give Sherese an opportunity to know who her natural mother is—and the time is now for her to stop runnin' from the Lord.'

"I hugged Mama for a long time and she kept saying how she wished you would talk to her, how she wished you would let her explain and tell you how sorry she was. Sher, their intentions do matter."

"Well, for all of their good intentions, I'm nearly suicidal right now." Sherese had uncrossed her arms, but her mind and heart still couldn't reconcile the deceptiveness of the whole thing.

"And exactly who would you help if you would even entertain those types of thoughts? It's not funny to play about taking your life."

Sherese rolled her eyes and defiantly said, "I'm not playing, and I would be helping me. Then, I wouldn't have to deal with all of this."

"Don't think you'd be helping yourself by burning in eternity. Instead of having a period of time on earth to deal with pain, you just might have it forever. You know the Lord."

"I'm not up for the fire-and-brimstone scare tactics, Syd. As a matter of fact, I'm also not up for this particular conversation anymore."

"Fine. I just thought you'd feel better talking about it." Sydney reached to turn the radio on.

Sherese turned to face her sister as she drove. "Oh, so does that work for you with your grief, because if I remember correctly, you haven't been up for talking either."

"Okay, you got me there. I just want to help, and I'm sorry that I have been so selfish over these past months. I understand if you don't want to talk about it. Just know that I'm here for you." With that said, her sister slid one of her sermons into the CD player.

"Thanks," Sherese muttered, thankful that the treacherous conversation was over as she closed her eyes to try to sleep.

When Sherese opened her eyes, she massaged the crook in her neck as she saw they were making the exit onto Route 81. Her stomach churned with nervousness as she realized that they were a little less than an hour from Natchez, her birthplace.

"You ready for me to drive the rest of the way? I know you must be tired," Sherese asked, now desiring to be in control of the wheel.

The closer they got to Mississippi, the more out of control she felt, so she figured driving just might make her feel better.

"Oh, I'm really not that tired. This trip has been good for me. I didn't realize just how much I needed to get away from Rochester."

Sherese couldn't believe Sydney's behavior. She acted like this was vacation instead of recognizing the daunting task that lay before Sherese.

Once Sydney reached for yet another one of her CD's, she happily chimed, "Sher, this is the recording that Rance Allen did live in Memphis at the convocation a few years back. Remember that? Girl, he set the place on fire!" She raised both hands up in the air for a second, emphasizing how much the message blessed her.

"Do me a favor? Could you please lay off the sermons until we get there? Oh, and keep both hands on the wheel, please." Sherese was annoyed and had an attitude.

"Why do you always have to lash out at me when I'm just trying to help?" Sydney asked as she turned the CD player off.

"I don't recall asking for help with this one, Syd."

"You're right, but this thing is too big for you to take on by yourself."

"No offense or anything, but I don't need your help."

"You're right about that, too, but I wasn't talking about *my* help. You need help from the Lord."

Sherese blew her breath out hard and loudly as if she were trying not to explode before she said, "Please, spare me. How much has the Lord helped you, Syd? From my observation, you are still devastated, depressed, and anxious. Don't you still have nightmares? What has the Lord helped you through? I want to know!"

Although Sherese knew that her words would upset and maybe even anger her sister, she also knew that there was more than a little truth to her words. While waiting for a response, Sherese stared at Sydney's profile with expectancy.

When Sydney spoke, Sherese was surprised by her sister's ability to remain calm under what must have felt like an attack on her and maybe even her faith. "I'm the first one to admit that I'm human like everyone else. For some time, I probably haven't seemed that way because when you feel like you're in control of your life, you can get prideful. I can honestly say that losing Vance has shown me that I'm not where I thought I was, but I can say that while I may be distressed and upset, like the scripture says, I'm not without hope. God has given me a measure of peace in the valley, and what He's done for me, He can do for you. I'm learning that I can't let my circumstances dictate who God is to me." Sydney sighed as she nodded her head.

Anger seemed to fester in every pore of Sherese's being with her sister's words, and she couldn't hold back her feelings anymore. "I'm so tired of the 'peace in the valley' speech every time something bad happens to me or somebody else. Remember, I've grown up hearing the same stuff you did. How could Mama and Daddy preach against lies, deceit, and secrets when they have turned out to be just as hypocritical as other people in the church?"

Sherese showed her displeasure in the way she hastily let down her car window, allowing the wind to cool her face off. "When I think about them pretending that I was their daughter, I just, I just—I can hardly contain myself. Then, the thing that really gets me is that they got me, and I guess I should be ever so thankful, but they got me and couldn't give either one of us the attention that we needed or deserved."

"What do you mean?" Sydney questioned.

"Come on, Syd. Don't tell me that it didn't stink most of the time in our childhood. Not only were we forced to wear skirts, not allowed to go to movies, not allowed to listen to anything but gospel, all in the name of holiness, but we were also never put first. Sydney, tell me that our parents didn't put the church folks before us, tell me," she demanded.

Sherese's eyes seemed to burn a hole through Sydney as she dared Sydney to tell her otherwise. Sydney took a deep breath, but she seemed to be at a loss for words. Pleased that she had won this round with her sister, Sherese continued on, reveling in her moment. "Mama and Daddy never came to the three art exhibits at the school where my work was featured because they always had something going on at the church. You yourself know that they only attended what—maybe three or four of the awards ceremonies you were in? You were in the top of your class every year. You have to remember how they were actually late to my graduation because Daddy was coming back from the state meeting."

"Yeah, I remember. Mama and Daddy aren't perfect. They have always done the best they know to do. You gotta cut them some slack."

"What I'm sayin' is that they put other people and things in front of us, and finding out that they deceived me only makes things worse."

"I understand what you're saying, but Mama and Daddy's intentions, as I've said before, were not to hurt you. Besides, they didn't really put anybody or anything in front of us anyway." Sydney paused for a second while Sherese crossed her arms in defiance. Sydney added, "Not really, anyway. They looked at it as putting the Lord first. You know that. If you're talking about them not always being able to come to our school stuff when we were younger, they've apologized for that. Like I said, at the time, they believed they were putting the Lord first by going to church and seeing about the members."

A look of disbelief came over Sherese's face. "You call what Mama said a while back after Sunday dinner an apology? Give me a break, Syd." Sherese sat erect in the seat to imitate her mother. With a mocking tone and an exaggerated southern accent, she said in a breathy way, "'Your Daddy and I wish we could've been more involved with you children's interests when you were younger. You know we were always proud of you.' That's not what I call an apology, Syd."

When Sydney didn't say anything right away, Sherese added, "The operative word here is 'could've' because that indicates that they really don't regret anything. They 'could've' if they wanted to, but they are still acting like they didn't have a choice. They always chose them over us."

"It may have seemed like that, but they only meant to put the Lord first. Besides, they knew that we would be okay."

"Are we okay though, Syd?" Sherese was tired of talking now, and based on her sister's loss for words, she must have been too. As usual, Sherese thought, she and her sister would simply have to agree to disagree.

CHAPTER 20

Sydney

He spake a parable unto them to this end,
that men ought to always to pray, and not to faint.

Luke 18:1

The "Welcome to Natchez" sign greeted Sydney and Sherese as they entered the city. Twinges of nervousness and anticipation raced through Sydney's body upon the realization that unlike the previous times she had come to Natchez as a child, their trip would now have a very different mission. The city seemed to somehow look very different to her, so she knew that it must really look different to her sister since Sherese now knew that it was her birthplace.

"Look at the antebellum homes, Sher. That yellow one over there with the white trim—it's so big. The columns are so beautiful and stately. I wonder what it must have been like to live in one of those a long time ago."

With a smug tone, Sherese responded, "Girl, please. We would never have gotten the opportunity to live in one of those. The only thing we could've done in those is cook, clean, iron, and say 'Yessa, Massa.'"

"Yeah, I guess you're right, but they're still nice." Sydney's voice trailed off. Despite Sherese's newfound pessimism and negativity, Sydney resolved that she would stay positive and refuse to buckle under the pressure. She knew that she hadn't been much of an example or testimony for Christ at work and even at church, so she viewed this situation with her sister as another opportunity that God was giving her to stretch herself spiritually.

"Ooooh, Syd!" Sherese perked up.

"What?"

Pointing out the driver's side window, Sherese shook her head. "Piggly Wiggly! I can't believe that's still here. Why on earth would someone name a grocery store Piggly Wiggly anyway?"

"Beats me, but I think it's cute."

"Remember how Mama Dee used to take us there during the summer? Seems like we went a couple times a week," Sherese reminisced.

Reflecting on the two weeks they spent in Natchez with Mama Dee during their summer vacations as children seemed like yesterday to Sydney. "Yeah, she would always buy us a peach to eat on the long walk back to her house. She would use the hose from her friend Bessie's yard to wash them off without even asking her. You used to gross me out, too—eating the skin off of the peach before you ate the inside. I hope you don't still do that mess." Sherese gave her sister a devious smile, which Sydney knew indicated that she still did it. "You better not ever let a brother see you eat a peach."

"Naw, it's all good. I've been told it's kind of attractive by a brother or two, I'll have you know." Sherese's smile broadened.

Sydney grimaced and changed the subject. "Do I make this left onto Main?"

"Yep, after that, take another left on Pearl Street, and then we'll be at the Natchez Eola. Is that how you pronounce it?"

"I think that's right." Sydney's thoughts were far away. "Boy, I miss Mama Dee. Natchez doesn't seem like the same place without her here. We had the best Grandmamma in the world. And we weren't the only ones to love her like that. Seemed like everyone loved her dearly; didn't matter if they were black or white."

"Yeah, she was like a Grandmamma from a book or something. She cooked, cleaned, and gardened and did it all like she loved every minute of it. You remember those collard greens. I didn't even like them until I had hers." Sherese thought for a few seconds and then recalled, "I could never understand it. Grandaddy used to give her a hard time, but she just quietly did what he asked of her. Oh, Pearl Street, here it is."

"Grandaddy was kind to us, but he could be a mean old somethin' to Mama Dee. It used to get to me real bad," Sydney answered.

"I remember seeing this building a couple of times when I was younger. I guess I never knew it was a hotel. It sits right on the banks of the Mississippi River, and it looks so historical and elegant. I'm glad you cancelled my reservation at the Days Inn after all."

"I thought it would be nice for us to try something new and old at the same time."

"Thanks, Syd."

Sydney felt the sincerity in Sherese's voice and demeanor, and it made her heart glad. After the disagreements and long trip, she was pleased that, at least her sister was satisfied with their accommodations.

Sydney noticed that Sherese seemed to temporarily lose her hard edge in admiration of the oil paintings and antiques in the hotel's lobby and hallways. Her sister's deep appreciation of art, whether it suited Sherese's own personal taste or not, was one of the reasons that Sydney had booked their reservations there. The website boasted of its arched doorways, Southern charm, massive columns, and of course, antique furniture and paintings.

"I love this hotel. It feels so warm and homey, yet it has class."

Sherese seemed pleased after they settled in the hotel room and showered until she started flipping through the menu for room service. "This is ridiculous! A simple cheeseburger and fries are

$12.95. A doggone grilled chicken and vegetable platter is $17.95, and there's an automatic twenty percent gratuity added to all orders." She slapped the menu down onto the desk in disbelief.

"Girl, you are truly your mother's child. You two are always in amazement about the price of things. You gotta realize—" Sydney stopped short of finishing her thought. It was hard to believe she was not their mother's child—in many ways they actually were so similar. By the sad look on Sherese's face, she hadn't missed the connotation of the comment. "I'm sorry."

"It's okay."

"She's still your mother, you know."

Sherese sipped some of her Coke. "Let's not go there, okay?"

Sydney nodded, but later as they ate their cheeseburgers, Sydney mustered up enough courage to question Sherese about her plans for the following day. The last thing she wanted to do was upset her sister. Sherese wiped the ketchup from her mouth and said before swallowing her food, "I'm gonna go over to the house in the morning when I get up."

"I know this is a stupid question, but you have the phone number and address and stuff?"

"Yep."

Sydney placed her glass of lemonade on the table and asked, "You're not gonna call first or anything?"

"Nope."

"You sure it's a good idea? I mean, what if she's not there?"

"Then, I'll go back."

Sydney finished chewing. "What if she's not at the address you have?"

"Then, I'll just have to find out where she moved to, huh?"

"You want me to go with you?" Sydney asked carefully.

"No way, Syd. You agreed to stay out of this, remember?"

Sydney put her hand up. "I know, I know. I was just making sure. You're not nervous or anything, are you?"

Sherese didn't answer but raised her eyebrows and tilted her head with a look that told Sydney that she was.

Although Sydney was curious to see and meet Rosa, she was somewhat relieved that Sherese didn't want her there because she was nervous for her sister.

Sherese went to brush her teeth. "Well, I'm beat. I'm gonna crash."

After climbing into one of the two plush queen-size beds, Sherese was asleep within fifteen minutes. Sydney was surprised to hear her sister snore, something Sherese did only when she was exhausted. Still, Sydney knew that this whole ordeal had been taking a toll on Sherese and that she needed rest.

As she brushed her teeth and put rollers in her hair, she thought about Sherese's adoption, and although it was shocking, it didn't change anything for her. She certainly felt no less of a bond with her. As a matter of fact, somehow her sister seemed closer to her now. Their mutual pain seemed to be bringing them together in a weird kind of way. It didn't matter that she and her sister didn't often see eye to eye on issues because the love was always there.

Before she got into the bed, she decided to call Chanel to find out how Zachary was. After calling her house and cell phone number, she decided that they must have been out or asleep, so Sydney decided to get some much needed rested.

While turning down her bed linens, she thought about Brian O'Leary. The memory of the gaunt face of his wife, Ann, tormented her. She desperately tried to quell the nagging feelings of rage, bitterness, and even sympathy that coursed through her veins, but they refused to subside. Now she knew the truth. The man who killed her husband wasn't the monster that she had imagined. He was a real person and people loved him as much as she had loved Vance, but she didn't want to feel sorry for Brian or Ann O'Leary. She hadn't cared or even wanted to know his story, but now that she knew, there was no taking it back. The truth be told, as much as she wanted to hate Brian O'Leary, she now pitied him and even that contined to make her angry and confused.

As she reached to turn off the lamp on the nightstand, she prayed long and hard for her sister's day tomorrow and their future.

CHAPTER 21

Chanel

Wives, submit yourselves unto your own husbands, as unto the Lord.

Ephesians 5:22

"Zachary's asleep now?" Tommy whispered, entering the house as quietly as he could.

Chanel stood up from the sofa. "Yeah, but you don't have to whisper 'cause that boy is out. He seems to feel better just to be back at home. He's definitely a lot more comfortable today than he was yesterday."

Tommy sat the bag down on the sofa. "I got some Popsicles and Tylenol for him. I even got some chicken noodle soup and saltines when he's ready for them."

"That's great, Tommy." She looked at him gratefully. "I'm so thankful that the doctor let him come home. I was so scared that it was that bacterial meningitis."

Tommy sat on the sofa without removing his coat or shoes, and Chanel wondered if he would stay the night. He sighed. "Well, thank God, but we still have to really watch him. Even though it's that viral meningitis, it's still pretty serious."

Chanel joined Tommy on the sofa. "I can't believe that we just have to let it run its course. It just seems like there should be something else we can do."

"You know the doctor said that antibiotics don't help, so we just have to be patient. The main thing is to watch his fever and make sure that he stays hydrated. Don't worry, he's a tough boy."

"Yeah, just like his dad." Chanel smiled. "I just never knew the flu could develop into anything like this."

"Chanel, I might be tough, but this scared *me*," Tommy sank back into the sofa.

"Yeah, I know. Me too." Chanel wondered if her husband was still angry about finding the e-mails. Instead, she decided to ask, "You want me to take your coat?" When Tommy didn't answer immediately, she asked, "Are you staying tonight—to check on Zach, I mean?"

He sat up straight up. "No, I'll be back first thing in the morning though."

"Tommy." She paused and then continued. "I need you to stay here with me." Chanel surprised herself for showing so much vulnerability.

"For what?"

"What do you mean, 'for what'? Our son is sick."

Tommy seemed to be thinking about what he should do until he began to pull his arms out of his coat sleeves. "I guess I won't do anything but worry myself silly if I don't stay here tonight."

Chanel exhaled with relief. She reached for his coat to hang it up. "Tommy, this is still your house too."

"I don't know about all that." He rubbed his hands up and down his legs anxiously. "All I know is that, no matter what, you and Zachary will always be taken care of." He stared directly into his wife's eyes.

Her stomach dropped as she realized that she really was losing Tommy. She couldn't think straight about anything. Her mind had been so occupied with Zachary and before that Sherese, Sydney, and the café. She had no idea if it was the right time to talk about everything or not.

She got up and hung his jacket up and walked to the kitchen. "How about some Coke and popcorn? There's gotta be something good to watch on that satellite TV we're paying an arm and a leg for," she called out from the kitchen.

"Naw, actually, I don't think I'm in a movie-watching mood tonight."

Chanel was startled to see her husband staring at her in the doorway of the kitchen when she raised her head from the refrigerator. "Oh, okay. Yeah, I understand." She went to put the drinks back.

"I don't wanna watch a movie, but I didn't say I didn't want a drink."

Chanel smiled as she prepared their soft drinks. She was glad that she, at least, had him there with her for the night.

"I know we've had a lot going on, but I can't believe that you haven't said one word about my dreds being gone. What do ya' think?"

She had been shocked to see her husband's bald head initially. "I noticed it, but I've been so overwhelmed with Zach, I didn't say anything. It'll take me a minute to get used to it, but I actually like it a lot. What made you do it?"

He smoothed his hand over his nearly bald and very nicely shaped round head. "I guess I just wanted a change, you know, a new start."

Chanel nearly gasped at his words. *A new start?* She didn't want Tommy to be starting over unless it was with her. "A new start? What do you mean?" she said trying to sound calm.

"It's time out for doin' these gigs that aren't really making any difference. I want my music to mean something. I mean, sure, people seem like they're happy when they're listening to the band play and all, but what about after they leave?"

Of course, Chanel thought, *he's talking about his music. What else could it have been?* She took a sigh of relief and told him, "I know how happy those people are even after they leave, Tommy." Chanel knew how happy Tommy made people when they listened to his music. Over the years, especially before they had Zachary, she had been front and center at as many of his playing engagements as she could. She would always find herself patting her feet, singing along, and smiling—and she had even danced a little a few times. Her husband's gift, something she had been in awe of about him at one time, had little by little become a thorn in her side. It dawned on her that maybe part of the reason was she hadn't gone to see him play in over a year. She was sorry that she had distanced herself so far from what was so dear to Tommy's heart.

Tommy leaned forward in deep thought. "But you know what I mean. How much of a difference can I make with the type of music I'm doing. It's not fulfilling anymore. I'm getting older and the sacrifices I've made with you and Zachary have been too many. I've been focused on the wrong thing."

Chanel was shocked to hear that Tommy sounded so mature and so grounded. "I have too, Tommy. I've focused on the wrong things."

He studied his wife's face and seemed to see her pain. "I'm sorry that I haven't been there and have put too much of a burden on you. When I read those e-mails, Chanel, all I could think about was killing that guy and you, but when Zachary got sick and I was in the emergency room holding his limp little body, none of it mattered. I realized that I've been really selfish and I don't blame you for steppin' out, I guess. It's just all screwed up and sad at the same time."

"Tommy, I—I" Chanel started.

"No," he interrupted. "Just let me finish. You've been tryin' to get me to go to church with you for a long time, and I've just thought that other things were more important. See, I remember my mom praying for me whenever I was in trouble, but I don't remember Jesus being a part of our everyday lives and decisions like He is for you. I've watched how you read the Bible, pray, fast, and go to church. Believe it or not, I've always respected that so much about you. I guess that's why I just know that I must've really pushed you over the edge to get you to start seein' that guy. I don't wanna mess you or my son up like that. I don't wanna be responsible for messing up a good thing," Tommy looked down and stopped talking.

Chanel waited a second or two to make sure he was done and got up to go kneel before him. "Tommy, first of all, you are not responsible for my bad choices. I was wrong and I'm sorry. But, you have to know that I did not sleep with that guy. He was a distraction. I was angry, and I was tempted. God only knows how sorry I am. I'm sorry for so much. I've repented to the Lord for looking outside of my marriage for comfort, but I'm asking you to forgive me. If I didn't know it before, I know it now. I love you, and I need you."

Although Chanel couldn't be sure, she thought she saw Tommy's eyes fill with tears. He put his rough hand on hers and admitted, "Chanel, I love you, but I just don't know. When I think about you and some other man, I lose it. I understand, yeah, but I can't see past that as far as you and me. I wanna believe you, but I keep seeing those e-mails over and over again in my head."

"I know, but just ask yourself if I've ever lied to you. I mean, think about it. Have I? I have a lot of flaws, but I don't lie."

While his head stayed bowed down, he admitted, "Naw, not that I know of. I just need some time to clear my head. What I do want you to know is that I had applied for a teaching job at a private school a buddy of mine told me about some time ago. It just so happens that the music teacher had to relocate, so I interviewed for the position last week. I got a call yesterday. The principal made an offer and I accepted."

"That's great, Tommy. Isn't it?"

"It's not a lot of money, but I miss teaching the kids. Besides, I can't feel like a real man and allow you to be the sole financial provider when I'm able-bodied—at least I can't anymore. My mom pretty much did it all when I was growin' up, and I used to hate that. Anyway, it's the last thing I wanna see my wife do. I don't want you to be stressed out, whether we're together or not. I think I can still pursue my dreams and have a stable nine-to-five job."

"I know things can get better between us with another chance. I've been praying about things."

"Well, that's good. I've been sending some requests up myself over the past few days in particular." Then, Tommy stood up, signaling to Chanel that he was done talking with her, for now anyway.

She, too, stood up and took their glasses to the sink. "Tommy, I love you." He stopped short, and in a barely audible voice, he responded, "Good night, Chanel."

CHAPTER 22

Sherese

So teach us to number our days,
that we may apply our hearts unto wisdom.

Psalm 90:12

"You sure you don't want me to come inside with you?"

"I think so." Sherese wiped her sweaty palms off on her new char-treuse skirt as the two sisters sat nervously in front of Rosa Harrison's house. Even though Sherese had said that she hadn't wanted Sydney to come with her, when she awoke, fear gripped her and she needed her sister.

"You know what you're gonna say?" Sydney asked carefully.

"I'm just gonna tell her that I know I'm her daughter. Why? What do you think I should say?"

"I'm not saying what you should say because I don't know where she is in her life right now. I mean, you don't have any idea?"

Sherese now felt silly as she thought about making the long trip, not even knowing if, in fact, the small brick house that she and her sister sat in front of was still her biological mother's home. Since Sydney had parked the car a good distance from the front of the house, Sherese was able to scan the neighborhood. The thumping sound of a car stereo's bass could be heard as well as the laughter from a small group of girls playing Double Dutch. Further feelings of uneasiness came over the sisters as they watched two men across the street make a secret exchange.

Sherese settled her attention on the empty bottles and litter that were strewn on the outside and all around the rickety fence that enclosed the aged two-story home. In spite of the chaos that seemed to surround the home, inside of the fence the lawn was neatly manicured and a large magnolia tree scented the block. With no warning, a sixtyish looking man, dressed in a plaid shirt and khaki slacks, opened the door to let a small white poodle out and went back inside. Sydney nudged her but neither said a word. Both wondered who the man was and if he were any relation to Rosa or them.

After taking a deep breath in and flicking her braids to her back, Sherese opened the passenger-side door. "Okay, I'm ready. I'll signal for you to come in if she's there."

As the intense heat from the hot sun beamed down, making her squint to see in front of her, beads of perspiration popped up around the frame of her face. The clicking of Sherese's heels seemed to be particularly loud on the cracked sidewalk as she checked to make sure that her legs weren't visibly shaking. Once she made it to the fence, Sherese noticed that it wasn't all the way closed, yet the well-trained poodle didn't leave the area. She pushed the gate open timidly, not sure how the dog would react to a stranger. When she realized that the poodle wasn't threatening, she slowly walked up the three steps to the front door.

Before she knocked, she took one quick glance back at her sister, who held her hand up in a wave gesture to her. After Sherese rubbed the perspiration from her sweaty palms one last time, she inhaled and exhaled deeply before knocking on the door. She waited for a few moments and knocked a little more loudly.

The same man who had let the poodle out opened the squeaky door and greeted her with, "I ain't got nothin' for ya' today. You gotta get me after the first of the month."

"Excuse me, sir?"

"Ain't you one of those people from the youth center takin' up donations?"

"No, sir."

The man scratched his head and mumbled, "Oh, sorry. What can I do for ya'?"

"Actually, I was looking for Rosa Harrison," Sherese explained, unable to disguise the nervousness in her voice.

"She ain't here, and if you're another one of those bill collectors, let me tell you this, Rosa ain't got nothin' to collect. That is, unless you want Rufus over there." The scent of menthol rub filled her nostrils as he pointed to the lackadaisical poodle.

Her anxiety was turning to aggravation as she said abruptly, "That's not why I need to see her, sir. Could you please tell me when you might expect her back?"

The man eyed her curiously and asked, "Who are you and what you need from my Rosa?"

My Rosa? Was this her boyfriend or husband? Sherese wondered, yet the only thing that would come out was, "I'm Sherese Hightower."

"Whatcha say, gal?" He pulled his glasses down on the tip of his nose.

"My name is Sherese Hightower, and—"

He interrupted, "I see. You wanna come in?"

"No, actually, I just need to speak with her. Can you ask her to call me as soon as possible, please?"

"Just come on it for a minute, so I can make sure I get the message straight."

Now Sherese was sure that the man's tone had softened. "No, thank you." She extended a small paper with her name and numbers on it, but the man wouldn't take it.

Instead, he said, "Hold on a minute." Then, he turned and slowly walked back inside of the house.

After waiting for what seemed to be an eternity, the man came back with a baseball cap and shoes on. He stepped outside and introduced himself. Now, it was his turn to extend his hand. "I'm Walter Finch, Rosa's husband."

Sherese wasn't surprised at the admission, yet it was very strange to shake her mother's husband's hand for the first time without even meeting her. "Nice to meet you, Mr. Finch."

He asked her to sit down in the swing on the front porch, but when she declined, he admitted, "Yep, I sure do see your mama's face in you."

"So, you know who I am then?"

"I should've known before you even said it, but my eyesight's gettin' worse by the day it seems."

"I found the address by her maiden name."

"Yeah, Rosa insisted on keeping her maiden name. I never heard of a Mississippi gal thinkin' like a big city Northern gal 'til I met her. Made me mad as fire when she plumb refused to take my name. It's the sort of thing that can hurt a man's pride if he's not real secure, you know what I'm sayin'?"

Sherese smiled uneasily. "Ummm, Mr. Finch, maybe I will take a seat if you don't mind my sister coming up here. She's in the car over there." She pointed in the direction of the car.

Mr. Finch pulled his glasses to the tip of his nose again, squinting to see Sherese. "Yep, that'll be mighty fine. That Darlene's oldest girl?"

"Yes, her name is Sydney. You know my mama?" Before she took a seat on the swing next to Mr. Finch, Sherese signaled for her sister to come to the front porch to join them.

"No, I don't reckon I do, but I heard enough about her from Rosa to think I do."

"Mama doesn't know Rosa's married."

"Yeah, I figured as much. She told me in no uncertain terms that she had burned a lot of bridges that only she could rebuild. Only thing was, neither one of us counted on—"

Sydney walked up, and he stopped mid sentence. After Sherese introduced Mr. Finch to Sydney, Sydney sat on the top step quietly and listened while they made small talk about the trip from New York and the weather. When there was a lull in the conversation, Mr. Finch told the story about when and how he met Rosa.

"It ain't a fairy tale-type story, the way I met Rosa, just so ya' know right from the start."

Sherese nodded. "I'd like to know."

He stared off into the clear, blue Mississippi sky.

"Joe McNamara had this big shindig back in 1967. That's when I first set eye on her. She was pretty, but not the prettiest gal I'd ever set eyes on. It was those mysterious eyes that reeled me right on in. As for Rosa, though, she didn't give me no time. She was hangin' with a rough crowd, a lot older than her. Me, myself, I got some years on her, but that group she was hangin' with was way older. Anyway, I went up to her to ask her if she wanted to dance and that little thing laughed so hard, she must've spit some of her drink on me. After that, my boys was laughin', and I couldn't stand that gal for embarrassin' me like that."

Sherese seemed to hang on every word Mr. Finch said, wanting to record it all in her mind forever.

"Well, nearly thirty years later, I saw her of all places, at New Hope COGIC, where I had been a deacon for years. I had just lost my wife a year before Rosa came to a Friday night service. Although I didn't immediately recognize her, when I caught a good look at those eyes, I knew who it was. Of course, I had to tell her who I was."

He chuckled heartily. "She didn't barely know who I was back in '67, so how she gonna know me fat, bald, and wrinkled? Anyway, her eyes didn't have much of a spark or mystery in 'em, but they had a glimmer of hope. Ya' know what I mean?"

The two sisters nodded.

"If it wasn't for the Lord, I'm tellin' you, I couldn't have gone on after Ernestine died. It was a blessin' to have Rosa come into my life. I was grievin' and Lord knows, Rosa was grievin'.'"

"Over what?" Sherese asked.

"Her mistakes."

"It's not really for me to say, but as you already know, she had some serious problems, some she caused and others she didn't. The thing was, she was tryin' real hard to get her life on track, and she told me she knew only the Lord could do that. I started pickin' her up and bringin' her to church. In no time, she made that walk down the center aisle of the church to get saved. I was happy as a lark, and truth be told, Rosa was, too, I reckon. Back in '97, I asked her to marry me, and it took some convincin', but finally she said, 'If you wanna touch the bottom, you might as well fill the pot.' I had no idea what that woman was talkin' 'bout then, but I came to understand. She told me that she loved me as much as she could love a man and agreed to marry me. So, ladies, on April 22, 1997, me and Rosa married at New Hope Church of God In Christ in front of the whole congregation."

"Why didn't any of us in Rochester know about Aunt Rosa's wedding?" Sydney asked, puzzled.

"Honey, Rosa didn't even tell her sisters and brothers right here in Natchez. It took me a long time to figure out why she was so private about her family, and quite some time back, I had to be at peace knowin' I'd never understand all there is to know about Rosa. I can tell you this though, I think a lot of it was just pure shame. She told me she came from a real good family, and she was the rebel, the black sheep, the wild one. When I mentioned callin' her family to meet me and come to the wedding, she told me in no uncertain terms, 'Are you outta your mind, Wally? No way, no how, am I tellin' my family to do nothin' more than they already done for me. How'd you think I'll look at almost fifty years callin' people to tell them I'm finally getting' my life straight. It's better to leave well enough alone.'"

Sherese's head was reeling from all of the information, but she had to know more. "Where is Rosa?"

From the sad countenance that came over Mr. Finch's face, Sherese didn't know what to think, but she held her breath anxiously waiting for a response.

Acting as if he didn't hear Sherese's question, Mr. Finch continued on. "Yep, she was full aware of all the worry she put on the family. She felt mighty bad about it. It took her a lifetime to shake that monkey off her back."

"Our mama told us that she had some addictions. Was it drugs?"

"That heroin is purely from the devil. You hear me? It's straight from the pit of hell. Rosa had just come out of rehab when she came to the church that first night. She came to New Hope because it wasn't in the same jurisdiction as your family's church. She knew enough to come to the holiness church."

"How long had she been on drugs?"

Mr. Finch stretched his legs out in front of him and crossed his feet while placing his hands behind his head. "Rosa says she was about nineteen when she first tried it. Her best friend…what was that girl's name? Oh, yep, Tammy, that was her name. She first introduced it to her, and Tammy's boyfriend gave it to her. When Tammy died at twenty-four from an overdose, instead of Rosa getting' straight like everyone expected, it messed her up. She didn't even go to the funeral. The thing already had a good grip on her, and besides, the heroin kept her numb to pain."

A sick feeling overwhelmed Sherese and she wanted to leave. The sound of Mr. Finch's drawl irritated her and she was getting depressed about what she knew of the life her mother had led. The more he talked, the more she somewhat understood Rosa's decision to give her up. Yet, she wondered why having a daughter wasn't a strong enough incentive to stop the drug abuse.

"Would y'all like some iced tea or water or somethin'?" he asked, sensing the heaviness of the conversation.

Before they could answer, a red Ford Escort pulled up directly in front of the house. A middle-aged bleached blonde with bright red lipstick and large hips got out of the car, fully dressed in white. Sherese and Sydney could tell from the stethoscope dangling from her neck that she was a medical professional.

"Howdy, Mr. Finch!" she cheerfully sang as she petted Rufus warmly. The dog's friendly welcome let Sherese know that the woman came there often.

"You're late this morning, Betty."

Betty examined the watch on her arm and placed her hands on her wide hips. "It's eleven forty-four, Mr. Finch, and I'll have you know, I'm early!"

They both grinned. "Betty, this here is Sherese, Rosa's gal, and Sydney, her niece. That would make this one my stepdaughter and this one here, my niece," he said, eyeing the women.

"Well, I'll be. Sherese, I heard a load about you before your mama took real ill. She's real proud of you."

All Sherese could do to hold it together was to smile and swallow hard, while shaking the woman's cold, plump hand. She didn't even know that Rosa was her mother a few weeks ago, and now she was overwhelmed.

"That Betty is a real pistol. We've had our share of run-ins, especially when she first started coming to check on Rosa. Who would've ever thought that I'd see the day when a white nurse would come over to this side of town to see about a black? I used to think she wasn't doin' right by Rosa. She seemed like she wasn't even tryin' to help make her comfortable. It's been almost two years now, and thank the good Lord, I really wouldn't want no one but her to see about my baby."

"Rosa's here?" Sherese was confused.

"Forgive me for lyin' to ya' when ya' first come up here. I just don't want no trouble for her. She's had so much."

"What is wrong with her?"

Mr. Finch stood up and faced the opposite direction of the two sisters. "Even though she stopped the drugs, she's got a lot of health problems and had a heart attack. All those years of doing drugs weakened her heart, and she's had a heap of small strokes that have affected her mind somethin' awful." He shook his head, "Never knew those drugs could do this kind of damage after stoppin' 'em."

"I'm sorry," Sherese said softly.

"Yeah, we all are, honey. Rosa is sorry, that I know. Anyway, she's partially paralyzed and got real bad liver problems. The worst part of it is that her mind and speech are no good. She's payin' an awful price for the abuse she done to her frail little body."

"Does my mother know this, Mr. Finch?" Sydney asked.

"When I last talked to your mama, Rosa wasn't quite this bad off. The last time I talked to your mama, Rosa left strict instructions that no one was to know. I'm tellin' ya' this cause I don't reckon it'll make a difference now. Ya' come all this way to see and talk to her and the least I can do is tell ya' what I know."

"Mr. Finch!" Betty called from inside the house.

"Y'all come on in, now. I want you to see her when Betty comes out."

Sherese and Sydney made eye contact and when Sydney saw that her sister moved toward the door to enter, she followed.

When Betty came out of Rosa's room, Mr. Finch asked, "Hey, Betty, is it okay to go in now? You done doin' what you had to do?"

"Mr. Finch, I'll need your help only for a minute, then you all can go on back."

Mr. Finch patted Betty on her shoulder. "That's why I love having Betty around here. She keeps things straight for me."

Betty smiled, "Thank you, Mr. Finch, but I think you're the one keeping me in check. I need you to come back to your wife's room for a second, if that's okay."

"If y'all don't mind, I'll just run back real quick."

In unison, Sydney and Sherese said, "Go ahead."

While Mr. Finch slowly walked to Rosa's room, the sisters sat down carefully on the orange-colored velvety sofa that seemed to have been purchased in the late seventies, but yet was in good condition. Aside from the dust that had settled on the plastic fruit in the ornate bowl in the center of the coffee table and the dust that clouded the stemware in the curio cabinet, everything was extremely tidy, just as the front yard had been. Newspapers were neatly stored in a rack that sat next to the sofa and framed pictures of unfamiliar faces seemed to decorate every space in the tiny living room. The small radio tucked in a corner played Southern gospel quartet music softly while the faint scent of coffee, as well as menthol, could be smelled.

"You okay?" Sydney whispered to her sister.

"I don't know yet." Sherese looked around anxiously.

"I can't believe that nobody knows Aunt Rosa is sick."

"Nobody knows because they don't wanna know. Besides, you know how most of the family is."

"What do you mean by that, Sher?"

"You know how most of us are too worried about going to church than to see about hurting people."

"That's not true!"

"It is true. Sometimes it seemed like we would've ignored and stepped over a homeless person to get inside the church. Besides, when it comes to Aunt Rosa, or should I say 'my mother,' according to the church, well, let's just say that I already know their take on her."

"What do you mean?"

"You know Daddy would be the first to say that it's her punishment for the life she lived."

"Shhhhhhh. Lower your voice, Sher." Sydney looked to make sure Mr. Finch wasn't in sight. "Now that's surely misquoting Daddy. He'd say it was a consequence, not a punishment."

When Mr. Finch came in the living room, he didn't sit down, but signaled for them to come into the room Rosa was in.

Sydney stood up, but Sherese remained glued to the sofa.

"It's okay, darlin'," Mr. Finch said sympathetically, waiting for her to follow.

As Sherese walked down the narrow, dark hallway, once again nervousness nearly overcame her. Outside of the entryway to the room, there was what looked to be a very old painting on the wall of Jesus tending sheep. On the small antique table directly below the painting, there was an open Bible. To Sherese's surprise, a high school senior photo of her rested on the inside of the Bible on the other side of the twenty-third Psalm. She was surprised but figured her mother must've sent it to Rosa.

Once Sherese laid eyes on Rosa's frail body, her lips trembled. "Hello," Sherese said in a soft voice.

"Wally? Wally?" Rosa cried.

"Right here, honey." Mr. Finch rushed to her side to comfort her.

The hospital bed seemed to swallow up Rosa as she lay helplessly, staring blankly at Sherese and Sydney. Her gray, coarse hair was brushed back off of her weathered gaunt face, and she had lost most of her top front teeth, making her look much older than her fifty-plus years.

While Mr. Finch checked the pillows that propped her legs up slightly, he said in a loud, clear voice, "Rosa, this here is your girl,

Sherese. She come with Darlene's girl, Sydney." He looked to see if the news made any connection with her.

The blank look on Rosa's face let Sherese know that her mother was not mentally intact, and from the looks of all the medications and her ghastly appearance, Sherese knew that Rosa probably didn't have long to live.

She searched her mother's face for her own likeness, and Sherese was disappointed until Rosa started to hum "Amazing Grace." Sherese noticed on Rosa's cheeks the same deep dimples that she had. Once she had identified that, she began to notice other similarities between her and her mother. The oval shape of her mother's face was just like hers, as well as the shape of their long slender fingers.

"I'd ask y'all to take a seat, but quite frankly, Rosa doesn't seem to be havin' one of her better days."

"Oh, sure. I understand," Sherese muttered, although she didn't understand anything. Her mind was still reeling from finding out that the mother she had known all of her life wasn't her actual mother. Now, she was faced with the fact that the woman she'd thought had been a crazy, strung-out aunt was her mother, and she was dying.

Instead of going back into the living room, Sherese raced back out to the front porch to get some air. With Sydney on her heels, she gasped for air once she made it outside.

"Sher? You okay?"

Sherese grabbed her sister like she was going to shake her, but instead, just held her arms tightly and then buried her face on her sister's shoulder as sobs racked her whole body. In an embrace that matched the intensity of Sherese's, Sydney held her and cried silently.

"Y'all don't need to leave in a hurry, now." Mr. Finch called out as he started to come out onto the porch until he saw the sisters crying and embracing. He quickly turned back around to go back into the house, but Sherese heard him and pulled away from Sydney.

She wiped the tears and said to Mr. Finch, "Please, come out. I'm sorry."

He let the screen door close anyway and insisted, "You two just take your time. I know it's a lot."

"Come on, Sher. Let's sit down for a minute on the swing," Sydney offered.

"I just wanna go now," Sherese said wearily.

"Okay, but let me tell Mr. Finch."

When he returned to the porch, he carried underneath his arms what looked like a scrapbook and a tattered notebook. "Sherese, I'm sorry that you had to find out about your mother like this, but I do want to tell you that she loves you. Every day is different. Tomorrow she might be able to talk to me 'bout somethin' she remembers we done. Anyhow, why don't you come back tomorrow? She might be feelin' better, but her mind is goin' fast lately. The doctor told her that those years of abusin' those drugs just plain and simple wreaked havoc on her body."

He patted the books he held, "Well, these are some things that Rosa had even before we got married. They're the most precious things in the world to her. Before she startin' ailin' real bad, she had been workin' furiously on these things. Before her last stroke, she told me to give these to you, if by some chance, you came to see her. I think she knew that you'd come and she also knew that she was real bad off." He extended the books towards Sherese.

Sherese accepted the two oblong photo albums. "Thank you, Mr. Finch, for everything."

"Don'tcha go thankin' me when I ain't done nothing. One thing though, just call me Walter. I know ya'll just met me, but it would make me feel good if y'all acted like we was family."

"Of course, Walter," Sydney answered.

"Y'all gonna be in Natchez long? I mean, you think you'll get back here tomorrow?" he asked.

"I don't think we'll be here long, but I'll try to come by tomorrow," Sherese responded.

"That would be mighty nice," Walter said, then he hesitated.

"What is it, Mr. Finch? I mean, Walter," Sydney corrected.

After reaching his hands deep into his front pockets, Walter looked kindly at the two women. "We have service tonight at our church, and a few of the women at the church have been kind enough to rotate staying here on church nights so I can be there. Anyhow, Pastor has had a real big influence on Rosa, and I just wanted ya' both to come to the service if ya' got no other plans, but I guess maybe ya'll got to see a lot of family here."

"Thanks for the invitation, but I won't be coming to church this evening." Feeling dizzy, Sherese was anxious to leave. "Like I said earlier, maybe we'll stop by here tomorrow before we head out."

"All righty then. Name of the church is Emmanuel COGIC. It's right off of Baylor on Lewis Street."

Instead of shaking Walter's hand, Sydney hugged him and thanked him for his hospitality. When he turned towards Sherese to hug her goodbye, she was already outside of the gate, avoiding eye contact with Walter as she threw her hand up, giving a brief wave.

Long or sappy goodbyes were not easy for Sherese, and even as a child she avoided them.

"You okay, Sher?" Sydney asked while sticking the key into the ignition.

"Yeah." Sherese knew that Sydney was probably as unconvinced that she was okay as she herself was because she couldn't even bear to look her sister in the eyes for fear that she would have a meltdown. She had learned too much in too little time, and as much as she appreciated Walter's willingness to open up with her about Rosa,

Sherese was angry and sad about the way her life was unraveling. Instead, Sherese sat with the books Walter had given her carefully centered on her lap as she gazed stoically ahead into the Mississippi afternoon sky, wondering why she couldn't muster up the strength to open them.

CHAPTER 23

Sydney

He giveth power to the faint; and to them
that have no might he increaseth strength.

Isaiah 40:29

"Maya, honey, I should be back tomorrow evening and you can stay the night with me one night this week if your mom says it's okay."

"She makes me totally sick! I'm tired of her, Syd! I wish she would just let me come live with you."

Sydney cringed at her stepdaughter's harsh words. Maya had never sounded so upset and angry. "Just be respectful, Maya. It will backfire if you're not," Sydney gently corrected.

"I don't care."

"Don't say that. You do care. You know your mom just wants what's best for you."

"She doesn't have a clue what's best for me," Maya sulked.

"I know it may seem that way now, but you'll understand it when you're older."

"If one more person says that to me, I think I'll just scream."

Even though it was over the phone, Sydney knew that Maya must be rolling her eyes in frustration, but she continued on. "Just be thankful for all of the things she does allow you to do."

"I just wish my dad were here. He would let me go to the party after the game. You know he would."

Sydney couldn't argue with Maya because she knew that Vance would've called Tiffany to plead his daughter's case. Despite her husband's decisive and sometimes even controlling nature, when it came to Maya, Vance would often cave, allowing his daughter to have her way. In Sydney's opinion, Vance had spoiled Maya and sometimes even undermined Tiffany, which Sydney was determined not to do.

"Every one of my friends is going to Keisha's party but me. It's not fair!"

"Your mom didn't say that you couldn't go, right?"

"She might as well have since nobody will even get to the party until ten."

"Well, sweetie, you just obey your mom. We'll talk when I get back. I'm gonna let you go for now, okay?"

She heard only a weak mumble from Maya until Sydney said, "You know how you've wanted to go to New York City to shop?"

"Uh huh." The enthusiasm in Maya's voice was unmistakeable.

"Well, just hang in there, and don't cause your mom any headaches. Then, at least, I can talk to your mom about New York."

"I love you, Syd."

"Love you too."

When Sydney hung up the phone, she was plagued by the familiar loneliness and despair that crept in without warning. She started to dial someone else's number so she could at least keep the emptiness away for a while longer, but when Sydney reflected on the number of calls she had made over the past hour, she was almost ashamed.

It was Friday, and she knew she needed to get some things taken care of before Monday. First, she talked to her boss about tying up some loose ends before taking her official leave of absence. Next, she tried to reach her parents who weren't home or at the church. After that, she called Chanel and was relieved to find out that Zachary was doing much better. Her final call to Maya was an awakening of a sort. Whenever she tried to fill the void inside with others, she still came up empty. Sure, she felt somewhat better while she was talking to them, but it was just a temporary fix. She had to figure out how to have peace all by herself.

She was slowly beginning to realize that on the outside she appeared to trust and rely totally on God, but she had used others as a crutch in her spiritual life—first, her father and mother, and then Vance. Now, she was exposed.

Sydney could recall many times when she went to Vance for prayer because, although she prayed, she was often plagued by doubt, not sure that God really heard her. Vance always came through for her, and his confidence and trust in the Lord exuded from his being. When her father's diabetes forced him into the hospital, Sydney recalled Vance's calming presence.

"I'm scared, Vance."

"Baby, I know you are. He's gonna be okay. The Lord is not through with your daddy. You just be strong, and keep your chin up."

"I'm scared to see him. What if he doesn't look like himself? Pray for me, please?"

Without hesitation, Vance took a small vial of his anointing oil from his glove compartment while they were parked in the hospital parking garage. He dabbed a small amount of the tip of his finger and placed it gently on her forehead.

"Lord, we thank You. We love You, Lord. We just praise You for all You are to us. I'm coming to You, asking You to give my wife comfort, courage, and peace. I'm standing on Your Word, Lord, and Your Word says that You have not given us a spirit of fear. Take away the fear, Lord. Touch my father-in-law in a mighty way. We know and trust You'll do it. Thank God. Amen."

Sydney remembered that the fear left her instantly after her husband's prayer. It didn't matter what the situation was. Vance had always been there for her, from the smallest thing to the largest. Even when Sydney was nervous about getting a root canal, Vance had surprised her by taking off from work to meet her at the dentist's office. He was her shoulder to cry on when she had to fire one of her subordinates and felt terrible about it. And before leaving for work each morning, Vance anointed her and prayed for her day. She knew that he always had her back spiritually. Sydney was now realizing how dependent she had become on him instead of the Lord. She had to believe that God heard not only the prayers of her father, mother, and late husband, but she also had to believe that the Lord heard *her* prayers.

Sydney had gone to Friday night church services her whole life because, as a child, she'd had no choice. As an adult, she went because that's what she had been trained to do; it was the right thing. Now, for the first time, she wanted to attend the church service she had been invited to—not because it was her routine or because it would disappoint her father or someone else. It didn't matter if Sherese didn't want to go with her. It didn't matter that she wouldn't know anyone there with the exception of Walter. She had a sudden burning desire to be around saints in the house of the Lord.

When she opened her suitcase to get out her plum sundress for the service, the very faint aroma of her late husband's cologne hit her unexpectedly. She found it hard to believe that she hadn't smelled it all of the other times she had opened the suitcase on the trip. Without retrieving the dress, Sydney slammed the suitcase shut and fell back onto the bed, covering her face with her hands.

"Hey, Syd?" Sherese asked cautiously.

Sydney uncovered her face. "I didn't even hear you come in."

"Oh, I just ran downstairs to get on the Internet to get directions to go to the church. I don't think I remember the directions Walter gave."

"Really? You mean you're actually going?" Sydney couldn't hide her surprise at her sister's revelation.

"You act like I'm the devil himself or something."

"You know I didn't mean it like that."

"Yeah, well, I guess I'm curious more than anything. I mean, the church has to be something else if Rosa got saved there, right?"

Sydney nodded in silent, stunned agreement, but Sherese changed the subject. "You look like you just saw a ghost. You okay?"

"I guess so. It's just that so many things remind me of Vance, and I just don't know how I'm going to go on. The pain that seems to zap every bit of my will to go on hits me every single day. Certain programs, things people say, foods, songs, smells, even scriptures make me think of how much I miss him. How am I supposed to go on? How am I supposed to get over it?"

Sherese sat down at the desk and sighed. "Ya' know? I really don't think it's something you're gonna ever get over."

"Well, how am I supposed to go on with my life when I don't think I can ever really be happy again. I know life isn't all about being happy, but I don't even know my purpose anymore. Things made so much sense with Vance. My life was planned out. What did I do, or better yet, what did he do to deserve this?"

"You can't really believe that God is punishing you or him through this, can you?"

"I just don't know what I believe anymore. My whole foundation has been shaken and now, this with you. I just don't know." Sydney's voice trailed off.

"You know what I think?"

"What?" Sydney asked.

"I think that God allowed this because He knew you could handle it. He knew that you could help somebody else."

A sarcastic chuckle escaped from Sydney's lips. "Girl, I can't help myself, let alone help somebody else."

"Maybe you already have, but you just don't know it." Sherese smiled warmly at her sister.

Even though Sydney wasn't totally convinced, she returned the smile. She got back up and opened her suitcase to get her things ready for the service. A renewed determination sprang up in her from her sister's encouragement.

"Sher, I don't tell you often enough because, to be honest, I'm always too busy trying to be the big sister who knows more, but you mean a lot to me."

"Syd, please—"

"No, let me finish. I don't know what I'd do without you. Please know that when I'm telling you what I think you should or shouldn't do, it's because I love you. I haven't always gone about it the right way when I was trying to let you know that, but losing Vance has really opened my eyes. I need to start letting people—no, you—know how much I love you, just the way you are."

"Love you too. We're both just gonna have to help each other bear these trials." Sherese got up and said, "Come on, now." Then, she changed her dialect to a Southern one. "Ya' wouldn't wanna be late for the church gatherin' tonight, would ya'?"

Nestled behind an old, abandoned warehouse, wearing a sun-bleached and chipped Pepsi advertisement painted on the brick, was the small white church. The sign read New Hope C-GIC, and Sydney couldn't help wondering why someone hadn't replaced the missing "O" on the sign. *Could an "O" cost that much,* she thought. The church sat on a small hill surrounded by a sea of tiny homes in an array of Miami-looking colors.

No sooner had she and Sherese stepped foot out of the car than they were met and welcomed by the resounding sounds of a praise and worship service, which had already begun. The church almost seemed to move rhythmically to the beat as the sisters entered the sanctuary. Sydney couldn't believe how the planks on the wooden floor actually vibrated to the beat, but she was more surprised to find out that the front door lead right into the sanctuary. With no entryway or foyer, Sydney and her sister stood, trying to find a seat, aware of all the people who continued to sing and clap but yet stare at them.

"Hi, ya'll doin okay? This your first time here?" a lady dressed in white, who appeared to be an usher, asked.

"We're fine and, yes, it is," Sydney answered.

The usher whipped out two cards from her front pocket and said, "Please fill out this visitor card, if you don't mind."

After Sydney and Sherese took the visitor cards and found a seat, Sherese whispered, "Why do so many people have Jheri curls here? That usher looked like she must've sprayed the whole bottle of whatever that stuff is on her hair! She looks plain hot."

"Don't you even start with that, Sher. Just fill out your card and enjoy the service."

The praise and worship leaders led song after song with enthusiasm and heartfelt praise to God, so much so that Sydney noticed her sister stood up to join her, clapping and singing to the call and response song, "I know the Bible is right" while the congregation sang back, "Somebody's wrong."

As they took their seats, Sydney noticed that Walter had come in and was helping to take up the offering. Their eyes met and they smiled at one another.

"Psssst," Sydney whipered to her sister.

"What's up?"

"Did you see Walter over there?"

"Yeah, I saw him. What's he got to be so happy about? You notice how much that man smiles? You'd never know he's got a sick wife."

Sydney thought about her sister's comment, but she knew how Walter could smile so much in spite of his heartache over his wife. She knew he was a man of great faith, and her determination to have a better and more optimistic attitude in spite of her situation sprang up in her in that very moment.

After the offering, the first lady of the church welcomed the visitors. Despite the fact that they were the only two visitors and there was probably a total of about fifty people in the whole congregation, Sydney and Sherese were welcomed as if they were royalty. To Sydney, it seemed as if everyone in the entire church came to give her and her sister a hug after the pastor's wife said, "We are a church that believes in lovin' everybody, and everybody is a somebody at New Hope Church of God in Christ. We believe that we have a new hope in Christ Jesus our Savior and we must always spread the love of our new hope. Show our visitors what I mean, New Hope."

After the big welcome, the first lady asked, "Would either one of ya'll like to have words?"

Sherese nodded no, but Sydney knew that protocol meant she should. "Praise the Lord, Saints!"

They responded almost in unison, "Praise the Lord."

"I give honor to God who is the head of my life. I give honor to the pastor of this fine church and the first lady. I give honor to the elders, deacons, missionaries, saints, and friends. I bring greetings from New Deliverance Church of God in Christ in Rochester, New York, where Superintendent Samuel L. Hightower is my pastor. My name is Sydney Ellington and I'm happy to be here today with my sister, Sherese. We were invited today by Deacon Walter Harrison." She paused for a few seconds while a few clapped and said "Praise the Lord."

She continued, "The Bible says we are overcome by the words of our testimony, so this evening I just want to thank the Lord for saving me, sanctifying me, and filling me with His precious Holy Ghost. You all pray my strength in the Lord."

As a flood of "amens" and "thank You, Jesus'" filled the room, Sydney sat down, smiling. Sherese nudged her, whispering, "Alright then, Missionary Hightower. You sound just like your mama."

Sydney noticed that Sherese made a point of saying "your" mama, and she silently prayed that something would be said or done that would prick her sister's heart. She desperately wanted Sherese to feel that their mama was just that—their mother.

Before Missionary Lewis, the first lady, sat down, she turned to her husband and asked, "Pastor, I hope I'm not too much out of order, but this daughter that's visitin' with us has made me want to hear some of your burnin' testimonies. What you think about that?"

The pastor nodded in affirmation as Missionary Lewis called for testimonies. One after another jumped up like popcorn thanking the Lord for a job, healing, finances, and even good grades in school. Sydney was really being blessed, and she knew that her sister especially was when a young woman who looked to be in her mid-twenties stood up to give her testimony. An uncanny silence came over the congregation when she stood up.

The young woman didn't say anything for a few seconds and briefly held her head down with her hand up to her lips, so the congregation seemed to want to encourage her to speak. Someone called out, "It's all right, honey." Then, someone else said, "You better tell it!"

Clad in a halter top which exposed her unprofessional-looking tattoo of a fox, she crossed her arms and began. "I wanna say first that I grew up in the church, but I strayed away a long time ago. I've been livin' a life that I know would make my mama turn over in her grave if she knew about it. My life has been about partyin', drinkin' and men."

Sydney heard someone way in the back of the church sing, "Lord, Lord, Lord."

The young woman continued, "I guess I need to back up. My stepfather was in the church, just like my mother. As a matter of fact, they met in church when I was about eight years old. He had a lot of respect in my hometown at church. I mean, that man was always prophesying or witnessing to someone. To make a long story short, when I was twelve, he started molesting me. I didn't tell anybody, but I'd just watch what a fake and a phony he was at church. I decided that I would never get saved since all saved people must live the way my stepfather did. I even blamed my mother for something she didn't even know about. I felt like God should've told her that he was hurting me. Anyway, I've been on a destructive road for a long time and have moved all over Mississippi getting into all kinds of bad situations. Last night, I was at a party and a fight broke out. A crazy man aimed a gun at me for no reason, but somehow the bullet missed me."

Tears started to flow as the girl stressed, "The gun was pointed at my head, but the bullet missed me. In that second, I knew that I had to repent for all my sins." With her voice trembling, she continued, "I don't know what it is, but I know after last night that God has a purpose for my life. I was at death's door, and God has given me another chance."

A host of "hallelujahs" and "thank You, Jesus'" broke out across the room as the pastor stood to his feet and walked to the podium.

"Before I sit down, I just want to say that I have forgiven my stepfather and my mother. I know that God is real, and I just pray that He can forgive me so that I can live the life that he wants me to live."

With that said, the organist and drummer played until people were dancing and shouting all over the church. Sydney rejoiced with the rest of the congregation over the soul saved, and she even danced a little until the Pastor began to speak.

He addressed the young woman and signaled for her to come forward, "Daughter, don't wonder if God has forgiven you. As Jesus said, you just go in peace and don't sin. Forget what's behind and you just press forward. The Lord has saved you and delivered you from the pit of hell."

The pastor then stepped down from the pulpit and stood facing the young woman. He took the anointing oil from one of the elders and dabbed some on his hand. When he placed his hand gently on her forehead, she was slain in the spirit immediately. One of the missionaries behind her caught her and another took a sheet to cover her body until she came to.

The powerful testimony along with pastor's words freed Sydney from the guilt she had wrestled so violently with about the argument with Vance. She asked the Lord once again to forgive her, knowing this time that she would accept the Lord's forgiveness for her harsh words that night. With uplifted hands in total surrender, Sydney felt that her life could somehow, someway begin again.

Having been so wrapped up in her own deliverance, praise and worship, Sydney had almost forgotten about her sister until she heard Sherese speaking in tongues and worshipping the Lord as she never had before. A joy that Sydney had never experienced leapt in her spirit as she thanked and praised the Lord for the outpouring of his blessings. Every burden had lifted from her, and she felt the Lord's presence as never before.

When the praise and worship had subsided, the pastor pointed to Sherese and signaled for her to come up. Sherese wiped her tears and went up to the front of the church to join the pastor.

"The Lord had done something for you today, Sis. Tell the saints what the Lord has done."

Without hesitation, Sherese grabbed the microphone, but she was overwhelmed with a joy she could hardly contain. "The young lady that testified blessed me. When I thought I couldn't open my heart to really and truly trust the Lord, her words spoke directly to me." Sherese could hear the "Amens" and the "Hallelujahs," but she continued. "What I've known all my life has been church. I've known church, but I had never met Jesus.

The pastor put his arm around her shoulder, "Glory be to God, you go ahead now, Sis."

Sherese started to cry, but she continued. "I have never really trusted Him for myself. I would go up to the altar and say I was saved out of sheer emotion and to please people, but not tonight. Some things have happened in my life that I can't handle alone, and no one can handle them for me. I mean, no person can help me, but today, I've decided to trust Him. The Lord's Spirit let me know that I need him like I need the air that I breathe. I've turned everything over— it's like I understand what that song means after all these years."

The first lady handed the pastor a tissue to give to Sherese, and he asked, "What song is that?"

"All to Jesus I surrender, all to Him I freely give." She wiped her nose again. "I thank the Lord for giving me a second chance. I thank Him for saving me and filling me with His precious Holy Ghost tonight."

"What you say!" the Pastor exclaimed as the church went up in praise again.

As Sydney cried tears of unspeakable joy, she glanced over at Walter who also was crying his own tears of joy. Her sister had gone through a lot in a short time, but she now knew that Sherese would be just fine.

CHAPTER 24

Chanel

The God of all grace, who hath called us unto his eternal glory
by Christ Jesus, after that ye have suffered a while,
make you perfect, stablish, stregthen, settle you.

1 Peter 5:10

Tommy had agreed to make the bank deposit and pick up Zachary tonight so Chanel could lock the café up and go straight home, something she could rarely do. Business at the café had really picked up all week and since Lena had called in sick for two days, Chanel had worked extra hard. She had no idea what had gotten into Lena, but her reliability was beginning to wane. Tommy had come in to the café to help the two days Lena was out sick but on one of the days when Chanel ran to the bank, Tommy had told her that Lena stopped in.

Chanel had asked Tommy, "I thought that girl was sick."

Tommy had shrugged his shoulders. "She looked just fine to me."

"What did she come in for?"

"She called first and asked where you were. I told you were out. Then, she said she might stop in for a minute."

"That's kind of weird."

"Yeah, well, all I can say is that with those tight jeans and heels, she didn't look like she was recovering from anything. I don't think I've ever seen that girl so done up."

Chanel thought that sounded unlike Lena, but then decided that she must have recovered from whatever ailment she had claimed to be suffering from. Although it had crossed Chanel's mind that Lena might want to talk to Tommy about what she may have seen, Chanel opted not to question her about the visit from Antonio. Some things were better left alone, she decided.

She was thankful that Tommy had come to help and had proven himself to be so efficient and patient, taking orders and helping her clean all week.

As she drove home, she reflected on how Tommy had dropped his rehearsals and recording schedule for two days to help her out in the café. He had been so efficient, but friendly with the patrons, idly chatting with them about a little bit of everything. No job seemed to be too menial to him either. He sterilized the counter and table tops, mopped, and Chanel had even joked when she saw him coming out of the restroom with a toilet brush, something he rarely did at home. He stayed extra late, doing more than she asked.

In spite of her tired and aching body, she would show her husband just how much she appreciated and loved him tonight. Although Tommy hadn't slept in their bed since he had come back home, Chanel was convinced that she wouldn't have trouble getting him back where he belonged.

When she went into the house, instead of going through her usual routine of kicking off her shoes, plopping down on the sofa, and going through mail, she instead decided to take a quick shower. Afterward, she applied her sweet-smelling body shimmer lotion, swept her hair over to the side, and squirted on Tommy's favorite perfume. Thankful that Tommy hadn't come in yet, she slipped Tommy's favorite yellow negligee on underneath her terry cloth robe.

Next, she laid out her husband's silk pajama bottoms and lit candles throughout the room. When she heard the garage door open, she knew her husband was pulling in, so she drew him a bubble bath.

"Chanel! Chanel!"

Chanel took one last quick look at herself in the mirror before racing down the steps, figuring Tommy must've needed some help with Zachary.

"Hey, honey. Where's Zachary?"

Tommy threw his keys carelessly on the coffee table. "I let Mom keep him tonight."

Chanel couldn't believe how perfectly her plan was coming together. Even though they hadn't eaten dinner, she figured that could wait as she suggestively let her robe fall open to reveal her nightie.

Her husband ignored his wife's advances and paced the floor, clearly agitated.

"What's wrong, Tommy?" Chanel asked as she pulled her robe together.

"What's wrong? Let me tell you what's wrong, Chanel. I can't believe that you have embarrassed me and yourself like you have."

"What are you talking about?"

"I'm talking about running into your girl, Lena. I was at the bank, and I ran into her. She's always sort of been slightly flirtatious with me, but tonight, she really laid it on thick."

Chanel gasped in disbelief. "Lena, who works for me?"

With sarcasm, Tommy mocked, "Yeah, Lena who works for you. Get this, she tells me she's always been really attracted to me. I tell her, 'Look, I'm happily married, and my wife would not appreciate this.' She then tells me, 'I don't think your wife really cares since she's got her own thing goin' on.' I said to her, 'What's that supposed to mean?' She then proceeds to tell me that everyone knows that dark-skinned brother who comes to the café is having some affair with you. What the—" Tommy stopped short of cussing.

"Oh, Tommy, that's not true." Chanel tried to get close to him, but he pushed her away.

"No! You actually let that brother go to your café? He knows where you work?"

"He only came once and that must've been what she's talking about. I didn't invite him. You gotta believe me. Lena just wants to cause us trouble because she wants you. Can't you see that?"

"You know what I see, Chanel? I see a woman who is successful in her business, is a role model and inspiration at church, and is even a great mom. But, I also see a woman who just lost her husband. It's over." With that said, Tommy picked up his keys and slammed the front door shut.

Chanel knew that it would be useless to go after him. She buried her head in her hands, praying about what she should do next.

———

"The first thing you need to do is get rid of that chick, Lena," Sherese said with authority as they walked into the closed café.

"I gotta agree with that. Chanel, I was worried about what she may have seen, but I wasn't sure." Sydney put her purse on the counter and took a seat on the stool next to her sister as Chanel turned on the lights and started one of the small coffee pots.

"I am totally shocked that Lena seemed so innocent. To think she's been after Tommy is scary. Even when I let the girl go, though, it still won't solve that fact that I was wrong. The whole thing with Antonio was just wrong."

"Well, it's none of my business, Chanel, but I am curious. What *exactly* did happen between you and Antonio?" Sherese eyed her questioningly.

Before Chanel could answer, Sydney added, "I know you said nothing happened, but what does that mean?"

As Chanel took three cups and saucers out of a top shelf, she explained, "I was attracted to him, and I'm ashamed to say that I was guilty of adultery in the sense that I was attracted to Antonio. I told him things about Tommy that I never had a right to. I don't know what I was thinking."

"Maybe you just *weren't* thinking," Sherese interjected.

"Don't make her feel worse, Sher," Sydney scolded her sister.

"My bad. You know I don't mean any harm as much as I've done without thinking," Sherese answered.

"That's one part of it. I wasn't thinking much. I mean, I felt like I was justified in talking to him as a friend. Before I knew it, he was romancing me, but I've gotta say it was more an emotional affair than anything else. We didn't sleep together, if that's what the two of you are getting at."

Sydney and Sherse seemed to take a sigh of relief simultaneously.

"But," Chanel continued, "I did kiss him."

"How was that?" Sherese asked.

Sydney nudged her sister. "Don't answer that question. The most important thing is to let Tommy know that you two didn't sleep together and how sorry you are. Let him know that it will never happen again."

"You all have to know that I've begged, pleaded, and cried, but Tommy won't move. I think the marriage is over, and I don't even think the issue is so much whether he believes that I slept with Antonio. I think he really knows that I would never allow things to go there, but I do think the violation of his trust is unforgivable."

"In that case, all you can do is pray and ask God to intercede. He can break up Tommy's stony heart just like he softened yours toward him," Sydney commented as she poured creamer into her coffee.

When Chanel went to pour Sherese a cup, she put her hand up. "My sista, I'll pass on the coffee. You got some of that cranberry juice?"

"Yeah, I forgot you're the weird one who doesn't drink coffee," Chanel teased.

As Chanel turned the sound system on, they heard CeCe Winans' soothing voice throughout the café. "You all never finished telling me about the trip. I can't believe that Zachary got that sick so fast. I'm just sorry I didn't make it to Natchez with you."

"Don't even give that a second thought, girl. You needed to be with him. If we would've known how sick he was, tell you the truth, we would've been right there with you," Sherese said.

"In that case, I'm glad that you didn't know. You needed to be exactly where you were," Chanel added.

"You know, I can say that you're right about that. I'm still overwhelmed, but I guess everything is starting to make some sense to me now. I've been able to talk to Mama and Daddy. I know they kept it from me because they love me so much and I can't hold that against them. I would've liked to have known sooner though. I just can't help thinking that maybe I could've done something to help Rosa before now. I am the only child she ever had. In a weird way, I'm upset that she wasn't there for me, but I'm even more upset that I wasn't there for her."

"You have time now, Sherese," Sydney reminded her.

"Please, Syd. Did you see how out of it she was? I don't think she knows anyone."

"Yeah, but God knows, and you can still tell her. Walter said that the doctors don't really know what she can comprehend, but they think that she understands more than she can respond and react to, so it's worth a try."

"So, Rosa's really bad off then?" Chanel asked with concern.

"The years of drug and alcohol abuse were just too much for her body. It's a miracle that she's even alive according to her husband, Walter. It's just real sad." A tear fell down Sherese's face, and Sydney and Chanel put their arms around her to comfort her.

After wiping her nose, Sherese admitted, "You know, even in the midst of all the shock and sadness, there's still one thing that Rosa did for me besides give me birth and give me to Mama and Daddy."

"What's that?" Chanel asked.

"She helped me to get saved in a roundabout way. I was so curious about the church where she got saved, I had to go see it for myself, never thinking in a million years that I'd end up getting saved. Here, Mama and Daddy raised me the best they could. I mean, I've grown up in holiness and been in the church all of my life, but through finding out I was adopted and going to meet my ailing mother, the Lord saved me."

Sydney squeezed her sister's arm. "God is just good like that, Sher. Satan wants to destroy us, and more than anything, take our minds. He wants us to turn away from God, but the Lord is so merciful because He'll give us chance after chance. He is more powerful than whatever Satan throws our way, but He gives us the choice as to whether we'll draw close to Him or run away."

"Y'all gonna get me shoutin' up in here talking like that. You're so right. It doesn't matter what it looks like. As long as we pray and seek Him with our whole heart, He will lead us in the right path. I mean, if you really think about it, God has seen the three of us through so much."

Sydney nodded. "God has really used both of you over the past months to help me. I'll probably be grieving in some way for Vance for the rest of my natural life, but the fog is beginning to clear a little. I couldn't really be used by the Lord when I was dependent on Vance for my spiritual strength. I think I couldn't come to this understanding without Vance passing away. His passing has revealed that I need to trust and depend on God for myself. I know Him in ways I didn't, and I can truly say that I've had a praise in the valley."

Sherese cleared her throat as if she had something to say. "I know you all have never heard me say what I'm about to say, but I would like to pray if it's okay."

Sydney and Chanel looked at each other and smiled knowingly as the three stood up in a small circle and joined hands.

"Lord, I thank You for being all-knowing and all-powerful. We thank You for leading us and guiding us. We really want to say thank You for joining us together. When we think about what we could've been without You, we know we couldn't have made it. I thank You for my family and friends. I thank You even for the trials that have made me draw closer to You. Forgive me for the times when I haven't thanked You and also for Your protection, mercy, and grace. You know the situations that the three of us are facing, and we know that only You can resolve them and give us peace beyond our understanding.

"We thank You for what You've done and for what You're getting ready to do. Thank God. Amen."

When Chanel opened her eyes, she didn't just see the two women who were her friends or her sisters in the Lord. She saw extensions of God's love, and she knew in her spirit that Sherese and Sydney saw the same thing she did.

CHAPTER 25

Sherese

Likewise, ye younger, submit yourselves unto the elder. Yea,
all of you be subject one to another, and be clothed with humility:
for God resisteth the proud, and giveth grace to the humble.

1 Peter 5:5

Each time Sherese prepared to go to church now, an unfamiliar twinge of excitement came over her. As she reached for her pearls, she knew that they would accent her pink suit perfectly. Instead of just looking like a saint, Sherese finally felt like one. For most of her life, getting dressed for church had gone from near torture to mere routine. Now, she genuinely wanted be in the house of the Lord, she thought, as she slipped on her pink strappy heels. It was strange to get dressed to go to the same church she had gone to her whole life only now it was with such new feelings of anticipation.

Before she left her apartment, she stared at the albums on her end table that Walter had given her but were yet to be opened. Although she desperately wanted to look at them, she had let fear keep her from finding out what her mother wanted her to see and know. Sydney had coaxed her on the way back from Mississippi to look at them, but she had remained firm on her decision not to look at them yet. Sherese finally felt ready to look at them, but she still didn't want to look at them alone. When she grabbed the albums before leaving, she knew that she wanted to share the experience of opening them with her parents.

———

"Mama! Daddy!" Sherese called as she let herself in the front door to her parents' home.

Fully dressed in her rhinestone-fringed pink suit, her mother seemed to be clipping her earring in as she commented, "So, you decided to wear pink too? You look nice, baby."

"Mama, you're the one who looks lovely."

"For a young gal like you to use the word 'lovely,' I must look all right."

Sherese kissed her lightly on the cheek, careful not to let her makeup touch her mother's fancy hat. "Where are Daddy and Sydney?"

"You know how those two are. They couldn't sit still and just wait for me. Sydney done gone with him to make sure that the deacons have everything right for the service. Thing about it is, he stayed up there half the night, supposedly doin' the same thing. What's that you carryin'?"

"Oh, these?" Sherese looked down at the albums in her arms. She hadn't planned on sharing them without her father, but since her mother was here alone, she knew that it was probably better this way anyway. She said a silent prayer and continued, "Mama, I know we have only talked on a surface level about the trip to Mississippi and Rosa, but her husband, Walter, said that she always kept these albums for me. He said that she had an idea that her health was getting worse, and she was really insistent that I get these. The only thing is, I haven't looked at them yet. I was hoping that you'd look at them with me."

Her mother put her purse down on the coffee table and she sat down on the sofa. "Of course, honey. Come on." Her mother patted the empty space on the sofa cushion next to her.

"We don't need to do this now, Mama. I know you don't want to be late for the service."

"Now, you know Bishop McKinley's coming from the second jurisdiction. He's late for everything. Besides, this is more important. Now, come on over here."

Sherese couldn't believe that her mother thought that looking at the albums was more important than going to church. She smiled nervously as she looked at her mother's face. Her mother looked equally nervous as they opened up the first album together.

The first page was a picture of a young mother holding a newborn baby. Underneath the picture, in childlike cursive writing, the caption read, The Love of My Life—Sherese Olivia-Rose Rayford.

"I've never seen this picture," Darlene said in awe.

Sherese picked the album up to examine it more closely. Rosa looked so young, and she looked so tiny. As her eyes moved across to the next page, there was a picture of a brown-skinned man with a somewhat ruddy complexion. He had a hi-top fade haircut and was holding a forty-ounce, smiling. Under his picture, it read: Albert Brooks. And under that, in almost tiny unintelligible writing, it read: Your daddy. Sherese turned to look at her mother and asked, "Mama, does that say, 'Your daddy'?" Does that mean it's my biological father?

"Let me get my glasses." Darlene opened her purse and pulled out her glasses as she looked at the print more closely. "That's what it looks like, but Rosa told me she didn't know who your father was."

"What if this is him? I mean, do you think I could find him?"

Darlene took a deep breath. "It could be. I just don't know."

Sherese's head spun so much that she couldn't even turn the page as she tried to grasp the possibility that the picture just might be one of her biological father. She studied it over and over again to see if she looked like him. The only feature that seemed to slightly resemble Sherese's was his prominent nose.

Her mother remained quiet, just as surprised and confused as Sherese seemed to be. When she finally turned the page, she saw an eight-by-ten picture of her in kindergarten, and on the next page Sherese saw what she knew was her first-grade picture. Page after page was filled with pictures of Sherese throughout her childhood. On the last page of the first album, there was even a wedding picture of her and D'Andre.

"Mama, you sent these pictures of me to Rosa?"

Her mother explained, "Yes. I knew that if my sister could've taken care of you, she would've. She just wasn't capable of doing it. When she trusted me to adopt you, I knew that was the most unselfish thing she could ever do. I also knew that she loved you, even though she didn't have you, so I always made sure to send pictures to one of my sisters to make sure Rosa could get them."

Sherese slowly picked up the remaining album, which consisted solely of her artwork. The first picture in the album was a picture of a chicken that she had colored with crayons. The teacher had written on the top of the paper, "Mrs. Hightower, clearly your daughter has an awesome gift!" Each page seemed to show the progression of her artistic skills. On the last page of the book, there was a pencil sketch that was unfamiliar to Sherese. It was an incredibly skilled picture of the sun setting behind mountains.

"Mama, I know I would've remembered this if I had done it."

"Hmmmmm. Let's look at the signature."

When they read the corner, they both gasped. The signature read: Olivia Rosa Rayford.

"I never knew Rosa had a gift like that. I'm amazed because I don't think anyone knew."

"Wow, I'm just speechless."

"Hopefully, it helps you to know that she's always thought of you. That's what she's tryin' to say. I tell ya', she always had a knack for surprisin' all of us, but this takes the cake."

"I guess we need to go on and head to the church, Mama. Service should be starting in twenty minutes or so," Sherese advised as she picked up the albums. As she went to get her purse, a paper fell from one of the albums.

"Baby," her mother said, "something fell out of one of them."

Sherese picked up the folded up and aged letter to open it. It was addressed to Sherese and written in pencil.

Sherese,

I always loved you.

Rosa

A lone tear fell from Sherese's eye as her mother wiped it gently from her face. "I know, baby."

"I love you, Mama."

"I love you, Sherese, more than you'll ever know."

"I know you do, Mama." Sherese hugged her mother. "You ready to go?"

"Almost. I got one more thing I need to tell you."

"What's that?"

"I know me and your daddy haven't done everything right, you know what I'm sayin'?"

Sherese nodded.

"I just want you to know that we tried our best to do right by you and Sydney. There's never been no difference between you, you know what I'm sayin'?"

"Mama, I know. Don't—"

"No, my spirit won't rest unless I tell you that. Whatever mistakes we done made along the way with you, I'm sure we done the same thing with Sydney."

"I know, Mama. I understand."

"All right then, I'm ready to go now, baby." Darlene patted her youngest daughter and headed out.

In an instant, the years of anger that Sherese had held in about her parents putting the church services and people first vanished. Just like that, her animosity was gone. She finally got it. Her parents' intentions did matter. They had always done what they thought was best for her and her sister. Sherese knew that it wasn't simply her mother's words that opened up her understanding. She knew that the Lord had broken up her once stony heart to make a soft place for her mother's words to land.

When they got to the car, Sherese decided to give her mother the painting she had finished a few days earlier. She had felt inspired and able to correct the eyes on the painting that earlier she had not been able to get quite right. As her mother admired the painting of her and her husband, she remarked, "How on earth did you make our eyes look so real and warm?"

Sherese smiled, knowing that she had captured her parents' true essence in more ways than one.

CHAPTER 26

Sydney

I have heard thy prayer, I have seen thy tears: behold, I will heal thee.

2 Kings 20:5

The church was packed, and Sydney still didn't see her mother or Sherese. Calling Sherese's cell phone had been futile because her voice mail just picked up. Her mother didn't believe in using cell phones, so instead of waiting any longer at the door, she took a seat in the pew next to Chanel, who asked, "You haven't seen Tommy, huh?"

"Sorry. Haven't seen him."

Chanel straightened Zachary's tie, and he bounced up and down on the pew. "Boy, if you don't stop this instant, you gonna take a trip to the bathroom to see your old friend."

Zachary stopped abruptly and asked with squinted eyes, "Who is in the bathroom? Who's my old friend."

Chanel whispered in her son's ear, "Good ole Mr. Switch."

Zachary let out a "Nooooo" the whole church could hear as Sydney swooped him up and into her lap. "You can't spank him," she said while planting a kiss on his cheek.

"Hhhmph, he better recognize what I'm sayin'. That boy's too big to be sitting on your lap too," Chanel said with attitude.

Sydney scanned the platform and thought that it was the first time she could remember so many pastors and elders on it. The deacons had to take extra chairs up to accommodate them. The congregation was no different. An extra row of chairs on the inside and outside of each pew had to be set up so that all of the people could fit into the sanctuary.

Sydney knew that the crowd spoke volumes about her father's character and reputation, not only in church, but also in the community. The church was not only full of COGIC members from across the city, but also with community leaders as well who were supportive of the vision her father had had some years ago. Her father had always wanted a youth center so that he could minister to the youth more effectively. He often said that you had to catch a fish before you could skin and cook it, so the youth center symbolized his way to "catch the youth" in the community.

As Sydney looked over the program for the service, she was relieved when she glanced up to see her mother and Sherese come in. She signaled for Sherese to come sit with her and Chanel.

"You and Mama took your time, didn't you? You know Daddy would have flipped out if you weren't here when the service started."

"Relax, Syd." Sherese turned to give her attention to Zachary. "Hey, what's happenin', lil man? Hey, Chanel, I haven't seen you in a minute." Sherese took her seat since the service was starting.

Sydney prayed, worshipped, praised, and listened intently through each part of the program, proud of her father's accomplishments. She knew that her daddy's ability to trust and depend on God was his key to success, and she prayed that one day she could have just a measure of his faith.

When the program was almost over, there was a section entitled "Remarks," but there were no names under it. Pastor after pastor got up to make remarks about Great Deliverance and Pastor Hightower, but it wasn't until one particular man made comments that shock came over the three women.

"Greetings in the name of our Lord Jesus Christ," the attractive man said with enthusiasm.

"I'm Elder Jack Simmons, coming in place of my father, Pastor Jack Simmons, Sr., of The Way of Holiness COGIC. As most of you know, my father has been very ill and is in the hosptal, but I'm believing God for his total and complete recovery from his heart attack." The congregation clapped in affirmation of this as he continued.

"He has asked that I tell Pastor Hightower what a blessing it's been to be counted as a friend for nearly thirty-plus years." Jack smiled and turned behind him to make eye contact with Pastor Hightower.

"He also wants you to know that he would do much more if he could, but would like to make a $500 contribution towards the new community center."

Sydney noticed that everyone seemed to clap but her sister, who had sunk conspicuously low in the pew.

"What in the world is wrong with you, Sher? You look like you just saw a ghost." Sydney frowned at her sister, whose face had lost its color.

"Lord knows, I'd feel better if I had." Sherese mumbled unintelligible words under her breath. *"Lord, help me. Jack the bartender is Jack the preacher? This cannot be happening to me."*

"What is *happening* to you?" Sydney asked, showing her agitation and confusion.

"I wish I could just get outta here. Any other time, any other day, I'd be outta here so fast."

"Girl, I don't know what just got into you, but you aren't leaving. Today is a special day for Mama and Daddy, and—"

"Oh, nobody's leaving, Sydney. I want to leave but I'm not. I just pray to God that he doesn't recognize me."

"Who?"

Sherese pointed again toward the young preacher.

"Are you talking about Jack, I mean, Elder Simmons?"

Sherese sat up a little. "You know him?" she whispered, pointing toward him.

Chanel joined their hushed conversation. "Know who?" she asked.

At the same time, Sherese and Sydney said, "Him!" as they looked toward the pulpit.

Sydney held her fan in front of her face and whispered to her sister, "You don't remember Jack? He was a bad little something when he was younger. Remember when we used to fellowship with Way of Holiness?"

Sherese nodded, and her sister continued, "He was the little boy who used to always be throwing spit wads, getting them stuck in the back of our heads when we were young."

Sherese seemed to be trying to remember him from her childhood, but when it seemed apparent that she couldn't, Sydney said, "The more I think about it, the more I'm thinking maybe you were too young to remember him. Anyhow, looks like he's turned into a nice-looking young man."

"Hhmmph," Sherese breathed out heavily, as if she hadn't noticed.

"What is it you have against him, Sher? That's what you need. A good homegrown preacher."

Sherese's face turned down in a frown.

"Shhhhh," Chanel whispered as Jack went to his seat and Pastor Hightower went to the podium to make his remarks.

"Words can't express my appreciation to you all for coming out and makin' me feel so good. The Lord gave me this vision some years back, and it makes my heart feel good to know that the saints helped this come to fruition. I want to especially thank Pastor Simmons' son, Elder Jack Simmons, for his kind words and contributions. Me and

Elder Simmons go way back and was friends before we became pastors. We both stay so busy, so we don't get together much, but I've been prayin' for him. And I want the church to continue to lift him up in prayer. We know our God is a healer and deliverer, right, church?"

Someone called out, "That's right!" Another said, "He'll do it!"

Pastor Hightower continued, "Yes, we certainly believe He can and He will. I know he's godly proud of his only son, Jack Jr., for acceptin' his callin' to be a preacher. I don't want to belabor the time, but I do want Elder Simmons to come on back up here and give us his testimony. This is what it's all about, church."

Sherse shrank further down in the pew again and Chanel nudged her. "What, may I ask, is wrong with you?"

Sherese mumbled, "I don't remember him as a child. Let's just say I know him as an adult."

"Where do you know him from?" Sydney couldn't hide her curiousity.

Chanel shook her head. "No, Sydney, she *knows him—knows him,* right, Sherese?"

A look of surprise came over Sydney's face as she finally caught what Sherese meant. "You slept with Pastor Simmons' son?"

Shame and embarrassment swept over Sherese's face, and although she didn't answer, Sydney read her sister's face. What Sydney saw made her stop short of questioning or scolding her sister. Instead, she patted her on the knee. "It's okay, Sher."

Sherese looked at her sister with admiration, love, and surprise. "Thanks, Syd. It was a huge mistake, and I'm sorry about it."

"I know, I know," Sydney comforted.

"I just hope he doesn't see me," Sherese whispered as Jack smiled and graciously accepted the microphone from Pastor Hightower.

"Praise the Lord again, saints. Well, I never thought I'd have elder in the front of my name, but all I can say is the Lord had other plans for me. I was determined never to follow in my father's footsteps, church. In fact, I decided, even though I had all the home training, that I was gonna party and have a good time in the world. The only thing was, I was doing all the things the world said were fun, but I wasn't having any. I even got to the point where I was a bartender, helping others to go to hell. Long story short, I was lost and headed for ruin when a series of events happened in my life that turned me to the Lord. One major thing that happened is my father becoming ill. It's made me really realize how fragile life can be. I realized that I'd been like Jonah. I've always known the Lord has had a calling on my life, but I had decided long ago that I would run from it like the plague. Just shows you how the devil can trick you, huh? Anyway, when I gave my life to the Lord, I realized that the first thing I had to do was to accept the job He gave me to do, which is to minister through preaching the Word to His people. Pray my strength in the Lord, saints."

As he handed back the microphone to Pastor Hightower, Sydney felt the sincerity in Jack's words. She didn't know what the circumstances were surrounding his and Sherese's encounter, but Sydney couldn't help feeling that there could still be something between them, both now being saved.

Just as Sydney thought her father would give the closing prayer, he asked, "Before we close out the service, I'd like to have my family join me. That includes you, too, Maya."

As Darlene joined her husband in the front of the church, Sydney was near the back of the church coaxing her sister to hurry up and come to join their parents. When Sherese realized that she couldn't get out of it, she reluctantly joined her family.

The family stood in front of the altar, and Darlene took the microphone from her husband. "Some time ago, I had asked my daughter to do a painting of me and Pastor, and I thought Sherese had forgotten about it until she surprised me by bringing it to me this morning. Pastor," she said, turning to her husband, "Sherese painted us this for a wall in the vestibule in the community center." Darlene handed the microphone back to her husband as she unveiled the first of two covered easels on either side of the front of the church.

"Well, I'll be," Pastor Hightower exclaimed, as the church stood to their feet in admiration of the painting of the pastor and first lady. Pastor Hightower added, "I believe that's the best I've ever looked."

Sherese whispered to Sydney, "Why is Mama embarrassing me like this?"

"Don't be silly, girl. This painting is spectacular! It looks exactly like Mama and Daddy." Sherese blushed at her sister's praise.

As the clapping died down, Darlene and Samuel embraced their daughter tightly and then he took the microphone again. "I've been surprised, but now I have a little surprise of my own. This has been an incredibly hard year for our family. We've grieved over the loss of my son-in-law, Vance. As you all know, Vance was a very vital part of our ministry, and quite frankly, I don't know if we would have the community center without his diligence and determination. As chairman of our deacons, he was directly responsible for helping us to get the funding and support in the community we needed to build it. I'm sorry that he wasn't able to see this day."

Pastor Hightower seemed to choke momentarily as he pulled his glasses off to wipe his eyes, which had begun to tear up. "But saints, our loss is heaven's gain, right?"

Sydney listened as the church responded emphatically to the pastor's moving words, and it seemed there wasn't a dry eye in the building, including Sydney's.

"Vance wasn't like a son, he *was* a son. He took mighty good care of my oldest in a personal way. At church, Vance would often be the first one here and the last one to leave. He was always concerned about the church building, but he also had a love and responsibility for the members. I'd like the deacons to come up to unveil the second painting, also done by my daughter to place in the community center."

As the seven deacons of the church came up, they surrounded Sydney and her family. Deacon McKnight, now the Chairman of the Deacon Board, took the microphone. "Saints and friends, there was no job too big or too small for Deacon Ellington. He was somebody to know, and if you knew him, he was a friend. I count it as a privilege to present this painting for the Vance Ellington Community Center."

Sydney grabbed her sister's hand tightly as she felt her knees go weak upon hearing that the community center would be named after Vance. When Deacon McKnight took the sheet off the easel, Sydney thought surely she would pass out. She heards gasps throughout the congregation as Sherese's painting of Vance was full of life and caught the very essence of who her late husband was. She stared at the sparkling black eyes of the man in the dashing blue suit, and Sydney felt the gentleness, kindness, and warmth that had brought her so much joy.

Sydney grabbed her sister and wrapped her arms around her with more vigor than she ever had as she sobbed tears of joy.

Sensing the Holy Spirit's presence, Pastor Hightower led the church into worship. "Praise the Lord! Praise the Lord! Praise the Lord. Hallelujah! Thank the Lord that death is not the end of the story. We don't sorrow as those with no hope. One day, soon and very soon, the Lord is gonna descend from heaven with a shout. Those of us who are left are gonna be caught up to meet Him in the air!"

With all of her weight, Sydney continued to lean on Sherese as she prayed. As Sydney cried, she finally began to release the weight of her grief. It was a burden much too heavy for her to bear alone. For the first time, she realized that the only way she could make it was by leaning on the Lord and casting her cares on Him. On this morning, Sydney knew that joy had finally come.

CHAPTER 27

Chanel

Be still, and know that I am God.

Psalm 46:10

Chanel was on a spiritual high after the service. In spite of the fact that she hadn't talked to Tommy in more than a week, she trusted that God would work it all out for her good. As much as she wanted her marriage, the Holy Spirit was leading her to be still now.

After dropping Zachary off at Olivia's, Chanel raced to the café. She couldn't miss the service at church for anything, so she had posted a note on the door letting everyone know that the café would open late. Ordinarily, she would never have closed the café without someone to open it, but she hadn't had time to find a replacement for Lena. Since it was Saturday, the café was bound to be busy, so she prepared her mind for the day.

When she went to unlock the café, the door was already open but all of the lights were off. She crept in slowly, knowing that Tommy was now the only one who had a key. She hadn't noticed his car so she gripped her cell phone, ready to dial 911. As Chanel scanned the sitting and kitchen areas, she walked carefully past the restroom to turn on the lights. Suddenly, she heard a noise in the bathroom.

She froze, not knowing what to do, until she remembered she had mace attached to her keychain. She took it out and aimed at the door, ready to spray. When the tall massive figure came out, Chanel screamed.

"Whoa!"

"Tommy! Oh, you scared the daylights outta me!" Chanel held her hands over her heart.

"I'm sorry. I just let myself in since I figured you'd be here soon."

Chanel turned on all the lights and flipped the closed sign to open as she said, "I didn't see your car."

"I'm sorry for scaring you. I parked down on the side of the barber shop since I needed an edge."

Chanel let out a deep sigh. "Oh, well, I was tired. I guess the good part of being scared is that it wakes you up." As Chanel removed her jacket, she asked, "How have you been?"

"I've been as well as can be expected without you."

Chanel couldn't suppress the tiny smile that tried to creep through her look of concern.

"You missed the dedication at Great Deliverance."

"Yeah, I know." He bowed his head for a second and then looked up at her. "But, I talked to Pastor Hightower a few days ago."

"Oh, really? How did that happen?"

"I went to see him. He's a real cool man."

"Yes, he is. What did you talk to him about?"

"I just talked to him about us."

Chanel wondered if he had told the pastor about her tryst with Antonio, but she was too afraid to ask. Besides, she decided that it was just a good thing that he went to speak to him. She knew that even if Tommy had confided any details about their marriage to him, he would never breath a word of it to anyone, probably not even her.

Before Chanel could say anything else about his conversation, the phone rang.

Chanel pressed the speaker phone button as she greeted, "Anchored in the Rock Café. Chanel speaking, may I help you?"

A hoarse voice said roughly, "I need to talk to you a minute if you have time for your Mama."

Chanel eyed Tommy who sat looking frustrated upon hearing his mother-in-law's voice.

"Nyla, how are you?"

"Listen, me and Orlando got kicked out."

"Wait a minute. Who's Orlando?"

"That's my husband."

"You got married?"

"You crazy, girl? Naw, but we common law."

Chanel took a sigh. "What do you want me to do about it?"

"Well, we need someplace to stay. What the devil do you think I'm calling you for?"

Chanel thought it was ironic that her mother would mention the devil. "You know what? I don't need to listen to this."

Chanel remained silent, looking up at the ceiling, and Tommy slipped a note he had quickly written on a napkin to her. It read: "Your mom can stay with us, but the Negro has got to get his own place."

Chanel grabbed the pen and wrote: "Us???"

Tommy smiled.

Even her mother couldn't mess up her great mood. The Lord had intervened and her husband was giving her another chance. Chanel looked up and said, "Thank You, Jesus!"

Nyla said, "Whatcha thankin' Jesus for?"

Chanel's attention turned back to her mother. She thought about the impact that Pastor Hightower must've had on Tommy. Chanel also thought about how she hadn't been a witness in her own home to her husband. If she acted ugly to her mother, especially in front of Tommy, what kind of witness would she be to him, she wondered? The worship experience had also opened her heart in ways she hadn't thought possible. She decided that she would no longer give Satan any victory in her life or her marriage. If she was to go forward, she had to forgive Nyla, even if her mother hadn't ever asked for Sherese's forgiveness.

"Well, Nyla, Orlando has got to find his own place, but you can come to our home as long as you agree not to smoke, drink or curse."

"How in the world do you—" Her mother didn't finish her question. Chanel knew that her mother must've thought about what dire straights she was in and decided against finishing her thought.

In defeat, her mother mumbled, "Yeah, okay. Wherebouts do you live? You probably live in Pittsford with all those high-minded folk."

"Nyla, do you have a car now?"

"Naw, I ain't got no car, but Orlando can bring me."

"Tell you what. I can come pick you up or you can just come to the café about nine o'clock tonight. You can ride with me from there."

After Nyla agreed, Chanel hung up, staring in disbelief. She couldn't believe that her mother had the audacity to ask her for anything.

Tommy seemed to know what she was thinking. "I know you must think that your mother has got a lot of nerve calling you to ask a favor as big as this."

Chanel looked into her husband's eyes and nodded as she folded her hands across her chest in disgust.

Tommy continued, "You ever think about how you'd feel if something happened to your mother? I mean, would you be okay? Would you be at peace, knowing that she had reached out to you and you didn't help?"

"That woman has never been there for me or Ramone. If she would've, he would be alive today, so yeah, I'd be okay."

Tommy searched Chanel's face for a hint of doubt.

"So, okay. Maybe allowing her to come is the right thing to do, but if I didn't know the Lord…"

"Yeah, but you do, so we don't even need to go there. Look, Chanel, you already know my story. My pops walked out when I was eight years old and never looked back to see about me or my brother. As much as it hurts and as angry as it's made me all of my life, the older I get the more I'd like to have the opportunity to know him. So many times, I've wanted to know about my family and even his likes and dislikes. You know, just stuff I can tell Zachary about his family on my side. I thank God for my mother because she did everything for us, but still, I'd like my father to know that I forgive him. I may not agree with what he did, but I still acknowledge that he is a part of me. If your mother never says she's sorry for her mistakes, you still need to forgive her—but not for her sake, for your own."

Chanel unfolded. She wondered when it was that Tommy had received so much insight and wisdom. Maybe there was more inside him than she had thought.

"I know you're right, but it's hard to forgive someone who doesn't even acknowledge any wrongdoing. My brother meant the world to me, and if Nyla would have just done some of what she should've done, I believe in my heart that Ramone would still be with me."

"Maybe he would, but then again, maybe he wouldn't. We can't really say, but the only thing we can do is realize that we all have choices to make in life. You couldn't control the choices that Ramone made and you sure as heck can't control the choices that Nyla makes. But, you can control the decisions that Chanel makes." He got up off of the stool and walked around the counter to pull his wife toward him. "Now, I don't wanna stand around here talkin' about your mother when we have some things we need to get straight between us."

Chanel started, "Tommy, I'm so sorry. I just—"

Tommy interrupted, "I've had some time to think about things, and I'm fighting for my family. I've been so wrapped up in myself that I wasn't paying attention to your needs and wants. You always seem so self-sufficient. It's like you don't really need me or anybody else."

Knowing she was guilty of this, Chanel tried to lower her hazel eyes from his, but he gently lifted her chin with his hand. "I believe that you didn't sleep with him, but I do think that you violated the trust that we have. It can never happen again."

"Never," she responded, while shaking her head.

"As for my part, talking to Pastor Hightower really was helpful. It's been nice playing in the band at the Christian Center, but I think I'm gonna try coming to church with you and Zachary, but no promises."

Chanel pulled away and jumped up. "Yes!"

"Did you hear me? I'm not saying that I'm gonna join there, but I have a lot of respect for your pastor. Besides, he said that he'd like for me to sit in when I come to worship with you all."

"Tommy, do you have any idea how much I love you?" Chanel embraced him again.

"I plan on letting you show me tonight when you get off work, so once you get your mother to the house, get her and Zachary settled quickly."

"It's a deal." Chanel winked as she heard a knock from the outside glass door.

Faintly, Chanel and Tommy heard Nipsy, an old man who delivered newspapers in the neighborhood and a regular customer, say, "Why y'all got the sign "open" and the door locked!"

"Oh, what am I thinking?" She ran to unlock the front door as she started up the coffee machines and percolators.

"See you tonight," Tommy called as he winked back at his wife.

As Chanel chatted with Nipsy, she could barely concentrate on the conversation because she couldn't believe how the Lord had perfectly worked the situation out. In spite of her mistakes, God had intervened and had mercy on her. Although she knew that she and Tommy had obstacles to overcome, she felt that they were surmountable. The whole ordeal gave her renewed optimism and appreciation for all she had been blessed with. It suddenly didn't matter what Tommy or even her mother, for that matter, wasn't. What mattered was that Tommy was still here. She had another chance. She forgave, and she thanked God that she was forgiven.

CHAPTER 28

Sherese

*Two are better than one; because they
have a good reward for their labour.*

Ecclesiastes 4:9

"You girls want something to eat?" Darlene asked as she pulled her low pumps off her slightly swollen feet.

"Mama, why are your feet so swoll up?" Sherese studied them with concern.

"We've been in church for a long time, baby," her mother said as she bent to pick up her shoes.

"I got them." Sydney reached down before her mother could get the heels and questioned, "Did you take your water pill today, Mama?"

"I'll have y'all know, I'm just fine," her mother said as she shuffled around the kitchen, opening and closing cabinets, searching for something to cook.

After Sydney put her mother's shoes up, she took a seat on one of her parents' dated, vinyl-covered chairs and kicked off her own three inch heels. "Mama, you need to rest. Stop worrying about everbody else and take care of yourself. You know we're not hungry. We ate at the church."

"Hmmph! I didn't much like that food today. I think that must've been Mother Florine's casserole."

Sherese watched her mother survey the cabinets. "Goodness gracious, Mama. You got the shelves ready to give way from the weight of all that food. You act like me and Sydney still live here."

Her mother quipped, "Ya'll here now, ain't ya?"

Sydney nodded, "Girl, Mama is always ready to feed an army or busload. The only thing is, some of that stuff has got to be expired."

"Y'all need to stop talkin' about your mama. It just ain't right."

Sherese slid out of her heels, careful not mess up her pink silk suit as she hopped up on the kitchen counter to sit down. "Seriously though, Mama, you and just about everyone else at the church have been complaining about Mother Florine's cooking for years, but nobody gets her outta the kitchen."

Her mother limped out of the room to change, temporarily disappearing from sight, but she said so that her daughters could hear her, "She's a real sweet lady, but she surely can't cook. I reckon nobody wants to hurt her feelings. Only person I know that loves to cook but can't in no way."

Sherese began moving her feet in a circular motion to relieve the cramps from the heels. Yeah, you may not be hurting her feelings, but you're hurting everybody's stomach."

"You're simply rotten, Sherese," her mother answered back.

"Nobody but you and Daddy did that to that girl, Mama," Sydney interjected.

"Now you need to hush, Sydney. What am I gonna do with both of y'all?" Darlene's voice was so faint that they could barely hear her.

"That was some kind of service, huh, Syd?"

"Sher, as you always say, 'It was off the chain!'"

"Oh, please help her, Jesus. You and slang don't go together, Syd."

"Okay, then I'll just say that it was indescribable. I'm still ready to shout. I can't remember the last time I saw Daddy so happy. I tried to let him know that we were leaving, but he was so busy talking, he didn't even see me."

"Girl, please. Daddy is on cloud nine. He probably won't be home for hours."

"Yeah, that's why it was best for us to leave him," Sydney said as she straightened the plastic placemats on the table.

"Syd, I don't know how, but things looked different to me today at church. I mean, it's the same church I've seen all my life, and I'm not tryin' to be funny or anything, but it looked different to me, you know?"

"That's what salvation will do for you."

Sherese smiled. "Yeah I guess you're right. The Lord really blessed me, but there is one thing I have to admit that's kinda buggin' me."

"What's that?"

"I just can't get over Elder Simmons Jr., better known as Jack, being there. I mean, to think that his daddy and Daddy know one another is weird. I didn't think I'd ever see him again."

"I'm scared to ask you for the details about it. Should I or shouldn't I?"

Sherese shook her head back and forth, and briefly covered her face with her hands. "Shouldn't, absolutely shouldn't."

"Well, don't tell me then. I know one thing; whatever happened between the two of you made you high-tail it on outta the church faster than I'd ever seen you do, and you've never been one to hang out at church."

Sherese reached for the cookie jar and grabbed a cookie from the canister and said through her munching, "Girl, I went as fast as my little feet could carry me. The last thing I was trying to do was see him."

"Now, there's nothing little about your feet," Sydney joked.

"See how she does me, Mama? See?"

"Y'all just a mess," her mother said as she put her hands in the pockets of her housedress.

Sherese offered her sister a cookie as her mother walked slowly back into the kitchen.

"No, thanks. I don't see how you eat those nasty ginger snaps." Sydney turned her face up.

Darlene grabbed the cookie Sherese had offered Sydney. "I don't know how you can say you don't like 'em. Child, you grew up on these."

"Mama, please don't remind me of all of them bologna sandwiches and ginger snap cookie lunches. To this day, I don't eat bologna and won't touch ginger snaps. You all knock yourselves out," Sydney said as she heard the door open behind her.

"Hey, Daddy! We weren't expecting you so soon."

Her father cleared his throat as he slowly put his hat on the hook. "I'm glad you all came on over here. I brought someone here I want you to meet."

Sherese was used to her father bringing guests home from church, but she wasn't prepared for the tall man who stood at the entrance of the kitchen as she sat on the counter swinging her legs with a cookie hanging out of her mouth.

"Hello, everyone!" Jack greeted warmly.

Sydney stood up from the table and extended her hand. "Hello, Jack. Oh, I'm sorry, it's Elder Simmons now."

"Please, Jack is fine."

"I guess you don't remember me, do you?" Sydney asked.

Jack studied Sydney's face intently. "You know, your father has been trying to get me to remember you and your sister from years ago, and I just can't remember. I'm sorry."

"All I got to say is, you better remember all of them spit wads you used to throw at our hair. We went over to your church for a whole week for vacation Bible school, and during review, you and your older brother used to torture all the girls."

He opened his mouth and exclaimed, "Yep, I think I vaguely remember that now that you say vacation Bible school. Sorry about the spit wads."

"Mmmhhmm. I thought you'd remember."

Sherese jumped off the counter and took the cookie from her mouth while her mother hugged and greeted Jack.

"Sherese, don't just stand there. Come and say hello to the nice young man. I think you were too young to remember him, but I know you'd remember his mother."

Sherese wiped the crumbs off her hands and extended her hand, but instead of Jack shaking her hand, he went straight for a hug.

Sherese jerked away, and she could've sworn that she saw a grin. She kept her composure. "How's that, Mama?"

"Remember, when I had you go pick up those lap scarves from Betty Mae Simmons?"

Sherese nodded.

"That's my mama," Jack chimed in happily. "So, you know my mama."

"I don't know her. I've just seen her before."

Darlene gave Sherese a look that told her she wasn't being polite. "You may not know her, but she certainly knows you. Betty Mae and I went to the women's convention in Houston together years ago. We had a real good time."

"It's a small world. I actually do remember you quite well for sure, Sherese."

When Sherese noticed how Darlene and Sydney smiled at each other, sensing the attraction Jack felt, she eyed him in a threatening manner.

"I told Elder Simmons to come over here because I wanted him to meet you girls. I figured y'all would still be here."

Sydney looked at Jack. "I'm almost thirty-four, and my father still insists on calling me a girl."

Jack smiled, "I understand why. It's because you look so young."

Sydney seemed to almost blush as Jack continued, "And, Mother Hightower, I know if he calls them girls, he must refer to you as a baby."

Darlene smiled so hard that Sherese could see the gaping holes of missing teeth in the back of her mother's mouth.

"I'm going to be going home now. I'm really tired," Sherese interjected, uncomfortable and irritated.

She grabbed her purse a little too quickly and kissed her mother and father on the cheek.

"It's nice to see you Jack. I'll be praying for your father," Sherese said when she neared the entrance to the door.

Jack stood in her way and wouldn't let her pass. "Pastor Hightower, I must be leaving as well. Again, I was blessed in the service. Mother Hightower and Sister Ellington, it's very nice to make your acquaintance again. Sister Hightower, may I walk you to your car?"

Sherese rolled her eyes as she marched out to her car.

When they stepped outside, Sherese fumed, "What are you doing? I am totally humiliated. What are you doing here? And why did you say that we already know one another?"

Without giving him a chance to answer, she continued. "I would've been more than happy if I would never have to see you again in life. I want you to know that I am totally and utterly embarrassed by what happened between us. I am sorry about what happened, and I've asked the Lord to forgive me. I'm saved now and I really don't want to be reminded about what happened. So just in case you think this is funny or cute or whatever, think again!"

"Whoaa, wait one minute," Jack held his hand up as Sherese got in her car and slammed the door.

He knocked on the window until she finally rolled it down slowly. "What do you want?"

"Listen, I just wanted to let you know that I'm sure I'm even more embarrassed and ashamed than you are. As a man, I am ashamed of my behavior. I don't want you to think that I go around taking advantage of women. It was a huge mistake. The Lord has really dealt with me about that. Not too long after that night, I got saved and turned my life around. Please believe that I was really genuinely interested in you, Sherese, and I thought that it would be more than what it turned out to be. I've thought about you. Not in the way you think though."

"Oh, really?"

"Yes, believe it or not, I've never done that before or since. I am so sorry because I knew you had had too much to drink, and I had had too much to drink. I never should've taken it that far, but you seemed—"

"I seemed what?"

"Never mind. It didn't really sink in until the morning after. Then, it was too late because, poof, you were gone! Please let me show you that I'm not an animal."

As Sherese listened, she couldn't ignore the smell of his cologne and the way his muscles bulged in his athletic-cut suit. As his massive but well-manicured hand rested on the inside of the opening to the window, Sherese noticed the monogrammed initials on his gold cufflinks. He was even more attractive now, saved and in his church clothes. Sherese wondered if he felt the same way about her, but instead she said, "What do you want from me? Forgiveness? I forgive you. Now are you happy?"

"Yeah, I'm happy if you're sincere. Please, can you come out here to talk to me face-to-face or better yet, let me sit in the car."

Sherese considered his proposition, and decided that she was just as guilty as he was, so she got out of the car.

Jack smiled as he took his suit jacket off and loosened his tie since it seemed he was perspiring heavily. He took a deep breath and smiled at Sherese who also finally returned a smile as she stood face-to-face with the handsome man.

An hour had passed and Sherese had hardly noticed her throbbing feet, still in heels, as she leaned against her car in the driveway of her parents' home. Jack was someone who, despite their horrible beginning, she would like to know better.

"What are you two doing out here? I thought you had both left over an hour ago?" Sydney asked as she came out of the front door.

Jack and Sherese laughed together as Sherese handed him her phone number, as she had done close to a year ago. He stared at the number for a few seconds and asked before going to his car, "You will answer the phone, won't you?"

"I'll answer," she batted her eyelashes as she slipped back into her car.

"Jack, why do I have the feeling we're gonna be seeing you around?" Sydney asked.

"Pray for a brotha, if you know what I mean," Jack smiled and called out to Sydney as he drove off.

Sherese felt her cheeks warm with embarrassment. "Call me tonight," she told her sister.

Sherese took her heels off and threw them into the backseat, excited and looking forward to Jack's call. She wondered if this was possible and if the Lord could turn something that had been so ugly into something good.

CHAPTER 29

Sydney

*When ye stand praying, forgive, if ye ought against any: that your
Father also which is in heaven may forgive you your trespasses.*

Mark 11:25

Sydney's palms were so sweaty that it was difficult to make the turn
as she pulled into a parking space at New York State Prison. She
couldn't believe that she was finally coming face-to-face with the man
she had had nightmares about for so long. Even her legs and hands
trembled noticeably when she pulled down the rear-view mirror and
smoothed her hair which was pulled back into a ponytail, purposely
avoiding any style of dress or hairstyle that would attract attention.
She took a deep breath and realized she wasn't ready to go in.
Although she knew that the Lord clearly let her know that she needed
to meet with him, she was afraid.

She picked up her Bible and turned to 2 Timothy 1:7. Slowly, she
meditated on the verse. "God hath not given us the spirit of fear; but
of power, and of love, and of a sound mind." Still, she didn't feel the
strength in her body to get out of the car to meet with Brian O'Leary.
She said the verse aloud, speaking to her fear. She said, "Satan, the
Lord rebuke you and all your evil devices. Lord, You have given me
power, love, and a sound mind. Thank You for power. Thank You for
love. Thank You for a sound mind." Now, she felt ready to face what
was before her.

Sydney had thought about asking Sherese or Chanel to come with her, but the Holy Spirit pressed her and she knew it was something that she should do alone. After she entered through the metal detectors, guards, and gated entryways, she was sent to a waiting room. She joined others, mostly women and children visiting with or waiting to visit with inmates.

As a guard entered, he brought the middle-aged man in and announced, "Brian O'Leary." Sydney froze. Again, the guard grunted with impatience, "Brian O'Leary." Sydney stood up, straightened her long skirt, and held her hand up to let them know she was there.

"Right here."

Sydney stared at the short man with disheveled and greasy-looking dirty-blond hair, piercing blue eyes, and turned-down mouth. This was the man. As the guard seated O'Leary at a table, Sydney couldn't help noticing the shackled hands and feet. She wrung her hands nervously.

"Hello, Mrs. Ellington," O'Leary mumbled, but avoided eye contact as the guard returned to the entrance.

"Hello, Mr. O'Leary."

"You can call me Sydney," she offered, trying to make eye contact.

"I guess you got my letters, Mrs. Ellington?"

"Yes, Mr. O'Leary, I did receive your letters." The only thing more noticeable than the pockmarks that covered his cheeks was the poorly done tattoo on his neck, partially hidden by his jumpsuit.

"Brian. You can call me Brian."

"Okay then, Brian it is."

He looked up at her face, but he still avoided eye contact. "Listen, I just wanted you to know that I'm so sorry. I know it won't bring your husband back, but I am so…" he stopped short. His face turned red as he tried to continue. "I'm gonna pay for this for the rest of my life. I wish it would've been me." Sobs escaped from his lips.

For the first time, Sydney realized the depth of Brian's agony and despair. He, too, was suffering. "I want you to know that I've been angry and hurt, which is why I haven't responded to you before now."

He nodded his head as if he expected her to say that.

"I know that you're sorry, and I'm sorry too. I want you to forgive yourself and live. I know that you have a family that loves you and needs you very much. Don't give that up for one mistake."

He finally made eye contact, and Sydney saw the tears fall down one after another from the man's worn face.

"I killed my son, you know? It's not just your husband."

"Your wife told me that there was an accident with your son."

"I wasn't watching him. I wasn't thinking when I got into the semi that morning when I was drunk either." He wiped the tears from his face with his cuffed hands.

"May I ask you a question, Brian?"

"Anything."

"Do you know the Lord Jesus as your personal Savior?"

"My wife talks about Jesus all the time, but I don't see how He can help me after all I've done now."

"He is the only one who can help you now or ever. You need to accept that He died on the cross for our sins and rose from the dead and sits on the right hand of God the Father. Apart from that, whether I forgive you or anyone else forgives you for anything, great or small, won't matter. Nothing else matters, Brian, but knowing the Lord. I know firsthand that He is the only one who can bear the weight of sin, guilt, and anything else that troubles you."

Brian searched Sydney's face for understanding. Sydney continued, "Do you understand that not one of us is worthy of God's forgiveness? If we were, we wouldn't need Jesus. When we accept Him as our Lord and Savior, He covers us with His grace and mercy. When we err, and all of us do, we simply need to repent from our sins and turn forever away from that mistake. He throws our sins into the sea of forgetfulness."

Sydney took a deep breath. "I want you to know that I forgive you. Accept that. You told me in one of your letters that if there was anything that you could do for me that all I had to do was ask. What you can do for me is to accept the Lord as your Savior because that is the best thing that can come out of this whole ordeal."

Brian nodded as more tears began to flow. "I appreciate you for taking the time to see me. I thank you for your forgiveness, and I want you to know that I'm really going to think about everything you've said to me today."

Nervousness fled from Sydney. "Do you mind if I pray for you before I leave?"

Brian bowed his head before he answered, "Of course not."

"Lord, I thank You for who You are in my life. I thank You for forgiving me of all of my sins. I thank You for filling my heart with forgiveness, Lord. On this day, I'm asking that You save Brian. Touch his life in a very real and immediate way, Lord. Let him know that You forgive him for all of his sins, not just some. Lead him and guide him in all spiritual truths. Give him peace and direction so that one day very soon he can be a witness and have testimony for Your glory. Bless his family. Give them courage and strength to endure this trial. I thank You in advance, Father. Thank God. Amen."

"Thank you, Mrs. Ellington…I mean, Sydney. You'll just never know."

When Sydney got up, the words "Thank you, Brian," that escaped from her lips caught her by surprise, especially because she really meant it.

Sydney relished the warmth of the sun as she left the gloomy prison, thanking God that her imprisonment was over. Her steps felt light and sure, knowing that her forgiveness afforded her the key to escape from the emotional prison that held her captive since Vance's death.

CHAPTER 30

Sydney

*Iron sharpeneth iron; so a man sharpeneth
the countenance of his friend.*

Proverbs 27:17

"Maya, you can put those books on the lower shelf in the front of
the counter."

Sydney hesitated as she wiped the perspiration from her forehead.
She was tired, but it was a satisfying, rewarding kind. The Anchored
in the Rock Café & Bookstore's grand opening was weeks away and
everything had to be perfect.

It hadn't been difficult at all to resign from her job when Chanel
presented the business proposition to her friend. Chanel had
dreamed of opening another café, but she needed the financial
backing. Sydney knew that the Lord had plans for her career other
than the ones the accounting department at KODAK had to offer, but
she didn't know what they were until she drove downtown past the
once-vacant lot that used to be where The Book Bungalow had been.
When they built a new building in place of the bookstore, it was a
retail store. As Sydney drove by the new building in the place where
The Book Bungalow had been located, she noticed a For Sale sign.
She slowed to jot the number down. The realtor had told her that

several businesses had tried but had been unsuccessful at creating enough overhead to survive in the location.

Logically, it didn't make sense for her to even consider buying the property, but she decided to pray about it anyway. She had prayed long and hard, but when she got up from her knees, she felt a total peace in her spirit. *Is God telling me to go forward?* She didn't know for sure, so she didn't speak a word of the idea to Chanel. Instead, she decided to fast. In her experience, turning down her plate and consecrating were the best ways to get a prayer through. When the hunger pangs came, she fought them by praying harder, seeking for the Lord's will to be done in her life.

A week later, while working in her garden surrounded by tulip bulbs, humming the melody to "Just another day that the Lord has kept me," Sydney's cell phone rang. She started to let it ring, but decided to pull her garden gloves off and answer.

"Sydney, hope I didn't catch you at a bad time. This is Patrice Thomas. I had to let you know the news."

Sometimes the shrillness in the realtor's voice slightly irritated Sydney, but when Patrice let her know that the building had been reduced by five thousand dollars, she understood the excitement in her voice. As Sydney ended the call, she felt peace and confirmation in her spirit. She would go forward and present the plan to Chanel about opening another location for an Anchored in the Rock Café.

Sydney had always known that Chanel's café was more than a business. It was a ministry. Sydney, as so many others, had found the café to be a place of refuge, inspiration, comfort, and relaxation. From the embossed scriptures printed on the napkins to the tracts left in various places in the café, the atmosphere was unmistakably Christ-centered. Even the Gospel music that always played softly throughout the café let patrons know what the establishment stood for. The peace that surged through her once restless soul made her know

know that supporting Chanel's vision for the ministry and business would be in the Lord's will for her.

Sydney dialed Chanel's number and decided she wouldn't put off what the Lord was directing her to do.

When presented with the idea of adding a bookstore to her café in addition to the other location Chanel had always dreamed of, Chanel was overjoyed. They would be co-owners of the downtown location. Little by little, God's plan began to unfold before Sydney's eyes. God seemed to be right in front of her directing and guiding her steps while opening doors as only He could do.

As the two women discussed their business, Zachary splashed in the large multicolored plastic pool in Chanel's backyard.

"Boy, you're getting me wet!" Chanel hollored as she pulled her lawn chair back further from her son's splashing.

Sydney left her chair close to Zachary, smiling at her godson who was oblivious to his mother's complaints. "This iced tea is really good, Chanel. You make it like they do in the South."

"Nyla did teach me a thing or two when I really think about it." Chanel stared up at the expansive powder blue sky, deep in thought.

Sydney searched her friend's face and then leaned her head back on the lawn chair, basking in the warm air and sun. "You know, Chanel, I didn't know if I could be happy again. It's strange though. I'm happy, but not the kind of happy I was before. It's a mature, responsible, accountable kind of happy."

Chanel leaned forward and slipped her large designer sunglasses off the tip of her nose to eye her friend. "What in the world are you talkin' about, girl?"

Sydney chuckled and explained, "I never knew that I was living my life like I was in control. If I wasn't, then it was Daddy or Vance.

Now that I've surrendered my life totally to the right one, the Lord, I can relax. I have this assurance that it's all going to work out. Before, I was so stressed about things, big and small. For the first time in my life, I realize that I have to truly seek Him myself and seek His will for my life. Nothing else can matter more. It's been rough, but it's a deep thing when you experience a new kind of happiness in your mid-thirties."

Sydney could tell by the somewhat perplexed look on Chanel's face that she didn't understand everything with one hundred percent clarity. However, Sydney could tell that Chanel's trials, along with hers and Sherese's, had matured her to a new level in Christ, no matter how nonchalant Chanel could be at times.

"Sister-girl, I'm not one for the heavy stuff, but I know the Lord is too good and faithful to fail us." With that said, Zachary went down in the shallow water and seemed to be struggling. The two women got up to grab him, and he laughed as if he had played a joke on them.

After exhaling a sigh of relief, Chanel whispered to Sydney, "I'm gonna beat him." Sydney tried hard to repress the smile that crept onto her face as she got the beach towel to dry her godson.

———

As Sydney worked diligently for the success of her new business venture, Maya showed a special interest in it as well. Maya volunteered to work weekends in the store with Sydney while attending Rochester Institute of Technology, and Sydney planned on training her to manage so that she could assist throughout her college years.

Tommy, too, had been excited, agreeing to have his newly formed Gospel jazz band, Spirit of Praise, play once a month in the back room of the bookstore, which was a cozy café section for bands, vocalists, and authors to minister to the patrons.

The Anchored in the Rock Bookstore & Café had promise, and Sydney was confident that it would become the best place in Rochester to get the latest and best Christian books and coffee to warm your soul.

Even as the rain poured down in buckets from the dismal sky, Sydney stood outside, not caring that she had just had a relaxer put in her hair as she watched the men raise the sign up in the front of the store. A tear fell as she thought of the goodness of the Lord. This was the fulfillment of a dream she hadn't even known she had. She had wanted contentment, peace, and the Lord's will for her life. This was the beginning of her letting the Lord totally lead her way. Things wouldn't be perfect all of the time, but she was now equipped to handle storms. Her expection and hope was in the Lord, and she would make it, no matter what.

CHAPTER 31

Chanel

The steps of a good man are ordered by the Lord: and he delighteth
in his way. Though he fall, he shall not be utterly
cast down: for the Lord upholdeth him with his hand.

Psalm 37:23,24

Nyla parked her knock-off designer luggage, tattered and worn, at the foot of the steps, waiting impatiently for her daughter. Chanel was positive that one of Nyla's no-good friends had traded the luggage with her for some liquor, drugs, or something worse.

With Nyla's deeply bronzed arms folded, her slender face, which always glistened a little too much, contorted. "Chanel, get on down here now, girl. I'm ready to pick up them keys from the rental office. The man say he's gotta be gone by five."

Purposely moving at a snail's pace, Chanel lingered on each step, determined not to have another conflict with her mother, yet sure that the time was right for a conversation, especially since her mother would be leaving. Nyla didn't know it, but Chanel was just as eager as Nyla was for the cohabitation to cease. It had been well over a year that Chanel and Tommy had put up with Nyla's unpredictable moods, constant laziness, and stubborn defiance toward attending church. The little compliance that they did get from Nyla in things like smoking outside usually ended in further aggravation. Nyla would smoke outside, but she would often carelessly drop cigarette butts on the newly laid bricks, littering their back patio.

Chanel took a deep breath, hoping for the best, but anticipating the worst from her mother. Yet, she had to say what she needed to say. Before she could make it to the bottom, her mother's raspy voice was at it again.

"Finally!" her mother spewed out as she picked up her bags and got ready to unlatch the door.

"Nyla, wait a minute." Chanel put her purse down on the steps and planted herself on the bottom step to face her mother. Before she could say anything, Nyla snapped. "Whatcha doin'? Thought we was gettin' ready to go." Her mother scratched the top of her head, tossling her thin and oily hair anxiously.

"Nyla, I just wanted to let you know a few things."

"Tell me on the doggone way, chile. I'm ready ta go!"

Chanel dug her fingers into the carpet, praying silently for the strength and patience to release the pent-up feelings brewing inside of her for so many years. "I need to say it now. Can't you just listen to me for a few minutes?"

"Jesus! Go ahead." Nyla gasped in frustration.

"Can you not use the Lord's name in vain, please?" Without waiting for an answer, Chanel continued. "I've been angry and hurt for a lot of years about the way we grew up. More than anything, I've been angry at you for the way you were with Ramone. I'm not tryin' to hurt you, Nyla, but you never made us a priority."

Nyla's glassy eyes stared at Chanel with a fiery intensity as if to caution her from continuing. "Don't cha even get started. Everythang always gotta be about you, don't it?"

Chanel breathed heavily. "How do you do that?"

"Do what?" she snarled.

"Always change the subject—always flip the script when it's something you don't want to talk about—something that hits too close to home."

"Girl, let's go. I'm ready to get outta here. I ain't got time for this. We ain't on no 'Dr. Phil' show," Nyla growled impatiently, while picking up one of her suitcases and starting to open the front door.

Chanel defied in silence by remaining still. "What I wanted to tell—" She hesitated and started again. "I wanted to let you know that I forgive you."

A loud *thump* startled Chanel as Nyla let the heavy suitcases drop to the floor. With her voice elevated, Nyla pointed her finger toward Chanel. "I ain't asked your tail for no forgiveness no how. If you feel like you can just say whatcha want cause I stayed with you for a while, you dead wrong. It don't matter if you don't like my ways. I'm always gonna be me, and I ain't askin' for no forgiveness from you or anybody else!"

"You're right. You're not asking, but I'm tellin'. I don't understand you and your selfishness, but it has driven a wedge between us." Chanel stood up. "I gave up a long time ago on having a mother who really cared about me."

Now, Nyla interrupted, "Wait—"

"No," Chanel said firmly. "You came to high school graduation drunk. My wedding was the same. You didn't even see Zachary, and we lived fifteen minutes away from each other. When Ramone died, you weren't the only one in trouble. I wanted to die. I was a child, Nyla. You didn't help Ramone, and you didn't help me to get through his death," Chanel choked back tears.

She waited for her mother to respond, but Nyla averted her eyes away from Chanel. "I'm sorry that, for whatever reasons, Ramone and I burdened you. I'm sorry that we couldn't do more for you. I'm sorry that you couldn't be a mom to me and that I could never even call you Mom. You may not want my forgiveness now, but one day—one day, you might want it. I want you to know that I forgive you for everything."

When Chanel realized that her mother stood as if in a daze, dumbfounded by her words, she added, "When you're ready to accept the Lord into your life, He'll be there and ready to accept and forgive you too."

With a slight tremble in her hands and voice, Nyla finally responded, "You're tryin' to be disrespectful, and I won't have that mess. That's why I don't go to church to this day. People tryin' to throw off on folks and think they better than somebody else. You just like all of them. You just ready to feel like you above somebody, but I know God loves me. I don't got to go to nobody's church to know that much, Missy. You don't know the stuff I done been through. You think you had it so bad. You had food and a roof over your head, girl. You ain't had no real problems. If I'm so bad, how'd you turn out the way you did?"

A faint smile crept across Chanel's face, knowing her mother hadn't meant to give her the backhanded compliment. Chanel had turned out pretty good in spite of her mother, but she knew Who to attribute it to. She knew it was by the sheer grace and mercy of God.

Chanel decided to let the conversation go and left her mother's question unanswered. She picked up her keys, purse, and one of Nyla's suitcases before following her mother out the door, knowing that it didn't matter anymore what Nyla did or didn't do for her—in the past, present, or future. She had let the anger go, and with forgiveness, she found herself in right standing with God. There would be no more depression about what she didn't have. No more jealousy toward anyone for what they had had while growing up and she had lacked. God had chosen Chanel in spite of herself and her upbringing, not because of it.

They rode together in silence as Nyla sipped on her water bottle that Chanel knew was filled with gin, but it didn't upset her as it had in the past. Her mother's stay with her had helped her come to grips with the fact that she couldn't change the past and she couldn't change her mother. The only thing she could do was to make an effort to always be there for her son. She would be a mother he could be proud of, and she would do everything in her power to lead Zachary to Christ at an early age.

In the meantime, all she could do for Nyla was pray that she would accept the Lord as her Savior. As Chanel drew nearer to her mother's apartment complex, she noticed men on the corner of Green Street and Broad loitering in front of the local bar called *Reggies*. Baggy pants, oversized shirts, and hand-held forty ounces were a staple in front of the bar. Suddenly her mother's sour disposition brightened as she saw familiar faces. She pressed the button to lower the window, calling out "L.J.!"

When L.J. yelled back something Chanel couldn't hear, her mother yelled out "Hey, L.J.! You crazy, boy!" while holding her "water" bottle out of the window with a smile so wide Chanel could smell the strench of alcohol that escaped from her lips and pores.

"You could've slowed down. That was my home peoples."

Thank God for saving me. With that one decision to get saved, the Lord has led me to make so many other positive life-changing decisions.

As she pulled up to her mother's complex, Nyla pulled her luggage out with more liveliness and vigor than Chanel had seen in a long time.

"You take care of yourself, daughter," Nyla said as she walked away.

Chanel knew it would probably be a long time before she would see her mother again, so she stood staring at Nyla, memorizing her frame, her walk, and her shabby luggage. Chanel thanked God for a second chance.

CHAPTER 32

Sherese

...joy cometh in the morning.

Psalm 30:5

"Hannah Olivia-Sherese Simmons, I dedicate you to the Lord Jesus Christ on this day." Pastor Hightower beamed with pride as he held his first grandchild, dressed from head to toe in a white satin christening gown.

He said over the microphone, "Darlene, who would've ever thought we could have such a precious grandbaby, honey?" Several members could be heard saying, "Awwww" while Darlene held an expression mirroring her husband's.

"Godparents," he addressed them, looking directly into Sydney's eyes, then Tommy and Chanel's. "I charge you to help the parents to raise this child in the fear and admonition of the Lord. Do you agree that you will do all that you can do to bring this child to know and love the things of God?

The three answered in unison. "We agree."

"Do you agree to assist in teaching this child the Word and the ways of holiness?"

"We agree."

Samuel raised his voice and asked, "Do you all understand that your example will be the biggest influence on this child's life?

"We do."

"Will you do all that you can do to make sure that the example this child sees from each of you will be a help and not a hindrance to her spiritual walk?'

"We will," the three answered soberly.

"Parents," he addressed Sherese and Jack. "Do you agree to love, nurture, and protect this baby as the Lord would have you?"

Jack and Sherese held hands tightly as they smiled at one another in agreement. "We will."

As Pastor Hightower continued to give Sherese and Jack the charge for the dedication, Sherese thanked God for her many blessings. Her whirlwind marriage could be topped only by the surprise pregnancy and birth of her baby girl. It was hard to believe that less than two years ago her life was turned upside down with Vance's death and then finding out that she was adopted. Once she accepted Christ as her Savior, everything paled in comparison. That was when her life really began. The old Sherese was gone, and she was glad about it. When the Lord told her to move, she moved, and she found that this was where her happiness was.

It seemed impossible for her to be married to Jack, especially considering the way their relationship had begun, but God had shown her something her mama always said. "What the devil means for bad, the Lord, He'll turn it around and use it for your good. You gotta trust Him." Sherese found this to be ever so true as the feelings she and Jack had for one another unfolded.

Sherese knew that he was the one the Lord had had for her because of the way he listened, protected, and loved her. It didn't even matter when he confessed to her right before their engagement, "Sherese, you know Dad has had a lot of health challenges these past couple of years. You already know that I've been called to pastor, but we always talked about it in the distant future."

"Right."

"Well, Dad is thinking that he may not be able to pastor much longer. He just doesn't have the strength. He wants me to be ready at any time to take over as pastor."

Sherese had felt his anxiety about having to reveal this to her, but she knew that the Lord had dealt with her mightily since she didn't do an about-face that very second. "Are you sure about this? It's what you want?"

"It's not about what I want, but I'm more than sure. I know that the Lord and I just want to make sure that you can accept this. It'll mean that you have a calling to fulfill in the ministry too."

"Yeah, I know."

"You think you can handle it?"

"Well, if can you handle a sista' goin' off on somebody if they cross me, then I can handle the rest?"

"Sher!"

"I'm not playin', Jack, especially if they ever try to mess with you or one of our future babies. I learned some things from my childhood and my daddy and momma."

"I know you did, but I can't have a fightin' first lady." He put his strong arms around her, burying his face in her braids. "You're much too pretty, inside and out, to be tryin' to go off on somebody," he whispered in her ear.

Sherese pulled away. "Jack, I can't promise what kind of first lady I will be, but I do love the Lord and I love you. I guess that means I'll have to handle the other stuff."

"That a girl," Jack said.

"You sound like you're talkin' to a horse, not your wife."

"Lighten up, Sher. I just want you to know that I'm here to protect you, and if it means protecting you from future church members, I'll do just that. I'm not promising that it will be easy." She laid her head on his chest, and he caressed her back gently. "I'm not gonna leave you out there by yourself, you know what I'm sayin'? You just agree to stand by me and help me. Let me worry about the church members."

Sherese relaxed, feeling in her spirit that Jack really would do just that.

Every day Sherese prayed for Rosa's healing and checked in on her by calling Walter, for whom she would be forever grateful to the Lord. She regretted that Rosa couldn't see Hannah, but she had to admit to herself that Hannah lacked nothing. Darlene and Samuel adored Hannah, and she had grown to love and appreciate them more than she ever had, especially since she was beginning to realize how difficult it really was to be a parent.

The mistakes, no matter how well-intentioned, that her parents had made were ones she vowed not to make with Hannah. Sherese knew that it would probably be hard at times, but she had to always put the Lord first and family second.

Still, more than anything, she prayed for her daughter's salvation as her mother had prayed for hers. With this gift, she knew that even in spite of mistakes, Hannah would have not only eternal life but would also understand and forgive any mistakes she and Jack made along the way.

As Pastor Hightower gave the closing prayer at the dedication, Sherese kissed her daughter's satiny sweet-smelling hair as she closed her eyes and listened intently.

"Lord, the birth of this baby, Hannah Olivia-Sherese Simmons is a new beginning. We thank You for her. We know that a baby is Your way of giving us another opportunity to do better, another chance to get it right. We thank You for it, Lord. Thank God, Amen."

EPILOGUE

Sydney, Chanel, Sherese

*They that sow in tears shall reap in joy. He that goeth forth
and weepeth, bearing precious seed, shall doubtless
come again with rejoicing, bringing his sheaves with him.*

Psalm 126:5,6

After Hannah's dedication, the congregation enjoyed several hours of fellowship and food to celebrate in the Vance Ellington Community Center. Sydney, Sherese, and Chanel agreed to go outside to get some fresh air since Darlene was tending to Hannah.

When they stepped outside, the faint breeze refreshed them from the smoke-filled air inside coming from the kitchen. Chanel coughed a little before fanning her face vigorously. "Syd, you ladies think it's possible for somebody to convince your daddy to stop letting Mother Florine cook? It's getting totally outta hand with her. That woman is gonna ruin the new kitchen."

"Shhhhh." Sydney held her finger in front of her mouth while she checked to make sure that no one was coming.

Sherese grinned, knowing that Chanel had only said what she herself had been thinking. "Syd, really, it'd be a good thing if somebody overheard Chanel. That woman burned almost every piece of catfish. I'm just too mad about that!"

Sydney finally chimed in. "Daddy was looking so nervous when he saw all that smoke billowing out of the kitchen. I could've sworn he was wringing his hands."

Chanel planted her hands on her hips. "Girl, my clothes smell like burnt grease, and this is a Louise Ricci Couture from Purseonality Boutique." She held the bottom of her peachy-colored rhinestone studded suit. "Do you know how much these things cost to have dry-cleaned?"

"That's what you get for tryin' to be so uppity, Chanel. You need to keep it simple like me and Sydney," Sherese said, now holding out her solid pink A-line dress after pointing to Sydney's tailored navy blue suit."

"You all need to spice it up a bit. Anyway, I was gonna go from here to check in to see how things were goin' at the café. I can't go in there smelling like this—nobody would even think of buying coffee, tea, or pastries."

"Maybe you just weren't meant to work today. Ever consider that, my friend? I'm much too happy today to even think about work." Sherese directed them over to the crumbling cemented front steps of the church where she sat between them, placing her arms around them.

"I never imagined that I could be so happy!" Sherese said.

"I can tell because your cheeks ought to hurt you've been smiling so much today," Chanel teased.

Sydney lightly placed her arm around her sister's back. "I'm really amazed at how God is working everything out. I'm really happy for you, Sherese. Just remember times like today when you hit the rough spots. There will always be trials, but I think we can really grow when we handle them the way the Lord would have us to."

Chanel had already put her arm around Sherese as well, but leaned forward to face Sydney. "Sherese, you mark my words, girl. Those are the words of a future missionary," she commented, trying to lighten the seriousness of the moment.

Sydney smiled. "Oh, Lord knows you need to stop, Chanel."

Sherese turned to her sister and said skeptically, "I don't know, Syd. You would look good in one of Mama's hats—like that purple one with the big feather in the front and rhinestones down the center."

Sydney looked up to heaven. "Jesus, please help them."

Sherese then added, "All I'm sayin' is that you never know what God has in store for you. I know there's just no way I figured my life could turn out like this. Never in a million years would I have guessed that Jack and I would end up married with a baby, considering how we met and all that's happened. And me—a future first lady? You know nobody but God could be in control of that!"

They all unlocked arms and Chanel leaned forward to make eye contact with her friends. "You all know I'm not good at remembering scriptures, but I do remember this sermon your daddy gave about bearing fruit. Remember he said that in the Bible it says that everyone who bears fruit has to be purged?"

"Okay, I'm not tryin' to be dumb, but tell me exactly what purge means."

"Purging is simply a cutting off, pruning, or cleansing process. You're on to something, Chanel. You know all this time I never thought about that sermon or those scriptures in that way. What Daddy was saying is that as believers who abide in Jesus, the vine, we have to be purged so we can produce more fruit," Sydney explained.

"In other words, through all of the pain and suffering we have as believers, God's in control, and not only that, he's going to get some glory and good things from us in spite of the trial," Chanel added.

"Shoot," Sherese said, "if that's the case, He's gonna get some crazy glory from the three of us right here!"

Chanel smiled, "You got that right, but in all seriousness though, Syd, whatever God has for you, it's just gonna get better and better."

"I hope so," Sydney said optimistically.

Chanel stretched her legs out in front of her and crossed her arms. "Hope nothing. There's no hoping to it. You know that scripture that says if you sow in tears, you're gonna reap in joy?"

Sydney nodded.

Sherese chimed, "Lord knows, you've had some tears."

"That's true, but I've got to admit that not all of my tears have been from missing Vance. I mean—most of them have been, but some of them are because I've been so remorseful about so much I didn't do or say. There's even more that I shouldn't have said. I've learned a painful lesson, and while I now know that God is not punishing me for my mistakes by allowing Vance to die, I do believe that through this, as awful and painful as it is, He wanted to reveal my mistakes to me. I've become really conscious about what I say, how I say it, and I don't think I'll leave an argument without making peace. I feel like I've been pressed, poked, and prodded spiritually. Just think, me, the one who's always giving the lessons has learned a truckload from all of this. Mama and Daddy always said that there are consequences to what we say and do. My consequence is that I didn't leave Vance that morning on good terms, and I said some messed up stuff to him that I would take back if I could. But I do know that he knew I loved him. I hang on to that. More than anything, I've learned that I need God's forgiveness just as much as Brian O'Leary."

"That's heavy Syd, but true. I mean, not about you, but about my own situation. I think about my own life and even Rosa's. I totally trust that God has forgiven me for my sins and Rosa for hers, but there are still consequences for decisions we make, good or bad."

Sydney, deep in thought, crossed her legs at the ankle as she reflected on the past. "Vance is a perfect example. He sowed spiritual things and now he has the reward of eternal life. For so long, I've looked at his passing as a cruel punishment, but I know Vance wouldn't come back here now even if he could. It was Vance's time, and I can't question or really understand God's timing. The only thing I can do is to make the best decisions I can with what the Lord has given me. Like I said, we're all gonna have our tough times, but I guess we just have to hold on to the good things and blessings in days like today."

"Yeah, you used to really get on my nerves with all of that kind of talk, but I'm really beginning to get what you mean. I'm so thankful for the Lord blessing me with a gift as precious as Hannah. I'm gonna do all I can to sow good things into her life because I don't want her to go through the things I've been through. Besides, I gotta be honest. I don't want to deal with all the drama Mama and Daddy have gone through with me," Sherese said.

Sydney nodded her head knowingly, but Chanel chuckled, "Girl, you better go lay out on the altar for at least a month cause I know you worked on your parents' last nerves!"

"Very funny, Chanel. You better be glad I'm saved," Sherese teased with attitude. At that moment, she heard Hannah crying frantically behind her.

Darlene, looking more than a little frazzled, held her wailing granddaughter. "Sherese, honey, I can't get Hannah to calm down for nothin'. She's been a little pistol. She starts screaming anytime one of the church members comes near her."

Sherese hopped up anxiously to cradle her wailing daughter, and she immediately quieted down. Darlene shook her head and leaned close to her granddaughter, saying, "Now ain't you somethin' else, little miss Hannah," before going back into the church.

"'Somethin' else' is just like her mama," added Chanel.

Sydney nodded in agreement.

Sherese joined her sister and friend back on the front step. "It doesn't matter if she only wants her mother now—I kinda like how she is."

"You're a good mother, Sherese." Sydney said with sincerity.

Sherese added, smiling, "Actually, I think the *three* of us are going to be good mothers to Hannah. I can't do this by myself. You know, they say 'It takes a village....'"

Reading Group Guide

1. Sydney believes she should "practice what she preached" by not allowing her stepdaughter to see her confusion, grief, and strain. Was this the right choice? Why or why not? How might it have been helpful to Maya (and others) for Sydney to be more transparent?

2. When Samuel Hightower wrestles with Sydney's choice of a man who was raised Baptist instead of Pentecostal, Darlene reminds him, "There's one church, and furthermore, holiness is a lifestyle, not a denomination." How do you handle denominational differences in your relationships with other Christians? How do your pastor and local church interact with other congregations in the community? What does Scripture seem to suggest about such denominational distinctions? (See Ephesians 4:5 to start.)

3. Have you ever felt as Chanel did when faced with Sydney's devastating grief? When is saying nothing better than saying the wrong thing (e.g., Job's friends)? When do we need to speak anyway and allow the Holy Spirit to mediate our meaning? (See Rom. 8:26,27.)

4. Do you call men? Why or why not? In your opinion, what is the "proper way to approach a sister"? What do you think is *God's* biggest concern in how a man and woman begin a relationship?

5. More than once, Sherese expresses unwillingness to "give her all to the Lord." Her reasons include disdain for hypocrisy in the church, reluctance to live a life of sacrifice and self-neglect, and

old resentments about feeling neglected herself as a pastor's child. What keeps *you* from giving your all to God?

6. Sydney's grief over Vance's death isolates her from family, friends, and church. How can someone like Sydney overcome such isolation? How can those who love such a person help her deal with the range of emotions involved in mourning a loved one—even after the initial grief has passed? (See Job 2:11; Rom. 12:15; 1 Cor. 1:3-7.)

7. It's the "small things" that make Sydney's grief hard to bear, and it's the little things about Tommy that really grate on Chanel's last nerve. What is it about the little things that matters so much? How can a person make them a blessing and not a curse?

8. Sherese *really* resists going to church. Even Sunday mornings are a burden to her. "Why do I have to go to church to get to heaven?" she grumbles. What does Scripture say about corporate worship? (See Neh. 8:1-13; Matt. 18:20; Acts 2:42; Heb. 10:24,25.) How important is church to you? Why do you think it is so important to God?

9. Sydney realizes that she never really had to *press* in her faith before Vance's death. Read Philippians 3:12-14 in your Bible. What experience do you have in *pressing on?* When did you discover what that concept really means?

10. All too aware of her own shortcomings, Chanel marvels at the authority with which she spoke to Sydney. "Why or how could the Lord speak through a person like her?" Consider biblical examples of God doing just that through unlikely candidates— and then answer that question for yourself!

11. "God has a way of allowing trials to open up our understanding of who He is." How did each of the three women featured in this novel discover that truth? How have you experienced it in your own life? (See Mal. 3:3; Heb. 12:7; James 1:2-4; 1 Pet. 1:6,7.)

12. Are you able to sympathize (or empathize) more with Chanel or with Tommy? Why? What experience have you had with adulterous temptations? What is it about such temptation that bothers you most—the sex (or lust) or the violation of trust? Why do you think Jesus said that lust was just as bad as the sex act itself? (See Matt. 5:27,28.)

13. As important as church and fellowship with other believers are, both Chanel and Sydney discover the need for a one-on-one relationship with God. Chanel realizes she doesn't need ritual or clergy to usher her into God's presence; Sydney realizes just how dependent on others she has been for her faith. How do you balance the need for corporate and individual fellowship with the Lord? Which comes more easily to you? Why?

14. Sydney feels a loss of identity when Vance dies; Sherese feels lost when she discovers she was adopted. Where do you get your sense of identity? Why? What does Colossians 3:1-4 suggest about our identity?

15. Sherese, like many P.K.s (Pastor's Kids), carries a lot of resentment about her childhood—because of a sense of neglect, unfair standards, and too-intimate knowledge of the "real" church. How can pastoral parents juggle the needs of their family with the needs of the church? Consider that question in light of Paul's exhortations in 1 Corinthians 7:1,7, 8, and in 1 Timothy 3:1-7, especially verse 5.

16. "Instead of just *looking* like a saint, Sherese finally *felt* like one." What does a saint look like? What does it *feel* like to be a saint?

17. "It's hard to forgive someone who doesn't even acknowledge any wrong doing," Chanel admits, but that is what Christ did for us. (See Luke 23:34; Rom. 5:8.) How willing are you to forgive someone without their repentance? What are the benefits to doing so—for you and for them?

18. Rosa would die bearing the consequences of her youthful mistakes; in contrast, God allowed Jack and Sherese to redeem theirs. What makes the difference? How do you live with the consequences when God does *not* choose to remove them? In what ways might God redeem even while allowing the consequences to remain? (See 2 Cor. 12:7-10 as an example.)

Prayer of Salvation

God loves you—no matter who you are, no matter what your past.
God loves you so much that He gave His one and only begotten Son
for you. The Bible tells us that "…whoever believes in him shall not
perish but have eternal life" (John 3:16 NIV). Jesus laid down His life
and rose again so that we could spend eternity with Him in heaven
and experience His absolute best on earth. If you would like to
receive Jesus into your life, say the following prayer out loud and
mean it from your heart:

*Heavenly Father, I come to You admitting that I am a sinner. Right
now, I choose to turn away from sin, and I ask You to cleanse me of
all unrighteousness. I believe that Your Son, Jesus, died on the cross
to take away my sins. I also believe that He rose again from the dead
so that I might be forgiven of my sins and made righteous through
faith in Him. I call upon the name of Jesus Christ to be the Savior and
Lord of my life. Jesus, I choose to follow You and ask that You fill me
with the power of the Holy Spirit. I declare that right now I am a child
of God. I am free from sin and full of the righteousness of God. I am
saved in Jesus' name. Amen.*

Compelling New Fiction!

Heavenly Places

Treva Langston's life has been turned upside down with the loss of her high-

powered job and her family's move to her home town full of memories of heartache and uncertainty about what makes her worthy.

Jillian, Treva's sister, understands the trials that come with self-doubt, and with the help of her women's prayer group, she invites Treva to ask God for what she can't do alone. Treva finds that the promised *Heavenly Places* she's always looked for have been in front of her all along!

Heavenly Places by Kimberly Cash Tate
Paperback, 978-1-57794-857-5

The Good Stuff

From the author of *Boaz Brown* and *Divas of Damascas Road,* Michelle Stimpson reveals a story about two marriages on the verge of divorce. Sonia and Kennard have the "perfect" life, but Kennard's emotional distance from the family makes Sonia believe that a good marriage is more than financial security. Adrian couldn't love her husband Darryl more if she tried, but he seems more interested in making money than babies. Theses two women are heartbroken and ready to call it quits when a common friend, Miss Erma, invites them to a prayer group. They discover marriage is more than wedding dresses and happily ever after—it is compromise, sacrifice, and patience. *The Good Stuff!*

www.walkworthypress.net
Coming Fall 2008
The Good Stuff by Michelle Stimpson
Paperback, 978-1-57794-856-8

Glory Girls Reading Group

Enjoy reading great books that glorify God? Join the thousands of women who belong to Glory Girls: Reading Groups for African American Christian Women Who Love God and Like to Read. For more information, visit **www.glorygirlsread.net**.

1/09

COLEMAN REGIONAL LIBRARY